Praise

Who is Killing the Great Capes of Heropa?

"The best non-comicbook superhero story I've ever read."
COMIC BASTARDS

"Cleverly alludes to the conflict between fantasy and reality at play — that this story about comics should be so similar to a murder mystery of the Sam Spade kind is just the cherry on the cake."
EMMETT O'CUANA, *The Momus Report*

"A compelling study of character driving an investigative narrative, and a cracking good read."
THE INK SHOT

"Plays with the conventions of comicbooks/virtual reality/dystopian fiction and the good ol' murder mystery."
RENEE ASHER PICKUP, *Books and Booze*

"A front-seat view into a quirky and imaginative world of super-heroes that feel love and pain in equal measure."
LLOYD PAIGE, *Huffington Post*

"I had an idea Andrez Bergen was going places — and his new novel fulfils that promise. An excellent book, don't miss it."
HEATH LOWRANCE, *author of* City of Heretics

"Equal parts homage and pastiche, Bergen peppers this bold mystery with superb nods to the four-colour world, while also densely building a universe in which he can play with confidence — and does."
RYAN K. LINDSAY, *author of* The Devil is in the Details: Examining Matt Murdock and Daredevil

"This love letter to the silver age of Marvel Comics will grab you by the tights and not let go till the final page — as complex as *The Matrix* and as immediate as a Jack Kirby splash page."
JACK SEABROOK, *bare*bones ezine*

"Andrez Bergen takes his childhood creations and mashes them up with various icons and tropes of superhero literature, resulting in a fresh, exciting look at crime fighters who don capes, masks and union suits to fight the forces of evil. I need two copies of this book — one to read and the other to bag, board and save."
STEFAN BLITZ, *Forces Of Geek*

"Reading *Heropa* is like going back in time — the nostalgia and childlike wonder is still there, but these are clearly more complex than you surmised. It's a pleasure to puzzle out the familiar faces hiding behind the characters' masks, and lovely to see that even through the grime and grit of Andrez Bergen's world, their eyes still have a twinkle."
PAUL O'CONNOR, *Longbox Graveyard*

"Filled with smart humour, stunning detail and credible allusions, *Heropa* captures the good-natured feel of the Lee/Ditko/King comic books while still feeling fresh and new."
ANDREW CYRUS HUDSON, *Comic Attack*

"If anybody else is as inventive and bizarre as Andrez Bergen, then they aren't half as good a writer or everybody would know their name. In *Heropa* pulp fiction is brought bang up to date and then slammed hard into the roots of its own mythology. Equal parts mystery, science fiction and comicbook fantasy, it's a stylish, creative, noirish romp full of darkness and fun. I don't know any other writer that could quite pull this off."
CHRISTOPHER BLACK, *Available in Any Colour*

"Twisted and warped with the best influences from pop culture — comicbooks and noir — this is one of the most original novels I've ever read."
SONS OF SPADE

"We're not in Kansas anymore. Or even Gotham City. Bergen's big-hearted meta-romp wears the author's mighty affection for comic-books past, present and future on its sleeve, and the call-outs, shout-outs and sly winks zip by faster than a speeding bullet — like a crazy, post-modern road trip with Jack Kirby riding shotgun, and everyone from Stan Lee to Raymond Chandler nattering away in the back seat. More fun than a box of old comics!"
KEVIN BURTON SMITH, *The Thrilling Detective*

"Bergen delivers a tale that is equal parts crime fiction and silver-age comics, with characters swimming in cultural winks and a mass-media homage that feels like the pious mutterings of an über-fan. But it's his unique style that propels the piece, gripping in an art nouveau sort of way, the clean architecture of an ornate age — long past — towering off the page. *Who is Killing the Great Capes of Heropa?* is a mad undertaking, and the madman pulls it off..."
NOIRWHALE

"In a world of silver-age superheroes, a murderous villain emerges as Bergen expertly combines the safety of our youth with the dangers of the present."
JAYDEN LEGGETT, *ComicsOnline.com*

"A mad, dystopian world, keeping Bergen fans on the hop with a virtual reality love story. Shifting parameters as the ground shakes under the reader's feet seems to be his strength — no need to be a comicbook fan to enjoy; the engaging characters will have you turning the pages in this story of true love in a virtual world."
MCDROLL, *author of* Feeling It

"A highly readable tale that gives us superheroes with a difference in a fantasy world gone sour, and does it with a lightness of touch that makes the pages seem to fly by."
STEVE DOES COMICS

"Reads like an open love letter to the golden age, blending in a gritty *Matrix*-esque, cyberpunk edge."
MATT KYME, *writer of* That Bulletproof Kid

"Great stuff! — as a huge comicbook fan, I really connected. It's funny, bizarre and very, very cool."
THE TROLLISH DELVER

"Whilst flexing his comic and cultural muscles to heroic proportions, Andrez Bergen manages to plant a razor-sharp tongue into a wickedly hardboiled cheek."
MIKE YOUNG & MARC CRANE, *creators of* LIL Comic

"Sam Spade meets the Justice League of America in a dystopian future where everybody's a superhero. Filled with clever references to the silver age of comicbooks, Bergen knows his comics and how to craft an entertaining mystery."
SILVER AGE COMICS

"A mixed-media love letter to the golden age of comics and the classic detective story, with nods to Batman and The Avengers along with tips of the fedora to Chandler and Hammett, *Heropa* is unlike any mystery you've ever read. Highly stylized and forever cool — like if Rorschach had been allowed to just gumshoe and smoke, without any giant blue dongs slapping you in the face to shatter the illusion."
JOE CLIFFORD, *author of* Choice Cuts & Junkie Love

"*Who is Killing the Great Capes of Heropa?* is a terrific, postmodern superhero noir. It's like Top 10 rolled into the Comicbook History of Comics, but with a wry Aussie humour all of its own. Action, mystery and yuks a-plenty, lavishly illustrated by real-deal comic artists. Get into it."
JASON FRANKS, *Black House Comics, author of* McBlack

"A little noir, a dash of dystopia, a pinch of alternate reality, and a heaped helping of creativity and talent make for the sledgehammer of a novel that is *Who is Killing the Great Capes of Heropa?* Prepare to change the way you look at superheroes."
BOOK REVIEWS BY ELIZABETH A. WHITE

"If Jack Kirby and Carroll John Daly had a child, science would cry and from those tears would rise *Who is Killing the Great Capes of Heropa?* Who knew hardboiled superhero pulp fiction could be so great?"
RYAN HUFF, *Geek of Oz*

"Andrez Bergen returns with a fast-paced romp that's equal parts comicbook heroics and hardboiled detective homage. Nobody is better than Bergen at this sort of highly entertaining hybrid — his is a unique voice, and if you haven't read his work yet, you really need to."
JAMES REASONER, *Rough Edges*

"Equal parts sinister fantasy-mystery and open love letter to the history of comicbooks, every passing hero reference will have you shouting excitedly at complete strangers with all the vigour of a Trivial Pursuit revelation. Ignore their cold stares, for you are right — that totally *is* Stan Lee."
DAVE BUESING, *Comic Book Herald*

"Bergen creates some of the most wildly imaginative places you will ever encounter in fiction and his characters are fascinating people who you'll want to hang out with...an entertaining and challenging read for comicbook lovers and the rest of us alike."
CHRIS RHATIGAN, *Death By Killing*

"*Who is Killing the Great Capes of Heropa?* is partly a homage to one of my favorite writers, Raymond Chandler, and a noir superhero crime fantasy inspired by a great love of the classic silver-age comic heroes. Jack Kirby meets Philip Marlowe? It's got my vote!"
BRYAN TALBOT, *creator/artist of* Grandville, 2000 AD, Sandman

WHO IS KILLING THE GREAT CAPES OF HEROPA?

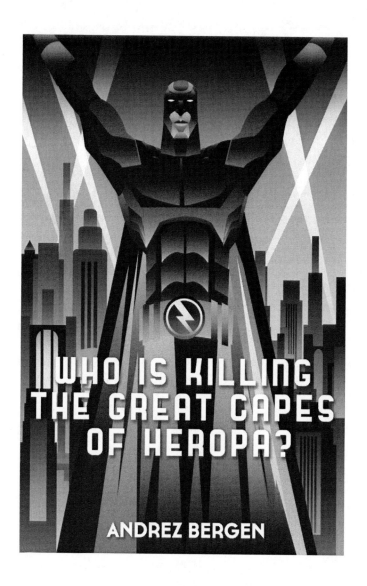

WHO IS KILLING THE GREAT CAPES OF HEROPA?

ANDREZ BERGEN

PERFECT
EDGE
BOOKS

Winchester, UK
Washington, USA

First published by Perfect Edge Books, 2013
Perfect Edge Books is an imprint of John Hunt Publishing Ltd., Laurel House, Station Approach,
Alresford, Hants, SO24 9JH, UK
office1@jhpbooks.net
www.johnhuntpublishing.com
www.perfectedgebooks.com

For distributor details and how to order please visit the 'Ordering' section on our website.

Text copyright: Andrez Bergen 2013

ISBN: 978 1 78279 235 2

A CIP catalogue record for this book is available from the British Library.

Design: Stuart Davies

Printed in the USA by Edwards Brothers Malloy

We operate a distinctive and ethical publishing philosophy in all
areas of our business, from our global network of authors to
production and worldwide distribution.

CONTENTS

ARTWORK CREDITS

Rodolfo Reyes cover & page ix

Drezz Rodriguez page xvi

Giovanni Ballati page 2

Israel Schnapps page 7

Juan Saavedra page 11

Kohana Yamadera page 28

Andrez Bergen page 37

Also by the same author:

TOBACCO-STAINED MOUNTAIN GOAT
ONE HUNDRED YEARS OF VICISSITUDE
THE CONDIMENTAL OP

For Cocoa, again

"We all do what we must, and live with what we've done."
Wolram E. Deaps, Tobacco-Stained Mountain Goat

PROLOGUE: THE KÁRMÁN LINE

"Aer—t," the radio receiver squawks inside her helmet. *"Aeri—st, re—ng me?"*

"Hello, you've called the Aerialist," the Cape says in response. *"She's not home at the moment, too busy falling from a ridiculous height. Please leave a message after the tone so the girl can get back to you — you know, after all the king's horses and all the king's men put her together again. Beep."*

God knows if anyone hears the quip. The only feedback coming through loud and clear is shrill static.

The Aerialist was aware of risks, but sabotage — someone cutting a hole in her jetpack to siphon out the fuel — had not been one of the hazards people bothered to mention.

Fifteen seconds pass and the drop is only one thousand, nine hundred feet shorter, according to the instrumentation on her wrist. Three hundred and twenty-six thousand of the imperial buggers to go.

The Aerialist is slap-bang in freefall, somewhere marginally past the Kármán line — in plain English about a hundred kilometres to impact on earth. Unless, of course, she hits something higher like Mount Everest (shaving off nine kilometres) or the top of the Empire State, four hundred and forty metres above terra firma.

Not that either place is optional here.

Flame-on! *she quips, laughing for just a moment.*

Inferring she's alit does, however, exaggerate the case. Objects light up when they fall at tens of miles a second, whereas her rate of descent clocks in around a few hundred miles per hour. Maybe seven hundred. Slower than a lead balloon.

That doesn't stop her brain racing, conjuring up the insane, expecting fire to lick up on the outside of the pressure suit. This suit takes the brunt of buffeting as she tumbles arse over tit. No hope. Nothing. Just falling till she hits the ground.

Never thought it'd end via such a lame whimper, *she further mulls, dizzy now.* Maybe I should've packed a parachute?

HEROPA

#100

While he may've felt like he'd been dropped on his head, he actually landed on his feet.

Even so, following on as this did from a spell of sustained darkness, Jack tottered in the middle of a sidewalk crammed with pedestrians. His body felt heavier, lethargic, cumbersome. When people began to shove past in brutal fashion, he beat one very hasty retreat to lean against a brick wall, overwhelmed and dazed.

There was a shop here, an archaic-looking place called the Big Trip Travel Agency, all posters of propeller-driven clipper planes, swirling bullfighters, and a dirigible marked with the livery of Latverian Airways, from which disembarked gaily-smiling, beautiful people in 1940s apparel.

The agency also grabbed Jack's attention because, back in his hometown, tourism had bird-dogged the itinerary of the dodo.

The man's heart was racing. He tried his damnedest to calm down, but this was bizarre.

In the reflection of one of the big windows, beneath a striped marquee, he'd noticed he was dolled up in a tight superhero costume — coloured a shade of dark blue, verging on cerulean — to which no one else here paid any heed. Peeling off the smothering mask, Jack inhaled deeply, coughed, and finally took time out to properly gawk. Revelling in the presence of no rain, he scanned a cloudless sky high above, and dropped his gaze to a metropolis — all flying buttresses, concrete and glass. This was something, he would allow that much. Not quite the Emerald City, yet hardly a place to sneeze at.

On street level caroused mint-condition antique vehicles snatched straight out of some tasteful car museum. Hurrying along the footpaths to either side were women in wild hats, kid gloves and fitted dresses with shoulder-pads, along with men in felt fedoras and double-breasted pinstripe suits who looked like they belonged in a photo with his great grandfather — which probably they did.

"Welcome, sir."

4

Outside Sam's Delicatessen, next door to the travel agency, an elderly gent had positioned himself in front of Jack. He was dressed in a jarring red military-style uniform with gold lapels, the only one of a horde of pedestrians to notice Jack's presence. The two of them looked like mismatched bookends in a sea of conformity.

"I'm Stan the Doorman."

Jack decided he liked Stan's eyes. They were warm and accompanied by a suave white moustache above a winning smile.

"You may label me the Doormat," the gent in red waffled on, "since there are some here who do just that — but I prefer to be considered a welcoming committee."

Jack looked at him for a few seconds, rediscovering anew the ability to speak. "Okay. Um. Can I call you Stan? That Cool McCool?"

"Of course. And appreciated."

"So — what is this place?"

"Everything has a starting point and your starting point is here."

"Cryptic."

"Actually, also very simple. Look around. Go on, then."

As if to encourage his charge, the old man performed a creaky, horizontal bobbin routine right there on the footpath, turning several times, so Jack hung on to his coattails.

This city was immense.

It stretched in every direction he could see, making him feel like a flea in a ridiculous blue suit of his own choosing.

The monumental skyline sweated neoclassical touches, its architecture early twentieth-century art deco colliding with Soviet formalism — offering tall, sharp-edged towers, soaring arches, looming statuary. Jack felt most of the places looked like enormous wedding cakes with kitsch columns and over-decorative façades.

One sculpture, a statue of some suited bigwig punching his fist heavenward, was in the vicinity size-wise of King Kong.

"Overboard," Jack muttered.

"Fear not. All this has happened before, and it will all happen again — but this time it happens in Heropa. It starts happening on a busy street in Grand Midtown. That corner skyscraper over there, the one that takes up all four corners of a city block, is the home of the Equalizers, and I suggest that you choose this particular building because there are people there who believe in you."

"Sure." *Whatever*, crossed Jack's mind.

The skyscraper the old man pointed out was dozens of storeys high. It ascended into a bullet-shaped peak a thousand feet up, with a glossy white exterior finish and mirror windows that caught distorted reflections of the neighbours.

"Come on then. I'll take you over. I am, you know, the building's doorman. Your first port of call," he chuckled.

"Handy. One thing, though — other people don't appear to see me."

"Give it time. The transition takes an hour or so. The Capes will have no problem."

Canvas awnings billowing in its doorways, a shiny, green, wood-panelled W-Class tram clattered past before they crossed a thoroughfare on which 1930s and '40s Packards, Buicks, Morris Minors, even a two-tone tan and chocolate-brown Summit Tourer from the 1920s, moved slowly.

These vintage jalopies honked one another while a traffic cop in jodhpurs, knee-high riding boots and white gloves, standing with rod-straight posture at the next intersection, used his whistle and energetic arm movements to control the flow.

After passing the crossroads they proceeded through a grassy square lined with elms and decorated by the occasional fountain and miniature pagoda, leading the two men to the tall, rocket-like building in question.

Stan grabbed a brass lightning bolt handle in order to push open a glass door that bordered on monstrous, and stood aside allowing entry.

"Welcome to Timely Tower."

"That's appropriate," Jack said as he brushed past.

6

"You get the inference?"

"I think so. Timely was the publishing company that predated Marvel Comics, right? From around World War II — they call it the golden age of comicbooks."

"I must say I'm impressed."

"Why so?"

"Many of our residents wouldn't have an inkling."

"Not that big a deal."

Stan scrutinized the other man as he closed the door with a quiet swish. "Sir, it's never wise to doubt any knowledge."

"Fair enough. Call me Jack, by the way."

"Don't mind if I do." Again with that debonair smile.

White marble paved the foyer inside, while shiny white walls were indented with chrome fixtures. Suspended above a bank of four separate metal concertina elevator doors sat a woven square banner several metres in size, showing a circle pierced by a simplistic lightning bolt that cut diagonally down from the top left corner to the bottom right.

Whoever designed the thing had been sparing with the colours, since it was cast only in black, white and grey.

"The symbol of the Equalizers," announced Stan, "designed by the great Israel Schnapps."

"Nifty — but shouldn't it then have an 'E' in the logo? That lightning bolt looks like an 'N' and," here Jack cocked his head to the right, "there's a 'Z'. Something Zorro would conjure up if he had a set of tapestry tools, don't you reckon?"

"I wouldn't know, sir."

"Jack. And you must have an artistic bone somewhere."

"None I'm aware of — at my age the osseous matter tends to accelerate into disrepair." Stan also crooked his neck. "However...now you mention it, I can see the 'Z'."

"But no 'E'."

"Sadly amiss."

"So, these people are expecting me, you say?"

"Certainly are."

"Which floor?"

"The Penthouse Suite — of course."

"Top of the heap, huh? Inside the bullet?"

"All the better to keep an eye on the city."

"Is that a good thing?"

Stan didn't respond. Either he'd missed the question or preferred not to offer up his two cents.

A half-moon shaped reception counter stood nearby. The guard sitting behind it would've been somewhere in the vicinity of forty to sixty — hard to tell — and his gaunt, expressionless face ignored them, so Jack ignored it back.

The guard was cradling a softdrink can of something called Dixi-Cola with red and blue ovals on a white background. He had his gaze fixed on a portable telly.

Jack stared at this small contrivance. "I thought TV wasn't invented till after the period we're supposed to be in — given the décor outside, I mean. Isn't this the 1930s?"

"Is it? I have no idea. But there is some debate about the true inventor of the television: Vladimir Kosma Zworykin, John Logie Baird, or Philo Taylor Farnsworth."

Having heard of none of these people blessed with three names, Jack remained mum.

"It was commercially available from the late '20s," the old

concierge went on, "so television wouldn't be out of place here by any means. The TV dinner, on the other hand, wasn't invented until 1945."

Hearing about any kind of dinner made Jack's stomach growl.

Over on the TV in the here and now, the monochrome picture rolled occasionally, but on it was an old guy in a clown suit with a ventriloquist doll on his knee. The wooden figurine was crooning a sad-sack jingle:

'Be a Top Man, flee the Bop Man, and drink a bottle or can of Tarax Top Ten flavours!'

By the end of this, Jack decided he'd had enough viewing time, so he turned around.

Inset beside one of the elevators, a little plaque read 'The Foundation Stone of this Building was laid by Mr William Eisner, President, Leland Baxter Paper Company'.

"Huh. I thought foundation stones had dates on them."

"Well, now, as I think we've established, dates don't matter here," said Stan.

The traction lift was one of those antique movie jobs with teak panelling and bulbous globes; these announced each floor as it passed in sluggish fashion. Jack had left Stan the Doorman in the lobby to do his real job, and after a month of Sundays and the piped-in, mind-numbing instrumental sounds of 'A Walk in the Black Forest', the cubicle reached the Penthouse Suite. This had its own private globe with a 'P' marked on it.

There was a lovely leviathan awaiting him.

Shoving aside the metal concertina door like a shower curtain, she smiled down with something Jack would have called benevolence, if he knew what it looked like. He took in a face composed of strong cheekbones; enormous eyes with purple irises, long lashes, and tiny, swollen lips that in most cases would infer a mild food allergy.

A full twelve inches higher than Jack, this particular giant was gift-wrapped in frills and ribbons, most in plum, with a big periwinkle bowknot on her bosom, a pair of long white satin gloves and one very short, voluminous miniskirt.

She also had a headband holding in check lavender hair spiralling down to her ankles — a touch of Wonder Woman interbred with far too much Sailor Moon, making her resemble someone dragged out of a manga comic and stuck on a pair of towering legs.

"I'm Pretty Amazonia," the woman announced with a tight smile that nullified the sultry effect of her mouth. "And a quick warning — before you conjure up any unwisecracks, I could break both your legs in quite the jiffy."

"Nothing comes to mind."

"Oh, dandy. You must be Southern Cross. We've been expecting you." Pretty Amazonia gave him the once over. "To be honest, I thought you'd be taller."

"Sorry to disappoint."

"I'll live. Well, come on now."

He followed the woman down a brightly lit passage along which were framed monochrome and primary colour pictures of heroes in action and/or hamming it up for the artist.

There were dozens of these; no photos, but drawings in black and white or red, yellow, green and blue — heavily outlined in black — with names attached like Lord Evolve-A-Lot, Kardak Da Mystic, Slam-Dunk Ninja, Babe Boon, The Soldier, Big Game Hunter, McBlack, Vesper, Mister Sniffer, Ace Harlem, Fraulein Helmet, Captain Atom, Cowboy Sahib, Flasher Lightning and Kid Squall, Sans Sheriff, Curvaceous Crustacean, Vege-Might, That Bulletproof Kid, Trick-Or-Teet, and Yarko the Utterly Greatest.

Some of the monikers fitted the costumes, while others looked like they were sorely mismatched and the designers colour-blind. Most made Jack want to chuckle.

Tucked in amidst the visual mayhem was a portrait of his newfound hostess, a classier rendering in black ink, pencil and minimal watercolour that accentuated her traits, including the nonplussed demeanour.

"Our rogue's gallery," said Pretty Amazonia as she sauntered ahead.

"That was you," Jack mused, in hot pursuit. "Huh."

Having passed a metal door with 'G.M.R.' initialled across it and the Equalizers' logo beneath that, Jack thought twice, doubled back, and was about to take a peek.

"Don't go in there," the woman warned.

"Why, is it dangerous?"

"No, just a white elephant — the Giant Map Room. Has a layer of dust as thick as my heels. C'mon — this way."

They came to a set of double doors that the woman pushed open, revealing a huge inner sanctum, mostly white.

A Spartan, unadorned milky ceiling was far above them, along with a second-floor balcony that steered close by the walls and gave a view from up there to the room proper, where they stood.

Hanging from a picture rail that did a circuit of this space were a series of replica white, lifesize plaster of Paris faces, cowls, visors and helmets, likely lifted from those jokers in the passageway. They looked like death masks. The way in which the decorations stared down at them made Jack lose count after a quick tot-up to twenty.

There was also a capacious, round white table with a carbon copy of the Equalizers' symbol in the centre. From this angle he made out the 'Z'.

Two-dozen chairs wrapped around the table, and next to that sat a couple of comfy ivory-coloured couches beside a glass-topped coffee table. On the table was a collection of cardboard cup-placemats with the same lightning bolt logo.

"Home, sweet home." She scrutinized Jack again. "You certainly travel light. No luggage. Just that mask in your hands you flaunt so nervously. Relax — I won't bite. Not yet."

"Who are you people?" he decided to ask.

"Haven't you heard? Thought Stan would've filled you in. We're the Equalizers — sworn protectors of Heropa City, guardians of the peace, et cetera, et cetera, blah, blah."

She laughed — making him decide straight away he liked her. Sure she was formidable, but she also had a solid sense of humour.

"This place is impressive," Jack said, as he wistfully struggled for more meaningful dialogue.

"What, Heropa? You'll get over it." The woman looked him over once again. "You know, you remind me of someone."

"I do?" Jack's tone was edgy. "Who?"

"The actor George Peppard, when he was younger — circa *Breakfast at Tiffany's*. If he'd excessively worked out, I mean."

"Okay."

"You have no idea who I'm talking about, do you?"

12

"No."

"Sad. So, take a seat. The others will be here shortly."

"What others?"

"The other Equalizers."

"Okay."

Jack eyed one of the couches and went on over.

There was an attractive hardback tome nearby, something about 1930s automobiles, which he reached over to grab. As he did so, a huge shadow appeared across the table's surface and someone tossed a newspaper onto it.

The broadsheet grabbed more of his attention than the shadow or the book.

A headline was splashed across the top, each word several centimetres in height and in thick caps.

PEOPLE'S SAVIOUR SLAIN!

Beneath the by-line — trumpeting that the article was written by some journo called Chief Reporter Gypsie-Ann Stellar — sat a sub-header in unnecessary inverted commas:

"Shots Fired From Grassy Knoll."

The paper was called the *Port Phillip Patriot*, with the price five cents and credits including Donald Wright (publisher), Jean-Claude Forest (editor) and Arthur Simek (designer). Its huge front-page sketch came close to inciting Jack, again, to burst out laughing.

In black and white, this one showed an advertising billboard of two happy, smiling kids with a superhero crouched between them. A mask covered the top half of the hero's face, shades of Captain America. He had a toothy, honest grin as he gave the thumbs-up beneath a slogan that read *Royal Vendetta, for Strong White Teeth!* and positioned just above his giant brow was the letter 'O'.

Impacted dead centre in this fifteenth letter of the alphabet was a ragged hole with two tiny legs dangling out, apparently lifeless.

"Bull's-eye," Jack muttered.

"An' the same guy."

"Huh?"

He glanced up to see a ton of bricks stuck together in the shape of a person. There were even patches of white cement smeared between the ochre-coloured bricks.

This arrival had on a giant-size trench coat that was open, displaying more paving across the torso, and propped up on the back of his great, stony skull was a small hat at a jaunty angle. The charcoal-grey straw number had an indented, fedora-style crown like every other man Jack had seen here, but contrarily sported a narrow brim, only about two inches wide, making it more 1960s than 1940s.

"The guy on the billboard an' the one *inside* it," the rock man was saying. "They're one an' the same. The Big O, as you can see from the symbol on his mask — a.k.a. Sir Omphalos. Not sure if we should be labellin' it irony, coincidence, or damn well freaky."

"Either way, this puts a dampener on proceedings," put in Pretty Amazonia, who'd settled on the divan next to Jack. He hadn't noticed the woman doing that — thought she was still on the other side of the large room. She propped her face in her hands, elbows resting on her knees. "Especially after what happened to the Aerialist."

"Think there's a connection?"

"They were definitely shagging."

"That so?"

"You know so."

"Do I?" The big man contracted cobbled shelving around his eyes. "Jealous rage? D'you reckon Stellar's capable?"

"That cow? Gypsie-Ann is one clever lady."

"Somethin' you don't have to worry yerself about."

"Precisely."

Jack lifted his gaze over both their heads and stared at the death masks. He'd been tuning out to this gossipy exchange between the two heroes, but after the rock man nodded he swung around.

"Oh, yeah — who the flying fig're you?"

Leaning too far forward, shuffling his mask from hand to hand, Jack failed completely any attempt to play it laid back. "Southern Cross," he said.

"How corny can yer get? Why the stupid name?"

"Tongue-in-cheek? We can't exactly see the Southern Cross anymore."

"He means back in Melbourne," Pretty Amazonia kindly interpreted.

"I know what he bloody well means."

"Course you do." She rolled her eyes.

The newcomer eased himself into the couch on the other side of the table, which groaned. Jack was surprised the thing didn't break in two.

"Reinforced," the man said, no doubt tipped off from the expression on Jack's face. He shoved his massive, fifteen-inch-long, shoebox-shaped right foot on the table on top of the news. "Yeah, all right, fair enough. 'Scuse the manners. I'm the Brick."

"So why the stupid name?" Yes, it was well-nigh impossible to resist the flip.

"What d'you reckon — yer nursin' an eyesight prob? Captures the spirit o' my charming good looks." He leaned over, holding forth a massive, four-fingered mitt as big as a pizza. "You seem okay, bub."

"Likewise." Jack thought the handshake was going to break every bone, but it was gentle. Apparently the walking/talking footpath again caught scent of the concern.

"Not invulnerable, eh?"

"Nope."

"Powers?"

"Some kind of weird blast thingy that comes out of the hand you nicely didn't crunch."

"Ah." The Brick took out a paper bag, rummaged, and stuck a long, dirty-pink stick of something into the slit of his mouth. He then offered one. *"Big Boss Cigar?"*

"Huh?"

"Big Boss Cigar."

"What the heck is that?"

"Caramel-flavoured candy — since we ain't able to indulge in the real McCoy here, figured I'd pretend to smoke."

"Think I'm fine without."

"I also have old school *Fags*. Ta-dah."

He conjured up a box, smaller than the size of a twenty-pack of cigarettes, painted in garish blue, red and yellow with a couple of cartoonish kids running across it.

"Tobacco?" Jack asked dubiously.

"Lollies from Melbourne's distant past, bub — we're not in Kansas anymore. In the shape o' wee li'l cigarettes. See?"

The Brick flourished a hard white stick in the air before Jack. It had a red tip, looking for the entire world like, yes, a cigarette.

"Oh, yeah."

"Our Mister B does love his sweets," remarked the Pretty Amazonia woman beside him.

"Ain't nothin' better, 'cept the ridgy didge originals."

The Brick looked over with liquid blue eyes, the only part Jack could see of the brute that was wet. He wondered about the inside of the gravelly mouth.

"Nah?"

"No, I'm fine."

"Suit yerself."

Jack then broached a subject he'd been too overawed to mention before. "Do you guys have a toilet?"

"No," Pretty Amazonia said in a singsong tone, "we use our pants." But when Jack thought about this, the woman swapped to irritated. "Course we do — just over there, the door behind the staircase. Have fun."

Jack stood up, hesitated, and hovered.

"Problem?" asked the woman, still annoyed.

"No, not really."

"Then, what is it?"

"Speak up, junior," the Brick encouraged behind him. "We won't bite'cha."

"All right. Um — how do I get out of the costume?"

Something resembling disgust crossed Pretty Amazonia's face. "It's a loo, not a bathtub," she said.

Jack scratched the side of his head behind his ear, a nervous tic. "You know what I mean. Don't you?"

"Kid can't pee in tights," the Brick guessed.

"Oh." The woman shelved her annoyance, and a smile flickered. "Cleverly hidden zip, at the back."

"Got'cha. Thanks."

A few minutes later the newcomer returned to find the two Equalizers squabbling about something. When they caught wind of his approach, they went silent.

"You have Equalizer logos on your toilet paper," he remarked.

"We do," the woman agreed, eyes on the ground.

As the Brick settled into his sofa it creaked in a tortured manner, and then the man threw his arms over the back of the couch. "How long you been here, kid?"

"Arrived today," said Jack, sitting down.

"Seen any action?"

"Nope."

"Anyone bothered t'tell you the ropes?" The Brick glanced at Pretty Amazonia with a lopsided grin. His face was surprisingly flexible for a thing composed of ceramics.

"Not really — I only just got here. Stan, downstairs, gave me a few pointers."

"The Doormat? Yeah, he ain't half bad fer a Blando."

"And Pretty Amazonia, here, about climbing in and out of costumes."

The woman smiled, but said nothing.

"Okay, easy." The Brick sat up and returned his leg to the floor. He raised one hand, as if preparing to count. "Heropa has rules. Stupid, dodgy ones I'm the first to whine about — like the Comics Code Authority all over again. One: no swearin'. Minor profanities like 'bloody' an' 'damn' are fine, but steer clear o' the 'f—', 'c—' an' 'sh—' words. You know the ones I mean, or do I need to spell 'em out?"

"I know. Weird rule, though."

"Like I says. Number two, honour. Yep, our very own *Bushidō*. Treat others — yer enemies, hell, even yer undeservin' peers — as you expect t'be treated in return."

"No worries about using 'hell'?"

"Sure, 'hell' is okay too. Y'can push the limits o' the honour fiddlesticks, but there's no cheatin' or betrayal — they expect yer t'be a fine, upstandin' role model. Now, there was a third rule, but I'll be bummed if I can remember that one. Four — no alcohol, no tobacco, no pharmaceuticals o' ill repute. Number five — what's number five again, PA?"

Pretty Amazonia smiled. "Thou shalt not kill."

"Hah. The Bible ref. No wonder I ditched it from me noggin. Fact is we're not s'posed to die — no matter how much we pummel one another. Rules is rules."

"Excuse me." That was Jack, speaking up.

Both heroes looked over.

"What?" asked the Brick.

"I get what you're saying," Jack assured, "but, then, who killed him, and how did he cark it?" His finger was resting on the newspaper picture of a pair of legs pinioning a billboard.

"That, kid, is a pearler of a question."

#101

Pretty Amazonia tucked their bums in comfy white seats at the big table that would sit about thirty — though there were only three people there. Attempting to balance this by spreading themselves thin around it, they had to raise voices to hear one another.

"Where's the Great White Mope?" the Brick asked from his region of the table.

Pretty Amazonia craned forward. "What's that, hon?"

"I said, where's Great White?"

The woman shrugged her broad shoulders. "Guessing he'll be along shortly, since he called the meeting."

"Huh?"

"He'll be here soon!"

"Prob'ly gettin' his jollies watching us wait." The Brick flicked a thumb at the camera suspended in a corner of the ceiling high above. "Whatever floats his boat? He has a boat, by the by."

Jack didn't quite catch that last comment. "He's a boat...?"

"No, no, he *has* a boat."

"I didn't see any harbour close by."

"There is one, but that's not what I'm talkin' 'bout. Hitler's pin-up boy—"

"Who?"

"Our rookie head honcho — the Great White Hope. Likes to lord'it up from above. Got a dirigible, half the size o' a bloody zeppelin, wrapped up in white silk o' course. Rocket Scientist designed the contraption fer him. Can't fly by himself, so gets round in that."

"Where does he keep it?"

The Brick pointed at the ceiling, again using his thumb. "Upstairs."

"And who's this Rocket Scientist character?"

Pretty Amazonia leaned onto the table so she was fractionally closer to be heard. "A disreputable bastard of a Cape who makes flying doohickeys for anybody that asks —hero or villain — in return for a favour. With the girls he has a saying, 'a jiggle for a jet-pack' — meaning they have to flash their titties, give them a wobble and entertain the prick. One of the reasons I've never flown."

"And with the boys?"

"Never did suss that out. Brick?"

"Don't ask me. I'm a land-lubber like you."

"Wasn't one of your rules — number two, right? — all about honour?"

"Yeah, but with the caveat t'treat others as you expect t'be treated in return. Rocket Scientist is downright dodgy."

Jack looked around at all the empty chairs. "So where is everyone?"

"We're it," the Brick muttered.

"What?"

"We're it."

"Three people?"

"Four," Pretty Amazonia said, "once our fearless new leader arrives."

"An' he's only been fearless since the Big O headbutted that billboard."

"True." Pretty Amazonia gazed at Jack. "The Great White Hope took the role of second-in-charge from day one, but Sir Omphalos was always *numero uno* and had the respect thing happening. He's the man we really followed."

"All two of you?"

The Brick chortled — the sound was like shale churning inside a cement mixer. "These days, yeah. In the ol' days this table was completely populated. Thirty o' us."

"More. Remember some people had to stand? Back when things were fun." Looking distracted, Pretty Amazonia had drawn off one glove and examined her fingers. Each individual nail was a different shade of neon. "For starters, there was Milkcrate Man."

"Hah, yeah. Points fer banal dress-sense — the guy got round in a long black derro coat an' busted up Docs, toppin' this off with a brown plastic milkcrate that never left his head. Ranted a lot 'bout Beelzebub. I liked 'im. Walked like John Wayne, banged into things, had an empty wine bottle permanently stuck in his mitt — you know how we're not allowed t'drink here."

"Hard to track down real wine out there anyway." Pretty Amazonia sighed. "Back in Melbourne, I mean."

"There is that," agreed the Brick.

"What was Milkcrate Man's special power? Did we ever find out?"

"Don't think it mattered a hoot."

"So, why the decrease in numbers?" Jack interjected, since he was feeling lonely.

"Decision made by the Big O," the Brick said.

"Sir Omphalos," tacked on Pretty Amazonia. "He thought thirty-odd members for a super-group was unwieldy. And he was right — in action we tended to trip up each other or get in the way. Some villains escaped because we accidentally bulldozed one another."

"Like the time I laid-out the Great White Hope," reminisced her friend.

"That was no accident. Anyway, Sir Omphalos said the best superhero groups had four members. The Fantastic Four, the Avengers at their more functional — God, even the Teenage Mutant Ninja Turtles."

"I'm not sure the Avengers were at their best as a quartet," Jack spoke up.

"Really, now?"

"Depends. Are you talking up the time from issue 16 in 1965, when Hawkeye, Quicksilver and the Scarlet Witch joined Captain America — and forgettable types like Power Man whipped them? Then again, I guess Roy Thomas, John Buscema and Vince Colletta's combo three years later — Hawkeye, Goliath, the Wasp and the Black Panther from issue 52 — was classic stuff."

Pretty Amazonia and her partner gawked at him in silence.

In that situation Jack felt exceptionally uncomfortable, his ears burned, and he was grateful when the Brick broke the hush.

"Bub, I don't worry easy — even so, dunno 'bout PA, but yer scarin' me."

The woman was kinder. "So he's more of a nerd than us."

"A truckload more."

"Speaking of which, what about you and your cars?"

"That's a diff'rent kettle o' fish."

"Horses for courses," PA muttered. "Moving right along, the Big O decided to make the Equalizers just such a group."

"Ahh."

"Ahh?" The woman laughed and now acted a little dismayed. "Don't you want to know which four?"

Jack was wishing he could be anywhere but right here. The spotlight sizzled. "Sure. Which four?"

The Brick took this cue to hold up his right hand, displaying all the digits there. He appeared to enjoy using them to count.

"The Big O, PA here, me, an' the Great White Hope — no real option with that last choice, sad t'say. Seniority carbuncle."

"But inviting me in makes five."

Pretty Amazonia shook her head. "No, learn to count — it recalibrates us to four. Remember, Sir Omphalos put his head through the giant ad."

"Ah." Sense. "Still, I don't get everything. From what you're saying, you were having a ball in spite of the crowd — it's not like anything is serious here. Why institute a big cut in the line-up?"

"The Big O figured things'd changed." The Brick stared at the floor.

"What things?"

"He lost faith in the outfit."

Pretty Amazonia went over to her friend and placed a hand on his shoulder. They looked at each other for several seconds.

"He didn't trust us no more."

"Why?"

The Brick gazed Jack's way with sad, puppy dog eyes. "Why? Easy — 'cos some whacko went an' murdered one o' our number."

"The Aerialist," Pretty Amazonia said, also hitting on despondence.

"A swell kid."

"As was Little Nobody — yet I hear none of you jumping to defend his honour."

That last comment came from above, the complete antithesis of the Brick's crunchy, husky baritone. This was smooth and rich.

Jack followed up his colleagues' Antarctic fix to view a man on the next level.

He was aged somewhere in his forties and had long, snow-coloured hair combed back straight, falling past the shoulders down his back. Precision-cut cream clothes with suede boots peeked out from beneath a radiant white cloak. While the notion of purity played across Jack's mind, the man's expression said this was less a cultivated, philanthropic fellow than an arrogant, self-opinionated Roman-emperor type.

"That probably has to do with the ignominy of Little Nobody's demise," Pretty Amazonia spoke up.

As Jack glanced over, she shrugged.

"Being stepped on in the middle of a fight with the Tick — well, we all knew it was a horrible accident."

The newcomer pursed his lips. "Why, because the Brick did the stepping?"

Jack swivelled to look at the Brick, and then his huge feet. "You stepped on someone?"

"Two people," the man said above.

"Hey." The walking slab sat back and held up his right thumb and index finger to indicate a size about half a centimetre. "They were *this* big. We were in the middle of a bout with the League. How could I see the bastards?"

"What league?"

"The League of Unmitigated Rotters." Once he knew he had their

23

attention that white-clad man up on the second level started to move. He glided slowly on the stairs, and Jack could've sworn his legs didn't move a single muscle all the way down.

"Ye ol' el grando entrance," he heard the Brick murmur. "Surprise, surprise."

Jack was still reeling with the idiocy of a name like the League of Unmitigated Rotters, but kept his trap shut as the late arrival came over and bowed in curt fashion.

"Southern Cross," he remarked, like he knew him.

"Yep."

"I'm the Great White Hope."

"Somehow that doesn't surprise me."

"Oh, indeed?" The man looked perky when he really ought to have been put out, given Jack's tone. "Welcome to our humble sanctuary. I trust these two misfits have shown you around as well as passed on our rather peculiar rules?"

"All sorted," the Brick said.

"Then let's get down to it, shall we?" The Great White Hope pushed out his cape in dramatic fashion in order that it ballooned about him, away from his buttocks, while he took a chair. "Good morning, ladies and gentlemen. Thank you for coming. I hope you brought your latte?"

Pretty Amazonia and the Brick deadpanned, "No."

"Do you see any cups?" The woman indicated the naked table.

"Bastard's blind," added her partner.

"Using 'bastard' is okay?" Jack whispered his way.

"Yeah, that's piss-mild language these days."

"Well," the Great White Hope barged on, oblivious, "this meeting will be very long, considering the fact I have a lot to say."

"Shock, horror." That was Pretty Amazonia.

Her boss shot over a glance. "Mmm, well. There is something playing on all our minds right now — there is the matter of death to discuss."

"Go on," said the Brick, suddenly serious.

"Well, for one thing, we've always — *always* — had a gentleman's agreement with the Rotters."

"What is this, the skies over France in 1917? A gentleman's agreement... Pfft."

"A gentlemen's agreement," repeated this leader as he stared down the Brick. "No one dies."

"Nonsense," Pretty Amazonia said. "Blandos are always copping it."

The Great White Hope smiled while he spiralled a hand in the air.

"Yes, well, that goes without saying — par for the course and all that! But we must never forget they are the very people we are sworn to protect." Here he rose to his feet and placed a hand over the place his heart possibly resided. "With great power, comes great responsibility." That out, he sat down.

Jack stared at the speaker. "Wow. Uncle Ben."

The man glanced at him. "Eh?"

"The quote. *Amazing Fantasy*, issue 15, 1962."

"I beg your pardon?"

"You do know you're citing from a classic comicbook? The one Spider-Man first appeared in. I think it's also used in the movies."

The Brick hit the table with his fist, taking out a chunk that clattered across pale parquetry. "I knew it! I knew the geezer was always nicking other people's lines!"

The GWH looked horrified. "Bah — I don't have to listen to this complete nonsense!"

"Course you don't, Napoleon," the Brick laughed. "You could go hide in your room again. Maybe brush up on more comic quotes while yer there."

"Better yet," Pretty Amazonia put in, "let's invest in a teleprompter."

This time the Great White Hope jumped to his feet.

"To hell with you. I'm going to find new recruits who actually appreciate this golden land of opportunity and adventure. This meeting is hereby adjourned. *Chrysophylax!*"

The man was gone in a blink. One moment there, the next M.I.A. Straight away Pretty Amazonia whistled and the Brick waved.

"Toodle-oo."

"Chrysophylax?"

"Nicked from Tolkien, some silly dragon," the Brick muttered. "Guy is obsessed with ol' J.R.R., case you hadn't noticed. In fact, why the joker hangs out in a world devoted to comics escapes me — wouldn't he be happier in some tra-la-la fantasy domain?"

Pretty Amazonia laughed. "This *is* a tra-la-la fantasy domain."

"No." The Brick held up a thick, knobbly forefinger. "There're diff'rent degrees o' fantasy. That guy's take gives me the willies."

"And Chrysophylax?" Jack asked again.

"Ah, 'Chrysophylax' is the GWH's open sesame, the ticket outta this wonderland."

"His password," Pretty Amazonia whispered in Jack's ear.

He nearly jumped — he hadn't seen her get up. She smiled down, apparently amused by the reaction.

"My singular knack."

"Teleporting?" While he couldn't smell brimstone, this told him nothing.

"Superspeed. You'd be surprised by what I can get away with."

Something — fingers? — caressed the inner thigh of Jack's left leg. The Brick was a small dot on the other side of the meeting table, and Pretty Amazonia hadn't moved an inch. Or had she? The smug look on her kisser tilted upward a fraction.

"See?"

"So much for honour," he mumbled.

"Live a little."

"You okay, bub?" the Brick called over. "Looks like you seen a ghost."

"Nah, I'm fine." Time to press on like nothing happened — even so, Jack kept his mitts covering his lap. "So, Brick, what's your password?"

"You kiddin'? If I say it aloud, I skedaddle outta here too."

"His is 'Geronimo'. Mine's — well? Mister B, are you going to play ball? Your turn."

"Hers is way too long-winded." The Brick blew out loudly. "Some Japanese gobbledygook like *Watashi, kanninbukuro no o ga kiremashita*. Sure I missed a 'na' or a 'wa' in there."

"No, no. You got it right, darling."

"Practice."

"And the meaning?" Jack asked.

The woman slapped her mouth into an exaggerated pout, and then prised it open to speak. "The phrase translates as 'I have reached my limit!' — it's pinched from my favourite *Pretty Cure* character, Cure Blossom."

"Pretty Cure? Is that why you use the Pretty Amazonia moniker?"

"Gawd, don't get her started," the Brick whined. "She's talkin' anime — but not decent mecha robots. Girls' stuff. Ouch."

"I get why you don't appreciate *PreCure*," Pretty Amazonia cut back, "since they destroy monsters like yourself every other week."

Andrez Bergen

#102

The three of them had swapped the boardroom for a patio —
stretched out on tri-colour banana loungers on a panoramic balcony
overlooking the city. Jack's seat was a '70s fusion of orange, tan and
brown. Behind him rose the bullet-shaped pinnacle of Timely Tower,
while in front, beyond a flimsy guardrail, was a view and a half.

Catching whiff of Jack's interest, the Brick edged up. "Three
hundred an' four point eight metres t'ground zero."

"That's how high we are?"

"Give or take a few feet. Never measured it meself."

While soaking up the sun they drank sham mint juleps served in
pewter cups, the Brick having advised that he swapped the usual
Bourbon whiskey for chilled, flat lemonade. Jack never experienced
a day anywhere near as perfect as this.

"If I were a cat," Pretty Amazonia mused, finishing her latest
round and placing the mug on a small table beside her, "I'd purr.
Looks like you brought the good weather with you, SC."

"As if. And call me Jack."

After over-theatrically sweeping off black, Manhattan-style
sunglasses to ogle at him, the woman huffed.

"In case it slipped beneath your radar, babe, I was being sarcastic
weather-wise. And we don't use real names here — even if Jack is a
fake." She raised a freshly filled cup in his direction. "Cheers?"

Jack frowned but returned the gesture. "Cheers."

"I have another gripe," interrupted the Brick as he sat up
completely, leading PA to stick her sunnies back on her nose.

"You're full of them."

"No wonder, out in this balmy weather and with this body — the
problem bein' I don't sweat, meanin' my inside temperature don't
regulate itself. I'm bakin'."

"Perhaps we should acquire glaze? You'd look a treat with some
funky colours."

"Ha-de-ha. Don't you know it's be-nice-to-gargoyles week?"

29

"Was that your actual gripe, or did you get distracted?"

"Yeah, I did, actually."

The Brick stood and threw a pail of water over his head. Jack was surprised to see a light veil of steam thereafter, and even more surprised to glimpse the Equalizers' logo on the bucket.

"It's the name o' the group," Brick was saying, "the Equalizers. I never did like the stupid moniker — what, we're only ever fated to play catch-up? We're never supposed to be leading? Geddit? Equal?"

"I get it," PA said. "What's your point?"

"C'mon, dollface, why don't we change now the Big O's gone?"

"Meh... Too much bother. Plus we'd have to update the stationery."

"So," Jack said in a loud voice while he reached over to a glass jug and refilled his cup, "you two ever considered sorting things out with a marriage counsellor? Much as I enjoy the bickering."

Both laughed, the reaction he'd been praying for.

"Cheeky," decided the woman.

"I try. And, since I have your attention, can you fill me in on some of the blanks?"

"Shoot," said the Brick.

"Well, for starters, you mentioned Stan — the Doorman — being a 'Blando', and I've heard the word lobbed about other times. What *is* that?"

Pretty Amazonia swapped merriment for boredom. "The Blandos are the Blandos."

"I feel a whole lot more enlightened."

"They're little people. Fodder," the Brick took over. "I mean look at 'em, even the Doormat, bless 'im — no superpowers, no personality. They're just plain bland."

"You're saying they're not important?"

"Damn straight."

"Like Christmas decorations," Pretty Amazonia helped out.

"Now you're losing me."

"Well, this's a huge city, right? Room enough fer millions of souls? Includin' the Rotters, there're about fifty o' us," advised the Brick. "It'd be pretty damned mundane an' empty if the Capes were the only inhabitants."

"And wouldn't be so much fun without an audience?"

"Somethin' like that."

"The Capes being people like us? Heroes."

Pretty Amazonia went to the barrier and crouched there, looking out over the city. A late afternoon sun was creating big shadows thrown by nearby skyscrapers. "The villains are also Capes — it's anyone endowed with a special gift."

"A gift?"

"Power."

"And these villains are members of the group you mentioned earlier — what was it, a League of Unrequited Rotters?"

She glanced over her shoulder. "*Unmitigated* Rotters."

"Unmitigated, yeah."

"Think I prefer unrequited," said the Brick. "Better bookend fer Equalizers."

"So what's the story with them?"

"The usual pleasantries — world domination, oppression o' the innocent, an' lust fer a bucketful o' gold doubloons."

"Led by Black Owl and his right-hand femme fatale Babushka, owner of outrageously bad Russian pronunciation." Pretty Amazonia stood up straight and stretched her legs. "You think her accent's real, Mister B? Sounds phony to me."

"If it's real, I'm Rock Hudson — boom-boom!"

The Brick laughed to himself, and then checked in the chuckles when he espied a blank expression apiece.

"Geddit? The actor? *Rock* Hudson? ...Oh, come on! You peeps need t'brush up on yer old movies — Sheesh."

"Don't worry about Mister B," PA confided. "His jokes are forever falling flat."

"Right," Jack said. "So let me get this straight — the Rotters are the bad guys? And our job is to stop them?"

"Mostly. Sometimes we play poker together when things get humdrum. Watch out fer Iffy Bizness — he's a devil with a deck o' cards. Cheats a lot."

"Yep, the arsehole's always trying to convince me to play strip-poker," Pretty Amazonia threw their way. She was waltzing toward the building, hefting several empty jugs.

The Brick paid too much attention to the woman's derrière, and then looked at Jack with what he took, amidst the rubble, to be a conspiratorial expression.

"She likes you, kid."

Jack leaned forward on the seat, fingering his lower lip between thumb and forefinger as he thought. "Is that a good thing?"

"Why ask me? Ain't nothin' more than a rollin' stone."

Jack held his gaze. "I have a feeling you know a helluva lot more than you like to admit."

"Awright, awright. Maybe yer onto somethin', or mebbe I'm thick as a proverbial brick — you decide." The man nodded in the direction of the open door while his voice dropped to a surprisingly soft level. "But be careful."

"Dangerous?" Jack quizzed with equal subtlety.

"Very."

"Neither of you boys knows how much."

Jack leapt up just as the Brick very nearly toppled over — where an instant before there was open space and furtive camaraderie, Pretty Amazonia had placed herself between the two men, a hand on each of their faces.

"Fu—!"

Far quicker than a flash, the woman's fingers covered Jack's mouth.

"Hush. No swearing, darling, you know the rules. You'll get kicked out of here."

Those intensely purple eyes were close to his, wandering up and down. Yes, she was beautiful. Yes, she also scared the willies out of him. This performance made Jack wonder if people had queued up to leave the Equalizers.

"Flippin' heck!" the Brick grouched as he pulled himself together. "I hate it when you do that!"

"You'll live," Pretty Amazonia said, still staring at Jack. She carefully removed from his lips one finger at a time. "No cussing?"

"Zero."

Jack backed away several inches, heart still racing.

"So, anyway," he said, shakily at first, "the Big O disbanded the Equalizers, hanging on to a skeleton crew to keep up appearances. What happened to the others?"

Pretty Amazonia considered for a few seconds, and then sighed. "They're still around, freelancing. Pop up now and then."

"No hard feelings about being given the flick?"

The Brick glanced at PA; she maintained a cool expression. "None that I know of."

"Everyone likes a grumble," added her teammate.

Just then Jack noticed something over the Brick's shoulder, high up in the sky. It was some kind of laser-light display visible even in daylight hours, and it painted there a huge, quivering circle with a lightning bolt through it.

"What the heck is that?"

After taking a look-see, the Brick swung back around. "That, kid, means it's showtime. Saddle up."

"Please don't tell me you have flying ponies."

"We're not the Four Horsemen of the Apocalypse," Pretty Amazonia grouched. "I wish. At least then we'd have an element of style and I could play Valkyrie. We're going in the *Rose* instead — follow me. Hopefully the GWH got over his temper tantrum and is here to pilot it."

#103

There was a gaping crater where once upon a time, according to Pretty Amazonia, a jewellery store called Harvey's Gems stood on the corner of Crestwood and Standard.

The place specialized in diamonds so had been frequently targeted by the city's marauding evildoers, though never before completely destroyed.

Around the crater was much debris including the shells of burned-out automobiles, blackened signage, and a lot of dead people.

Police officers busied themselves cordoning off the living with bright yellow tickertape. The blood splashed around — from inert, mostly dismembered bystanders — looked real enough. With carefree abandon the Brick and Pretty Amazonia played hopscotch amidst body parts while their recently returned leader, the Great White Hope, tried to find a parking spot for his blimp.

Looking about, Jack felt his stomach lurch and he eventually threw up brown bile, only partially a compliment of the imitation drinks.

Trouble was the mask.

Since the Capes were in public, hardly incognito, Jack had been instructed to wear the thing. This was a tight, full-face hood with holes only for the eyes, so he had to — out of necessity — roll it up fast to vomit.

On top of these travails, the mask made him feel a bit of a sore thumb, since he was the only person in the posse whose costume included one. The Brick got about in salmon-coloured undies, Pretty Amazonia had her frills, and the GWH his stainless whites. No masks. Sir Omphalos wore a mask — but he was dead.

"My, my. If it ain't little Miss Nancy Drew." The Brick nodded his great skull in the direction of a skinny woman who'd arrived at the scene in a mandarin-orange car, registration GEN 11. "1940 Ford 11A Super Deluxe Convertible Coupe. Neat-o."

"You and your wheels," Pretty Amazonia sighed.

"Them's enough to drive you mad, eh?"

"No — but your poorly steered wordplay drives me to distraction."

They watched the approaching woman while Jack pulled his mask back down, a sour taste in his mouth. She flashed an ID at a police officer and promptly marched over.

Around thirty or thirty-one, this lady had short, straight brown hair shaped like a 1920s Hollywood actress's bob. On top was a small hat with minimal veil that didn't reach further than the forehead. She had hazel-coloured eyes, looked workably attractive, and wore very little in the way of cosmetics.

To make up for the lack of attention to her face, the newcomer wore a smart, box-cut chartreuse tweed suit and pumps.

Her face grabbed Jack. There was a mix of honesty and obsessiveness there, plain to see — and in profile she had a striking aquiline nose that'd give Sherlock Holmes a run for his money.

"Hello, Brick. Pretty Amazonia," the woman said as she stopped before them.

The Brick paved a smile. "Gypsie-Ann."

"Who's your kewpie doll?"

"His name is Southern Cross," muttered PA, annoyed.

"Well, I guess the flag's a giveaway. Bit obvious. But isn't there a star missing?"

"Who cares? SC's our replacement for Sir Omphalos."

Gypsie-Ann presented the three with a birdlike expression, more hawk with that nose than sparrow. "Is he now?"

Jack couldn't put his finger on exactly why, but he felt this woman was hiding a certain amount of distress beyond the window dressing.

"Well," she barged on, "what's the scoop on Sir O's demise?"

"We were hoping you'd tell us," Pretty Amazonia said in a voice very flat.

"Why me?"

The Brick shrugged. "Yer the ace reporter."

The woman considered both Capes, and then settled her frigid glare on Jack.

"No leads I haven't already written about in the *Patriot*. Three spent cartridges by a grassy hill, right in the area witnesses say they saw a muzzle flash around the time O bought it. He was flying overhead, waving to kids on the cricket oval, apparently winged — and flew straight into the billboard, breaking his neck. No positive IDs for the shooter. Police Forensics believes the weapon used was a Tavor TAR-21 assault rifle."

"I don't even know what that is," PA said.

"Something exotic for these parts."

"Own a firearm yourself, dearie?"

"What's that supposed to mean?"

"Well, it's common knowledge the Big O was having it off with the Aerialist."

"Is it now?"

"And seeing as how they've both kicked the bucket only a few weeks apart, one could get to wondering."

"As one does," the reporter mused. "Like why Sir Omphalos disbanded most of the Equalizers straight after the death of the Aerialist — yet kept within arm's length the three members he trusted least." She shook her head. "Anyway, enough recrimination. There's a state funeral tomorrow. Are you going?"

"Haven't been invited."

"Funny, that."

"Is she a Blando?" Jack quietly asked the Brick while the women traded barbs.

"What, Lois Lane here? No bloody way. This is her shtick — super snoop. A Cape without bein' a Cape, so to speak."

The reporter surveyed the carnage. "Back to the here and now, in case you've forgotten — there's a crime to investigate. And I'd say, straight off the bat, this is the work of Iffy Bizness."

"How do you figure that?" scoffed Pretty Amazonia.

"The high Blando death toll — plus he conveniently left his calling card over there."

The woman pointed to a black, diagonal, oval-shaped sticker stuck on a street sign next to the crater. This sticker measured only a few centimetres across, with white writing, and was a fairly amateurish job.

"Could be old," Pretty Amazonia feebly protested as she peered closer. "Huh."

"Looks new to me — straight off the roll he carries with him."

Some rotund city bureaucrat in a morning suit, spats, a pork pie hat and a plump red face waltzed over from the kerb, surrounded by an entourage of well-dressed cops. Their badges shone.

"Oh crap, it's Big Bill," observed Gypsie-Ann. "I'm out of here now. Service — tomorrow."

As the reporter scuttled away on her heels, the fat man walked straight up to the Brick.

"Mayor Brown," PA whispered to Jack.

"That's his name?"

"Well, yeah, I suppose partly — the Brown bit — but he's also the mayor of Heropa, dummy. Keep your ears open. You may learn something trivial."

"He's one of us?"

"Are you kidding? Blando-city. Shut up and watch."

"Brick, Mister Brick," Big Bill wailed like a Greek grandmother at a funeral. "The city needs you to bring to justice the fiend that did this!"

A swarm of cameramen had arrived and started taking pictures with large flashbulbs.

"In this moment of need," the mayor now yodelled, holding two yellow-stained fingers heavenward, "we need the Equalizers!"

"Yeah, yeah, whatever," the Brick muttered, unmoved, but then he rolled his baby blues once coerced into shaking the mayor's hand before the press corps.

Mayor Brown edged closer still, and when he did Jack noticed the round, lightning bolt logo of the Equalizers on a small metal button affixed to his lapel. There were lots of small pinhole marks in the material around it, leading him to suspect the mayor frequently threw the badge on and off.

"Was that Miss Stellar I saw just now? Listen in... You couldn't put in a good word with her, could you, on my behalf? She seems hell-bent on ruining my reputation. Some of the lies she prints — scandalous!"

"Same song and dance at every crime scene," Pretty Amazonia was saying in a low voice. "Usually we let the Great White Hope handle Big Bill. Where is that loser, anyway?"

Jack wasn't listening.

He was watching the so-called Blandos — police and ambulance staff — as they went about cleaning the surrounding mess. He'd seen something pass between these people, and could've sworn there was a scowl and a dark look or two thrown the Capes' way.

Then he noticed it — a small black sphere, two-thirds the size of a soccer ball, on the ground a few yards away, with the same 'if?' from the sticker plastered on it. Jack went to pick up the ball, but recoiled before he touched its surface.

"Uh, guys..."

"What now?" PA complained when she, the Brick and the mayor

looked his way.

Jack pointed out the object on the ground. "I think I found this Iffy Bizness."

"Well, well," the woman muttered, realization settling in. "Heads will roll..."

GO WEST

#104

The Brick had set about making tea in the expansive kitchen of Equalizers HQ while he absent-mindedly chewed at one his Big Boss Cigars. The teapot was a vintage number — square-shaped, brown and beige, with hand-painted geometric designs.

"Japanese," the man said when he caught drift of Jack's attention. He was drying cups using a tea towel decorated with Scottish highland tartans, and then hung it on the wall. "A prezzie."

"I was wondering where you dragged that thing up from," commented Pretty Amazonia, who'd sat down on a blue metal stool, one too small for her, over by the kitchen table.

"The pot, or the towel?"

"What do you think?"

"I'll go with the pot."

"Suit yourself."

"Yep. So. Homicide victim number three. Head blown clear off. We now know the murders're indiscriminate — doesn't matter a hoot whether yer a good guy or an utter bastard."

"This could have been an accident — maybe he blew himself up in the process of pulling the heist?"

The Brick stopped what he was doing to look at Pretty Amazonia. "A cheat an' liar he may've been, but incompetent? Nah."

"Well, at least he was still wearing his mask."

"Some kind of lucky," Jack muttered from his place perched on the kitchen bench. "Is that like dying with your boots on?"

The woman crossed herself, a surprising gesture. "The police never found his boots."

"Where's the Great White Hope?"

"Off sulking in his quarters," the Brick said, retrieving a carton from a stainless-steel refrigerator that looked big enough to house a dairy. "Missed all the fun. Milk?"

Jack nodded. "Sure. For a leader, he spends a lot of time flying solo."

"One o' the reasons the Big O was our original boss. Sugar or honey?"

"I'll go with the honey."

"Good call. One squirt or two?"

The Brick held up a plastic container with a nozzle on the end.

"Ah, gimme two."

"Sweet-tooth, huh? Learn somethin' new about'cha everyday."

"Mister B stopped trying to suss me out a long time ago," said PA, tagging the observation with a laugh.

"Nothin' more to know, m'dear."

"Oh, you would be surprised."

The Brick again looked at her, serious now, while he handed a cup to Jack. "Actually, nah — I wouldn't be. At all."

Innocuous as it sounded, the Brick's comment wound the woman up. Her eyebrows lost their separate arches and became a shared straight line across her face — an integral part of a fast, angry burn.

"You think you're not an open channel?" she sneered. "You and your teapot."

This obscure rebuttal had its own effect.

The Brick moved quickly, fist clenched, to stand over Pretty Amazonia. Jack gave her ducats for bravado — she sat there on the stool with her chin up, a challenging look on her mug. Then again, she could afford to. With her speed she would be able to beat a retreat before the Brick started swinging.

Jack shifted his legs uncomfortably. "Nice tea."

"Grand," said the Brick, offering not so much as a sideways glance. Both parties inched closer to fisticuffs right there on the chequered linoleum floor — with sufficient tension brewing to serve a room full of guests after dinner.

"What kind is it?" Jack hedged.

"Mariage Frères."

Jack peered from one angry face to the other. "Okay, guys, take it outside or try getting back to the here and now. Better yet, calm down — won't you?"

The Brick glared his way. "You tellin' me, sonny jim?"

Jack sipped at his tea. "Asking."

"Right-o."

The Brick unclenched his fist to flex the fingers. His face, however, remained a clenched gathering of pebbles. Smouldering, Pretty Amazonia pulled her lips together in an indignant pout.

Jack decided changing the subject might help, since he couldn't see it making things worse.

"So, what's actually going on in Heropa with these murders? And have you given any serious thought to changing the locks on this place?"

PA heaped a cranky glare on Jack. "Which part of 'none of this is real' do you not get? It's all just idI shenanigans."

"IdI? — You mean idInteract."

"Der."

"What rock've you been shelterin' under? Pun intended," the Brick guffawed. Obviously Jack had distracted them from pummelling one another — just so they could channel the mockery onto him. Things could get worse after all.

"*Surely* you know about idIocy?"

In honesty he couldn't say he did — Jack was not altogether up on what went down in the big wide world of Melbourne, having buried himself away for two years — but a wild guess wasn't off the table.

"We're talking idInteract gaming with the cheat mode switched off?" He remembered the deaths of the Big O and Iffy Bizness. "Safeties inoperative. Making them very, very illegal?"

Just to be sure, Jack studied both colleagues. Acknowledgement filtered through in their faces and the truth settled in to roost. He felt brave enough to take another stab. "So Heropa is idIocy?"

"Not exactly."

PA stood, stretched her legs and arched her back — already she seemed in a better mood. "Let me give you a lesson in the basics: IdInteract is the state-controlled stuff, government-licensed. Legit."

"I do know this," Jack fudged. "I'm not as stupid as you think."

"Bear with me, SC, so there's no confusion."

"About me being stupid or not?"

"About anything you like."

"All right."

"Good boy. Now, let's get back on track. IdI's role, as you must know, is to entertain the masses, keep them addicted — but never kill the losers. Think of extreme sports without the bruising. Players create a whole world of advantages for themselves to make the game easier, usually via cheats — activated from within the game or created by third-party software and hardware. Things like enhanced abilities, superhuman strength—"

"Increased sexual prowess an' a killer libido," intercepted the Brick.

"—and so on." Pretty Amazonia wiped away a knowing smirk.

"I get the gist," Jack said. He hated to be lectured.

"Well, number one on the idI agenda is an automatic shut-off that stops a player from being fatally or seriously injured. We could debate the issue of trauma, since a load of officially-approved horror merchandise is ultraviolent and gore-central — but let's leave that to the Australian Recreation Classification Board."

"Who're in the pocket o' the pols, big biz and the profits made from them there horror," the Brick added.

"Yep."

Heading to a sink after finishing the tea, Jack rinsed his cup and noticed it had the brand name IMPERIAL DALTON stamped on the bottom, with smaller print reading *Morris René Goscinny*. An obligatory Equalizers hallmark hogged one side of the chalice.

"So, horror aside," he mused, staring at the silly symbol, "idInteract basically comes down to ego-stroking shenanigans with a nanny complex — anything goes, so long as you're safe."

"Basically."

"Sounds like here."

PA proceeded to touch her toes. The manoeuvre was a striking one, given her towering height.

"Except for the nanny," he heard the woman say as hair tumbled over her face and she was upside down, placing palms flat on the floor.

The Brick grinned. "That's where idiotic stuff comes in."

"Exactly."

PA had bounced straight back up to her full seven feet.

"IdInteract games are legal, whereas idIocy is not — this is bootleg, obviously idiotic street stuff with cheat mode and all safeties switched off. I don't condone that merchandise either — absolute madness. If you ever try it, SC, I'll kick you. You hear me?"

"Yeah, yeah."

"Better. Just saying. Anyway, platforms like Heropa sneak through somewhere in the middle. Usually idI and idIot lurks are private affairs for a single player. Our one is networked, so we all get to roughhouse together. We're not constrained by the boring restrictions of permissible produce — we can take risks and dice with death, but have rules and regulations to keep the anarchy of idIocy at bay."

"Why take the risk at all?"

"Adds an edge," said the Brick. "If Superman falls off of a skyscraper nobody cares, since the bastard's invulnerable. But if Daredevil takes the same plunge, equal chance he survives or is dead-meat. Human condition, an' all that."

"Okay, fine, if this is the case — what happened to the Big O and the Aerialist? Not in Heropa, but back in the real world."

"Haven't seen for meself. Been here the past few months, no time-out."

Jack glanced at Pretty Amazonia. "You too?"

"Mmm."

"Any guesses, then?"

The Brick scraped one stone finger along his paved left temple, like he was scratching. "I'm guessin' their brains were fried, going by what we saw of the bugger that was Little Nobody."

"After you stepped on him?"

"Yeah, yeah, rub it in, bub."

"So dying here kills people — pretty much — in Melbourne."

"In all likelihood," agreed PA. "The risk factor right there."

"But they shouldn't have died, since you people are supposed to have rules that stop the anarchy riding roughshod over your doormat."

"Yeah." The Brick frowned. "But anarchy stepped over the threshold. Somethin's changed."

"Then it's unequivocal, dangerous. I didn't sign up for self-mutilation."

"What did you sign up for?" PA asked.

Jack looked at her. "A comicbook world in which people didn't really die or vanish. They picked themselves up, made a quip, brushed themselves down, and moved on to the next adventure."

"The way it used to be — so long as you were a Cape, not a Blando." The woman put a hand on his shoulder. "You don't understand. You missed that part of Heropa, when things were light-hearted and fun. Everything now is out of whack."

"Could always go home, bub," suggested the Brick, screwing up his cement face and looking like Michelangelo had taken to one of his least-loved works with a mallet.

Jack thought about the notion for a few seconds.

"Never said I was doing a runner — and even though I didn't pop in for all the intrigue and back-biting going on, let alone impending homicides, I'm in no rush to return to my old digs."

"Why?" PA asked.

"For one thing, there's a mystery here to unravel."

"Oh, hurrah." The woman's eyes glittered from some inner amusement she wasn't one to share. "Why else do you think we're sticking on here, darling? Not for the scenery."

#105

Jack's first full day in the supposedly exciting city of Heropa was shelled out at the requiem for a man he'd never met.

He stood with the Brick and Pretty Amazonia on the tiled rooftop of a three-storey apartment building overlooking a main thoroughfare.

The metropolis had come to a standstill.

Thousands of people mostly in black lined the streets below, a majority morose, as immaculately dressed, sombre-faced police, musicians and dignitaries in morning suits filed past on the road proper. Prancing at the head of the VIPs was a tall, moustachioed man in a tuxedo and top hat.

"Donald Wright," Pretty Amazonia said. "The real power-broker in Heropa. Chief Justice, publisher of the *Patriot*, head of the Television Board of Control, Chancellor of Metro College, and a million other things. Wanker — you'd like him, SC."

A discordant marching band of children plodded along, deconstructing 'London Bridge is Falling Down', followed by more professional practitioners. When the bands weren't carousing, music played on loudspeakers — sight unseen — spitting out a blend of Gregorian chanting and despondent organ recital.

At a hiccup in the middle of the parade, a gorgeous sportscar appeared. Painted British racing green, this low-slung, well-rounded beauty was driven at a mundane pace that sullied the name and purpose of the sleek vehicle. The cop behind the wheel also stood out like a sore thumb since his starched blue uniform clashed with the shiny moss green.

"The Big O's 1957 Jaguar D-type XK-SS," confided the Brick, "with a Tony Nancy leather job an' Von Dutch's locking glovebox — identical to the one owned by Steve McQueen. Legendary stuff, only sixteen built, an' blended road-racin' science with art. Won three straight victories at Le Mans in 1955, '56 and '57. The chromed bumpers're a nice touch, if I say so meself."

"Blah, blah," PA said, evidently annoyed.

"Well, sad thing is Heropa state requisitioned it. Prob'ly rot away in some museum nobody frequents. And y'know what gets my goat more? That flatfoot there can't drive it prop'ly — the insult makin' a man outta Mac. Lemme at the creep!"

Precisely then, a coffin appeared several metres behind the Jaguar.

It was carried slowly, conjuring up howls and much tearing of hair. A small woman ran from the crowd to throw her body at the casket; the trio could hear shrieks a hundred metres away. Cops had to drag her aside.

Next to Jack, the Brick shifted uncomfortably. "Nuts — the croc tears're in full flow."

"Not fair. They adored him. Don't love us, though," Pretty Amazonia sighed, while toying with her long hair. "Even the Reset doesn't appear to have fixed that. I thought they'd forget and move on. Isn't it the way things are supposed to work?"

"Prob'ly helps havin' Gypsie-Ann an' the *Patriot* remind 'em in the mornin' paper."

"Maybe that's the answer."

Jack noted six sturdy police officers carrying the casket. A flag was draped across the top of this box, but not the Equalizers banner as he expected. Instead, he made out a navy blue number with a sailing ship dead centre inside a yellow rope, two crossed swords behind that, and several golden stars around the lot.

"What's the flag?"

"Heropa City's."

"Why not the Equalizers' one?"

"Dunno. Didn't ask us t'be pallbearers, neither," the Brick complained.

"Or choose the music. This dirge is killing me."

While the others continued their complaints unabated, Jack focused on the ceremony unfolding below.

He could see anguish en masse, one very public display of

emotion that affected him in ways he hadn't expected. Pretty Amazonia was right. These people did adore the Big O.

"Will you guys shut up?" he muttered.

#106

Turned out the Equalizers had to pay their rent for the penthouse aerie on the second of every month. Given how mundane banking could be, and the fact that dealing with Blandos was boring at the best of times, they rotated the chore. Jack's recent apprenticeship meant he jumped to the top of the short queue.

"The Blandos won't remember whether or not we settled up last month," Pretty Amazonia told him as she handed over an ox-leather, Dinah-brand Gladstone belted with lanyards, "but it's our duty to be honest."

When he opened the bag Jack spied stacks of one hundred dollar notes. There had to be thousands of bucks in there.

"Want to count?" the woman inquired, having taken stock of his observation.

"No, I trust you. Why d'you trust me?"

"Well, what are you going to do with money that's only legal tender in Heropa? Skip out downtown? By the way, you might want to be more discreet."

"Huh?" Jack thought she meant about theft.

"The costume."

"What about it?"

"Usually we wear civvies out there on the streets when we're not on active duty."

"Why? The Blandos care?"

"I wouldn't give a toss if they chucked a wobbly, but this is one of our customs. We play by old comicbook rules, secret identity and all, even if it's a given the secret doesn't matter. Brick's suits will be ten times too big for you, but I'm sure we can nick one of the Big O's outfits — he won't need them again — just till we get a tailor in to cut something specific."

"I don't know if I dig the idea of wearing a dead-man's duds."

"You'll live."

Jack looked at the woman's fine head of purple hair crowning her height. "I almost hate to ask, but given the colour and length of that mane, how d'you play it straight — and how do you hide seven feet?"

She gave him a lopsided smile — it could have meant anything from jest to warning. "Believe me, you don't want to know."

#107

Jack was in a line behind several grey-looking, inconsequential types. No wonder the Equalizers called them Blandos.

He yawned and stared instead at the architecture holding up the domed ceiling dozens of metres above. Now that was impressive. Not just the masonry, but also the sense of depth. So much space would never be found in Melbourne, not with its twenty million forlorn souls squeezed into every nook and cranny.

A row of six ceiling fans up there spiralled slowly, creating a pleasant draft, but the back of his neck ached from all the craning, so Jack looked down and straight ahead to see how much longer he would be stuck in this place.

The man in front of Jack peeled away in silence, not so much as a "thank you" to the girl behind the grille.

Which placed Jack at the front of the queue, one hand on the counter, gazing at the girl behind the grille as she gazed back at him.

He lost everything in mind — the banking, the building, other people, the money in the bag, how to breathe. Behind tortoiseshell cat's eye spectacles all he saw were a pair of wonderful, emerald-green eyes, the most precious articles in the world. In any world.

"May I help you, sir?"

It took Jack a second to realize she'd asked this, and he prayed she hadn't been forced to repeat the jingle while he was knocked out — in thrall to her peepers. The comment at least kick-started his diaphragm.

"Yeah. Sure. I — um — I'd like to make a deposit."

Jack wished he'd worn only his costume so she might have enthused — "Oh, you're one of those wonderful heroes, aren't you, the Equalizers?" — but instead he had over the top a herringbone wool three-piece suit by Walter Plunkett that was too roomy and garnered no reaction whatsoever.

This forced him to remember — forget the eyes; the girl was a Blando. If his teammates were correct, she wouldn't get excited and even if she did, it'd be fake-and-bake.

After he pushed over the Gladstone and the bag was opened to check, Jack watched the woman's downturned face. Age, about nineteen or twenty. Skin? Perfection, nary a blemish. Small, pixieish nose supporting the brown, black and orange frame glasses, arched eyebrows above those, and one compact, extremely kissable mouth — the whole caboodle lightly skirted with makeup that accentuated every little thing in subtle style. Then there was blonde hair, parted on the left side, proceeding in neat waves to her shoulders. The ends defied gravity and curled back up an inch.

Her eyes were the killer; so magnetic Jack had to avoid looking at them. He tried to focus instead on the girl's magnificent carnation-pink lips.

"Would you have your passbook?"

"Ahh — yep. Here you are."

Jack swallowed hard as he slid the bankbook across.

Their fingers brushed, and he noted a slight colour appear across her cheeks. In return, Jack's face burned. Briefly peering down to rediscover the girl's hands — slender and superb — while she sorted through the bills, Jack winced. He didn't know where to stare so he adjusted his gaze to the clothes.

The girl wore a fitted navy blue box-cut jacket, with a series of grape-rose coloured buttons, one inch in diameter, boasting rhinestone accents. The bottom hem of the jacket, visible just above the counter when she stepped back a moment, flared to produce a Peplum effect.

A mother-of-pearl badge affixed to the left lapel read 'Miss Starkwell'. The badge swivelled away from Jack, along with the sublime face. Instead, he beheld a profile that once again knocked off his cotton socks.

"Oh, Mister Winkle," she was saying to a cadaver at the next stall, a gaunt man pushing ninety. "I have a deposit here for $5,000. I hope you wouldn't mind confirming the amount."

"Certainly, Miss Starkwell."

The Gladstone exchanged hands, pristine to ancient.

"We won't be a moment, sir," Miss Starkwell assured, all professional.

A middle-aged gentleman with a droopy brown moustache, bulbous nose and very little chin sauntered up to the woman's side and placed his mitt on her shoulder. He poorly balanced a smirk that tottered toward patronizing, and those fingers on the navy blue held Jack's attention.

Unsure why, he felt angry.

On the newcomer's grey blazer sat a gold nametag with 'Henry Holland' inscribed. Apparently he was the manager — his badge looked like it'd cost a month's salary.

"Everything fine here, Louise?"

"Yes, sir."

Jack noticed the girl didn't look up at her boss. In fact she hardly moved and was evidently uncomfortable.

Meanwhile, Henry's contemplation sauntered over Jack and the other customers like they did not exist, since he was more intent on manhandling his employee. Those digits on the shoulder, nails cut far too short, had started to knead the material there.

Jack considered pulling away the metal grille and ripping the man's arm out — what did it matter? He was only a Blando — but super strength was not his stuff.

All he could maybe do would be to blow a hole through the bars, in the process blinding or maiming everyone around — including Miss Starkwell. Jack didn't know the extent of his power yet.

Thankfully, Mister Winkle had finished a plodding count of the cash.

"All done, Miss Starkwell," the walking corpse croaked while he laboured under the Gladstone's weight and placed it upon her desk.

"Thank you, Mister Winkle."

They were so damned polite and formal to one another Jack considered he might fall asleep standing up, but there was no denying the mischief of that creeping hand on the girl's shoulder.

Finally, she brushed off the thing.

"Thank you for your concerns, Mister Holland," Miss Starkwell said in a frosty tone. "Now, if you don't mind, I'd like to finish up with this customer."

"Yes, quite right, of course." The man clicked his heels and went back into his gloomy office.

"My apologies, sir, for the delay."

The girl's expression was certainly warmer than the one she'd just tossed her boss — but that was precisely when the wall caved in, amidst much racket.

People ran about screaming and shouting as bricks, mortar, and a cloud of dust settled.

Standing by a yawning hole leading out to the main street was a huge character about three metres in height. He was made up of iron hexahedrons, each the size of a Rubik's Cube, fixed together to create a man.

At least, Jack gathered this was a man.

His head, stuck on top of a short, thick neck, mimicked the shape of a hammerhead shark's — again made up of the metal cubes. The eyes were the only organic part of him, but since they sat on the sides of his head he was forced to tilt it to the left, then to the right, in order to see ahead. The design was so unwieldy that, out in the real world, he would've been the first victim of Darwin's natural selection.

"I-AM-BULKHEAD!" this gatecrasher roared, like it was meant to mean something, from a slit mouth cut between two cubes in what represented a face.

The roar echoed and resonated before it reached Jack's ears and ended up sounding more tinny than imposing.

"Course you are," Jack muttered.

He'd turned to face the beast with the vague intent of shielding Miss Starkwell and the elderly Mister Winkle, rather than any assertive pretence leaning toward heroism. If he could have, Jack would've hightailed it to the exit in an instant.

The metal man's left eye studied him for a few seconds, and then he swivelled his head so that the right eye could do the same. "I'm here for the dosh, the swandooly, the contents of the big safe in there."

"And I thought you wanted to make a deposit."

While he may've been cracking foxy, Jack was also playing for time — trying to run through options, or the lack of them, while stalling the big bastard.

Bulkhead's right eye blinked several times. "Why'd you believe that?"

"The grand entrance, and all."

Jack continued to think hard as he spoke. He could try to take out the fiend now — straighten his right arm and let him have it with one of those kooky power surges he'd supposedly been blessed with, according to Gonzo. Who cared if he wasn't in uniform?

"Smacks of big bucks," Jack rambled on in half-hearted fashion, "since you're going to have to pay for the damage."

The eye that regarded him hardened, if possible.

"Oh, a wise guy, huh?"

"Just looking out for my investments." Who knew from whence the bravado was flowing? *Skedaddle*, a more sensible side of Jack whispered in his ear.

Testing out the power blast was risky. There were dozens of people inside this bank scattered round them, and it really didn't matter that all of them were Blandos. Besides, the bank clerk Louise sat behind him — while Blando material she may've been, he couldn't shake those eyes.

He didn't get another second to procrastinate, since Bulkhead barged forward at surprising speed and bowled him over.

Jack bounced off a bench, using his head as a cushion, and was pretty much out for the count before lifting a finger. Bulkhead leaned over him, ripped the buttons away from his jacket and shirt, focused in on the Eureka Stockade flag on the costume beneath, and flattened his mouth.

"Hah, a Cape — thought as much. You had me worried the Blandos were getting out of line. Investment and all, like you mentioned."

He raised an ironclad fist and Jack decided on the spot he was a dead man, but that was before Miss Starkwell — Louise — figured into the action.

She was suddenly on Bulkhead's back, hitting him across the noggin with a steel typewriter. The villain threw up hands to protect his head, and then swatted her aside.

From where he lay, Jack couldn't see what happened to her, but he fretted and tried to rise. Bulkhead returned attention to him on the ground.

"Crazy dame," the villain muttered. "G'night, sweet prince."

With the flick of one huge iron finger, he knocked Jack out.

#108

When he came to, Jack was tied to a chair in the middle of a dark room that would've been somewhere in the vicinity of a thousand square metres in size.

These people had their very own banner on the wall, showing a big black bird with three legs.

Beneath the flag was a row of windows, red-lit and without a view. Probably they were red to compliment the surrounding black. Chains hung from the ceiling with no apparent purpose other than making the place look more dangerous, but a worrisome iron maiden decorated one corner.

"That's our filing cabinet," said Bulkhead, standing before him.

On the other side of the room, either aesthetically balancing the filing cabinet or offering a place in which to hang spare capes, there was an incongruous metal clothes-locker, and a few feet left of that was a Corinthian-style pedestal boasting a silver trophy cup with handles. 'Villain of the Month' was inscribed on it in big letters Jack could soak up from the chair.

Bulkhead followed his gaze. "Bet you do-gooders don't have one of those."

"I live in hope. You wouldn't have personalized toilet paper, by chance?"

"Of course not."

"Just checking. So," Jack surmised, "these are the digs of the League of Unmitigated Rotters."

"That they are."

"Gotta ask — who thought up the zany name?"

"What zany name?"

"The League of Unmitigated Rotters."

"Who knows?" Bulkhead chuckled, and the resulting sound scraped his prisoner's ears. "Someone who left for greener pastures, no doubt. But tradition is tradition in Heropa."

"So I'm learning. It doesn't exactly inspire fear or respect."

"What, the name?"

"Yeah."

"You think 'the Equalizers' inspires respect?"

"Point taken."

Jack's right hand felt clammy and cold. When he bent his head to take a peek, it was encased in a mitten of dull metal — in fact, the thing resembled a helmet that'd been refashioned with some creative gaffer-taping.

"That's right," his captor announced. "Your superpower is nullified. Could've been more original — pinching the same mojo as the Faceless Phantom. To shame."

"Bombastium?"

"Yep."

"Is it real? I never heard of bombastium before Heropa."

"Dunno. Don't get all technical — try it out if you don't believe me."

"Safer not to?"

"For sure."

"How'd you know my power?"

"On file."

"I'm in your books already? That was quick — I arrived two days ago."

"We don't mess about."

Jack gazed again at the silly banner on the wall. "What's the story with the three-legged chicken?"

Bulkhead glanced up as well. "That's not a chicken — any fool can see it's a crow. Don't you know your ornithology?"

"Looks more like a chicken. Who's the shoddy artist?"

"Dammit, it's a crow."

"Well, why the three legs?"

"I don't like you. You ask too many goddamned questions."

"Okay, just the one more. This is a super-villain group, right? Where is everyone? I see only you. Singular."

The giant shrugged. "Past their bedtime."

"Yeah, right."

"No, seriously — it's late and past their bedtime. If you could keep things down, I'd be much appreciative."

"I'll try."

"Good boy."

"By the way, you didn't misplace any of your number, by chance?"

Bulkhead eyed Jack with a single peeper, this time the leftie. "Whaddaya mean?"

"I had the pleasure of acquainting myself with Iffy Bizness. Well, with his head at any rate — the rest of his body I'm yet to meet."

"Dead?"

"People usually do die in those circumstances."

Bulkhead squinted. "You killed the prick?"

"No. Blew himself up, we think. Can probably read about it in the papers today."

"Friggin' unbelievable. Well, now."

The villain momentarily hung his head and Jack thought he might be in prayer, but then he raised himself again and had a crafty smile between the metal cubes.

"Tell me, you ever copped *Peter Pan*?"

"Er — no."

"I'm talking up the Disney movie, not the book."

"Neither, to be honest."

"Never read the book myself, personally, and not sure it reads the same as the movie. In the movie there's this part where the Lost Boys and Wendy's brothers — I forget their names — are captured by Red Injuns. They have this policy of letting each other loose after every bout — point being it's the rumble that matters, not the aftermath. Without each other, things'd get boring. So, we're going to cut you loose."

"No roughing up?"

"Well, now, never said that, did I? Figure you need a few half-decent souvenirs to show your mates."

His gleaming leer told Jack he would not enjoy the experience.

A few hours later, just after dawn, Bulkhead excused himself to go wake up fellow fiends Schlock Tactile and Kid Calmdown.

After much pointless carousing, including the pulling of Christmas bon-bons and a fight over the enclosed paper party hats, the three of them did a drive-by in their slick, retro-futuristic black Phantom Corsair six-passenger coupe, to drop Jack off at Timely Tower — unhitched the bombastium mitten and pushed him out a car door (which had a picture of the three-legged chicken on it) as they hooned past at thirty Ks.

Jack bounced a few times, collected a couple more souvenirs, brushed himself down, and took the elevator to the penthouse — after commiserating words in the lobby from Stan the Doorman. "It won't always be like this," he said. "You can do some genuine good in the world, but you need to hold onto your beliefs. Now, go patch yourself up."

Pretty Amazonia must've woken with the racket he made coming in the front door. He was surprised he didn't wake the entire building. The woman appeared on the balcony above the shared living quarters, dressed in a boudoir gown of gold lamé that was remarkably homely. She shook her head, descended, and then whisked him to a brightly lit bathroom.

"No one bothered teaching you to use your hands to protect your face?" she muttered, while she bent over and dabbed antiseptic on swollen abrasions.

"My hands were tied down at my waist."

"Excuses."

Jack couldn't see out of his right eye, but attempted a grin. This hurt more than the effort was worth.

"You really are tall, aren't you?" he remarked.

"The Brick says two hundred and thirteen centimetres of man-eating, gut-crunching terror. So, you met the Rotters, huh?"

"Charming fellows."

"They do have their moments." PA acted like an old hand with the treatment as she gently checked each wound on his face. "Strip," she then commanded.

"Do I have to?"

"Don't worry, even I wouldn't attack you in this state."

Very carefully, with a barely repressed groan or three, Jack unbuttoned his shredded suit, and then yanked off the costume. While doing so he got dizzy again and almost collided with the white porcelain sink. He was so close, he could read the royal blue brand name: HILLMAN.

"Isn't Hillman an old clothesline manufacturer?" Jack muttered, just as Pretty Amazonia's firm grip on his arm ensured he didn't receive additional head injuries.

"I have no idea. Are you delirious?"

More swabbing ensued.

"Stand up straight and stop slouching — anyone would think you'd never before been in the nud in front of a girl. Okay. There. Most of these contusions will heal overnight — part of the charm of this place. Your brain, however, will take a while longer to let go of the pain."

"You were a nurse back in Melbourne?"

"Who's to say I wasn't a doctor?" Jack was surprised to see a grim look on her face. "You've got to learn you can't ask me questions like that, not here."

"I can't ask your real name?"

"You know it already, hon. Pretty Amazonia. PA to my friends."

He winced as she dabbed a deep cut on his chest. "Ouch."

"You could've saved yourself this grief by using your password. Why didn't you?"

"I thought we needed intel on the Rotters."

"Liar."

Jack stupidly smiled again. "Okay. I forgot I could do that."

PA rolled her eyes. "Oh, my Lordy. So what did you find out from your accidental incursion into enemy territory?"

"Not much, but I think they're clueless about the deaths of Sir Omphalos and the Aerialist — they weren't even aware of what happened to Iffy Bizness."

Pretty Amazonia tossed a final cotton swab into Jack's friend the Hillman sink, and gave him the once over.

"There. Done. Now, SC, get to bed — doctor's orders."

#109

The next morning, Jack scrutinized his reflection in the sparkling, full-length mirror of another bathroom upstairs.

This was an art-deco looking glass, styled like a huge triangular shield with bevelled edges. The good-looking face returning same scrutiny was about twenty-five: chiselled features, neat blond hair, blue eyes. Nary a freckle nor blemish in evidence. Not a bruise in sight from the previous day's fun and games with the Rotters.

A perfect façade with white, straight teeth and a heroically dimpled chin.

Below that was a strong, stable neck, further down the blue costume riding atop sinewy musculature. Jack held up his right arm, flexed the bicep, and was so impressed he was tempted to go fetch a tape measure. This was like getting cosmetic enhancements without breaking the bank.

All up? A living, breathing dead-ringer for Jack Kirby's late 1960s drawings of Steve Rogers — a.k.a. Captain America — which was, anyway, what the original Southern Cross illustration had aped.

The flag emblem sitting on his hearty chest was pretty much the same one used at the Eureka Stockade fight north-west of Melbourne in 1854 — where the rebellious gold miners had stitched together five eight-pointed stars representing the *Crux Australis*, better known as the constellation Southern Cross. They'd joined these via a white cross on a dark blue background, one star at each end of the cross and a single star in the centre.

In his costume's case, however, the middle star was missing. Jack had no idea why this was so. Skewed memory?

Whoever'd been the artist of that original sketch of Southern Cross — the superhero — had obviously been clutching at straws for a symbol of Australianism. To be honest, he might just as well have used the Vegemite logo.

When Jack had once bothered to investigate further, the *MADE SIMPLE Self-Teaching Encyclopedia* told him the Eureka Stockade was

66

a failed rebellion that lasted just one day. Then again, it ended up inspiring male suffrage and was identified with the birth of democracy in Australia — something everyone had since been deprived of.

Jack returned to the face of this hero, which now annoyed him.

If he looked too long at the flawless mug in the mirror, he felt there was every possibility he'd go blind. He pulled on the mask, and that was somewhat better. It covered everything bar the eyes.

"Done with the preening?"

Jack lifted his gaze in the mirror's reflection and found Pretty Amazonia standing in the doorway to the bathroom.

She wore her bows and ribbons, leaning against whitewashed wood with her arms crossed, and Jack noted the woman nearly reached the top of the doorframe. Her expression was blank, aside from a vaguely upturned mouth.

"How long've you been there?" he asked, without turning.

"Long enough. You all right?"

"Sure."

"Any aches or pains?"

"Only the ones in my head you warned me about. What's up?"

"We have a group meeting, another humdrum affair organized by our fearless leader. Lose the mask — we don't need to follow formalities indoors. But let's grab coffee this time, so the bugger's jokes don't fall flat. Otherwise, it's downright depressing."

THE ORIGIN OF
SOUTHERN CROSS

#110

Back in Melbourne, the environmentally lashed, overpopulated last city on earth, Jacob Curtiss lived it up at Hikari Mansion.

Even so, let's not fiddle round misleading you but leap straight to the point — Hikari Mansion, near the corner of Hope and Elizabeth Streets in the northern suburb of Preston, was a Housing Commission dump.

Likely it'd been named, with perverted jocularity, in homage to the Japanese concept of a 'mansion': myriad apartments thrown together in the single building, with each separate flat containing one tiny room and a more compact bathroom. Jacob Curtiss therefore really resided in a box and this box was about twenty square metres.

He'd shared the place with his mother and father, before they were taken away. "Sedition," the uniforms had said as they shuffled off his parents, with their wrists and ankles shackled, black plastic bags over their heads.

That was when he was thirteen. He'd lived alone in the box for two years.

Jacob had no TV, no electricity — it was cut off when the bills weren't paid long before — and he stopped going to school on his fourteenth birthday. Figured nobody would notice, or weep, and he'd been proven right.

There were twenty-three other boxes the same size on this floor, twenty-four apiece on the other fifteen storeys of the Housing Commission block. They were shoved full of families and couples and kids and elderly types too afraid to communicate with one another.

Sometimes, when he needed a sense of space, Jacob would trek to an abandoned locomotive graveyard half an hour's trudge from Hikari Mansion, close by the ruins of Batman Station. There was a gutted carriage there, stripped of anything valuable, parked on uneven gravel since the iron tracks had also been plundered. Usually

Jacob sheltered beneath the car with a large sheet of plastic, listening to the rain on top, watching it spatter and torment the mud and eternal puddles.

Most of his time, however, the boy was home.

In his particular 20^2 cubicle, Jacob hoarded things, mainly books. A number of these had been left behind by his parents, like the dog-eared, constantly underlined and asterisked Penguin Classics paperback of Thomas More's *Utopia*, which belonged to Jacob's father. The others he collected from derelict houses, junk piles and rubbish bins, many of the books water-damaged — yet legible regardless.

There was a black-bound hardback of *The Maltese Falcon* by Dashiell Hammett, published by ImPress Mysteries, New York, with an old price sticker on the back in Indian rupees (175 Rs).

He had eighteen of the full set of twenty-five volumes of the *MADE SIMPLE Self-Teaching Encyclopedia*, published far back in 1964, yet still in relatively good nick despite the mould.

One of Jacob's favourite tomes was a hefty hardcover from 1970, titled *This is Australia*, by M. Sasek: a simple picture book with vivid red binding that had a painting of a girl holding a koala. She was dressed in a check one-piece with a boater on her head.

Another prize was S. D. Robinson's *The History of Art*, published through Wyeth Press in Boston, 2011. This boasted either a legitimate previous owner's name or a dadaist pisstake — 'Dick Mutt' — scrawled inside the front cover in thick black ink. Some of the pages had been loose, but he sticky-taped these into submission.

Not to forget the *Unabridged Illustrated Encyclopaedia of Classic Cars: The Globe's Most Fabulous and Innovative Cars and Hot Rods, 1920 to 2000*, edited by Buster Camshaft. Given the length of this tome (it clocked in at six hundred pages), the publishers were able to fit the exceptionally long title on the spine.

But Jacob's pride and joy was another kind of printed matter.

Several plasti-board boxes sat in the middle of the room, packed with hundreds of ancient comics from the 1960s. These particular containers, unlike the residential boxes hereabouts — which were sterile and lacklustre — sheltered a sense of wonder.

To deter the constant humidity and dampness, every issue was individually wrapped in a plastic sheath, each a full sixty microns thick, seven and a quarter inches wide by ten and a half inches high, bearing a one and a half inch tuck-in lip.

Between books, the boy would slip out a random comic, throw himself on the worn floral carpet that pretended to hide the concrete slab beneath, and flick through pages defining an alien realm in which justice was king and superheroes fought the good fight to uphold dignity and equality. There was laidback humour in them, too, a sunny-side-up sense of cheeky bravado — since the world wasn't the dystopia that existed just outside the door to his box.

Jacob read by plasti-wax candlelight or, depending on the time of day, via the distorted illumination courtesy of a giant Hylax neon advertisement outside the only window. And he knew a happiness he otherwise didn't think could exist.

On the walls inside his box, on every bit of existing space of the dirty beige wallpaper, between bookcases and stacks of books, were paintings of superheroes and monstrous villains in action and in flight.

Since Jack wasn't the finest artist, these were glorious, idyll-defining eyesores.

On the rare occasion, Jacob broke away from escapist paperwork and murals to stare at the single, square mirror above the sink.

This was filthy, stained with toothpaste, soap, morsels of rotted food. He hadn't cleaned it since his mum went away. Beyond the gunk, he could make out his reflection: overgrown, mousey-brown hair past his shoulders that hadn't seen scissors or a brush in two years, join-the-dot freckles scattered across a pale face. The tiny beginnings of downy hair on the chin. Skinny as. Shorter than other kids the same age.

His dad's razor-set lay abandoned at the bottom of a plastic basket next to the sink, but the remaining blades were rusty and he'd wasted the can of shaving foam doing decorations on the window last Christmas.

Jacob regarded his brown eyes. They looked hollow, dark rings beneath, nothing to sustain them aside from reading matter.

While roving about the box, the boy usually wore one of his father's t-shirts, a faded black number a couple of sizes too big, threadbare, unwashed for months — it still somehow reassuringly smelled of his dad's cologne.

Even though the screen-printed writing on the tee sat in reverse in the mirror, he could recite the slogan in his sleep:

'Go to Hell? I'm Already There.'

#111

There was a letter that Jacob read and re-read, on dozens of occasions — so many times that it was worn out and the words faded in the folds. This correspondence had been written using a manual typewriter on foolscap, and the writer resorted far too often to semicolons, but even so it caught his imagination and went thus:

TO: MR STAN LEE,
PUBLISHER, MARVEL COMICS

Dear Stan,
Please find enclosed an idea.

I suppose I've directed this letter and the accompanying idea to you personally because of the admiration I bear towards you in the creation and fermenting of such ideas as The Fantastic Four, Thor, The Avengers, The X-Men, et al. That, and the hope that you will see something of use in the enclosed idea, or perhaps pass it on to someone else to consider it. P'raps even just glance at it?

I've been an ardent fan of Marvel since 1974, at the tender age of nine, when I chanced to pick up my first copy of Captain America; and ever since then I've wondered why Australia couldn't have its own icon of superherodom. Britain has gained Union Jack and Captain Britain; Canada has Vindicator/Guardian; Africa the Black Panther. Yet we down here in Australia find ourselves cheering on Americans, Brits, Canadians, Africans, Irelanders, Norse myths, heroes of Grecian antiquity — but no Australians. At times it gets frustrating because there's no-one from

"here" to follow. Marvel at least recently gave
us the character of Gateway, but his is a minor
role, and the only one in each of the major
comics production houses. Australia is a country
of over sixteen million people, of which 90%
live in the cities. Is one person all we would
have in the superhero market?

So, with these details in mind, we come to
that accompanying piece of Australianism, that
you could perhaps utilize or develop upon if
ever you get the compulsion to create an Aussie
counterpart to your very own Captain America. I
call him SOUTHERN CROSS. Why Southern Cross?
It's an idea with a long history, beginning 'way
back in high school with those absent-minded
doodles that appeared on my lecture pads;
evolving into the characterization pictured
overleaf. The "Southern Cross" is actually a
constellation visible only in the southern
hemisphere, and it appears on the Australian
flag. The version of it employed on our hero's
tunic is a derivation of the rallying flag of the
Eureka Stockade in the nineteenth century —
Australia's first and only rebellion, and
revered ever since as a libertarian struggle
against repression (in this case, British rule).

The letters 'S' and 'C' that appear on our
hero's back are fashioned into the shape of
boomerangs (another Australian symbol); his
costume is navy blue, with white detailing; his
power is ambiguous — it's the one thing that I
couldn't resolve, even after all this time! An
idea could be that the character had a mutant
power of repulsion of any sort of blow struck

against him... Thus you could play with the notion that, although he's a national hero, Southern Cross is also a mutant, and gets caught up in the whole mutant hysteria?

Anyway, do with him what you will; hopefully, use him. If not, get some sort of idea from his draft and create something else! Just remember that there are a large number of Marvel fans down here who could do with a "home hero". Earlier this year I spent a week in Los Angeles, and a week in New York, and was struck by the increased awareness most Americans now possess with regard to Australia — so couldn't Marvel lead the way and extend that awareness by a foray into the untouchable grey zone down under?

I have my fingers crossed. And my toes. Thanks for bothering to read this slightly long-winded letter. One thing I'd really appreciate is to hear from you or your colleagues by return — giving an indication of what you think about my idea, and also if you could fill me in about the possibilities of writing something (anything!), okay?

Thanks,

Yours faithfully,

Wally Deaps.

Andrez Bergen

#112

As it turned out, Jacob found Heropa while wandering a rain-drenched street (Grandview Road) just beyond the ramshackle, junk-cluttered entrances to Hikari Mansion.

He'd been scrounging for something to eat, having rifled through various moss-green plastic rubbish containers, while evading police and security types, but found most of the bins filled with murky water — nothing edible nor potable.

That was when a fossilized hippy/homeless man — in all probability the geezer juggled both the professions — sidled up to him with a handful of soggy paper flyers.

This man, sixty-odd, had on a tattered vinyl poncho with peace symbols all over it in various shades of discolour. He had dreaded hair and a dreaded beard in which Jacob could not spy a mouth, and he stank of mould, incense and mothballs. The mouth was confirmed by wafting breaths of something unbrushed for an agonizingly long time.

"Looking for escape from the madness, my boy?"

"Not interested." Jacob circled past, hoping to put some space between him and the stench — he pictured some indoor acoustic guitar circle singing 'Kumbaya' to the accompaniment of god-awful bongo drums.

"Wait, wait. Hold your over-excited horses — whoa, Nellie!"

The Hippy thrust a sagging, half-torn flyer into Jacob's hand before he had the chance to snatch his fingers away.

Jacob looked at the message; worried it might carry some breed of smell bacteria and wished he'd brought along a pair of salad tongs with which to hold the thing. There was a poorly drawn picture of a masked man, a bit like Batman's sidekick Robin as he was conceived in the 1950s, smiling, with no worry in the world.

The caption beside this junior hero's head was written in bold caps that said HEROPA and, in smaller lettering — the ink of which was starting to bleed — *Escape to a new life of heroes and adventure!*

77

"Come along anytime," the Hippy urged, at the same time that he leaned closer with stinky fumes.

Jacob tottered away, trying hard not to screw up his face. "Got no money. Can't afford it."

"Heropa costs nothing."

"Everything costs something."

"In this case? Only your leisure."

There was the hook. Free, and a timewaster to boot. Jacob finally looked into tired, slate-coloured eyes. "What's the catch?"

"No catch. But you look like you could use a romp, if not a bite to eat. Too young to get about with that hangdog countenance you're folded up in. This here is everything you ever dreamed about in comicbooks."

"Who says I dig comics?"

Grey peepers sidled down. "The t-shirt, my boy. The t-shirt." He pressed a finger into Spider-Man's print-faded forehead. "I can tell you have a hankering for some place better than this nightmare in motion."

#113

The ink-bled address scrawled on the flyer ended up being a ruse.

The place was an old, boarded-up milk bar that hadn't seen custom in at least a couple of decades. Jacob had kicked the door with what — frustration? A sense of bitter reality? Of course it was a hoax. What'd he expected? Escape? There was no escape. The world was the world.

Jacob walked from beneath a sheltering doorway, back out into the deluge. His clothes were already soaked through, his skin itched. Precisely the moment a tiny woman approached, wrapped to the nines in torn plastic garbage bags.

"Heropa?" she inquired.

"You were scammed too?"

"No scam. It's real. But you need to go some place else. First up, a question: How did Peter Parker become Spider-Man?"

"You're kidding?"

"Fine. See you." The little lady turned about.

"He was bitten by a radioactive spider. Any fool knows that."

She chortled while coming back. "Not so many fools as you'd think. Go here." The Bag Lady showed him a different address, and retracted it as he reached over. "No, you remember. Safer that way."

"For who?"

"Everybody."

"Who's everybody?"

"You'll find out when you get there."

"That address?"

"No, silly. In Heropa."

#114

The address the Bag Lady offered up led him to an empty lot. A man hidden in a waxy, plasti-board crate in the corner of the open space, secure from the downpour, asked a different question after Jacob politely knocked.

"What were the names of Batman's parents?"

"Thomas and Martha Wayne."

"Listen carefully," the unseen Box Man's voice said from within. "I'll give you the next directions only once. I don't care if the rain is making a racket and you can't hear me properly."

"I can hear you okay."

"Aren't you the lucky one?"

Third port-of-call was a three-storey, nineteenth-century redbrick warehouse down a flooded laneway. There were beaten-up old skips, fallen walls and rusted shopping trolleys littered about that together prevented access by any means other than foot. This was tricky enough, since it required a lot of climbing and much slippage.

The place had corrugated steel on some windows, but similar dressing on the others had obviously been torn away for salvage, and there was a helter-skelter of planks and plastic sheeting stuck on.

The warehouse, too, was a red herring.

The by-now-customary point-man — in this case a middle-aged punk with a misshapen umbrella and a leather jacket that was probably really vinyl and way past its use-by — intercepted Jacob and quizzed him with another teaser, this time pinched from an old cartoon ('Who was Popeye's girlfriend?' — Answer, 'Olive Oyl').

The Punk passed on a street number in the same neighbourhood.

Wildish goose chase this may've increasingly resembled, but the fact was Jacob had little better to do with his time, and at least the wayward search killed his appetite. He wondered if these watch-people hovered there twenty-four hours a day, if they had rotating shifts, and whether or not they got paid.

At the fourth address the question was dead easy ('What is Superman's weakness?' — Answer, 'Kryptonite, magic or lead') and at the fifth obscure ('When was the first issue of *The Fantastic Four* published?' 'According to the cover, November, 1961').

Outside address six Jacob stopped, waiting to be accosted, but nobody showed.

Before him was a dilapidated Victorian terrace house, street number 43, two floors of bluestone and perhaps an attic above that. There were a brother and sister joined at the hip on either side, in equally shoddy condition.

The gate was missing most of its pointed bars and let out an almighty creak when he shoved against it. After that he weaselled past an overgrown, very dead bush with zero foliage, and went up five steps to the verandah, where most of the floorboards were absent and the cast-iron ornaments long-since plundered.

Stepping carefully from remaining slat to remaining slat, Jacob reached the heavy-looking wooden door and pushed. Of course it was locked, or barred.

Above eye-level on the warped upper panel where a window probably used to be, there were three sketches of apparent female superheroes done in charcoal or pencil and rendered in a style that would've made Japanese kids' book illustrator Ryōji Arai proud.

Too high to have been done by a child's hand unless the tyke had a step-ladder, just above their heads was a silly plastic knocker that looked like a lightning bolt — far newer than the ancient door — so he swung it twice, and then a third time for the hell of it.

Nothing happened for a minute or so. Jacob had no idea how long, exactly, since he didn't own a watch.

"Password?"

The question had come from the other side of the thick door, so soft the boy barely heard it above the ruckus of the rain. "Huh?"

"Password." That voice, louder now, had a hint of irritation.

"What password?"

"Come on, come on, haven't got all day."

"Heropa?" Jacob guessed.

"Bzzzt—! Push off."

"The Hippy sent me."

"I don't care if the Green Lantern gave you an invite. Get lost."

Jacob walked carefully in a circle out there on the verandah. "Wow, you're a wanker, aren't you?" he said in a loud voice as he dodged holes.

The voice inside sounded angry. "Beat it!"

Jacob turned to go. "So much for comic fantasies."

"—Bingo! Comics it is. Why didn't you say so before?"

"What?"

"The password: comics." The voice had taken on a warmer, conspiratorial edge. "Okay, one more question, a doozie, but if you get it, I'll open up. What was the Red Skull's real name?"

"Depends. Johann Schmidt, Albert Malick, or George John Maxon?"

"Sheesh, I dunno — I would've been satisfied with only Schmidt."

The door creaked open a few centimetres and another teenage face appeared before Jacob's glare. This boy had squinty rodent eyes, sunken cheeks, severe acne, and lips looking like they'd recently been employed to suck on a lemon.

"Was there really three Skulls? I just heard of the one."

"You going to tell me the next address, or do I go home?"

"C'mon, lighten up," whined that mouth surrounded by the damage — acting as if these two kids facing each other on a reprobate's doorstep had upped the ante to chumminess. "Your journey's over! What're you waiting for? Come on *in*!"

Just through the entrance was a long passageway, one so dimly lit it was impossible to see the high ceiling above. Water dropped onto Jacob's shoulder when he stepped inside, having fallen from somewhere high up there in the darkness, and that reminded him.

"He had a daughter, too, who used the Red Skull name."

"Huh?"

"Sinthea Schmidt. Look into it."

"Oh, you'll fit right in. Follow me — or, as Igor would tell his master Frankenstein, 'Walk this way'." The other boy pretended to drag his left leg as he went ahead.

Jacob followed the Rat on squeaky boards. He noted a succession of tiny rooms, with people in them — dead or asleep, he couldn't tell — lying on chesterfields and covered by tatty space blankets. Each individual had two small machines beside him or her, an IV drip, and something that looked vaguely like a lunch bag.

Cabling linked the machines, burrowing from one room to the next. Often, accommodating this communal technology, there were holes crudely punched through the brick walls.

The place looked like an opium den Jacob had seen in a Sherlock Holmes comic published by Dell — what was it called? 'The Man with the Twisted Lip', he remembered.

"These people high, or something?" he asked, louder than he'd planned.

"Or something. Ohhh, really something."

The two of them trudged up a steep set of wooden steps, several of which were worn smooth or broken, and on the next floor entered a small living room with battered furniture.

The only other decoration that clung to one wall was a tattered poster for Aldous Huxley's *Brave New World*, rendered in some kind of cubist hand.

"I'm not sure that's the best sales-pitch for what you're trying to hawk," Jacob observed, eyes on the poster.

"Dunno what you mean."

The opposite wall to the adjoining house had a door — apparently, they were linked.

"Take a seat, tiger," the Rat suggested.

Still suspicious, Jacob sat down.

#115

Ten minutes later, there was an addition next to the Rat.

This man had a black overcoat on its last legs, a Ralph Steadman-designed *Fear and Loathing in Las Vegas* t-shirt, black pants gone in both knees, and fourteen-hole Doc Martens wannabes. Thirtyish, with long, green-dyed hair and a faraway look. Jacob decided straight away to label him Gonzo.

The Rat had pulled up an ancient red and white handle-backed diner chair, a simple mix of 1950s rusted metal and vinyl, but Gonzo settled on an overturned maroon plastic milkcrate.

"So, what shall it be?" Gonzo inquired.

"Here." Jacob took out an old pink satin purse that had belonged to his mum.

"Kinky," the Rat decided.

Jacob scowled. "Not the purse. Jeez. This."

He extracted a twice-folded sheet of yellowed A4 paper and carefully flattened it out on the scratched and beaten coffee table between them.

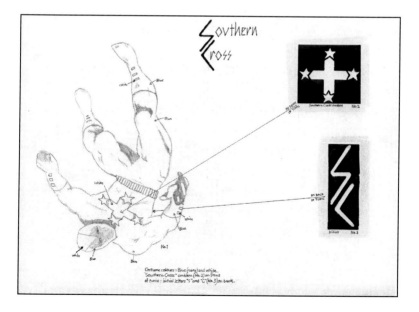

This was a lead pencil drawing of an upside-down superhero without a cape, with little details written in blue ink, arrows pointing this way and that. It said 'Southern Cross' in bigger letters on the upper right-hand side of the page, next to more detailing in cerulean blue: two boxes that showed a stars-and-stripes logo for the front of the costume, and a boomerang motif of the hero's initials, SC, supposed to go on the back.

"Swanky." That was the Rat again.

"Any special name?" Gonzo asked, wiping green wisps away from his eyes.

"Like it says there." The boy pointed at handwritten text at the top of the picture. "Southern Cross."

"Southern Cross? That's a bit tacky, isn't it?"

"Think it's been done before too, boss," the Rat piped up — to which Gonzo hung his head.

"I'm not your boss. How many times do I have to hammer that into your oblivious skull? Boss, no. See? Easy." The man lifted his eyes back to Jacob. "And you want this exact costume?"

"Pretty much."

Now raising his eyebrows, Gonzo pushed surprised. "Even the '80s boomerang-style font for the back of the duds?"

"*Passé*," the Rat agreed.

"Well, we can ditch that. The flag'll do — unless you think it's dated too."

"Flags are always old hat, which is why they work. And I think we'll go for cerulean blue instead of navy." Gonzo squinted as he turned the piece of paper over. "There's no mention here of powers."

"Hadn't thought about that." Jacob shuffled nervously on the sofa, *Brave New World* still in his field of vision. "Listen, this is the real deal, right? Not some sort of cult that preys on losers like me?"

"It's real enough, buster," Gonzo said, all prickly.

"Better quality than the flyer?"

"Depends which one." Settling back on his crate, the green-haired man looked Jacob over. "Tell you what, let's give you plasma blasts.

The last Cape using them, the Faceless Phantom, quit six months ago. Arsehole was a beer-killer, and no one will notice. Anyway, he used his eyes."

"If this person was faceless," Jacob piped up, "how could he have eyes?"

"Don't worry yourself about that," Gonzo replied. "We'll endow this power to the right hand. In your hour of need, all you need do is aim at a target, think about unleashing the power, and—"

"Hey, presto!" announced the Rat. "Va-voom!"

"Right," Gonzo agreed, even if his expression betrayed annoyance that some thunder had been stolen.

"Can I have any power?"

"Within reason, yes. But only one. And each has its Achilles' heel. Yours is the fact that plasma blasts can go through anything, except for bombastium."

Jacob felt his left eyebrow raise itself. "Bombastium? Something like adamantium, I'm guessing."

"Stronger. Nothing beats it for elasticity and strength, since this is a vibranium/adamantium mix. Also, did I tell you no one can fly in Heropa? Nup? It's one of the golden rules — no Cloak of Levitation here. Unless you sneak past that rule with the available technology, which some unruly people have done."

"Can I opt instead for invulnerability?"

The Rat shook his head. "Nobody gets invulnerability."

"Mate, you won't be needing it where you're going," added Gonzo. "Capes never die. Only the Blandos give up the ghost."

"Only the stupid Blandos!" came a squeaky echo.

"In Heropa?"

"Heee-*bloody*-ropaaa!" The Rat pumped his fist.

TWILIGHT OVER HOBOKEN

#116

Jack went back to the Warbucks & Erewhon Union Trust Bank, on Fawcett Avenue, a couple of days after his unplanned rendezvous with Bulkhead.

The incentives for doing so were to pass on his gratitude to the teller, Miss Starkwell, and make sure she was okay. A Blando she may've been, but Jack kept remembering the girl's eyes and her heroics with the typewriter.

In fact, the eyes were the real reason for this visit — thanks be damned.

He wore something new, a grey wool suit with red and ivory pinstripes that he'd been fitted with by a tailor in the suites of Equalizers HQ. On the back of his head Jack had a gun-grey felt fedora.

When he arrived, though, Miss Starkwell wasn't at her desk. Jack asked the old guy, Mister Winkle, to have her paged.

While waiting, he pretended to do some browsing, even if — in actual fact — he was steeling his nerves.

The wall Bulkhead crashed through was completely repaired and looked like it'd never been scratched. Instead of appearing brand spanking new, the wallpaper there had deteriorated with age. Jack moved on, to study an oddball lump of metal on a perch over near the main entrance.

"*Twilight Over Hoboken.*"

"Huh?"

Jack jerked about to find himself face-to-face with Louise — Miss Starkwell — and her cat's eye glasses. Once again, he found it difficult to breathe.

The girl was decked out in a sleeveless, knee-length flapper dress in varying blues divided by a diagonal ivory lightning bolt. There didn't appear to be any injuries to her body. She had a small, business-like smile, but there was no hint of recognition in her glorious, emerald eyes.

She was merely being friendly and informative to a customer.

"The sculpture you're admiring, sir. It's called *Twilight Over Hoboken*. By the famous Italian-American artist Pierre Picolino — do you know him?"

"Can't say I do. I don't see it."

"What don't you see?"

"The twilight."

"This is an abstract piece. You're supposed to imagine it."

"Still."

"There's always something there, sir, if you look closely enough."

Jack, somewhat overwhelmed, gazed at the girl's face. "I'm beginning to realize that. Please, call me Jack."

"All right. You're the gentleman who asked for me?"

"I am. I wanted to say thanks for the other day."

"Oh! I'm so glad I could be of assistance."

Jack could see she had no clue what he was talking about, but she covered nicely.

"Yeah, well, it's always nifty to get good customer service these days, you know?" Jack, on the other hand, covered poorly — he had to stop the ramble in its tracks. But there was one more thing to pursue. "Listen, what time do you finish here?"

"The bank closes at four, and I usually stay on an hour after that." Those eyes darted his way. "Why do you ask, sir?"

"Jack." He swallowed with difficulty. "And I'd like to take you out for a drink."

"A drink?"

"Tame stuff. Coffee only. I'll be a complete gentleman, I swear. We can talk about *Twilight Over Hoboken*." Was that panic in his tone? God, he hoped not.

"I don't know. This is highly irregular."

"Go on — be a devil," Jack dared.

"A devil?" The girl laughed softly.

It was a joy to see some of the veneer flake away. She peered over at Mister Winkle, and then nodded the smallest fraction.

"At five o'clock, then."

"On the dot." *Unbelievable,* crossed his mind.

#117

They were perched on maroon-and-cream hound's-tooth pattern cushions, atop barstools made from rosewood and gleaming chrome, inside a diner pretending to be a streetcar. The place was called Quality Street.

Since the evening was pushing chilly, Louise had donned a tight sweater, a red and gold cotton scarf, and a chocolate-brown beret. Jack did notice she'd added red to her lips as well, but he was more preoccupied trying to stop his right leg from jigging nervously.

"What do you want to know about Pierre Picolino?"

"Who?" Jack had gone completely blank.

"*Twilight Over Hoboken.*"

"Ahh — the artist!"

"Your excuse for whisking me off here."

"Oh, yeah."

Miss Starkwell took a small bag off the stool beside her to place on the table. After clipping it open she whisked out firstly a small paperback, *Run for Love*, and then a packet of Paul Jones blended cigarettes and an ostrich skin-covered cigarette lighter. The girl flipped the lid of the lighter and rotated the flint wheel with a dainty thumb to create flame. Jack was mesmerized.

"You can't smoke here," he finally managed to utter.

"Really?" Louise glanced about. "Oh, I'm sorry — I didn't see any signage."

"No, I mean you can't smoke here. In Heropa."

Louise looked at him with wide eyes that suddenly sparkled in merriment, and she laughed in a boisterous manner.

"Oh, go on! Next thing, you'll be telling me our chain-smoking mayor's introduced some kind of tobacco-prohibition! God forbid!" The flame hit the end of the cigarette in the corner of her mouth, and she quickly inhaled. Smoke drifted out lazily a few seconds later. "I needed this. My boss drives me crazy. I only smoke at night, you know."

"Mister Amsterdam, was it?"

"Holland. Henry Holland. The man cannot keep his hands to himself."

"Yep, I noticed."

Jack sipped at his coffee, when in actual fact he wanted to try one of the cigarettes. The iconic character on the packet — some joker in an admiral's hat — was gazing at him from the table. Jack wasn't sure. Perhaps this rule against smoking applied only to Capes?

"So," Miss Starkwell mused, the cigarette gently held between teeth before she snatched it away with her fingers, "are you *really* interested in art, Jack? Or was there some other reason for inviting me here? I'd hate to find out you're casing the bank."

This was a surprise. The longer the evening wore on, the wilder the girl became — and they hadn't yet got to any alcohol. He began to wonder if she could break those rules as well.

"No, no, I'm not really the bank robbing sort. Bad with guns. Never touched one, actually. I did want to talk art, which I do dig — though I haven't brushed up before against this Picolino fellow. I'm into a painter called Roy Lichtenstein."

"The pop artist?"

Jack froze mid-sup. "You know him?"

"Sure. Lichtenstein's *Drowning Girl* is famous — snatched, as it is, from a twelve-cent girls' comicbook."

Louise did a quick sketch of the painting on a paper napkin; it took her less than a minute, but she skipped the added-extra *ukiyo-e* waves and dialogue bubble.

"See?"

Jack felt gobsmacked. This particular Christmas decoration had her art history down pat. "How do you know this stuff?"

"This 'stuff' is not exactly a state secret. Why are you so surprised?"

"I'm not sure."

Louise caught the waiter's attention and silently ordered two coffees from afar. "I hope you don't object to another round?"

"Anytime."

"Watch how you say that in proximity to me — I'm notorious for my caffeine intake." The girl slid over a sham-crystal ashtray he hadn't noticed before and butted out the cigarette. Then she blew one last puff toward the ceiling.

She looked edgy, and he doubted caffeine was the culprit.

No way this girl was a Blando — she had too much going on in her headspace. Surely she was a Cape too. Memory loss?

Then it came to him.

Amnesia.

Happened all the time in comics, old soapies and dodgy romance novels. Sure, it was a rare occurrence in the real world — but they weren't there anymore and didn't need to play by its rules. Maybe she'd banged her skull, or had the memories plundered by some diabolical Rotter?

"Getting back to your boss," Jack said, while he contemplated this theory, "why do you stay at the bank if he's such a sleazy bastard?"

"I don't know. By the middle of the afternoon I'm fed up, and every evening I resolve to quit — but by the time I wake up in the morning, I've forgotten most of what happened the previous day, I'm over the crankiness, and ready to begin afresh. Starting the cycle all over again. I wonder if I have some kind of illness."

She exhaled loudly.

"I know I paint Mister Holland out to be a jerk, but he's not. Not completely. Every morning he also starts off charming and gentlemanly, like he's turned over a new leaf, but whenever two o'clock comes round, he starts pawing me again."

Jack remembered the first time he went to the bank was just after lunch. One-thirty.

After both left the diner, the Equalizer was surprised to find he was so wired on caffeine that he decided to walk Louise all the way home, through quiet city streets. It took half an hour to get there and they arrived before midnight.

Louise lived in an apartment in a four-storey brownstone facing a main road — the nearby sign said East 71st Street — though there wasn't much traffic that time of night. It was a neoclassical building, with Grecian architectural features, number 169.

She pointed out a divided-frame window on the second storey, over a darkened shop called Brooklyn Antiques that took up the entire ground floor. "There's my room."

The two of them walked up a short set of steps to the double front door, under an arch beside the closed shop, and paused while the girl rifled through her purse to fetch keys. Before unlocking the door she smiled, removed her glasses, and leaned Jack's way.

"Don't you want to kiss me?" she teased. "It's okay, I don't taste like an ashtray anymore — I sneaked a few breath fresheners on the way home."

Jack couldn't move a muscle, so she did the kissing. She tasted of peppermint, smelled gloriously of citrus fruit.

#118

Later that night, around two a.m., the Brick took Jack with him to a seedier section of town that had neons everywhere and women on the streets dressed like hookers — which is what he cottoned on they were.

"Do we need this kind of realism?" Jack muttered, gazing at the mimed kinkiness through a triple-glazed window that helped soundproof the vehicle. "Isn't Heropa supposed to symbolize a better place?"

The Brick nodded, just as he brutally shifted the gearstick. "Human nature prevails."

"I thought Blandos weren't human."

"Never said no such thing."

They were in the Brick's V12-powered, two-seater 1938 Delahaye 165 Cabriolet, a burgundy-coloured, capsule-shaped French number with dashes along the bodywork that split up its exterior profile, and concealed engine bay vents and door handles. Chrome fixtures ran along the sills to wrap around the rear-end brake lights, making the vehicle look like it would've been more at home in the 1930s *Flash Gordon* flicks starring Buster Crabbe.

This car's lean didn't favour the right, the driver's side, since the Brick had built up the suspension and added a four hundred kilogram counterweight under the passenger seat — meaning the crate hugged the road only an inch or so above terra firma.

Inside was all white leather upholstery; on the burgundy dashboard two large, round Jaeger gauges gave the speed as well as the tours per minute. Perhaps an afterthought, a couple of furry dice dangled from the rearview mirror, and up on the dash was a sun-faded dime novel displaying a cowboy in a mask. Feeling ill as he followed the cheap tome's sliding path left and right while the Brick swerved this way and that through traffic, Jack finally deciphered a title (*Rawhide, With Two Guns*) above the author name Clay Harder.

"Good book?"

"Scintillatin'."

"So why all the mystery, Brick? Where're we going?"

"I got a call from an ex — ex-teammate, that is, before you crack foxy. Bloke's a freelancer these days, has been since the Equalizers downsized."

"Friend of yours?"

"Teammates and friends're mostly chalk an' cheese."

"And I thought you cared." Jack laughed. "What's the scam?"

"Death of a mutual acquaintance."

His passenger glanced sideways at him. "Another murder?"

"Mebbe. Here we are, Sunset and Camden." The Equalizer slammed on the brakes and Jack had to stop himself from ploughing into the dashboard. The Brick's parking was as neat as his exterior — one wheel up on the kerb and the car's rear-end poking into oncoming traffic.

He slapped Jack's shoulder far too hard with one of his earthenware fists. "Don't worry, tiger. Anythin' happens, it'll be fixed by tomorrow."

Jack wasn't sure whether the man meant his shoulder, or the car.

After locking up, they walked beneath a huge collection of electrified, luminous tube lights that together formed a moving skipping girl, and turned down an alleyway marked La Montagne.

On one of the walls was some stencilled Cyrillic graffiti, the very first tagging Jack had seen in this city:

Улица Марата

The two men ascended a steel fire-escape behind a redbrick Victorian-style factory building and, after pushing through an open iron hatch and promenading a corridor lined with other, less substantial doors, stopped before number 1793.

The Brick politely knocked.

A few seconds on, a voice called out from within: "May I inquire who's there?"

"You may, buster. Doesn't mean I'll soddin' well answer."

The door opened and a man in a long black robe — it reached the floor, very priestly — looked out at them. "Brick. Thank God. My prayers are answered."

"Well, I received 'em loud an' clear. Dunno if any dippy deity had a hand in that."

"Oh, you and your ribald commentary. Come on in."

As Jack passed by the possible padre, he took note of pale hair, cadaverous skin and white lips. The guy more resembled a ghost.

The Brick turned around in a large, dishevelled living room. There were five or six toy poodles yapping about their heels — Jack kept losing count — and a colossal painting of a weeping willow dominated one wall. On the plaster opposite was a framed movie poster for *Marat/Sade*, with the actors' names — Patrick Magee, Ian Richardson and Glenda Jackson — in a shaky red font, resembling blood.

"Junior, this is Exegesis. I likes to call him Exy — easier to pronounce on the fly. Exy, yer lookin' at our new recruit Southern Cross."

"Very nice to meet you," the anaemic man said, shaking Jack's hand with the kind of jellyfish grip his dad had always warned him about. "Please call me Exegesis, if you don't mind. I'm very lenient with the Brick's iconoclastic behaviour, but I prefer not to encourage it in others. Bravo with the flag."

"Um — cheers."

"Exy found our body. He an' the corpse're old Grail Quest buddies." The Brick caught Jack's eye. "Don't ask." He turned back to the other Cape — which is what Jack now realized the man was. "So, whadda we have here, bub?"

"I do think it's best if I show you."

"Lead on, Duff Beer."

Exegesis frowned, but then busied himself manoeuvring little dogs out of the path — expertly using a broom — as he led his two visitors down a corridor, stopping at a closed door at the very end.

This he opened with great flourish.

Beyond was a rather large bathroom, poorly lit, that had dozens of burning tea candles arranged helter-skelter on the floor, the toilet seat, and on a bench by the basin.

Slumped within a bathtub in the centre of the room was a naked man.

The diorama rehashed the famous painting, by Jacques-Louis David, of murdered French revolutionary leader Jean-Paul Marat, right down to the towel wrapped around his head and the slit throat — except this particular dead démagogue was holding a biro instead of a quill.

Exegesis put a warning hand on Jack's shoulder, stronger this time.

"Stay away from the water. It's electrified."

He pointed at a chrome and black metal rotary fan submerged beneath the man's legs, with the cable winding out and up to a plug in a socket. Jack hadn't noticed that in the flickering candlelight.

The Brick rubbed his chin, thoughtful-like. "Classic overkill."

While he did this rubbing, Jack flicked the power switch. God knows why Exegesis hadn't done this before. Probably, he liked his sense of the dramatic.

"So, who's Marat?" Jack asked.

Exegesis glared at him. "Rabble Rouser. The man's name was Rabble Rouser." He pondered for a few seconds, before speaking again. "And one might think this were an accident — if not for the note."

"And the fan."

"Well, the fan could have fallen in by itself."

"True."

"What was the bugger writing?" the Brick asked.

Before anyone could answer, he bent over to take a piece of paper from the man's left hand. It was wet and the ink had smudged, but they could read the four words there fairly easily: 'I am a fraud'.

The Brick shoved the note into his overcoat pocket. "He got that right. There'll be no fancy funerals here."

"Suicide?" Jack suggested, dubious.

"Not the best way to enter the Lord's domain," said Exegesis, "and Rabble Rouser was not your standard suicidal personality. I'd say this incident has more in common with the death of Marat, already alluded to by Southern Cross."

"Murder." The way the Brick uttered the word made it more statement than question. "Given he had his throat slit, on top o' the live-wirin'."

"I would further allude that that fiend Doctor Satan is involved."

"Course you would — yer always do. Any proof this time?"

"Sadly, no."

"Then what's bugging you 'bout him? — 'Side from the name, I mean."

Exegesis gazed heavenward, channelling some mysterious rapture. "Let me quote to you from Matthew 24:27: 'For as the lightning cometh forth from the east, and is seen even unto the west; so shall be the coming of the Son of Man'."

"Eh?" said the Brick. "Who's comin' from the east?"

"He does not mean to affirm that the 'Son of Man' will come from the east."

"West, then? And who's he? Doc Satan?"

"Of course not! You are entirely missing the point. *He* is Matthew, as in the Matthew from the *New Testament*. In the Gospel of Matthew, he is described as a tax collector and was one of Jesus's original disciples in all four gospels and in Acts."

"The guy wrote and starred in these shenanigans? Bit of an Orson Welles, huh?"

Exegesis had ditched cloud nine for visible bristling and a great gnashing of teeth.

"It is highly unlikely the two Matthews are the same, and this has absolutely nothing to do with Orson Welles. My God. Matthew-the-Apostle lived decades earlier than Matthew-the-scribe. Now, back to my point: The 'Son of Man' won't come from the west, but He will come in a sudden manner, like the lightning — rapidly, unexpectedly, in an unlooked-for quarter will be His coming."

The Brick appeared well and truly bamboozled, a feeling Jack shared. "Think yer losin' me, Exy. Who the heck is this Son o' Man?"

"I can't say."

"Fat lot o' good that confession does us."

"Look, I hate to be a fly in the ointment," Jack spoke up, "but do we need to know any of this ecclesial hogwash? Marat here is dead."

"*Rabble Rouser*," Exegesis reminded him. "But, indeed. Electrocuted. The Good Book mentions lightning — in all likelihood the two are connected."

"Or not." Jack glanced at his teammate. "Are we done?"

"Hang on, kid." The Brick went around the tub, pushed aside the plastic curtain, and with patience peeled something off the windowsill.

"This is interestin'," he said, as he held up a small black oval sticker with the tag 'if?' printed on it — identical to the one they'd found at the Harvey's Gems jewellery heist. "Murdered by a dead man."

After notifying the police, the Brick and Jack drove in silence.

At that time of night, Stan the Doorman was home in bed, but the Timely Tower security guard — or a carbon copy — sat in his same position, sucking on a Brown's Iron Bitters as he watched the rolling black-and-white portable TV. This time they heard a male glee club advertising ballad about a fly:

Boppie the Fly, I'm Boppie the Fly
Straight from rubbish tip to you.
Spreading disease, with the greatest of ease...

The Brick slammed the concertina door — "I hate that commercial, I feel fer the bug," he muttered — and they took the elevator to the penthouse accompanied by 'A Walk in the Black Forest'.

Squeezing his eyes shut, Jack groaned. "Hate to say it, but the ad's gotta be better than this mundane tune. Don't they play anything else?"

The lights were on when the doors finally parted and Pretty Amazonia was there, trussed up in a flowing purple satin nightie. According to her, the Great White Hope had tucked himself in early.

The Brick gave the woman an abbreviated version of what had been discovered and, for her part, she looked uncommonly serious while tuning in.

Then the Brick showed her the sticker.

"Interesting," PA mused, adjusting the bodice on her gown. "You think someone wants to infer Iffy Bizness did the deed?"

"Double-R hadn't been dead long enough. I'd say it's someone messin' with us."

She nodded. "While you were out, we got a message from that Blando cop Kahn, at City Hall."

"What'd Dick Tracy want?"

"To let us know they found another dead Cape."

"Double-R."

"No. Someone else."

The Equalizer frowned by lowering a layer of bricks low over his blue eyes. "Who?"

"Sir Dagonet."

"Crap."

"My feeling exactly."

"I thought that bastard were adept at hightailin' it from trouble — guy was more court jester than hero. Foul play?"

PA raised one eyebrow. "Unless you call being spit-roasted in your own armour an accident, I'd say yes."

"Jesus," Jack mumbled from where he sat propped up on the arm of a sofa.

"Stop it, kid — yer remindin' me o' Exy. Once a lifetime's religious hokey pokey is enough."

The Brick walked over to the big window that dominated the shared living space of Equalizers headquarters. Dawn was only minutes away.

"So. Another Grail Quester bites the bullet. Reckon there's a connection?"

"I don't know," said Pretty Amazonia. "Those people are socially retarded."

Jack held up his hand. "What is this Grail Quest stuff?"

PA sighed. "You know medieval re-enactment festivals?"

"Sure. Heard of them, anyway."

"Same thing — on a twee idI level."

The next evening, when Jack went out for a stroll, a newsboy was standing on the corner, a Grit satchel over his shoulder, holding aloft a paper while he shouted.

"Extra! Extra! 'Nother Cape found dead! Suicide verdict questioned!" As people bustled past, the kid's eyes found the Equalizer's and he rushed over. "Want one, mister?"

"How much?"

"Five cents."

Jack dropped a coin in his hand and stood beneath a streetlamp to read. The Marat picture took up a fair chunk of page one of the *Patriot*.

They'd nailed it.

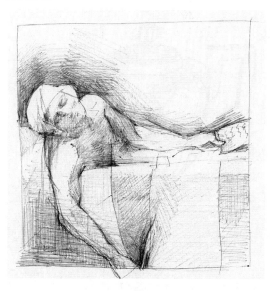

#119

"Grab yer mask, kiddo. The Sandman's amiss, an' we're up," the Brick grouched from the open door to the bedroom, before vanishing with surprising speed.

Jack struggled to a sitting position, swayed unsteadily, and realized he had on his costume. Handy. Where the mask had got to, however, was another matter. He wiped sleep from his eyes, thought about Louise, smiled, and stepped off the bed.

Eventually finding the mask scrunched up under that same piece of furniture, Jack considered himself lucky it was made of an oddball fabric that didn't wrinkle.

He tucked the thing into his belt and went upstairs to the giant hangar in the roof, where his three teammates were twiddling thumbs, already settled in on the dirigible.

Predictably, the atmosphere was strained — Jack could sense they'd again been quibbling — which meant all was well in this world.

"SC, where were you last night?"

That was Pretty Amazonia piping up, albeit in a tone of feigned indifference, without looking his way. She was staring instead at sweet nothing through the porthole, perhaps studying rivet formations in the hangar wall.

This made Jack think again of Louise.

"Getting acquainted with the city."

About their second kiss, once more on her doorstep, longer, but on this occasion initiated by both at the same time. He felt overwhelmed with his bravery — never thought he had such enterprise in him. His face overheated just rewinding it.

She hadn't recognised him again — this was like dating *Groundhog Day* style. They'd once more discussed *Twilight Over Hoboken* and he'd reissued the invite, this time with more confidence since he now knew she liked him.

"Do tell," PA said in the same flat style — a worrying one. Jack glanced at her.

"All aboard?" hollered the Great White Hope from a comfy, leather-bound captain's chair up front. His passengers were forced to content themselves with unpleasant canvas seating.

"Nah, bwana." The Brick crossed and then uncrossed his gnarled, rock-ribbed legs. "I left me stomach at the breakfast table. Whaddaya reckon? Course we are. Let's go."

"So — the game is afoot!" their leader declared in an over-energetic, gleeful manner that made Jack more tired.

The ceiling slid across with loud grating that could be heard inside this iron carriage suspended beneath the blimp's rubberized cotton fabric, and in seconds their transport lurched through the exit and hung above a shining city of cement and glass.

When Jack took a glimpse out of a small round window, at the drop to the pavement thousands of feet below, his stomach churned. He tightened the seatbelt and again looked across the aisle at Pretty Amazonia.

"PA?"

"What?" The woman had moved on from rivets and was preoc-cupied with the passing outside world.

"Are there any Capes who've gone missing?"

Silence. Then, "How do you mean?"

"Like, well, disappeared."

"God — dozens of them."

"Huh?"

Having sighed loudly, the woman peeled off her white satin gloves, took out a nail-trimming kit, and began to file. "Haven't you checked how many heroes there are in the rogue's gallery?"

"You mean that hallway with all the pictures at HQ?"

"Yes. So, haven't you?"

"Haven't I — what...?"

"Counted? Darling, sometimes you have the attention span of a gnat. I have. Totted them up, I mean."

PA honed in on a particularly troublesome nail on the ring finger of her left hand.

"Bugger," she said with a frown, and then her eyes darted over to her teammate. "Yep, well, there're eighty-nine people on the walls. Eighty-nine previous and current members of the Equalizers. You'll be number ninety, once we get your mug shot sketched up."

The woman placed the nail file in a plastic sleeve, and straight after took out several different bottles of coloured varnish. One big flask had the words 'Miracle Liquid Nail Formula #35'.

"We've kept track of thirty-seven of those people. Five are dead, and only one of them an accident so far as we know — Little Nobody. Capes come and go; I guess people get bored or find new ways to entertain themselves...and they stop coming back. More recently, they simply die."

The blimp was drifting a hundred metres above the crater they'd explored a few days before, the one on the corner of Crestwood and Standard, where Harvey's Gems once stood.

The Brick whistled — Jack had no idea how the man did that with a gob full of stones.

"Well, well. Will ya lookit that."

All of them were already gazing downward, even the pilot.

"Looks like the same hole to me," Jack said, stifling a yawn. "Cleaner, maybe."

"That's precisely our problem, dodo," PA snapped, slipping into one of her intemperate moods precisely as she stuck the gloves back on.

"The cleanliness?"

"No! — What am I going to do with you? The problem is the hole itself. See? Everything in Heropa is supposed to Reset after twenty-four hours, always in the middle of every night. It's how we've been able to lay waste to most of the city, get some kip, and wake up to the renovations."

"Then that crater shouldn't be there?"

"Nope," said the Brick. He winked at Jack and subtly made two horns on top of his head with his thumbs, as he nodded at PA. "We ought'a be navel-gazin' Harvey's Gems again. Reckon Harvey'll be put out."

"Who exactly is Harvey?"

"Dunno — the Blando that runs the joint?"

PA rolled her eyes. "I think it's just a name — like Tiffany's."

"Got one more question," Jack said.

"God. What now?"

"You mentioned the city rejigging—"

"Resetting."

"Resetting, yeah. Do the Blandos also reset? I mean, do they rejuvenate or reanimate themselves, or whatever, like the city does every night?"

"Pfft. Who knows and/or cares?"

"Me," the Brick complained. "Never thought 'bout that before — I'm gonna get zombie nightmare creeps after you tuck me in tonight."

"Once they're dead, they're dead," the Great White Hope spoke up from the nearby cockpit. "Blando casualties get rebooted, like we do, but the fatalities stay put. Same with the Capes, actually."

"So — in what way do you tell if someone's a Blando?"

"Let me think now," Pretty Amazonia said in a mocking tone. "P'raps, maybe, by how yawn-inspiringly boring they can be?"

"Any other way?"

"I'd say that's sufficient, wouldn't you?"

"Well, sure thing," interrupted the Brick, "there is the obvious ID. They all have a lower-case 'p' tattooed between their shoulder blades."

"You're kidding me."

"Nup. Right here..." The beast struggled to point out an exact spot; unlike PA, flexibility was not his forté.

"Why?" Jack asked, feeling more than a little horrified.

"Dunno. Guess it's a quick an' easy reference t'see if someone's bona fide or not — when they're picking up the pieces at fight scenes, I mean."

"You say it's a 'p'. If you call them Blandos, and you're going to resort to that kind of crap, why not use a 'b' — for Blando?"

"Mebbe depends what angle you look at 'em. Like, if yer upside down, it'd read as a 'b', right?"

"Actually, that would make it a 'd'."

"Don't get all pedantic, kid."

A Citizens' Band radio set, positioned in the single alcove above their pilot's head, beeped hysterically, causing the Great White Hope to snap up the mic.

"Top of the morning to you," he declared in jolly manner. Jack realized this was the man's painful attempt to kid around.

"The Equalizers?" crackled a familiar, whining voice over the communal speaker.

"Roger."

"This is the mayor. We have a situation."

"Check that," said the GWH.

"A diabolical situation!"

"Er — What kind of situation, sir?"

"Yeah, tell 'im to get to the bloody point," the Brick grumbled.

"The League of Unmitigated Rotters," the single speaker squawked, "is laying siege to the Museum of Antiquities."

"The museum?" Pretty Amazonia, who'd taken out a mirror to check her eye makeup, paused mid-burnish. "That lot are getting cultured on us."

Jack was surprised they bothered with a museum dedicated to antiquities, considering Heropa was only about five years old.

"I believe the fiends are after the treasures of Pharaoh Rama-Tut," nattered the mayor.

"Understood. F.A.B., sir." Their pilot hung the microphone back on its hook.

"F.A.B.?" Jack queried, leaning forward to see out the front window.

"Full Acknowledgment of Broadcast," the Great White Hope said.

"That's not what F.A.B. means — the Big O told me it's 'Fully Advised, Briefed'," cut in the Brick.

"And here I was thinking we meant 'Fabulous'." Pretty Amazonia had apparently finished her makeup repairs and inspected the job. "Not bad."

"Regardless, flight path set in for the Museum of Antiquities."

"Which means," said the Brick in a low voice, "he'll be steerin', since there's no on-board autopilot."

Fifteen minutes later, they descended into a wide boulevard on which most of the traffic had stopped and people were outside their cars, staring in one direction at a big building on a small hill. A ring of blue-clad police officers and their cars, bulbous roof lights swirling, surrounded the slope. They barely noticed the arrival of this big, white dirigible.

"Heads up."

Pretty Amazonia seemed to be finally paying attention as she leaned over next to Jack and looked at the building.

"I see Chop Suey and Sinistro. Down there, loitering next to that — what kind of car is the Mediterranean-blue number, Brick, the one with all the curves?"

"Late 1930s. Chrysler."

"Yeah, I think it's a '39 Chrysler Royal."

The Brick and PA stared at Jack.

"Dear God," the woman muttered, "not another motor-head. Stick to your comics, darling."

Jack blushed. "I defer to the Brick, of course."

"Whatever. See the two Rotters? Next to the blue Chrysler."

"Spotted," said the Great White Hope. "They will be acting as look-outs — no doubt there will be more of the devils in the museum proper."

"No doubt." PA blew out her cheeks.

As their blimp came lower still, settling just a few feet above the asphalt of the expansive thoroughfare, two figures that had been skulking behind the automobile took off and raced into the building via its grand portico. This place had a dazzling dome slapped on top and could've filled in as Everymuseum.

"Brick, Pretty Amazonia, you're up," their glorious leader announced. He swivelled a lever, opening a door behind the Brick. "Take Southern Cross with you. Time he learned the ropes. I'll stay here to co-ordinate activities."

"Course you will," PA remarked. She looked Jack in the eye. "I'll be brief, SC — Sinistro sticks to the shadows, literally becomes a shadow, gets his kicks scaring kids like you. And, for God's sake, watch out for Chop Suey's hands — they're ten fingers of death. One time he nearly karate-chopped our erstwhile giant here in two."

"Yeah, that wasn't fun. Little bastard." The Brick stood beside the door and bowed. "After you — an', kiddo, be careful o' any other Capes we meet out there. If in doubt, ask."

"Or scream," the woman behind Jack helpfully suggested.

With that, they jumped. PA and Jack landed without much ado, but the Brick's descent was announced with the loud crunch of broken paving.

"Oops."

"Elegant," his tall teammate muttered.

"Mebbe I should go on a diet?"

The coppers were armed with an array of nasty-looking weapons, some of them new, but most World War II vintage — things like bazookas, Vickers machine guns and .45 Thompson submachine guns ("Chicago typewriters," the Brick said). The officers kept these in check as the trio passed through the cordon and after that walked up a neatly trimmed driveway toward the museum, past pampas grass and palm trees.

"Mister B, you take the rear," Pretty Amazonia instructed; apparently she was second in charge or had decided to appoint herself thus. "I'll head straight inside. SC, you hold down the entrance. Anyone comes out, smack them one."

"Even you?"

"You won't see me."

And she vanished — no password, just pure speed. The Brick lumbered away at a more sedate pace, leaving Jack on the doormat.

For a while, all was peace on earth.

Zero was happening on a front lawn that looked as well-manicured as Pretty Amazonia's nails, and Jack could hear nothing special within the building. Eventually, however, a tall, wiry-looking individual in a baggy black leather costume approached from inside.

He wore a midnight cowl loosely covering the top half of his head, tied in a knot at the back. Incongruously, so far as Jack was concerned, he had on a pair of thick, square eyeglasses and the Equalizer could see mutton-chop sideburns poking out from under the mask.

"Hope you don't mind me asking," Jack said, as the man came closer, "but why the specs?"

"These are my night-vision goggles."

"It's daytime."

"One does like to be prepared," pontificated the man. "I am *Black Owl*."

"Oh, hoot-hoot."

The Cape's mouth fell open, possibly in an attempt to catch passing flies. "How dare you! Don't you realize who I am?"

"Some lame-arse clay pigeon in a recycled Zorro mask?"

"This is not a Zorro mask. I made the cowl myself."

"So you're a seamstress to boot."

"Good Lord — who the devil do you think you are? I am Black Owl, leader of the League of Unmitigated Rotters!"

"Charmed." Jack yawned. "Listen, mate, I still haven't tried this out, so by all means make a report and get back to me with the details."

He levelled his right arm and pointed it at the flying owl logo on the man's torso. Then he thought about what he really wanted to do to the pompous arse. The recoil and pain surprised Jack most — made him think he'd dislocated his elbow — and the flash was subdued cobalt in colour.

The result? Black Owl, on the receiving end, took artificial flight and disappeared somewhere down the next street.

"*Sugoi* shooting."

Jack turned quickly to discover a ballerina on the boardwalk.

There, in the middle of a promising ad hoc battle zone, about six metres from him, was a superbly postured, picture-pretty girl with pale, luminescent skin and brunette hair pulled back severely into a small bun that was wrapped in a floral garland.

She was dressed in a black leotard sporting a frilly tutu, with white tights and *pointe* shoes — looking like the goddamned Black Swan. A domino mask sat on her nose, across which were inscribed musical notes, and Jack noted she had one blue eye and one brown.

"Sugoi?" he asked.

"Japanese. It means 'great', impressive. That kind of jazz."

"Okay. So tell me — are you a hero, a villain, or someone who's misplaced their ballet studio?"

"Funny," the girl said, plumbing sarcasm, but she was kind enough to present him with a charming smile. "Black Owl is a valiant fighter — too valiant for Prima Ballerina to allow him to be defeated."

"You always refer to yourself in the third-person?"

"Sometimes. If it suits."

"Well, since you're narrating, what's the plan? You're going to dance me to death?"

"Oh, a comedian."

"No, just stating the obvious."

"More obvious that you know."

The girl placed her arms in an 'L' position — the left one out straight beside her, the right pointed Jack's way — and for a split second he believed her intention was to throw at him what he'd done to Black Owl.

Instead, she pirouetted on one leg several times, so swiftly her body became a blur. When she finished the rotation, the dancer struck a pose, her arms crossed low in front and one-foot forward.

"*Bras Croisé*," she announced. Jack couldn't help himself — he gave a round of applause.

Seconds later, she'd moved on to a series of linking steps consisting of three small hops, executed both with the back foot and the front foot in tandem, sideways, forwards, backwards, turning.

"*Pas de bourrées*," Jack heard the girl say in the sweetest of voices while he followed the rhythmic footfall and began to feel drowsy. "*Ichi, ni, san, ichi, ni, san, ichi—*"

That was when something struck his back from behind. He ended up on all fours on the cement, shaking his head to clear it.

"*Arabesque*," that candy-coated tone declared. "*Dō itashimashite!*"

A hand grasped Jack's arm and yanked him to his feet — he was staring up, at close quarters, into Pretty Amazonia's purple irises.

"Don't look at her feet, her legs, her arms," the woman hissed, "don't listen to her voice. Prima Ballerina uses everything she has like a Siren. Just bloody well shoot her and be done with it!"

"Understood."

Jack swung around and aimed the dancer's way before he had time to properly look or listen — right when the Brick blundered across his path. The cobalt blast that exited Jack's fingertips struck the Equalizer in the shoulder and he staggered sideways.

Jack scrambled straight over. "Crap, Brick — you all right?"

"That...hurt," he muttered. "Don't worry 'bout li'l ol' me, I'll live."

Vaguely reassured, Jack looked past the man, but the street was now empty. Glancing over his shoulder, he spotted only Pretty Amazonia hunting about for prey.

"Looks like they did a runner."

"The sewers." The Brick straightened, as he rotated his *gleno-humeral* joint. "That's the bastards' standard escape route."

"Not all of them." Jack pointed over to the blue '30s Chrysler, where a shadow on the bonnet had surprising enough dexterity to open up the driver's door.

"Sonuvabitch — Sinistro." The Brick made a fist, but before anyone else could move, the automobile exploded with a definitive ka-boom. It rained down fragments of engine, upholstery, whitewall tyres and a bent black fender, along with a shade shorn in half — minus its physical body.

Jack yanked off his mask to stare at the burning spot where the car was once parked, and the dissected shadow now lay. "Bollocks, Brick, is that supposed to happen?"

"Um. Not so far as I know."

Pretty Amazonia twirled a cautious circle out on the street, just as the police and the crowd surged forward, and then suddenly she was standing over her partners. "What the blazes happened?"

"Me an' SC been askin' ourselves the same thing."

There was another blinding light, this time a flashbulb instead of a bomb — reporters had surrounded them.

"Get your mask back on," Pretty Amazonia urged. "Move it!"

A moment later, the miniature zeppelin was hailing them from afar. "Brick! Pretty Amazonia! Southern Cross! Report in!"

The Brick's clenched fist eased up and he instead popped a thumb into the air for all to see. The thumb sank, as he replaced it with a raised index finger and saluted the blimp. More camera flashes ensued. "A-okay, El Bastardo."

"Bastardo's a usable epithet here?"

"Sure, since it's bogus French."

The police began assembling their hardware and pushing the crowd of onlookers away from the museum entrance and the smouldering parking spot. Amidst a sea of grey, brown and black fedora and bowler hats, Jack noticed a red Stetson.

"I want one of those," he mumbled, straightening his mask. "You too can stand out in a crowd."

#120

The following afternoon, Jack loitered on a corner next to the bank, hoping to meet Louise Starkwell on her way out — if only to shake things up and avoid another *Twilight Over Hoboken* episode.

Back still aching from the 'Arabesque' kick Prima Ballerina had kindly shared — there was dark bruising around his coccyx — the Equalizer wondered why Heropa's overnight Reset hadn't fixed that up.

He'd ended up leaving the Southern Cross get-up back at HQ. The thing chafed in general; he felt liberated without it.

And this time, when she came out the front door of the bank — wearing a simple black dress and a big black bonnet wrapped by a beige silk scarf that dangled down past her left elbow — Louise recognized him. Her face lit up, making his heart skip in ridiculous manner.

"Jack, you're a breath of fresh air," she decided, as she straightaway linked her arm through his. "I wasn't sure I'd see you again."

"You're kidding, right?"

"No, actually, I'm not."

Louise peered up at him with a shy smile, while Jack was sure he responded with a dopey look. She remembered?

"You *are* here to see me, aren't you? This isn't an evil coincidence?"

"None that I'm aware of. But let me think some."

"Watch out, or I'll start harassing you with obscure art."

"Oh, no!" he laughed, beginning to relax. Confused he might have been, but there was no mistaking the happiness that washed through that. She remembered him.

They trudged slowly along the sidewalk, crisscrossing shadows and twilight. "Are you hungry?" Jack finally found the courage to ask.

"Famished."

"I know of a restaurant near here — this place comes highly recommended, though I'm not a hundred percent sure the person who recommended it can be trusted." True, since he'd filched the information from the Brick. "Name of the Holyoke. D'you know it?"

"No, but I'm already intrigued by the contradictions."

The restaurant actually wasn't half bad, a cosy establishment on a quieter street, down a flight of stairs, tucked away in a basement. Booth tables were separated from one another by Japanese-style partitions made of wood and paper, and the place was romantically lit — difficult to see anything further than three feet. Given Jack was half that distance from his date, he was hardly going to get upset.

He did wonder, however, why the Brick would patronize this eatery alone — or if the man dragged along someone special. The thought of the Brick as a concrete Romeo brought a smile to his mush.

"What are you thinking about, with that grin?"

Jack looked straight over at the girl. "How beautiful you are." This sounded like the right thing to say, was partially true, and even in the miserable light, he could see her blush.

They proceeded to gasbag aplenty, not just about art. The conversation turned to food, cooking, fashion, music, cinema and the workplace. Louise had insight into each of these topics — seemingly from a practical perspective — whereas Jack had only read up on most and fanaticized about others.

He learned the girl loved going to see an ensemble led by popular Heropa bandleader and radio personality Cake Icer, and her favourite movie was *The Long Kiss Goodnight*. Jack hadn't heard or seen either. The novel she'd read the most times was Radclyffe Hall's *The Well of Loneliness*.

"Critics hated it," Louise announced, while adjusting her glasses, and then she lit a cigarette. "One British journalist said he'd much rather give a boy or girl prussic acid than let them read this novel. To be honest, I'm not sure I like the book either, but there's something in there that captures my attention."

"What's it about?"

"Lesbianism in Edwardian England, class differences, Christianity, spiritualism, World War I, cross-dressing." Louise winked. It seemed to Jack everyone was doing that in his general direction. "A smorgasbord, really."

The girl went on to say she despised red roses but loved yellow ones, she smoked 16mg Paul Jones cigarettes — only at night, Jack recalled — and liked to drink Bollinger champagne. She had two glasses over dinner. Her preferred toothpaste was Ipana, and she adored fashion designer Walter Plunkett.

"You know, I have a Walter Plunkett suit," Jack decided to bring up.

"Really? The man is an illusionist with his sense of line, harmony, and of challenging both. Oh, my — you'll have to show it to me."

He neglected to mention it was an overlarge hand-me-down from a dead man (the Big O), that he'd worn the threads on the first occasion they met, when Bulkhead attacked the bank — a time Louise appeared not to remember at all — and that the suit had been summarily destroyed.

After a lengthy hesitation, Jack's hand fell onto the girl's, and they entwined fingers.

Louise found out Jack had no particular preference for toothpaste, dress-sense, music, film or flowers. He didn't smoke or drink. He had too many books he loved to narrow down specific examples, and favourite food went unanswered.

An entrée of California rolls and a generous serving of pasta intervened, but Jack bypassed the seventy-two-ounce King Henry VIII steak the Brick had suggested.

"You don't like talking about yourself, do you?" Louise decided, well into the evening.

"Not really," Jack admitted. "I also don't have much to say."

"I'm not sure I believe you. That would make you the complete antithesis of most of the men I've known."

"That many, huh?"

"A fair few."

"Are you disappointed this time round?"

"No." She squeezed his hand. "It's a nice change."

"Thanks. I think."

The conversation then pivoted to childhood toys, something Jack felt he could participate in. After mentioning some plastic rocket ships and anonymous toy soldiers he'd owned — recycled hand-me-downs from the neighbours' kids — Louise nattered on about her favourite soft toy tiger, Mister Hobbes, a velveteen cat called Perri-Purr, and a doll named Tarpé Mills that still took up prime real-estate on top of her bed.

Jack couldn't help wondering if she'd had a childhood — he very much doubted this — and the notion made her 'memories' far more tantalizing than his genuine experience of growing up.

Not that he told her much about this. Jack kept almost everything under the cuff, since he recognized there was nothing with which to dazzle the girl. To the contrary, she'd likely do a runner. So, instead, he encouraged Louise to talk about herself, and every minor such detail made him more enamoured.

After the dinner plates had been cleared, Jack placed his wallet on the table-top and decided to teach Louise how to play an old game that'd kept him sane on long, lonely nights by himself in his box in Melbourne: Three Coin Hockey.

While their waiter simmered nearby — either he fretted about the surface of the table, or the unnecessary delay in his tip — the girl first frowned, pondered, and then smiled. Within five minutes, she giggled a lot as they played, and inside fifteen minutes started to win.

The ideal proposition to work off their excess culinary baggage was another meandering walk to the girl's apartment. Their conversation had trickled off. Louise's right hand was in Jack's left; they looked at one another and beamed more often than they needed to speak.

On the way, the two of them passed a shop with its shutters

down. Painted across the metal, in slaphappy manner, was the second batch of graffiti Jack had seen:

BOPS GO HOME!

Nonsensical tagging appeared to be a growing fad in the city of Heropa, although they saw no more over the next thirty minutes, and finally Louise's brownstone reared above.

Jack counted the stairs to the front entrance: one, two, three, four, five, six, seven, eight, nine, ten. Ten steps were nothing to fear.

"Can I come up?" he ventured, braver still this time.

"I'd love you to. But I wonder if my father-in-law will be in bed. Hard to say — he works such odd hours."

Jack stopped dead in his tracks. "Father-in-law? Then that would mean you're—"

"Widowed." The girl shrugged. "Not all of us are old hens."

"Really? Christ...I'm so sorry."

"Don't be. My husband died some time back, stupidly, in the middle of a Bop fight."

Jack glanced at her. "A what?"

Maybe he asked too softly, or possibly she wasn't listening. Either way, Louise continued as if Jack hadn't spoken.

"Ages ago. I remember him, and I know I was in love, but mostly the memories seem like they belong to someone else. I don't feel much — strange, I know. The Prof says it's one way of dealing with the trauma."

Jack tried again. "I hope you don't mind me asking, but what's a Bop?"

"A Bop?" Louise regarded him with an expression close to amazement. "You know, Jack — a Cape, of course. Everyone knows that."

"He was a Cape?"

This time, she laughed in husky fashion. "God, no! He was in the wrong place at the wrong time, when those awful people decided to have a brawl."

Obviously.

When would Jack get it through his thick skull? If her husband were a Cape, he more than likely wouldn't be dead — at least according to the old rules. Jack nodded, but had other things in mind. Killed in a battle between Capes? He had to think about that, and played for time.

"What was his name?"

"His name?" A shadow passed across Louise's face, as if she'd been caught sleeping. "Honestly? It's the past. I'm all for the here and now. C'mon. You really do want to meet the Prof."

"The what?"

"Not the what, silly, the *who* — Professor Sekrine, my eccentric inventor-cum-father-in-law."

"Don't you mean father-in-law-cum-inventor?"

"Hah! What a silly slip-up!" She laughed again. "Although, p'raps, he might've invented me. I should ask."

Jack studied her. "Louise, I doubt anyone could invent you."

"Are you dissing or flattering me?" The girl blushed. As far as Jack was concerned, she looked still prettier while doing so. "Well, what's the verdict?"

"Both?" he hedged.

"Humph! Perhaps I should turn you away."

"Homeless again," he said, with a smile belying how close to the truth it felt.

For her part, Louise seemed to sense some of that. "Of course I'm kidding!" She leaned over and kissed his cheek.

"Care to repeat that?"

"Maybe." Her eyes held onto his.

"You mentioned this professor's name was Sekrine, but yours is Starkwell."

"Starkwell's my maiden name. I stopped using Sekrine after my hubby passed away. Seemed like a good idea at the time." She blinked a few times. "So, hop to it — otherwise we'll fall asleep here in the stairwell!"

"Now?"

"No, tomorrow." Louise edged the glasses down her nose in order that Jack could better observe as she rolled her eyes. In any case, she still had a smile.

"Well," he said, lacking any solid argument, his byte of bravado having scarpered, "didn't you say this professor would be caught napping?"

"I think I said likely. Sometimes he works all night, pottering away on his devices. The Prof runs the antique shop here during daytime hours, though often I discover him kipping at the till. Come on, you'll like him. And if he's hit the sack, well, we can play quiet. Right?"

"Right." Jack had to laugh. "What kind of play are you talking up?"

"The mind boggles."

Louise took his hand in hers; they ascended the ten steps, whereupon the girl opened the letterbox. Finding nothing, she unlocked the big front doors, they pushed one of them inward, closed it as silently as possible, and proceeded up a set of extremely squeaky stairs.

"Well, I think it's safe to say we've woken up the entire building," Jack decided.

"Shhh."

On the landing, the door to his right swung open and a man with seriously competitive tall/dark movie-star looks drilled him from inside its gateway. This neighbour had on a purple satin dressing robe with a swirl pattern and tassel-end belt.

"Everything all right, Louise?" he asked.

In spite of the effete dinner wear, the man looked ready to bludgeon Jack to death — if this turned out to be the girl's father-in-law, he decided he was in serious trouble.

"All perfect, Mister Phillips." Louise presented him with a charming smile that seemed to tame the beast. "Sorry for disturbing you. Good night."

"G'night."

Once the door closed, Jack followed the girl to its partner on the left.

"Friendly neighbour," he remarked, grateful the man was just that.

"Handsome Harry. Your tone makes you sound like the Prof — he says you can't trust someone looking so good who lives in this neighbourhood. Not jealous, are you?" Louise laughed softly, a gentle guffaw. "Harry's harmless. He watches out for me, and even better keeps an eye on the old man."

Louise quietly unlocked, and then opened the door. Vague lighting flickered within, making the girl stop to sniff.

"I smell fire."

"Nonsense, my dear — hardly the smell of a furnace, but the aroma of Vita-Rays! Welcome home."

The door swung completely open, allowing Jack to feast lowered eyes on an elderly man who only reached his shoulder. Distracted as he was, he banged his forehead on a dangling lightshade. Now he understood how Pretty Amazonia perceived the world — like a clodding giant.

"Nothing's broken, is it?" he worried aloud.

"Nothing important," said Louise, with an affectionate hand touching Jack's forehead.

The living room here had a bull's head on one wall, a zebra rug over the floor, three-tiered shelving on a singular pole, a legion pallet table on wheels, two globe lamps either side of a huge rectangular mirror, and one claw-foot bathtub sofa. Behind the couch was a filigree-pattern, mod-style lattice partition.

In the centre of this flashy spread stood the tiny old gent.

Pushing seventy, the man had unkempt white hair, skin like parchment and wild silver eyebrows, skittish and all very mad scientistish — but he also had a capacious grin.

Less concerned about the crack on the skull than the mention of

Vita-Rays — deployed in comicbooks as an integral part of the Super-Soldier Serum that created Captain America — it dawned upon Jack that the way the old man used the term made them sound like nothing more than incense. This had to be coincidence.

"Well, now. Hello there," the elderly gent said, rubbernecking Jack's way. "Please, come inside, and do mind your head."

"Once bitten," Jack agreed as he absent-mindedly loosened his necktie. "It's sweltering in here."

"That would be the Vita-Rays."

"Prof, this is Jack. Jack, this wonderful gentleman is the Professor."

"Nice to meet you, sir."

"Please, please, call me Prof. I haven't the faintest idea what my real name is — forgotten ages ago. Paul? Fred? José? Truman? ...nothing rings a bell."

Louise's father-in-law shook Jack's outstretched hand and continued to smile, but he felt some kind of searching going on in the man's gaze.

"Jack, was it?"

"That's right."

"And you know Louise how? Through the bank? You're a fellow employee."

"Not exactly."

"Prof!" The girl gave out an exaggerated sigh while she bolted the door, and then hung her jacket. "Leave the grilling for later. Please?"

"Yes, of course — perhaps I should parboil my questions?"

"I have a soft spot for stir-fried," Jack said.

"Ahh, but without the parboiling the carrots may not be completely cooked when seared with the other vegetables. If the carrots are subjected to parboiling first, they will be tender along with the rest of the stir-fry. The soft spot you prefer."

"Can't argue with that."

"The Prof," Louise said, as she deftly removed Jack's coat, "is an amateur chef, among other talents."

"Don't let her fool you. Louise applies the term 'talent' so loosely." The Professor continued to study his visitor's face. "Definitely not a banker," he mused, "since you have a chin. I'd say a detective, but one of those canny fellows would have avoided the lightshade."

This discussion was becoming too personal for Jack's liking. "You mentioned Vita-Rays," he politely cut in.

The Prof suddenly clapped his hands — "I did!" he shouted, while Jack backed away — and, straight after, the man's eyes slit with a blend of understanding and mischief. "A detective, after all," he decided, and then poked his guest in the chest. "For Heaven's sake, take a seat. Put your feet up. We're not heathen here!"

"Better do what the Prof says, Jack," Louise whispered in his ear. "My lovely father-in-law has a robot sofa chair over there that he made, with retractable arms and hooks — it forces people to sit down. *Really* uncomfortably."

Jack flopped onto the nearest settee, of which there were quite a number. Luckily there didn't appear to be gadgets attached to this particular choice.

"Coffee?" Louise asked, from over near a doorway that led to an expansive kitchen.

"Sure." He nodded. "Love one."

"Tea for me," spoke up the Professor, as he sat close to Jack on the other side of a small, low oval table. "All that caffeine keeps me awake."

"In case it escaped your notice," Louise called out while waltzing into the other room, "tea has more caffeine than coffee."

"Ahh, then that's what keeps me awake all night," he chuckled.

"Louise says you're an inventor, sir."

"Sir? You make me sound like a schoolmaster. Prof will do," he insisted, at the same time reaching over and patting the Equalizer's knee. "And, yes, I suppose I am an inventor in my free time, away from the ball-and-chain the antique store has become. Are you interested in the sciences?"

"More the outcome than the process itself."

"I say, that's very cluey of you."

"I know my limitations. What do you make?"

"Oh...this and that. Mostly silly gadgets. I'm currently working with Vita-Rays."

"You mentioned. What exactly are they?"

"I'm not quite sure. More importantly, there's a loose connection on my printed circuit projecto-analyzer. You wouldn't have a screwdriver handy, by chance?"

"Er...not on me."

Jack gazed at the other man, unsure if the Professor was deliberately playing it vague, or genuinely absent-minded.

"*Mens sana in corpore sano,*" the old man muttered. "A sound mind in a sound body — that is my goal in life, Jack. My dream."

#121

Louise was asleep beside Jack on top of her twin-size, scrolled iron bed. Propped up against the bars was the brunette doll Tarpé Mills, looking straight at him.

They'd played it above-board, engaging in conversation with the Professor and waiting patiently for him to go to bed. Even so, Jack judged from his twinkling expression and slight smile that the old man had suspicions regarding what was afoot. Likely, he knew a lot more than his guest.

Aside from furtive kisses on the doorstep and much recent hand play, Jack had never before touched a girl. Even the doll staring back was unnerving.

He didn't tell Louise that; couldn't. He was certain his clumsiness and apprehension were evidence enough, but the girl proved patient and considerate, helping him through the audition.

Louise had removed her glasses, slowly unbuttoned her dress, stood before him in a white satin slip and stockings — and then unbuttoned his shirt, too, as he had not moved a muscle. Given the earlier revelation about her husband's death, Jack thanked lucky stars he'd ditched the costume.

Throughout everything, he was held hostage by her gaze, which said so much in a myriad of subtle forms: tenderness, happiness, sadness and mischief each had their moment in the emerald sunlight of those eyes.

For a long time after, they sat on the iron bed in an embrace, simply holding onto one another. When she came closer still and kissed his mouth, he wanted to hang on to her forever.

"You're a gentle man, Jack," Louise murmured, between kisses. "Thank you."

Eventually, the girl fell asleep on his arm.

Jack stayed awake, studying every facet of the face close beside his. So happy he felt swamped — this kind of joy was far beyond him — the man swivelled his head and instead examined every inch of the ceiling. The sound of her breathing had a calming effect as he did so.

Finally, Jack slipped his arm out from under Louise; he lifted himself onto one elbow and stared briefly at the serene profile on the pillow inches away.

Easy enough to push aside her blonde tresses, to make out — in the poor light — a 'p' on the back of her neck, beneath the collar-line.

Beside the bed, Louise had a round fish tank with seahorses in it. Jack leaned over, dipped his finger, and quietly returned to dab at the p. The ink there was as indelible as a tattoo.

Jack eased her hair down and tidied it, glanced at Tarpé Mills, gave her a smile.

Okay.

PATRIOT CLAIMS

#122

The *Port Phillip Patriot*, located at 335/1000 Broadway, occupied a twenty-two-storey art-deco office tower. Compared with the bulk of the city's surrounding architecture, this rendered the building a pygmy, but what the place lacked in height was made up for with largesse unto itself.

Take, for example, the long-winded slogan above the entrance, hand-carved across two metres in a flowing font, all inlaid mother-of-pearl and gold leaf:

A great crag rising from the sea, clinging with sea flora and fauna, tinted in sea-green, touched with gold.

This went some way toward capturing the wayward spirit that hallmarked the interior.

Jack rode to the tenth floor in an elevator of polished brass, copper and jade. Decorating the walls in the corridor up there were etchings of sea snails, skate, crabs, turtles, carp, scallops, seaweed, sea horses, mermaids and other marine paraphernalia. They made him feel like he was stuck in an aquarium built by Frida Kahlo.

He knocked on a door that had a panel of frosted glass, with the simple words 'G.A. Stellar, Chief Reporter' neatly arranged across it, *sans* marine life.

"Yeah?" he heard. Jack took this as a summons to enter.

The room beyond the neat door was its obverse — all disarray, stacks of paper and books, unclosed filing cabinets, and a broken set of Venetian blinds. A big pin board hung crookedly, crammed with various pictures and newspaper clippings.

In the middle of the room, beneath a rotating ceiling fan, was a wooden desk suffering under the weight of a huge metal typewriter that rode roughshod. There were unfinished cups of what once possibly resembled coffee, and they surrounded a black candlestick phone that had the number 214782 sticky-taped to its trunk.

The place looked devoid of intelligent life, until Jack spotted a patch of hair bobbing about on the other side of the desk, too low to see a face from the door.

This person was obviously preoccupied, so he cleared his throat. A pair of eyes instantly swept over the desk.

"Well, that's subtle."

"Miss Stellar?"

"That's the moniker — overwork it and I'll throttle you."

"Do you have a minute?"

The reporter breathed out in loud fashion and slowly stood. At first Jack caught her aquiline nose, but then she turned to face him and it disappeared.

"So who are you, and what do you want?"

"We've met before."

"We have?" Her eyes conducted a once-over of his blue pinstripe. "Nice-looking suit you have there. Tailored. Quality material. You've got a budget. Banking?

"No. I work with the Equalizers."

Stellar's previously pert mouth formed a round circle. "That so?"

"I'm Southern Cross."

"You know, you're not supposed to go round telling people that."

"I know. We met briefly outside Harvey's Gems."

"The heist? I remember. It's not often we have a Cape making a house call — next time phone ahead, and I'll pretend to tidy up."

"Funny."

"Hilarious."

They stared at one another for several seconds, until Jack broke the silence.

"I have a favour to ask."

"Strange thing to bounce off someone you met only once — and on that occasion she called you a kewpie doll."

"You're forgetting the daggers you steered my way."

"Oh, I steer those at everyone. So — what are you asking?"

"You're a reporter."

"That's what I claim. Others maintain I'm a hack."

Jack noticed a calendar on the cluttered wall, positioned behind the desk. This was opened at September and had a picture — another of those monochrome sketches that dominated everything in Heropa — of Reichenbach Falls in Switzerland. Jack knew this because the name of the place was printed beneath the picture.

"Go on," the woman urged, with an impatient edge.

"I'm looking into the death of a Blando."

"Really?" The reporter leaned forward. "Now you interest me. Why?"

"Long story."

"I have time. It's also my job to listen."

"It may be nothing."

"Allow me to judge."

"You know, you do like pushing people."

"Usually after lobbing those daggers."

"Well, okay. I'm after two things, actually — also information relating to the death of the Aerialist."

Stellar sat back, annoyed. "And I thought you were interesting."

"Well, that's where number two comes in — another death, this time of the Blando." Jack sat on the few centimetres of clean desk, over in the corner nearest him. "I'm guessing nobody bothers to keep any records of Blando fatalities."

"Not true — we do. To a point."

"What point would that be, Miss Stellar?"

"Gypsie-Ann."

"Okay. Call me Jack."

The reporter raised her eyebrows. "You do like breaking your rules."

"And the point you were talking up?"

She nodded. "The *Patroit* compiles the names of the people killed in Heropa, but often these lists are too big to publish in the obituaries section, and some people are never identified."

"Why's that?"

"You can imagine the shape of many of the corpses. We have gophers, our cadets, who try to find the owners of body parts, but they're not always successful. Still, we keep a database here on everyone we can."

"I'm looking a few months back."

"That could be tricky. We have a twenty-four-hour window in which to find out the names — after that, friends and family, as well as our cadets, simply forget they existed. The Reset. A clean slate."

"But if that's the case, how does the *Patriot* — a paper run by Blandos — report things from the day before, without also forgetting?"

"Easy. The morning edition goes to press in the evening, before midnight, and it's delivered before dawn."

"A simple system."

"It functions. Events here change daily, thanks to the Capes, but you'll find some articles we run — about the mayor and his corrupt minions — are the same every day. I get creative and change wording — the next morning's news is fresh to everyone at the newspaper aside from me."

Gypsie-Ann then pursed her lips, clearly annoyed.

"Lately — lately — that's been changing. One of the copy-editors this morning pulled me up for running similar articles two days running. Embarrassing stuff."

"Excruciating."

She broke out in a smile. "Sarcastic tongue you've got there."

"Special training. Anyhow, I've been told Blandos don't revive like the rest of Heropa after those twenty-four hours you mentioned."

"Injured ones recuperate, but you're right — the dead stay dead."

"Why is that?"

"No need? Plenty of other people to act as fodder for you fool Capes. The same rule applies to us — possibly it has to do with live organic matter versus dead. I haven't worked that out yet. But

Blandos' memories are wiped, whereas ours are not."

"Then how about a Blando remembering a death from months ago?"

"That would be...highly unusual."

"Not impossible?"

"I never use the word. Can you be more specific about the John or Jane Doe?"

"A bystander killed in a tussle between Capes."

"Well, that goes without saying. Anything more solid?"

"Name of Sekrine."

"S-E-K-R-I-N-E?"

"I think so."

"First name? — I assume Sekrine is the family name."

"I don't know."

Stellar blew out loudly again and looked at her visitor.

"Without luck, this will take forever to find, if I find it at all. We have no computers here — there're none in Heropa. They like to keep things old school. So, everything's on paper, stored away in the archives. I need some incentive. What's the slant?"

"I don't know yet. But I do need to find out the circumstances of his death."

"So it's a he? You could've told me that before."

"Does it help?"

"Nope." The reporter glanced at the door, and then nodded to herself. "Tell you what, how about you doing the legwork? Here's a key to the archive, which is on the thirteenth floor. I'll write you a note to give the guard there. But if you find anything untoward — you tell me right away, and it's my story. Deal?"

"I'm not sure. This is personal. It mightn't be something I want written up in a neat little article."

"Deal or not?"

"You sure are pushy."

"I know. But I'll be discreet — won't run with anything without your approval."

"Deal."

Gypsie-Ann passed over a bronze barrel key with a decorative open eye attached to the end, and then began scrawling something on a scrap of paper that had a coffee ring across it. As she did so, the woman once again pursed her lips — obviously a habit. She handed Jack the letter.

"There's something else. See this?"

She held up her right thumb, which was wrapped in a peeling Band-Aid.

"Paper cut, I get them all the time. This one I did yesterday — but it hasn't healed overnight like it should do with the Reset."

Jack grinned. "Funny you mention that — I still have bruising from our tussle with the Rotters two days ago. And I'm not talking up phantom pains."

"Trouble with the idI hardware?"

"Injuries hanging round, Blandos recalling the day before yesterday. Sounds like this Reset thing is on the blink."

"Interesting."

"Speaking of interesting, I read your article on the death of Rabble Rouser."

Stellar studied him. "Don't tell me you're another critic."

"No, not at all. But I was curious — how'd you figure out it wasn't a suicide?"

"Ah, the theory."

The woman smirked as she stood, circled the desk, swept up a letter opener — a *katana* blade in six-inch miniature — and held this against Jack's neck.

"It's hard to cut your own throat, especially in the manner established by the police coroner, Doc McCoy — a slash from right ear to left, like this."

She softly moved the letter opener around, still touching the skin, and Jack found the demonstration unpleasant.

"That kind of self-mutilation would normally be done by a south paw, whereas Double-R was right-handed. At least, it's fair to assume he was right-handed since that was where the pen was sitting."

"Smart thinking."

"Saw it once in a movie. Besides, why electrocute yourself after cutting your throat?"

"And the note?"

"Likely incidental — did you know him? The man was a no-hoper. Maybe he was drafting up an autobiography."

"Of four words?"

"As I say. No-hoper."

"What was your opinion of the Aerialist?"

The reporter smiled. "A nice girl." She speedily held up a hand when Jack moved to speak. "Hold your horses — I know what people say about O and her."

"Was it true?"

"To be honest, it's possible. I resolved never to ask."

"Because you were involved with the Big O."

"Old news. But — yes. A lot of men, and women too, fell for the Aerialist. She had something special, and it wasn't just the pretty jetpack."

Jack nodded. "What about Sir Omphalos?"

"To my mind, Sir O took her under his wing because he was paternal rather than a potential *innamorato*. He was an honourable man I trusted completely. Others chose to see things...differently."

"Do you resent them for that? Or him?"

"No. It's the nature of this place. The Capes go on about honour and virtue, but most of the time their behaviour scrapes base level."

"You're a Cape too."

"But never worn one."

"What was the Aerialist's power?"

The woman laughed. "I haven't the faintest idea."

"No one seems to know. How'd she die?"

"Flying in pursuit of a Rotter, out past the stratosphere. Fell sixty-two miles to earth. As you can imagine, there was very little left afterward, but definitely no fuel — leading us to speculate someone sabotaged her jetpack."

Jack leaned forward through the rubbish on the desk and placed his elbows on the wood, in the midst of the disorder, chin in his palms.

"You're game!" Gypsie-Ann muttered.

"Considering I used to rummage through trash cans, trying to locate my next meal, this is nothing." Jack shrugged. "Back to the Aerialist — could it have been an accident? She simply forgot to refuel?"

"There was a witness. PA saw her fill up the jetpack before the mission — not that PA is particularly reliable. But, by all reports, the Aerialist *was*. A very, very good Cape. The full five years in Heropa, originally with the Crime Crusaders Crew, and then one of the founding members of your Equalizers. It's my belief that O was grooming her to take over leadership of the group."

"How did the GWH feel about that?"

"A good question. What's your interest in all this?"

"Bear with me."

"You'll answer my questions in return?"

"Sure — I'll tell you everything I know."

"Deal."

"Can we get back on track?"

"Ready when you are, Jack. Do you know about her old *nom de plume*? No? The Aerialist used to call herself Bullet Gal. Handy with a firearm. A pistolero — but no maestro."

"That so?" Jack thought some. "The Rotter you mentioned, the one she was chasing when her jetpack ran out of juice. Who was it?"

"Jetstarlet."

"Another woman."

"We don't know."

"Meaning...?"

"We don't know. No idea. This Cape was never seen previously, and hasn't been heard of since. Knocked over a bank and flew into the wide blue yonder. Sir O sent the Aerialist to tail and intercept this person. She died."

"Jetstarlet sounds like a girl's name."

"I never allow things like that to confuse me. Proof comes first."

"Of which you have none."

"Currently? You're right."

"Can you tell me more about him — about the Big O?"

Gypsie-Ann smiled thinly. "He didn't like being called the Big O." She scratched at her left ear. "What is this, two hundred questions? You want a job at the *Patriot*?"

"Just trying to get up to par here. What was your take on Sir Omphalos?"

The reporter sat down in her chair on the other side of the clutter and peered back at Jack through piles of paper and old coffee cups.

"O was an idealist — you know he helped create Heropa?"

Jack raised his eyebrows. "No."

"Well, he was one of the chief architects of all this." The woman waved at the mess. "Not that he was satisfied."

"He wasn't?"

"Hardly. O told me he felt the original vision had been tainted — 'polluted', in his words. That's why he broke up the Crime Crusaders and rolled out the Equalizers, equal being the key word. By this, he meant equality for all people, not just the Capes."

"For Blandos too?"

"He hated that word, 'Blando'." The woman's eyes moved around the room and finally settled on the window. "Far more than he disliked being called the Big O," she added, with another narrow smile.

"Is it possible someone didn't appreciate his vision?"

"Vision. Nicely put. Are you asking me if that was why he was assassinated?"

"Maybe."

"Well, you're not the only one who thinks so." Gypsie-Ann glanced over.

"What was he like?"

"A wonderful man."

She sat up straight and looked Jack in the eye.

"He had wit — you know the bugger plundered the Equalizers' lightning bolt logo? Pinched a symbol used back in the 1930s by the British Union of Fascists. The only differences being it's black-and-white and back-to-front."

"I thought Israel-someone-or-other did the logo."

Gypsie-Ann laughed. "Oh, the Israel Schnapps nonsense? Another of O's jokes. Israel was the birth name of Ira R. Schnapp, who designed the *Action Comics* symbol and the Comics Code Authority seal you once saw on all the comics from the 1950s. Knowing O, though, I suspect he also decided on this particular banner and rumoured designer combination to remind himself of a path not to follow: Fascism and censorship."

"That makes me more fond of the thing," Jack decided.

"Nice to hear. Want to know more?"

"Please."

"O loved his classic Hollywood movies as much as he did the comicbooks of the twentieth century — not merely American ones, but British and Australian. Hence the commingling here. That said, O decided Heropa was too much skewed in favour of the 1940s golden age of comics. He preferred the silver age, you know, from the '60s. This imbalance, he said, was the handiwork of his programming partner."

"You know who that was?"

"O never mentioned him by name. But definitely a man."

"Do you reckon it may've been someone who also became a Cape?"

"Again — I haven't the faintest."

Gypsie-Ann sighed.

"You know what I dislike about Heropa? There are no insects. One of the minor details they forgot — or chose to ignore — when they designed the place. Back in Melbourne, my father was an entomologist, so I grew up with bugs all over the house. Until one day he vanished, the house was requisitioned by the State, and the rest of the family tossed out on our ears."

The reporter turned passive nostalgia on its own ear and stuck an attacking scowl on her mush in the space of two seconds.

"Now...well and truly my turn to conduct a grilling. Things recently have been out-of-whack. Not just Capes being bumped off, but Blandos acting differently, remembering things from the day before. What's going on?"

"I don't know."

"Don't know, or won't tell me? I'll find out eventually, you do realize that?"

Jack believed her. "If you do — can you tell us?"

"I'm not sure you deserve any more intel — our relationship is already heavily weighted in your favour. So, can you tell me who the Capes suspect of perpetrating these murders?"

"We don't know."

"What do you know?"

"Honestly? Next to nothing."

"Well, that's unfair. I blather on and you suck it all up, only to play dumb when the tables are turned. How about next time letting me know in advance that you're intending to give me the short end of the stick?"

"Sorry."

"Sorry? You'd make a good reporter. Get out of here."

#123

At the chief reporter's prompting, Jack changed into costume before he went to the archive — she said it'd give extra-added kudos to her request to allow him permission to see the files.

Spot on.

The middle-aged guard very nearly bowed down to the ground when he saw a Cape alight from the lift, and his hands were shaking as he accepted the letter.

But Jack found nothing in the archives, even after five hours' sifting.

Gypsie-Ann was right — there would never be enough time in a week to find what he searched for, especially given the slipshod manner in which filing of fatalities had been done. There were thousands of names in there, sometimes listed alphabetically by first name rather than family name, and often files were thrown in without any order at all.

Having a surname alone was next to no use.

Jack wondered if it would be a good idea to quiz the Professor — he'd know his son's given name and perhaps a specific date of death. But wouldn't that make him suspicious? And, on second thought, the guy couldn't recall his own first name.

What exactly was it Jack was trying to uncover here?

After checking the physical files, he turned to older newspapers over the past six months, preserved on 35-millimetre microfilm, using a clunky, motorized 16/35mm roll film reader.

While the Equalizer researched, he grabbed several paper cups of coffee and had to roll up the lower half of his mask to drink. Now he understood why heroes like Batman, Daredevil and Captain America opted for the half-masks that exposed their mouth and nose — it was far easier to drink, eat and breathe. Jack, Spider-Man and the Black Panther had it hard.

When he settled up for the day and locked the door to the archive, a younger guard awaited. This individual appeared to be less deferential, almost bothered.

"Mister Wright wants to see you," he announced.

"Who?"

"Mister Wright — the owner of this paper and the archive you just ransacked."

Jack looked at the guard for a moment. "So, what does this mean to me?"

"It means you go to his office and you pay your respects." Touchy.

"All right." Jack didn't have anything planned till he was supposed to meet Louise at eight. "You friendly enough to give directions?"

#124

The quarters of Donald Wright were a stark contrast to Gypsie-Ann Stellar's.

For starters, they were plural — several rooms joined together — with the main office ten times the size of his employee's. Jack guessed Wright had taken over two entire floors. He checked in through a receptionist named Mavis, a personal assistant (Smedley), and then another couple of security guards.

The plaque outside this head honcho's personal abode was glistening gold, the door made of cedar — with intricately cut, gorgeous patterns that hurt Jack's eyes.

When he opened it up he found a stadium-sized space with a sweeping spiral staircase to the next level wrapped around a three-metre tall mess of twisted nuts, bolts, steel and rubber on a marble pedestal and the title 'Clobber Creation' on a brass nameplate.

Otherwise this was full of smaller knickknacks: statuary, paintings, rugs, tapestries, chandeliers, antique sideboards and well-dusted sofa chairs. Over by one grand window was a tall, antique wooden stand that had six identical black bowler hats propped at random angles.

Half of a wall, the one to the right as you entered, was crammed floor to ceiling with 1960s memorabilia. Attached to the plaster were old vinyl 45s by Henry Mancini, Quincy Jones, the Animals, the Easybeats, Dionne Warwick, Horst Jankowski, Nancy Sinatra, the Peanuts and Cilla Black. Hung from a curtain rail was a large plastic 'Twister' game mat, sandwiched between one of Twiggy's miniskirts (signed by the model in black texta), a poster for the World War I film *The Blue Max* starring George Peppard, and a framed DC comic of *Showcase* #4 featuring the Flash — with the subtitle "whirlwind adventures of the fastest man alive."

Opposite that was a contrasting diorama covering two walls, sourced from the 1930s and '40s, articles like old shop signage, a vintage taximeter, Japanese matchbox labels, pages torn from old newspapers with comic strips like *Dick Tracy, Flash Gordon, Ginger Meggs* and *Li'l Abner.*

A centrepiece spread was a black-and-white movie poster for Joan Crawford and Walter Huston in *Rain*, with these words dashed across it: 'You Men! You're All Alike! Pigs! Pigs! I Wouldn't Trust Any of You!'.

Stretching across both walls, at head height, were a series of framed original comicbooks including *Action Comics* issue 1, from June 1938 — featuring the first ever appearance by Superman — and *All Winners Comics No. 1* (summer 1941, price ten cents), showcasing Captain America, Bucky, Sub-Mariner, a duo of Human Torches, and two other male heroes Jack couldn't place. Strangely stuck in the centre of the golden-age row was something else Jack didn't recognize: *Speed Comics* issue 17 (April 1942), with an all-star cast of nobodies named Black Cat, Shock Gibson, Biff Bannon, and a hero on the cover that was the spitting image of Captain America — yet also wasn't, since he had a red skullcap and mask instead of blue, and some sort of yellow shoulder decoration.

Above the comics there was a Soviet-style image of workers raising their fists, placed in the centre of a scattered collection of postcards showcasing vamping Hollywood actress Jean Harlow.

But the main feature in this room was a wraparound desk as big as a small bus, boasting a marble surface that was clean and tidy aside from burnished silver in- and out-trays, a hefty Ming vase on the side, a bust of some composer like Beethoven, and a double-lamp on a curving stand.

In the centre of the wraparound sat a middle-aged man in a leather throne that boasted enough space for three people. It was backed by a curving headrest, itself a frieze looking like a ripped copy of the Elgin Marbles.

The man had a black moustache above a taut scar of a mouth and was smoking a cigar wedged in a cigarette holder. He was on the phone. His scalp, hairless, was as polished as the desktop. Somewhat more bizarrely he had a nervous-looking squirrel monkey leashed to his shoulder with a lollipop stuck in its gob.

"Wright talking! My answer is no! I will not lend your bank any more money!"

The man slammed down the receiver, puffed on his cigar, looked up, and discovered Jack in costume. His fury vanished in an instant.

"Ahh, you must be that new fellow Southern Crossed."

"Cross."

"Perfect, perfect. That's wonderful. Well, don't just stand there! Come on in."

Jack walked over and stood to attention before the desk.

"Relax, baby," Wright crooned, in a patronizing tone his guest didn't appreciate. "I like the stars — they're sweet. Take a chair."

So he did.

"I'm Donald Wright — among other things, the publisher of this newspaper. This here is Miami Beach." He nodded to the twelve-inch monkey perched on his shoulder. "You look thirsty. Me too. Parched. Pointless business dealings with tardy financial types. What's your poison?"

"I'm sorry?"

"You know, the '60s or World War II."

"I still don't follow."

"Which era do you prefer?"

"Are you talking comics?"

"I'm talking up comicbooks, baby. Don't you know comics are the funny ones?"

"Then, I guess I'd say the '60s."

"You guess? Thought as much, but you don't sound so convincing. Me? I'm partial to the period too, as you can see from my collection of curios — but the late 1930s and the decade after offers more to catch my fancy."

"Four times more," Jack observed.

"Indeed."

The ringing phone interrupted Wright's flow. He scooped up the handset with an angry flourish.

"Haven't I told you never to interrupt me when I'm talking business?" he barked at somebody on the other end of the line. "When will you learn to know your place?" Straight after, the man hung up. "Now, where were we?"

"The '30s and '40s."

"Of course, of course. This was the golden age of newspaper strip comics as much as the comicbook, the time they begot Buck Rogers, Batman, the Flash, Captain Marvel, you name the iconic hero. The Soviets and fascists were taking on the capitalist West, the cars were superb, the men's fashions sweet and, *ahhh*, the noir: Chandler, Hammett, Cain." Wright seemed, then, to remember his manners. "Can I buy you a drink, kid?"

"No, I'm fine."

"Sure about that?" The publisher absent-mindedly stroked his pet.

"I'm sure."

"No?"

"No."

"Alrighty. Let's get straight down to the practical details, parched or not — nasty business, these killings."

Jack looked over the desk, in the publisher's remote direction. "Which ones, sir?"

"Well, the Capes, of course. Everyone is a suspect. Do you good people have any leads to pursue?"

"No concrete ones I'm aware of."

"There's a pity, SC-baby. Do you mind if I call you that? People gossip, you know, when there's an information vacuum." Wright flicked through a thick dossier in front of him. "Son, I need a friend. A reliable person on the inside, an extra-vigilant cat, keeping an eye on activities as they transpire, and all that kind of shenanigans."

Jack stared at him. "You mean like anonymous source material — or a spy?"

"Neither. More an observer, seeing the wood for the trees, or in spite of them. Plus, I'll loan you the axe."

"I'm sorry, sir." Jack stood up again. "I don't believe that's my job."

"Is that so?"

"So, indeed."

"Then what, may I ask, do you believe your job to be?"

"Helping people."

"Good Lord, baby — you're an idealist!"

"Another one. Is there a problem with that?"

"No, but it is rather astonishing. Say, don't get all tense and soft. I suppose I should have guessed from the flag there on your chest."

"D'you mind if I ask — are you a Cape or a Blando?"

The man guffawed. "Wouldn't you like to know?"

"Yeah, I would, actually."

"Spare me the details. They are for lesser men...like you." Straight after, Wright waved his hand as he returned attention to the ledger. "All right, Southern Cross, you're dismissed now. Get out — there's a good kid."

For a few seconds, Jack entertained a mad impulse to hop up on the ink blotter, swat the monkey, yank over the publisher, push him to the desktop, and peel down his shirt collar to see if there was a letter 'p' there. Surely, in this body, he had the strength to wrestle an old man and his bulging-eyed pet.

But the impulse passed and he ran along as requested.

#125

That night, Jack and Louise found themselves again in the girl's large bedroom.

The door to the passageway was closed, but the blind at the window remained at half-mast and this allowed in a certain amount of street illumination and moonlight.

On the windowsill were an assortment of small, hand-carved figurines of gods and their associated hangers-on. Jack recognized a clear lead glass Virgin Mary and a rotund, rosewood Buddha. Their cohorts on the sill were carvings of Takehaya Susanoo-no-Mikoto, a Shintō summer storm god, and the elephantine Hindu deity Ganesha.

Louise obviously liked playing it safe, regardless of spiritual persuasion.

There was a big-framed painting on the wall above the bed, an unusual one displaying World War I-era biplanes indulging in a dogfight amidst gloomy-looking clouds.

"My father was a pilot," Louise said, as she got undressed. "That picture belonged to him."

To the left of the window, in the large space leading to the bedroom door, was a bookcase jammed with classic hardbacks: *Moby-Dick, Great Expectations, Pride and Prejudice, The Old Man and the Sea, Gulliver's Travels, The Age of Innocence, The Crows of Pearblossom* — and, yes, *The Well of Loneliness.*

Otherwise, there wasn't all that much in the way of furnishings except for suitcases, wooden crates and boxes. A vanity table, made up of slapped together old pieces of wood, was cluttered with cosmetics and perfumes.

On a small table by the bed, between the fish tank with seahorses and a loud, ticking chrome clock, was a vase with wilted yellow roses. A wind chime, made of shards of bamboo tied together with wire, dangled from the overhead chandelier.

"You're so beautiful, Jack."

Louise kneeled on the carpet beside the bed on which he sat. She was dressed only in a beige chemise — having removed her earrings, glasses and stockings.

Jack placed a hand on each of her cheeks and moved in to kiss the girl's mouth. She stood again, leaning into him, blonde hair falling across his face. Her breathing quickened as he daringly moved his fingers down her neck, across her chest, and on over the flimsy material that covered her stomach. In return, her hand rubbed the bruising on his back.

"Ouch," he mumbled between kisses.

He explored her chin, her cheeks, and then her throat, became fascinated with the nape of her neck and rained more kisses there, while his hands located the girl's buttocks and gently squeezed.

Louise arched her back, peered heavenward, and let out a great sigh.

"Oh, Lee," she moaned.

Both people froze.

Straight after, Jack's hands fell away, and then he backed up on the bed, staring at the girl's upturned face. Louise, for her part, still looked at the ceiling; still breathed in jerky, ragged fashion — but she was gnawing at her lower lip as a tear rolled down the closest cheek.

"Oh, God," the girl finally squeezed out.

"Louise."

Jack tried to catch her eye, but she didn't, couldn't, look at the man in front of her.

"I'm so sorry."

Blinking several times, unsure of what to say or do, Jack rubbed his right index finger and studied the foreign joints, the strangely well-manicured nail. "That was his name? Lee? — Your husband's name?"

"Yes."

"Okay."

Finally, Louise lowered her face and peered his way. "Please forgive me, Jack. Please. I'm damaged goods. You shouldn't be with me."

"It's okay."

He braved himself, reached over, put arms around her, drew her closer. "Louise, really — it's okay." Told the truth. "In all honesty, I think I'm way more damaged than you. This evens things out a morsel."

"Do you mean that?"

"Yes."

"I'm not sure I believe you. You're just saying that."

"Believe me."

"God, I *am* sorry."

"Forget it." He gently kissed her nose, and she looked at him.

"You know what? You're amazing."

"I wish I could say 'of course'. Far from it."

"It's true anyway. Thank you." Louise broke into a grateful smile, disarmed and relieved, if still nervous. "Heavens, I thought — well, I thought you'd hate me."

"Never, ever possible."

The two of them ended up spending the rest of that night lying side-by-side on the bed covers, occasionally nestling up to the other, but mostly taking turns reading aloud passages from different books selected at random.

That was how they fell asleep, with an opened copy of *The Count of Monte Cristo* on Jack's stomach and Louise's face pressed against his, Tarpé Mills's against hers.

#126

Jack had to be up early and back to Timely Tower by eight a.m., since their fabulous ringleader had scheduled a red-eye get together.

He wasn't certain why one should feel either fatigue or wired on caffeine in a make-believe place like Heropa, but even after three espressos the fatigue was winning and he struggled to keep it together.

Flashbacks peppered his more lucid moments — of waking up on Louise's pillow and gazing into her green eyes. Of her looking back with an earnest, open expression. Of her saying, in a soft voice, scared, "I love you."

Jack and the Brick were the only two at their round table when eight segued by. According to his cinder-block teammate, Pretty Amazonia was ill.

"Not fair," Jack decided.

"Tell me 'bout it."

"Do people actually get sick here?" Jack asked.

"Blandos do — they run the full gamut o' illnesses we have in the outside world, somethin' t'do with makin' it more realistic, poor sods. But Capes? Nah. We have our own probs back home, health or otherwise. PA was out late. Figure she's feignin' illness, an' catchin' up on beauty sleep."

"And she needs it."

The Brick chuckled as he looked at his rocky left wrist, like there was a timepiece there, when in fact a watchband would never circumnavigate its width. "Anyways, where's the Great White Dope? The loser called this meetin'."

"I heard that."

The Great White Hope, bedecked as ever in stainless white robes, did his smooth-descending-the-stairs trick from the balcony.

"Nice to know yer hearin', at least, is intact."

"It's nice to know you care."

The Equalizer had reached the bottom-most step, but remained in that spot as his gaze swept over Jack, like he was inconsequential, and affixed itself on the hulking man to his right.

"By the way, perhaps you might be courteous enough to help me understand — why stick with a name like the Brick, when you could better resort to the Dick?"

"Oh, gee, the bozo has a wily sense o' humour — he even rhymes. Hurrah."

Stifling a yawn, Jack lifted his fourth coffee and decided to hose down some of the tension.

"What's up, GWH?"

The remark earned him that piercing grey stare, but this at least meant he amounted to more than a hill of coffee beans.

"Please, Southern Cross, use my full name. Don't you realize how much the acronym 'GWH' irritates me?"

"Actually, sorry, I didn't. Everyone else uses it."

Very discreetly, the Brick winked at him. At least, Jack thought he winked — it was difficult to tell amidst the masonry.

"Yeah, it irks our boss. Makes 'im sound like some kind o' dangerous, illegal drug. GWH-slash-GHB — geddit?"

Jack didn't get it at all, but shammed. "Sure."

For his part, the Great White Hope plumbed unhappy. "Dear God. Do I really need to listen to this nonsense first thing in the morning?"

"Course not, bub. Y'could kick us out on our arses right about now — only, I seems to remember we're here by yer explicit invitation."

"Ahh. That."

"Ahh, that," the Brick mimicked.

Their all-white host finally drifted across the marble foyer, and then lingered to stand over the other two Equalizers. In close proximity, Jack noted the GWH had some weird, eerie personality clout, leading the Brick to renounce his breezy charms and slouch instead to examine his feet. His partner wondered if he was searching for remnants of Little Nobody or the Tick between his toes.

Biting the bullet, Jack peered up at their leader.

The GWH held him with those cold grey peepers — no, Jack changed his mind, mark them down as refrigerated.

"What's the scam?" he hedged, equally ruffled.

In response, the GWH barely moved. "Scam?"

"The rort — you know, what's up?"

"What makes you think anything is up, Southern Cross?"

"So, you invited us down bright and early for drinks and polite conversation?"

The Brick raised his head. "That sounds half my cuppa. Drinks — without the yabberin'."

"You two fools are incorrigible. No wonder you get along well."

The Great White Hope sighed, loud and long. It appeared the whole of Heropa disappointed him.

"I had hoped you would learn the proper ropes, Southern Cross, our true calling — not the self-indulgent gutter paths trod by your 'mate' here."

"Dunno, ol' boy. I'd call self-indulgent the amount o' time you spend on yer hair every mornin'." The Brick guffawed his rumbling, heavy bass laugh. "Oh, yeah — an' what about the pristine wardrobe, huh? How much dosh an' effort do you waste there?"

The Great White Hope stared at the ceiling. He apparently had nothing to say.

"So, anyways, where's this hooch you promised?"

"What hooch?"

"The hard stuff, el firewater, *capiche*?"

Jack laughed. "Gotta admit, I'm pretty thirsty myself."

The GWH did his menacing-stare trick as he again focused on Jack. "Well, you can't drink."

The announcement caused him to shrug. "I know we can't — I'm only kidding round. No Capes can drink alcohol here, I remember."

"No," the Great White Hope said in a smooth, honeyed tone bordering on contemptuous, while he slipped silently across the floor, "I'm not referring to the general alcohol restrictions in Heropa.

You, my boy, would not be allowed to imbibe *anywhere*."

This made Jack's heart skip around a bit — he wasn't sure if it sped up or slowed down.

"Whaddaya mean by that crack?" the Brick demanded on his behalf.

"Well, correct me if I'm wrong, you blockhead, but the meaning is clear enough," continued the GWH. "Southern Cross is too young to drink. Back in the real world, he's only fifteen. Young enough to be your son, my cobblestoned friend."

Jack glared at his leader. "How the fuck do you—" Like a shot, his hand covered his mouth, far too late. The profanity had slipped out before thinking.

Yet nothing happened.

He didn't eject or unboot or whatever the hell they called it. There was no slap in the face back to Melbourne. His eyes darted over to the Brick's, who appeared equally astonished.

"What?" Jack whispered.

"Fuck?" the Brick said in a soft, testy tone. Then he smiled in broad fashion. "Fuck!" he threw to the ceiling, his head tossed back. "Shit, bloody, anal... CUNT!"

Nothing.

The three men stood in a circle beside the table, in the middle of their headquarters in puritanical Heropa, and it now looked like they could swear like sailors on shore leave.

"You sly dog," the Brick suddenly decided, appraising the GWH anew. "You set up some kind o' force field round this room, so's we can get away with murder while in here — about time we put our powers to good use. You sly bugger."

The Great White Hope held up his right hand. "Not me. But, as you can see, the rules have changed. Things are in flux."

"Yeah? That so...? Luv'ly. Or should I say 'shit a brick'? You know how long I've been meanin' to throw down that quip?"

Stomping over to a trunk covered with a beautiful throw-sheet, the Brick yanked off the material. There was a padlock beneath, instantly broken to smithereens, and then the man delved inside the box for a bit.

Finally, he stood up straight — with a silver cocktail shaker in one mitt and several unopened bottles in the other.

"Well, if the ol' restraints are passé, I'm fer havin' a drink. Wanna join me?"

"I told you. This boy is a minor."

The Brick stopped to study the Great White Hope. "So, who cares? How old're you again, kid?"

"Fifteen," Jack admitted, embarrassed and reasonably humiliated. It felt like someone had wrenched away his gut. What if the GWH somehow got word to Louise? What if she found out?

Panic set off alarm bells somewhere in his belfry, and in the middle of them darted the flashback again, his eyes close to hers, the slight hint of peppermint and citrus. "You mean the world to me," he'd whispered, just as frightened, and he meant it.

The Brick's next sentence switched off the clamour.

"Then you're old enough."

Cutting back to the here and now, Jack glanced over at his partner, was silently grateful.

"Kid's an adult, in my book," the man went on. "Been in action already, kicked arse, got kicked himself in the bum. Been on the receiving end o' some serious shit. *Fuck* it." He chuckled — "Lordy, I do like the new world!" — and then thumbed the patio outside. "You comin', bright eyes? We have a party t'get started."

Beaming, Jack nodded. "For sure, Mister B. Ta."

"Then go grab the ice."

Somewhat deflated, their lionhearted leader trudged in the opposite direction, toward the stairs. "Inconceivable," he hissed to no one in particular.

They could even see his legs move.

#127

Jack was less recuperating, more reeling, from his first ever drunken binge when they got the scoop.

"SC — wake up. Come on. Wakey-wakey."

Pretty Amazonia shook him roughly, and went so far as to throw in a couple of jarring slaps. He came to half-on, half-off a lounge chair, outside on the balcony.

The sun was low in a sky tainted pink. The Brick lay spread-eagled on the tiling at Jack's feet, an empty martini glass stuck in his fist. He was snoring like an outdoor generator.

"I don't feel well," Jack grumbled, about to close his eyes again.

"Not my problem. Pull yourself together — we have business." After slapping him awake one more time, the woman studied an array of scattered bottles. "That's alcohol?"

"We can drink!" roared the Brick, suddenly awake, as he reared up into a sitting position and attempted to drain emptiness from his glass. "Way o' the new world — halle-friggin'-lujah!"

The notion of any similar celebration far from his mind, Jack felt ill. "I'm never drinking again," the disoriented Equalizer said to nobody.

It seemed impossible to recollect everything he and the Brick had yacked about while toasting one another into oblivion. The Brick reciting cocktail recipes was one tangent — a Luis Buñuel surrealist martini being the standout — and, later on, the big man offered fatherly advice over his shaker, something about women being an enigma. Had Jack mentioned Louise? He couldn't remember — and prayed he kept his trap shut.

Pretty Amazonia squatted down beside her rock-ribbed colleague and carefully prised away his glass.

"Hon, much as I don't want to rain on your party — I'm going to rain on your party. We got a call from the mayor. They found the Great White Hope."

"Yeah? Where was the Great Gazoo off sulking this time?"

PA deliberated a moment.

"Remember the statue they dedicated to the Big O yesterday? Ten-metre granite thing with his arms outstretched, over on the Boardwalk?"

"Don't 'member nothin' right now, babe."

"God, I'm there with you," Jack muttered. "Never drinking again."

"Well, both of you must remember how put-out the GWH was — come on, use those pickled brains. Him going on about being the new leader of the Equalizers, yet having no monument to call his own."

"Oh, yeah. That I do recall." The Brick smiled as he reached for the cocktail shaker, which was lying abandoned under Jack's chair.

The woman stopped him. "Not now," she said. "Later."

"Why?" The Brick sounded like an annoyed drunk.

"Good reason. The GWH is dead."

Both men looked at her, stunned, but the Brick still got in his usual word first.

"What?"

"He's dead."

"Yeah — you said."

"So I did."

"How?"

Clearing her throat, PA pressed lips together and focused above her large partner's skull. Then she spoke. "Someone strung him up from the arms of that statue — the Big O's — and crucified him there, his eyes gouged out."

"Jesus," Jack exhaled, hangover misplaced.

"I'm thinking that's precisely what the perps wanted to replicate, except for the bonus extra with the eyes."

"See no evil?" he suggested.

"And there was a message."

The Brick rubbed his skull, likely trying to rejig his brain. "What message?"

"Messily painted on the plinth beneath the GWH, spiralling round the column."

"Well, don't keep us in suspense — what'd it say, dollface?"

"I have no idea."

"You fergot yer glasses?"

"No, I have no idea what it said. I can't begin to pronounce the paintjob, but I can spell it for you: H-O-U-Y-H-N-H-N-M-S."

"What is that? Welsh?"

"God knows, but we're dealing with creative types—"

"Horses fer courses," the Brick muttered, looking bewildered.

"—and now they've had their way with the GWH," PA steamrolled on, ignoring him, "we're likely next up on the agenda."

"Poor bloody bastard. All that handiwork is goin' t'do serious damage to his unsullied image." He grabbed back the cocktail shaker and partially filled a glass with the last drops of a Vesper. "When'd they find him?"

"Just before five o'clock."

"What time's it now?"

"Six. The last time you saw him?"

"We had a meeting at eight this morning, the one you slept through, an' he stomped out about eight-thirty."

"And you passed out when?"

"The kid lasted only a couple'a hours. Me? Sheesh, now I'm strugglin'. Reckon, last time I checked, it was three in the arvo. Guess I lost it after."

"So he was butchered some time between eight-thirty and five. Daylight hours, in a very public space, while you boys were having your soirée."

"Hey, fair crack o' the whip, dollface — also while you was indulgin' in mootably deserved forty winks."

The woman looked away. "Mmm."

"Makin' all'a us appear incompetent, an' the GWH the beneficiary o' that lapse." The Brick finished his drink in an instant. "Okay, well. Blame games aside — let's get them facts. Any witnesses?"

"The mayor says none."

"Is that possible?" Jack wondered.

"Dubious, if you ask me."

"I was asking."

Lobbing his glass over the railing, the Brick stood up. "Pity the statue can't blab."

PA almost smiled. "If it did, we could replace you. So. What on earth are we going to do? For all his faults, the GWH did lead us."

"You think so?"

"I'm trying hard to be generous, since he's dead. Anyway, we need a new leader."

"No way I wanna be boss. You?"

"Not my style."

Jack panicked. "Don't dare look at me."

"Kid — we're not."

Seemingly thoughtful, Pretty Amazonia stared out over the city as the sun set. "Maybe we should play it democratic for a while?"

#128

After they inspected, and then identified, the mutilated corpse on a slab at City Hall's morgue, Jack cut loose from his cohorts under some pathetic pretext. He got changed in a public toilet upstairs and met Louise outside the Warbucks bank.

They'd made a date to go see a movie.

While Jack was tempted to suggest *Bijou, the Monster from Mars!*, Louise chose a musical, a monochrome number with lots of dancehall rollicking and a man in top hat and tails, spinning his partner across a landscape that looked like a cinematographer's gaudy version of nirvana. Louise held his hand throughout, and at one stage she rested her cheek on his shoulder.

Before and after the film, Jack said less than usual.

Too much circulated through his head — most of all, he kept visualizing the Great White Hope's empty eye sockets, along with special guest star vignettes from Marat in the bathtub and the rolling, decapitated skull of Iffy Bizness.

On top of these apparitions, he was nursing a killer hangover, and gradually the girl got it. Louise adapted to his mood, could probably smell the stale alcohol, and distanced herself.

Following on from an obligatory post-screening coffee, they said their goodbyes without so much as a hug — just an awkward, puzzled exchange.

#129

The Brick was babbling on about some motorcycle while he drove, and he promised to give Jack lessons on the thing the very next morning.

"I'm talkin' up me Orley Ray Courtney-revamped 1930 Henderson. Rare as hen's teeth: four-cylinders, 1300 cc — bliss on ten-inch wheels. Fer starters, picture a chassis wrapped in an elegant shell that begins with a rounded nose and grille, like a '34 Chrysler Airflow, and finishes up on the wee backside reminiscent o' an Auburn Speedster. Along the way, it's a Coke-bottle-shaped, goddamned art-deco miracle."

"You sound enamoured," his partner mused in the passenger seat.

"With seductive curves like this, what's not t'love?"

"Think I need to see the thing to get the affection. I'm having trouble imagining it, and looking like a Coke bottle doesn't sound pretty."

The Brick was chauffeuring them both across town to meet Pretty Amazonia.

The man drove his car like you probably can imagine — lead-footed — but otherwise played it remarkably safe in terms of plying traffic. The other automobiles were much slower and boxier, and the Brick slid his car between them with a good millimetre or two to spare.

"You'll be amazed, kid. Lucky also I have the best motorbike mechanic in Heropa, Alex Raymond, t'keep it tuned. Cars're more my speciality."

"Like '60s comicbooks are mine?"

"Vaguely related. Speaking o' which, I been meanin' to badger you, kid, somethin' that reporter Gypsie-Ann brought up. You know there's a star missing from the Southern Cross on the togs yer wearin'?"

"That's related?"

"In a roundabout fashion."

While he was in costume, Jack at least didn't have to don the mask, seated there in the passenger seat behind tinted windows.

He was wearing rounded 1970s Persol Ratti sunglasses — not for any fashion statement (Jack had no idea about style, brand or vintage), but because he continued to suffer ill-effects from yesterday's drinking binge and had found the pair in the Big O's dresser — which still hadn't been cleared out.

Louise had taken pole position in his battered mind. He'd resolved to apologize, even if he couldn't explain the nature of said apology. She deserved better and he felt like an arse.

"This isn't a Kiwi thing?" the Brick rattled on, oblivious. "You know, their flag having had four stars while ours has five?"

Jack realized he had to respond. "Nope, nothing New Zealand about it. I swear." He marked the shops they passed, along with people on the sidewalk, others crossing the roads, more parking their cars. Joe-average citizens in suits, hats and skirts, hunched over elderly types, and kids with school bags and caps. All of them pursuing a private early afternoon mission, some personal course of action no one else knew about. "I guess it was aesthetics — balance."

"Y'guess? You dunno? Correct me if I'm wrong, but ain't that there the Eureka Stockade flag stuck on yer chest? I 'member from history class the thing havin' five stars. The one in the middle's missin' — ain't it?"

"I didn't design this suit."

"No?" The Brick looked sideways at his partner. "Then who did?"

"I wouldn't want to bore you, mate."

"Since when did you worry yerself 'bout that? And, well, hey, I got the time if you got the stamina — we won't meet PA fer another half hour thanks to this here toddler-gridlock. Takes a lot to get me noddin' off."

"That true?"

"Well, a bit."

They detoured round a timber W-class tram that hogged the

middle of this particular thoroughfare, but again got caught up in traffic.

Jack glanced up at the hopper windows on the side of the tram and saw a bunch of passenger faces running the gamut from annoyed to asleep. The driver, in his peak cap and white gloves, seated behind a round cornered windscreen at the front, focused somewhere dead ahead — presumably at the backside of a grey, metal-clad van that had the words 'Mitchell Armored Truck Co.' stencilled across it.

"You ever been to Richmond District, Brick?"

"Not since they locked-down the place."

"Two years ago I busted in there — pretty easy thing to do when you're desperate and scavenging," Jack mused. "You get to know the breaches in the fence and you're up on the clockwork patrol routes by security. Either that, or you end up in the clink."

"At the very least — they don't like people breakin' their li'l rules. Much as I hate t'play the age card...what were yer folks doing durin' these bloody risky high jinks?"

"Arrested. Taken away."

"Any reason?"

"Sedition."

"Ah. That classic. How old were you?"

"Thirteen."

"Seen 'em again?"

"What do you think?"

The Brick nodded at the road ahead. "Got'cha. Go on, kid."

"Well, yeah, I found this weatherboard house in a back-road in Richmond, name of Duke Street, if I remember right. The area was a shit-hole, like the rest of the neighbourhood, this house no different. Leaning to one side, about to collapse, just like its brothers. Nothing special."

"Presumin' yer gonna fill me in to the contrary, lemme hop in first — why then bother takin' a look-see?"

"Funny thing. The house had a corroded brass nameplate

screwed into the woodwork, beside the front door, barely readable, but I could make out the name: 'Deaps'."

"The hell, you say."

"The hell, I do. Figured anything to do with Wolram E., the big banana running Melbourne, shouldn't be sneezed at."

"One hundred percent agreed. What'd you find?"

"Initially? Sweet FA. After jacking the bathroom window and attempting to prowl the deserted place, I stuck my foot through the floor, plus a door fell over when I pushed too hard. Came across a stack of rotting mail behind the door, years and years old, addressed to Alice and Patrick Deaps. Nothing with 'Wolram' on it. Figured the name was a coincidence."

The Brick eased the car into a corner. "Guess."

"When I was snooping round the back, I got caught in a real heavy downpour, so I busted into this ramshackle shed they had in the yard. Inside, wrapped up tight in several sheets of blue tarp, protected from the rain, the snails, and also probably the decades, were boxes of old comicbooks from the 1960s. Hundreds of them."

"Man, oh man, what a natty discovery!" the Brick enthused — Jack could see the dollar signs in his eyes. "DC? Marvel? Dell? Not Harvey, I hope an' pray."

"No Harvey. Silver-age Marvel. Plus black-and-white reprints of their stuff, in a British rag called *It's Terrific*, some Dell titles, an old issue of DC's *The Flash*, when Barry Allen wore the costume. Batman too."

"A treasure trove. Sounds like one o' them archaeological digs they used to indulge in, like the one with King Tut."

The Brick had taken out a Big Boss Cigar, started chewing, and then chucked it out the window. Instead, he slid a bona-fide cigar into his mouth, something Cuban from the looks of it. He bit off the end and lit up.

"'Scuse the smell. I'm still listenin'. How's this relate to the costume?"

Jack tried not to cough, did anyway, and wound down his

window. "Getting there," he said, breathing in fresh passing oxygen mixed with automobile exhaust. "Sandwiched between issues of *Thor*, I found this letter addressed to someone named Wally Deaps. It had Marvel's company address in New York on the stationery, along with a picture of Spider-Man and a U.S. stamp, but the postmark was illegible. Inside the envelope was a note signed by the secretary to Stan Lee—"

"Get outta here? Now, I reckon yer pullin' me leg."

"Nup. It was there, all right, along with a folded up, hand-drawn picture of a superhero."

"Stan Lee done his own art? Thought the guy was scribe only."

Jack frowned. "Well, no, maybe I said that wrong. They were returning a picture this Wally Deaps had sent them."

"Ahhh."

"Anyway, after lugging these boxes back to my place — it took several trips — and somehow not getting nabbed by the cops, I read through every issue. A few times. I lost count how many times I've done so since then. But it became clear that the artist of the drawing in the Marvel envelope, this Wally character, had nicked his image from the cover art of *Captain America* 102 — originally concocted by Jack Kirby and Syd Shores."

"Can't say I know it."

"One of the comicbooks in this Richmond stash, a 1968 issue in which Cap is tossed aside by a Nazi robot, the Sleeper, while Agent Carter looks on, dismayed."

The Brick sighed in loud fashion. "Yer losin' me precious attention span, kid. What in Sam Hill are ya on about?"

Jack laughed — somewhat abashed, as they put it in old tomes. "Well, yeah, yeah, I know. You're right. Not important. Comicbook stuff."

"Glad we got somethin' straightened. Remind me to bore you more to death about cars — fair's fair. But go on."

"Okay, I'll get to the point — this plagiarist did a pretty good job. He reversed the cover and changed the costume. The new outfit was supposed to be darker blue, with the white-starred flag from the Eureka Stockade stuck on the chest — minus the centre star, like you and Gypsie-Ann picked up on. He also had a mask covering all the face aside from the eyes — made him more like the Black Panther than Cap. 'Southern Cross' was scrawled at the top. So, when I came here and they offered me the option to be anybody, I gave them that picture. Besides, the concept struck me as funny."

The Brick furrowed the cobbling shaping his brow. "Lemme remember — 'cos all the smog an' rain and shitty weather in Melbourne've eliminated any sign o' the real constellation it's named after — like ya already mentioned."

"That, plus I was nicking someone else's design they'd, in turn, nicked from a great artist — Jack Kirby. Bet this Wally kid never pictured a living, breathing version of his pirate copy."

Andrez Bergen

THE CRIME CRUSADERS

#130

"Before the Equalizers came into being, there were two rival crime-fighting groups plying the trade in Heropa," Pretty Amazonia said. "One of them was the Felon Fighters, run by Capitol Hill, the other the Crime Crusaders Crew, helmed by Major Patriot."

She tossed a picture onto the linoleum surface of the small table around which the three Equalizers sat. They were in a crowded bar called the Kublai Khan.

"This is a group caricature of the Felon Fighters — done by another Cape, Kid Drawalot."

The Brick swivelled a drawing that looked like it'd been composed by Thomas Nast, all puny bodies, overlarge heads and insanely big grins, to get a better look. "Neat-o," he muttered.

It went without saying that three Capes in full regalia drew stares from the other patrons — but Jack wasn't sure whether this was because (a) Capes were increasingly rare, (b) the customers fretted about the place coming under attack from other, rival Capes, or (c) they didn't like these superpowered cretins they labelled Bops.

Jack was certainly feeling cretinous. He had a dull pain in the back of his head and felt like half the grey-matter in his skull had been vacuumed out — the useful bits at any rate. Having a hangover in a virtual-reality world simply wasn't fair.

He peered about the room over the top of people's heads.

There was a wall, next to the bar proper, upon which was pasted a huge, reproduction sixteenth-century map titled 'The Kingdome of China'. The bored, dark-haired barman beside it sported a pencil-thin moustache, a bowtie and a tuxedo — making him a dead-ringer for Mandrake the Magician.

"Could we get a drink?" Jack asked a nervy waitress hovering nearby in a tight silk *qípáo* dress, and then he turned to the other Equalizers. "Beer?"

"Yep — gimme three. Brick Lager."

Jack sat back. "You have your own brewery?"

"Nah, it's a Canadian drop. I like the name."

"Figures." Pretty Amazonia raised a hand. "I'm in too. Don't worry — I won't play recondite like Mister B and order gallons of Amazon Beer. Just the one Mountain Goat will do."

"Three Bricks for him and a Mountain Goat for her," Jack told the waitress, "and I'll have a sarsaparilla with a generous scoop of vanilla ice-cream. Cheers."

The Brick choked on the dregs in his glass. "A spider? Junior, sometimes you worry me."

"Hey, I need time to recuperate from that last dabble with alcoholic excess. The trick is how I'm going to tuck into a spider while wearing this bloody mask."

"Bah! Costumes...tights... That's kid stuff. Who needs 'em?"

PA had perked up. "You're still suffering?"

"God, yeah."

"Brick, how about you?"

"Never better."

"I'm thinking the Reset's given up the ghost." Jack rubbed his eyes. "My back is still black and blue from the other day, and twenty-four hours has not in any way helped my hangover."

"But Mister B is okay."

"He's the Brick. He doesn't feel anything."

The craggy Equalizer feigned a broken heart — "Mebbe I should go get sensitivity lessons," he whined — and then gratefully accepted his replacement beers.

Jack returned attention to the picture on the table.

"You people never bothered to invest in a camera?"

Brick put chunky hands in the air. "Not us — them. Me'n PA came later."

"I like it," Pretty Amazonia decided. "Old-school vibe and all. The artist captured them pretty well. This is one of Heropa's edicts — photos are out. Haven't you noticed?"

"Not exactly true. I've seen cameras."

"But have you spotted any happy snaps?"

"No," Jack admitted.

"Precisely. The rule gets scuttled when it comes to TV and cinema — you can't exactly make animation without a camera, and we don't have computers with which to create CG. But no still-photography." PA moved on, unfazed, "Here we have, from left to right, Escape Goat, Doc Fury, Air Gal, Capitol Hill, Vic Torrious, Crimson Skull — he's the one kneeling there — and Mer-Maiden."

"They look chirpy."

"Chirpier times. Here's another sketch, this one of the Crime Crusaders, done round the same timeframe." The picture was laid down with more care but still had the ridiculous proportions.

"Some of these guys look familiar," Jack observed.

"So they should. The original Crime Crusaders were Sir Omphalos, Bullet Gal, Big Game Hunter, Milkcrate Man and the Great White Hope, along with Major Patriot here, in the centre, acting as big boss. When the Felon Fighters moved on to better pastures and the Crime Crusaders disbanded, the Big O, Milkcrate Man, Bullet Gal and the GWH set up the Equalizers — at which time Bullet Gal also changed her costume and name to the Aerialist."

The Brick yawned.

"Big on their gals, eh? Yeah, yeah, I know the history."

"SC doesn't. And there is a point to this little rehash — look at the picture again, both of you. Three of the four founders of the Equalizers are dead."

"Oh, yeah."

"You reckon there might be a link?" Jack asked.

He was staring at the tumbler of black fizziness before him, in the midst of which rolled a scoop of white.

"I'm not sure what I think," PA confessed.

"Can't I take off my mask for a couple of minutes?"

"No. Roll it up if you need to appease your stupid sweet-tooth."

"Hardly the same — that's just mean."

"Nah," the Brick was saying, still focused on the picture. "Milkcrate Man? No way." He leaned on the table and of course it tilted, very nearly flipped, spilling some of his precious beer. "Oops — tarnation!" he muttered.

Luckily, PA hadn't noticed the misdemeanour. "Maybe. Verdict's in the air. And what happened to Big Game Hunter and Major Patriot?"

The woman sat back on the bench seat to take in both her partners.

"Remember — the Major was leader of the Crime Crusaders Crew, yet he wasn't a shoo-in for the Equalizers."

"Prob'ly both o' 'em got bored an' left," the Brick suggested.

"Maybe."

"Wish I scored a dime fer all the maybes we're liberally sprinklin' about. Y'know, I heard tell that the Big O an' Major Patriot were two o' the original programmers, the designers of Heropa. Dunno if it's true, tho'."

Pretty Amazonia finished her beer and scoffed.

"Let's steer clear of hearsay. We need some kind of lead here, and I'm saying that Milkcrate and Patriot are two people we should check into — for their safety, if not some connection to the murders."

"Why? As I says, they prob'ly done a runner."

"Even so."

"So, are we's on the prowl fer superheroes or demented-lookin' children like these in the pictures?"

"Laugh it up, big boy."

Straight after, Pretty Amazonia frowned and, by turns, grimaced, looked horrified, and finally pushed angry.

"What is it, dollface?" the Brick asked, alarmed.

"Listen — they're playing Olivia Newton-John. Hear that? 'Xanadu'. Dear God, no. Turn it off!" she shouted at the waitress.

Repressing a grin, Jack looked again, long and hard, at the smiling façade of Bullet Gal in the Crime Crusaders pic.

"Why'd she do that?" he finally asked.

Surprisingly, PA intuited his meaning.

"You're asking why Bullet Gal changed name and costume?"

"Yeah, I guess."

"Nipper has a point. No one ever told me — what's the hearsay on that?"

The woman fidgeted on her seat. "I haven't the time for this."

"What's your hurry?" Jack asked.

"She's late fer her meeting with the Women's Canasta an' Mah Jong Society," laughed the Brick.

With no further word the woman vanished, leaving the two others to foot the bill.

"Guess she don't like our ol' Olivia," the Brick decided while he and Jack divvied up their cash. "PA was right — there are still things 'bout her I dunno."

Andrez Bergen

#131

That evening Jack found Pretty Amazonia ensconced in the lofty hangar above Equalizers HQ.

Lying on her front on the concrete, flicking through a big book of manga and listening to Giacomo Puccini's *Madama Butterfly*, she twirled a metre-long coil of lavender hair round her forefinger.

Once Jack made some shoe-scuffing noises to announce his presence near the ladder, her eyes ventured up and over.

"Well, well," the woman mused. "Look what the cat dragged in. What brings you here?"

"Me? On the prowl for a decent cheddar — I thought *you* were running late for your thingamajig with the Women's Canasta and Mah Jong Society."

"Ahh, the Brick and his zany sense of humour." She smiled, closing her book. "I gather I owe you some money."

"Forget it. Our shout."

"That's kind of you, hon, but are you sure Mister B agrees? He can be a miser and you might have to prepare yourself for another kind of shouting."

"No worries."

"Your funeral. I'll pay next time, then."

"Sure. PA, can I ask you a personal question?"

"Depends."

"Yes or no?"

"What, am I supposed to take pot-luck and pray it's a question I'm inclined toward?"

"You could always refuse to answer."

"Ahh. An escape clause. I like that. All right."

"I was curious. What happened between you and the Aerialist?"

PA frowned, although perhaps she was merely focusing on Maria Calas's version of 'Un bel dì, vedremo' that played, sight-unseen, around the large space. "Am I that easy to read?"

"The comic there's probably easier."

177

"I doubt it." She flipped through the pages. "This is written in the original Japanese."

"Ah. Magical superhero girls' stuff."

"No, no — desperate love. *Candy Candy*, by Kyoko Mizuki and Yumiko Igarashi. Famous in Japan and Europe in the 1970s. Didn't really hit it off in the U.S. or Australia."

The woman reclosed the manga and sighed.

"The Japanese call these slice-of-life stories. Unrequited affection, lost first love, heart-rending triangles, and tragic sacrifices aplenty."

PA rubbed her eyes. She looked abruptly a decade older.

"Unrequited affection," she repeated, to no one in particular. Jack suspected she'd forgotten all about him. "That's pretty much what I felt for the Aerialist."

What was it Gypsie-Ann had said about women as well as men falling head over heels for the Cape? "You were in love with her."

"Mmm." She shrugged. "Kind of. Silly, I know. I could kick myself for being so stupid. She was never going to be interested in me. But you never met her, SC. The Aerialist was warm, funny, vibrant. Beautiful, too, a redhead with a fiery temper and a passion for life and living that knocked you out. This place has been a vacuum ever since she — well. You know."

"Since she died."

"Yeah. Brutal, but that. She could hold a pencil, too."

"Huh?"

"The kid could draw — whipped up this one of me in about two minutes."

PA went to the back of her book and extracted a piece of pad paper, which she then lobbed. It spiralled across the smooth surface of the floor to Jack's feet.

"Nice shot," he said as he picked it up and studied the lead-work. Torn out of some ring-pad, the page had creases and a coffee-cup stain. "I see she liked to exaggerate."

"I think she preferred to capture the spirit," PA mused. "Definitely, that's how I see myself."

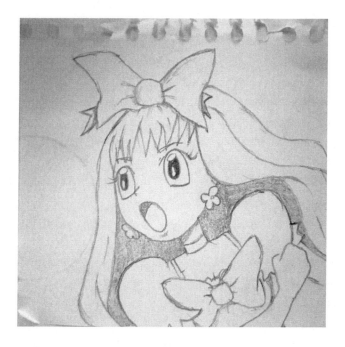

"What, twelve years old and anatomically over-the-top?"

"The kid nailed the shōjo manga influence."

"I guess."

Jack wandered around beside the walls of the hangar, taking in the contours of the GWH's white dirigible, the OS-2 *Magnetic Rose*, that was parked there. He wondered if the *Rose* would be flown again — it'd ended up an unspoken shrine to a man none of the Equalizers actually liked.

"You mentioned unrequited affection," he mused.

"Mm-hmm. I believe we also mentioned cheese."

"You said something else a few days ago, just after we met, about the Aerialist having had a fling with Sir Omphalos."

PA slowly sat up, wrapping herself in her arms.

"I was angry. The rumour was common knowledge among us Capes, and I began to wonder if this might've had some truth. They were...close. She never told me what their relationship entailed, and I guess she had no reason to — it wasn't my business. But everyone in the Equalizers talked about it."

"Any proof?"

"No, nothing to frame up and stick on the wall. Why all this interest?"

"I'm curious. How did you feel about the possibility they were together?" Jack stopped walking and looked directly at her. "About the Big O and the Aerialist having it off, I mean."

"I told you before — it made me angry."

"I didn't believe you."

"What makes you so intuitive?"

"Am I wrong?"

"No." The woman paid a surprising amount of attention to straighten the bows on her short skirt. "You're right. Honestly? It made me sad."

"Jealous too?"

"Maybe." PA now chewed the corner of her mouth and stared back his way. "Are you implying something?"

"Well, it's a good reason to have bumped off the happy couple."

"Don't kid around — I thought we suspected Gypsie-Ann Stellar or Milkcrate Man."

"*You* suspected them."

"So, what, you're now a budding detective in your free time?"

"Hardly. I want to be able to trust you."

"You don't?"

"Help me do so."

"How? Trust isn't a magic trick I can conjure out of thin air." PA swept up her manga and slid out of the tome another sheet of paper, this one far better quality stuff, an ink drawing on Magnani stock. "This is her when she was Bullet Gal," she said, handing it over.

"You mean the Aerialist."

"Yes."

"Shouldn't it be framed up and hanging in the Rogue's Gallery?"

Something resembling a sheepish look passed across the woman's face. "Strictly speaking, Bullet Gal was never a member of the

Equalizers — she'd changed character to the Aerialist by that point."

"So you souvenired this picture."

"Was it wrong of me?"

"Well, it doesn't help with our trust issues." Jack studied the

Cape in this portrait. The subject looked laid-back, with a sardonic smile and a swagger she somehow exuded while sitting down. And — yes — the Cape was beautiful. "Lady liked her guns, huh?"

"I heard she was pretty good with them, too."

"With a name like that, I guess she had to be." Having passed the picture back, Jack sighed. "Now, about trust."

As she carefully replaced her prize inside the book, PA nodded, eyes glittering. "All right. Cards on the table. I've kept your secret."

Crap, Jack thought. Another one who knew his real age — maybe the Rat had blabbed? He seemed like that kind of unreliable git.

PA was looking straight at him, now exuding an expression difficult to decipher.

"How long do you intend on seeing her?"

Jack lost his train of thought and stared back at the woman. "What?"

"You heard me, my sweet."

"See who?"

"That pretty blonde thing you've been shagging — the Blando."

"What?" Jack repeated, stunned.

"Don't project dumb. I know."

"The hell you do. You've been spying on me?"

"No spying — not *per se*. More keeping an eye out from a distance, just in case."

"Same thing. Jesus." Jack stared at the high ceiling, his heart pounding. "Are you now going to blackmail me?"

"No! What kind of opinion do you have of me? Babe, we're on the same team."

"Are we? Where's the trust?"

"Getting back to my point..."

Pretty Amazonia silently slid to her feet and walked the short distance to her teammate. The front of her costume was dusty from the cement, and she placed arms around him to hug, sharing the dust.

Not only that, but Jack felt like a child being crushed by an overzealous aunt who'd previously feigned indifference.

"We need to be able to believe in one another," the woman said. "At least that much."

"It'd help if we were a compatible height."

"You ought to invest in a pair of Liftee Height Increase Pads — they'd give you an extra couple of inches for under two bucks, plus postage."

"Yeah, right."

PA relinquished her grip, but looked down at him with a worried expression.

"Sleeping with a Blando is against the rules. They'll cart you straight out of here, if they find out — throw you back to the wolves in Melbourne."

"I'm not sleeping with her," he mumbled while brushing himself down.

"Call it what you like. Honestly? — I don't care. As much as I bag out Blandos, I really don't give a shit. I won't tell anyone. But you need to trust me in return. Listen to me."

PA placed her hands on his shoulders, pinning him to the spot.

"She's not real. You do remember that?"

"She's more real to me than anybody I ever met."

"It has no future."

"Doesn't matter."

The woman sighed. "What are you going to do? Tell her you're an interloper from another world — a real one — and that this world is a fraud? Make her understand everything she's ever believed in is rubbish? Or are you going to string her along and lie to her, the basis for any good relationship?"

"I'm not lying to her."

"Does she know the truth?"

Jack remained tight-lipped and silent.

"Then you're lying to her. If you really love the thing — really — she deserves better. You would've got away with this back when the Reset was working. I know too many unscrupulous Capes that did.

Had a one night stand, disappeared in the wee hours, and the Blando never remembered a thing."

"This isn't a one night stand."

"Of course it isn't — with the Reset on the blink, you need to deal with consequences."

"I'm not afraid."

"God, I am." PA shook her head. "All right. Just don't get in too far over your head. Once one is here — in Heropa — for a while, it's impossible to go back. To Melbourne, I mean. Things get messed up. Not because you're a humdrum John or Jane Smith there, with next to no rights and zero powers. The fact is the real world is a horrible place that keeps getting worse."

"I seem to remember."

"Sure. We all do. It's been in a downward spiral ever since the Catastrophe. I get so utterly depressed whenever I go back, half my mind there, half in Heropa. If I felt out-of-sync before, these days I feel like a total outsider. Once you've seen and clutched at the stars, it's not easy to return to oblivion. There's nothing for me in Melbourne, and I would not risk my place here for anything. Anything."

"Thought you said this world isn't real."

"It isn't. But Heropa is an escape hatch. So I'm not going to kill anyone, or compromise my standing. I need you to trust me on that alone."

Jack looked at her hard. "You don't make it easy."

"I know I have an attitude from hell."

"Attitude sounds perky. I'm seeing more a chip on the shoulder. Speaking of which, can I have my arms back?"

The woman lifted her hands in over-theatrical fashion. "Voilà. So now the question is — could you try to trust me?"

"Try? That's all you're asking?"

"It's a start."

"No catches?"

"None I can think up on the spot."

"All right. I will. Try." Surprising himself, Jack meant what he said.

"There's a boy. You're a good man, hon, better than I expected. And, if this works out, I'll owe you one."

"Just promise to say nothing more about Louise. I don't need you lecturing me."

"That's her name?"

Silence.

"My lips are sealed, sewn, glued — you name it."

PRANCE, PRANCE, PRANCE

#132

When the Brick exited the building not long later, Jack couldn't decide why, exactly, he followed.

There were too many mysteries circulating, no clear-cut answers.

Thirty seconds between them, each man passed a sleeping guard in the dark foyer, the muted portable TV creating dancing monochrome shadows in one corner.

The Brick carried an umbrella and declined to take his car — perhaps he felt it was the perfect evening to promenade the city, wrapped in an overlarge trench coat with a straw hat and a pair of sunglasses his only disguise. Oddly, the ruse seemed to work. No one on the streets noticed this hulking behemoth passing them by.

For a while, the Equalizer walked beneath a wooden trellis overpass that shook and groaned whenever one of the peak-hour trains scuttled along. Jack hung back several metres, far enough to remain anonymous (he was wearing a suit and hat), unless the Brick actually looked his way. The man didn't. He focused ahead and occasionally up at the brilliantly lit city skyline. There was a zeppelin, hundreds of feet in length, sliding through a network of spotlights and heavy cloud-cover.

They passed a boarded-up haberdashery. Most of the other shops, although still in business, had closed by this hour and some had their metal shutters down, others lights on in their window displays. It started to rain.

Slowing down as he passed a row of lit-up store windows, the Brick inspected a Smoke Mahout window display in a pharmacy, hats on show in the LaValle Millinery Shop, a bookstore called First Editions, and finally Mount Hollywood Art School.

The rain was getting heavier and Jack had already raised his umbrella, but the Brick took longer to open his. After a few short seconds sheltering beneath it, he shrugged, closed it again and laid it on his shoulder — even went so far as to skip the next few steps along the pavement. The lamppost was probably lucky that the

Equalizer didn't try swinging around it.

The Brick reopened his umbrella, grinned boldly to no one, and stomped off.

From the darkened doorway of the pharmacy close by his left, Jack heard a voice, all quiet-like. "Hey, mister."

Since the rain had eased off, the Equalizer dropped his brolly and examined the shadows. The first thing he noticed was a glowing cherry, and then an individual stepped out into the yellowish luminescence, cigarette dangling from his lips.

"There's only two things in this world that a 'real man' needs: a cup of coffee and a good smoke. Got the ciggie, but not the Joe. Can you lend me a dime?"

Jack noted that the fancy coat the newcomer wore was hardly down-at-the-heel. "You don't look short of a buck."

"Still. Won't tell the big fella you're following him, if you do. C'mon — help a fella out." He lifted an upside-down red hat, as if that was where Jack was supposed to drop his donation.

He had no time for this. He took out his wallet and deposited a dollar bill. "Get yourself a Thermos to go with the coffee."

"Sweet."

When he turned around, Jack realized he'd lost sight of the Brick. The street was dead quiet in both directions.

"Think you'll find the guy went up there."

The charity-case pointed across the road and up to the third floor of a tenement building. It had big windows with blinds drawn, 'SATORI DANCE STUDIO' stencilled in orange letters on the glass.

"You're kidding me."

"Nup. Favour for a favour"

"I didn't get your name, stranger."

"Didn't give it."

The man faded back into the doorway, so Jack took that as his notice to move on. Having checked for non-existent traffic, he crossed the street and found an iron staircase leading off the footpath.

He ascended the steps quietly, three at a time, and finally came to a small, covered balcony with a door that had the number three on it and the name of the studio, along with splashed black paint that formed a rough *kanji* symbol.

Jack could make out music within. Something orchestral — melancholic, yet oddly uplifting, all strings and horns and a softly tinkering harp.

The large window was just to his right, spattered with droplets of water, and he noticed a gap: about an inch, between closed blind and the sill, through which light escaped. Jack leaned over to put an eye to the glass.

There was, indeed, a studio, with a rotating wooden fan up on the ceiling, oak flooring, handrails attached to two of the walls, and a large, simple framed poster bearing two names (Alessandra Ferri and Massimo Murru) beneath the French words *La Chauve-souris*.

Otherwise the place was empty — aside from a duo dancing together across the boards, doing some kind of ballet routine in time to the music.

The man lifted his partner into the air and she affected a handstand, legs scissored; with effortless ease she wound herself around the man's neck and their faces came close, almost a kiss.

Swivelling into her beau's embrace, the woman was then spun several times, and she deliberately fell into his arms. He whisked his partner full somersault, landing her behind on her toes — from there to lean in for a desperate hug. Their faces again touched.

The music reached a crescendo, all clashing timpani and violins, just as the girl, perspiring, and her partner — who couldn't sweat — clung to one another and smiled. Yes, it was moving, mesmerizing, astoundingly beautiful, and other superlatives that should not have been possible.

Jack had to drag himself away from the spectacle. The man was the Brick, and he could dance.

The Brick's agile partner may have worn something different — a white, full-body leotard that hugged every immaculate curve — but Jack recognized the domino mask she was wearing, and her different coloured eyes.

"Snoop."

Jack swung about, spooked, even as he felt an inordinate amount of anger.

"Think I'm bloody justified in saying the same of you."

"Shhh. Fair enough."

"The Brick and Prima Ballerina. How—?"

"Long? About a year."

Pretty Amazonia had precariously perched herself on the wet, flimsy balcony railing, long hair — Tyrian purple in the evening illumination — waving in a soft breeze. She possessed something of a cheerless attitude, and Jack had to resist the impulse to push her over the edge.

"Now you know our Brick's skeleton," she said. "They breed like rabbits. We all have them. Soon enough you'll hear the pitter-patter of little skeletons."

"So I'm learning. Heropa has more secrets than a grave."

"Oh, very pithy, Jack."

"What's your secret?"

"If I told you, it wouldn't be one."

"That's unfair."

"That's life."

"But why does the Brick keep this — this relationship — hush hush?"

"With good reason. Remember when you first arrived, and he told you the rules of Heropa? How he skipped past the third one, pretended he forgot?"

"Vaguely."

"Number three dictates no sexual relations between members of the Equalizers and the Rotters. It's expressly forbidden."

"Why?"

"Don't ask me."

"Who conjured up these dumb rules?"

"A bunch of idiots, I agree, but we have to carouse by them. Anyone finds out, those two," Pretty Amazonia nodded in the direction of the window and the score they could still hear, "will be given the boot from Heropa. The sad part is they believe no one knows."

"Who does? Know, I mean."

"Me. Bulkhead. Now you. So we keep this under the cuff — the three of us. Like our other secrets. Mister B doesn't need to know, agreed?"

Jack could make out the rousing music inside. "Okay."

#133

The next morning might've been mistaken for a showpiece of domestic bliss, since the Brick, Pretty Amazonia and Southern Cross were at a table in the big kitchen, tucking into pancakes.

The moment Jack dribbled maple syrup down his sleeve — he'd been wearing the SC outfit, without its mask, as pyjamas — he remembered to ask a question that'd been bugging him.

"Where do you lot get your costumes cleaned?"

The Brick groaned. "Didn't yer mum ever tell you to wear nothin' special at the brekky table?"

"Not lately."

"Dollface, mebbe we should invest in a bib fer the kid."

"It'd be difficult finding one to co-ordinate with the flag. Personally, I hand-wash my threads," said PA more helpfully.

She delved into a cupboard beneath the sink, and then held aloft a box that had a cartoonish yellow face on it and purple stripes.

"I tend to find that Mr Sparkle brings out the colours. As for our Brick here, well he has a few pairs of undies he tosses into the washing machine, along with everything else. They don't sparkle. We're often picking off the lint for hours on end."

"What's it matter?" the Brick piped up from behind the pages of the *Patriot*, pretending to be otherwise occupied. "None of this is twenty-four-carat anyway. Back in reality you're plugged into an idI machine, prob'ly napping in a pool o' pee since yer ceroscopy bag's broke."

"*Colostomy* bag — and unbelievable. You know that tact is a lost art?"

"Just tellin' it like it is."

"Telling it like a crusty degenerate, you mean."

"Say, lookee here," the Brick ignored her, "there's a special on athletic iron boots, only $6.95 a pair."

Jack wasn't listening to the old married couple.

A big electronic doohickey in the corner — all stainless steel, black plastic knobs and bulb diode lamps — had grabbed his attention. It had the letters 'XZ-12' in bold black on the top.

"So what exactly does this worrisome-looking contraption do?"

"It's our coffee machine."

"Oh, well, that's all right then."

#134

At eleven o'clock, Jack was summoned from his quarters. For the past two hours he'd been fighting a losing battle inside the pages of *The Well of Loneliness*, and gratefully made the descent to the boardroom.

There was a tall stranger next to Pretty Amazonia — not quite her height, but somewhere in the vicinity of six and a half feet. He had a pouter pigeon's swollen chest and wore a costume rather like a nineteenth-century cavalry uniform.

This consisted of a pale blue short jacket with heavy horizontal white braid on the front and braided knots on the sleeves; a matching over-jacket slung on one shoulder, royal-blue-coloured trousers, and black riding boots. He also had a fur busby hat tucked under his arm. Topping all this off? Short, curly black hair, a waxed moustache, and sideburns that complimented a ruggedly handsome face.

"SC, this is Saint Y," Pretty Amazonia said, by way of intro-duction.

If he didn't know better, Jack would say she was smitten — she didn't even offer him a chance to shake the tall man's hand, since she was clutching onto his right elbow, fondling the busby beneath it.

"He's here to do your picture," she added in breathy fashion. "The man is handy with his inks. Do you have time? Say you have time."

While she spoke, the woman's eyes remained on their guest — making Jack wonder which man she was addressing.

"Well, sure," Jack relented, deciding he was the recipient. "Nothing planned today, so no hurry. I'd hate him to whip out a $1.98 draw-any-person-in-one-minute Magic Art Reproducer."

"Mmm," PA agreed, obviously not listening.

"Pleased to make our acquaintance," Saint Y finally drawled in an accent pushing eastern European, possibly Russian.

Jack frowned. "Yeah, ours too."

"You are the dummy?"

"Eh?"

With a fabricated smile on her mush, PA leaned closer. "Mannequin, darling."

"I guess."

Saint Y broke free from his hostess' grip, suddenly conjured up a set of pens from some unseen pocket in his uniform/costume, and then flourished them about like he'd rediscovered his missing sabre.

"Huzzah! Then we are ready to do the art."

"I'll leave you boys to it," PA murmured, having trouble tearing her gaze from the Hussar with the pen set. "Don't forget to come see me before you go, Saint. Upstairs."

"*Uvidimsya*, pretty one." Saint Y delivered up one of the more urbane, possibly most devastating grins Jack had witnessed — and then the man reversed course. "Now, my young friend, to do the art," he commanded, serious. "Mask on, if you please."

The Equalizer was directed by the Hussar to the centre of the room, positioned before a bare wall. Once there, he stood sheepishly, arms dangling by his sides.

"Strike the pose," the Hussar commanded.

"Huh?"

"I am wanting to draw you as a hero, not the wallflower."

Jack thought some, and then mimicked the fighting stance from his favourite comicbook cover — one composed by Jack Kirby for *Captain America* issue 109, fists clenched, bursting through a newspaper and ready for action. He hadn't cottoned on that this would be a difficult one to maintain in repose, since he had to balance on his right foot, thrust forward, while the left, behind him, touched the floor with only the toes.

"Ahh, that is good. Please do not to move."

Sure, the Hussar's English grammar left much to be desired, but at least he spoke the language. If he resorted to his native Russian, Jack would've been stranded without a linguistic paddle.

"You're kidding?" the Equalizer mumbled.

"I am not."

Taking out a sketchbook, again from some place Jack couldn't perceive, Saint Y started drawing in quick fashion.

"Your mind, my young friend — it is elsewhere. On the woman, perhaps?" the artist inquired.

"None of your business."

"Suit myself. Do you mind if we do the listening to the Beatles? I find their harmonies help me to make the art."

"Okay — I guess."

Jack had no idea who he was talking about and, seconds later, realized he wouldn't find out on this occasion.

Having stuck on a pair of earphones, the Hussar's shoulders affected a repetitive spasm in time to music Jack couldn't hear at all. The man even did a spot of out-of-tune harmonizing, singing something about a sky with diamonds in it.

Every time Jack swayed or tottered, the Hussar yelled at him. This one-sided harassment went on for quarter of an hour, then thirty minutes.

An hour later, obviously unable to bide her time waiting in her quarters, Pretty Amazonia wandered back with the big bow on her bosom shoved down, displaying a fair amount of cleavage.

"Well, that's subtle," Jack muttered.

"Please to not move," barked the Hussar, a fraction kinder in front of the lady.

"Sorry."

Working at a frantic pace now, paying absolutely no attention to PA's attempts to distract him, the artist leaned against a wall and stared hard at Jack.

"We need some filler, some — how do you say? Props?"

"Well, there's this." PA tossed a newspaper onto the table. Jack saw it was the one announcing the Big O's death. "Published the same day SC arrived in Heropa, and captures the changing of the guard. Appropriate enough, I'd say."

"Enough," Saint Y agreed, licking his lips as he thought.

Much tearing of the newspaper subsequently took place, along with more frenzied sketching and inking, and then the Hussar ripped off a page and held it up for all to see.

"Is it not magnificent?"

Pretty Amazonia beamed. "You can do anything with words and pictures," she gushed, while Jack more simply stared at the finished depiction.

"Do I really come across that menacing?"

"I took the liberty to adding fire in your eyes," the artist said, "otherwise you would be looking like the little boy lost."

#135

In the early afternoon, after Saint Y left and Pretty Amazonia hung the picture, the Brick whisked Jack away on his Coca-Cola bottle motorbike. They wound up at a grandiose park that covered two city blocks and was forested with oak trees, wattles, maples and gums.

There was a pond, dead centre, where children played with toy boats, and ducks canoodled. The temperature would've been around twenty-three, the sky blue, sun perfect. The two men sat together on a wooden bench, partaking of hotdogs in their civvies.

"Christ, I never thought the simple act of sitting down would constitute bliss," Jack sighed.

"That's why you get yer picture done relaxin' in a settee — like I did."

"I think the Hussar would've blown a fuse if I tried."

It still surprised Jack that people didn't spot the Brick when he played incognito in his trench coat and hat. Nothing could hope to disguise a round, paved patio that constituted his face — the sunglasses sat there like outdoor furniture.

"I love the food here," the Brick announced as he scoffed down the first of his three dogs. "Never ate so well back in Melbs. Most of this stuff is impossible to find these days."

"Even if it's not real?"

"Tastes real 'nuff." Number two disappeared.

"There is that," Jack agreed, focusing on his single hotdog. The mustard created a minor nose-rush and the bread seemed stale. His teammate was right. This was eating like a goddamned king.

The Brick had already finished his third round and sat back to observe the kids over by the water.

"Y'know, we have this game I like t'play when I'm bored — which can be too bloody often in this stuffy glen."

"Go on."

Jack ring-pulled a can of Tarax Dixi-Cola while the Brick tore open a pack of something named Cracker Jack.

"It's *Whaddaya Reckon This Person is Really Like Out There?* — a mouthful, I know, but by that I mean the authentic, real-deal us."

"Back in Melbourne?"

"Yep, merrily kippin' while connected up into them idI machines."

"In a pool of pee."

"Got it."

Jack followed a radio-controlled yacht tacking across the glassy pond, which narrowly avoided a water lily. "How does this game go?"

"All about hypothesizin', really. Fer starters there's our Pretty Amazonia. Towerin', voluptuous, gift-wrapped, tresses down to her toes. In actual fact, prob'ly a mousey, frail little librarian lezzo, with short hair, glasses, an' tiny tits — sportin' a name like Lula Mae Barnes."

"Man. You are a terror."

"Did I ever tout otherwise?"

"Not really, except for when you bat your baby blues."

The Brick leaned back, a triumphant look on his face. "Part o' me effervescent charm."

"Part of something, that's for sure." Jack glanced at his partner. "Anyway, speaking of PA, you know she was all eyes on Saint Y? A man. There goes your theory."

"Really now? Good t'see the dear move on."

The lapidarian Equalizer stuck into his gob a great handful of molasses-flavoured, candy-coated popcorn and peanuts. Jack had to look away from the bedlam.

"Back to this guessing game. What about the Great White Hope?"

"Weak-sister nobody, cruddy dress-sense — oh, wait, that described 'im perfectly well here in Heropa, rest his blamed soul. Well. Whaddaya know?"

The Brick held aloft a plastic ring he'd apparently found in the box of snacks.

"The prize in the Cracker Jack. Want it?"

"Uh-uh — you're more likely to need a ring than me."

The Brick's blue eyes flicked over. "That so?"

"I'm poking fun," Jack said, perhaps too quickly.

"Go lightly, kid. Not sure either comment soothes me soul."

"Brick, what do you think about love?"

The Equalizer didn't blink as he gazed at his partner. "There's somethin' socked outta leftfield. This some kind'a Bizarro World test?"

"No. Just curious."

"So it's legit? Nuts — I reckon the thing's overrated."

"You don't believe in love?"

"Hard to. Makes me feel ill, thinkin' 'bout the implications, let alone saying the word out loud."

"Well, yeah, yeah, I know it can come across pathetic. But seriously, if we look at the general concept, do you think it can overcome — well, barriers?"

The Brick narrowed his eyes. "What kind o' barriers?"

"In general, like I said."

"Then lemme give you a general response: hippy shit. And yer defo askin' the wrong slab o' cement."

The man shoved the ring into his overgrown coat pocket.

"Gettin' back to the game, which is far more fun, there was this Rotter before yer time, name o' El Stencho. Pretty crass. As his name implies, he used obscene odours to win friends an' influence people, got round in a stinky sombrero. Had very li'l in the way o' teeth. Prob'ly he's a dentist in Melbourne. Dunno what happened to him — haven't seen 'im in a while. I'm wonderin' if dentistry got more attractive than Heropa."

"How about you in the real world?"

"Hmm. Lemme get back t'you."

"That's cheating."

"Not really — the game's all 'bout guessing. I know who I am. You give it a shot."

"I wouldn't know where to begin, unless the main idea is to be insulting."

"Ahh. Quick learner."

Jack remembered the drinks his partner had put together the other day, the cocktail recipes he'd flouted. "Bartender?"

"Brother is. Go on."

"Okay. Weedy and couldn't fight your way out of a wet paper-bag. Desperately craving a cool car, but the only wheels you have are a hand-me-down bicycle from that brother."

"Interestin' deductin'," said the Brick in noncommittal fashion.

"Thanks."

"Nothin' else?"

"Nah. Still working on it. And me?"

"You? Easy. Young — yep, I already had insider tradin' on that particular nugget — but yer obviously a babe in arms lookin' for somethin' you'll prob'ly never find. You seen a lot, but who hasn't in this day and age? Still have hope round your neck, chokin' like a garrotte."

"Gee. Ta."

"Hey, I am the Brick. Got a reputation t'uphold — terror, an' all."

"So, why're you telling me this? Is there a point, or do you get kicks out of offending your teammates?"

"Bit'a both?"

"That's sad."

"Well, now." The Brick rubbed his blocky chin. "There is another element — the game's taken on a brand-spankin'-new dimension. What d'we really know about any o' these people?"

"Who?"

"The Capes, kid."

"Got'cha."

"An' the answer? Nothin'. Sweet FA. They're just sham window dressin', avatars. Question now being — who, among all of 'em, is killin' the great Capes of Heropa?"

"What's to say it's a Cape doing these executions?"

"Well, fer starters — there's no one else here. Boom-boom."

"You sure about that?"

The Brick looked at Jack. "Why? You got other ideas?"

"Disgruntled civilian."

"A Blando?"

"Yeah."

The Equalizer chuckled. "Oh my, and one flauntin' an axe t'grind!"

"Seriously. You and the other Capes insist that the regular people here — the Blandos — are part of the woodwork, that they don't think for themselves, but how do you account for someone like Stan, downstairs at Equalizers HQ?"

"The Doormat? He's off-colour. Diff'rent."

"More like us."

"No way."

"But you're saying there are degrees of Blandoism — some being more fluff than others."

"Ain't gave it much thought. Is Blandoism even a word?"

"Is now."

"Point."

"Brick, how many of these people have died in battles between the Capes?"

"Again, dunno."

"You given some thought to the notion that our killer might be one of them, exacting comeuppance for years of indiscriminate killing?"

The Brick squeezed out a contralto chuckle. "Yeah, right."

"Haven't you noticed anything? What was used to kill the Big O? A gun. Somebody sabotaged the Aerialist's jetpack and Double-R was electrocuted — after having his throat cut. The GWH was crucified. The weapons of choice for Sinistro and Iffy Bizness? Explosives. No special powers necessary. No costumes."

"But this's nit-witted, you talkin' up some kind'a Blando conspiracy theory. What, you sayin' there's some kind'a vendetta goin' on here, *Dirty Harry* style? — A Blando fifth column?"

"I'm not making any assumptions. Just throwing round alternatives."

"Careful — you might poke out an eye. Geddit through yer head, junior — these are not real people. They're inconsequential electronic blips in a computer."

"What if one of those inconsequential blips just got angry?"

"Nah, impossible. Blandos have no will o' their own, no identity, no surprises. We'd be wastin' our precious time lookin' for spooks in this lot."

"You know what they call us? Bops. That's not a term of endearment. It's a slap."

"Yeah, but words is words. Actions're...diff'rent."

Right then, Jack and the Brick noticed a small pair of shoes before them.

Their combined scrutiny followed up two skinny legs, past a pair of shorts and a half tucked-in shirt, to a redheaded boy's face, maybe ten, with a dirt-smudge on one cheek and a yacht tucked under his arm.

"Beat it, kid. Yer blockin' my view."

"Excuse me, but you're Mister Brick, right?"

The Equalizer's response sounded uncharacteristically anaemic. "Er... No."

The kid thrust out the boat and a marker.

"Don't care what anyone says — you're all right. Can I have your autograph, right here on the bow?"

#136

Jack went directly from the park to Louise's apartment block.

He realized it was too early in the day for the girl to be home, but reasoned that the antique shop downstairs might be open, enabling a chat with her father-in-law.

When he pushed open the door and a bell attached above announced the arrival of a customer, Jack back-patted himself for a guess proven correct.

The store was rammed full of old furniture — secretaires, shelves, clocks and paintings — along with piles of books and magazines, and chaotically organized bric-à-brac that included a moose's head next to a hanging kimono, boxes of 78-rpm records, a suit of tarnished armour that had a woodcutter's axe leaned up against the right leg, several ancient willow cricket bats, and a statuette of a black bird of prey.

He browsed the bigger hardback and paperback tomes, along with the vintage magazines, always curious.

There was a worrisome mathematics book titled *A Treatise on the Binomial Theorem*, along with the November 1887 issue of *Beeton's Christmas Annual*, containing a novel by Arthur Conan Doyle (*A Study in Scarlet*). One copy of *Life Magazine*, dated July 12th, 1963, had actor Steve McQueen and his wife Neile on a motorbike together on the front cover.

Sadly, there were no American comicbooks, only British ones from the 1930s — *Tiny Tots* and *The Beano* — along with three from the early '70s (*Cor!!*) and a single copy of an Australian-published version of *The Phantom*, dated 1948, with a flimsy, matt-paper cover.

"Jack!" The Professor, emerging from a backroom, came over and shook the Equalizer's hand with a lot more energy that he expected. "My apologies for the mess."

"No need. This is a pretty nifty shop."

"A pigsty, that's what it is — but the customers like that. Plus I'm too busy to pay attention to the cleaning. Come into the office. Far more spacious there."

Jack followed the Professor to a backroom in which Vera Lynn crooned 'We'll Meet Again' from a teak wooden radio. He shifted some cartons and gestured for his visitor to take a seat on a divan.

The Professor sat down across from him. The man was so small he looked like a diabolically aged child.

"I'm so happy you came to visit. I have a question for you."

"Go on," Jack said, waving aside some of the dust in the air.

"You may find it foolish."

"I doubt that."

"You're a good man."

"Not really. Anyway, what was the question?"

"Oh, a silly one, I assure you: Who is your preferred superhero?"

Jack shot a look at the older man. "What, here?"

"No, no, of course not. In comics, my boy. I'm a *Phantom* aficionado myself — the hereditary crime fighter from deepest, darkest Africa. 'Ghost Who Walks, Man Who Cannot Die', and all that wonderful brouhaha."

"I noticed you had a copy in the shop."

"That issue out there is a double. I have another copy, in better nick, beneath my bed. You should see how many I store there! Alas, Louise does not approve."

"Because of what happened to her husband? — Your son."

"Ahh, she told you." The Professor shook his head. "No, more because she sees it as both a childish pursuit and a fire-trap. All that paper." The man laughed. "Anyway, I do believe it's your turn to speak."

"About what? Are we still discussing favourite superheroes?"

"Yes, please. May I hazard a guess?"

"Go ahead," Jack laughed.

"I would wager you prefer your Spider-Man or Batman."

"Nice try — both of them have their moments, but I'd go with Captain America."

"You like the pretty stars and stripes?"

Still laughing, Jack shrugged. "Well, yeah, I do dig the costume."

"Oh, come now, you strike me as a gentleman with better taste. Those showy red boots and gauntlets? The little wings on the head? The chainmail? Really."

The Professor reached over and manhandled Jack's suit jacket.

"This is far nicer. What is it — Frederick Scholte?"

"Phineas Horton. He's our local tailor, whiz with a needle."

"Wool-blend?"

"Mm-hmm. With cashmere."

"I must meet this Mister Horton. I am in dire need of a new wardrobe. Anyhow, I detract. You were talking about the good Captain."

"And his kitsch costume."

"I recall something along those lines."

"Well, honestly? I think the costume is beside the point."

"Go on."

"The Captain America they reinvented in the 1960s swayed me with his personality, not his wardrobe. A man out of place, out of his time, looking to fit in — a humble guy, once weak but now blessed with great strength, who wants to do the right thing but is coming to grips with guilt related to the death of his partner. The world has changed and he doesn't understand it — reflecting the crisis of confidence in the U.S. at the time. Even though Cap may be old-fashioned, he's a symbol of hope — for everybody — and maintains that despite all the evil tossed his way."

"Defending the little man. A simple but worthy pursuit. Never once led astray?"

"How do you mean?"

"By the prejudices of the era, or the people publishing the comic?"

"Sure. You've got to sift through this stuff and place it in context. The Soviets and geriatric Nazis get a bad rap, but overall Cap was a decent human being, and Jack Kirby drew him so damned well — even if the character, along with the suit, was too patriotically

American."

"Hence the name. Interesting."

The Professor commenced filling a corncob pipe from a tin marked Capstan Navy Cut. It sat precariously on his lap.

"Now that we have superheroes out of the way — what is it to be human, Jack?"

Well, this was an offbeat tangent. Why not?

"The way I understand it, Homo sapiens developed in Africa, broke away from there to take over the world, dominated every-thing — then, finally, depopulated most of the place."

"The sad Homo sapien genome story in a prize nutshell, to be sure, and let me add we still share ninety-nine percent of our DNA with chimpanzees." The man poked about his pipe with a match-stick — tamping, Jack guessed. "No, I'm thinking on a more philo-sophical level — what is it, exactly, that defines us as human?"

"Haven't thought much about that before now."

"Go on, then."

"I don't know. Breathing?"

"All animals breathe."

"Good dress-sense."

"Debatable."

"Thinking, then."

"What's to say some of our animal friends don't have the capacity for cognition?" The Professor dropped his match on the table, fished out a pigskin-and-nickel lighter, and lit up. He burned his hand in the process and stuck a finger in his mouth. "Ouch."

"All right." Jack raised an eyebrow. "The ability to learn from something and avoid doing it again."

"Well said. I liked the droll flourish. One lesson that always escapes me." The Professor held up his pipe in mock salute. "A condition reflex. Something animals are also capable of — remember Ivan Pavlov's dogs."

"Whose dogs?"

"Oh, it matters not — I prevaricate."

"I think you also expect better responses."

"Or barks? No, no. Let's continue, shall we?"

Do we have to? Jack thought.

"Shall I steer us via the psychological characteristics that all people are supposed to have in common? The 'human condition' that tells one the sum total of experience existing as a human being? Do we look at the nature of humanity, which is the act of tending for kin and befriending others? Self-awareness as the litmus test of humanity? Indeed. The qualities of introspection and the ability to reconcile oneself from the whole — in terms of knowledge, attitude, good and bad taste. 'I think, therefore I exist', and all those other throwaway philosophical nuggets?"

The man puffed at his pipe and exhaled towards the ceiling, waiting.

"I have no idea," Jack finally admitted.

"Well, think about it. Humans search for purpose and thrive on new stimuli, correct?"

"I guess."

The old man's eyes twinkled. "You'll have to do better than that, Jack."

"Okay — yeah, they do."

"Then humanity is all about a sense of curiosity, sapience, an ongoing search for the meaning of life, and obviously an anxiety about death. Living life demonstrates to us what it's like to live, and thereby shows clearly the nature of being human."

The Equalizer stared at the Professor for a while, soaking up the commentary, feeling bamboozled — thank Christ, Louise stepped in and broke the highbrowed moment.

"Hello, you two. Who's up for coffee?"

Jack jumped to his feet. "Actually, I was hoping you might be up for dinner."

"That'd be lovely. What about you, Prof?"

"By all means, children. The night is young — for the young. I need to close up shop, and then joyfully potter through mundane accounting. Go and have fun."

Taking Louise by the arm, fetching his hat, and walking her out of the store, Jack finally relaxed.

"Know any decent places round here? I'm lost."

"Sure. There's always Jim Hammond's over there." Louise pointed across the road at a place painted on the outside various shades of red and orange, mimicking fire. "Cheap, really sweet people, and they do a great barbecue."

"Do we need to B.Y.O. fire-extinguisher?"

Louise nudged him. "Oh, you!"

"Okay. Yum. I'm up for that."

"C'mon, then."

They entered a small restaurant with darker, smoke-grey walls covered in charcoal sketches of propeller planes and sailing ships.

"Miss Louise," said a handsome older man with curly hair who looked vaguely Italian. He was wearing a white t-shirt with black pants and wore an orange Atlas apron over the top. "Always a pleasure to have you." The man smiled broadly.

"Sorry we haven't been in for a while — you know how life goes," Louise answered in pleasant if breezy fashion. "Jack, this is Mister Burgos, the owner of the restaurant."

"Karl," Burgos said, while he proceeded to crush Jack's fingers with a grip of steel.

The rest of the staff also knew Louise, and a waitress showed them to a scenic table over by the front window.

"Thanks, Tara. Could I trouble you for an ashtray?"

"No worries, Louise."

"A glass of Bollinger too. Jack?"

"Coffee would be great."

The waitress nodded. "Today's special is the barbecued lamb — it's a real humdinger. I'll scoot back with the drinks."

Louise took out her packet of cigarettes and lit up while Jack examined the menu.

"It was such a surprise to see you when I got home. In a good way."

Louise had a smile that took up most of her face. Jack'd never seen an expression so infectiously uplifting — except, perhaps, the last time they'd met.

"Likewise," he said simply.

"So. Here we are. Tonight, can we do something different?

"Sure."

"Tell me about yourself."

After a few seconds' hesitation — during which time he realized he couldn't wrangle out of this one — Jack almost mentioned his adoration for comicbooks, but then remembered the Professor's warning.

"Not much to say, really."

The girl sat back and exhaled a puff of smoke. Her smile was dead in the water. "Oh, I don't believe it."

"I love books."

"Yes, we *have* established that."

Jack looked away. He didn't know what to reveal — and then something came to him. "Okay. My parents died when I was young."

Louise instantly leaned forward to place a hand over his fingers. "Really? Oh, no. I'm so sorry. God. Mine too."

"It's okay."

They ordered a dinner of barbecued lamb and actually said little more of note. Occasionally, Jack felt Louise's emerald eyes on him, but he focused on the meal gracing the table.

His partner ordered two more glasses of champagne and talked for a while with Karl, the owner, who leaned in too close — and had Jack fidgeting uncomfortably.

Other than that, he kept thinking about his mother and father, about how quick he'd been to say they were dead. Maybe it was true. Probably they were — and yet he had no idea. He felt like he'd betrayed them.

After dinner, Jack played it honourable. He deposited the girl on her doorstep, pecked a cheek, told her what a swell evening he'd had.

Then he virtually ran away.

#137

Next day, Jack got Gypsie-Ann on the line at the *Patriot*.

"Any news on the Blando lead?" he asked, following thankfully abridged unnecessary pleasantries.

"I thought you volunteered for the leg-work?"

"Got a few other angles I have to pursue."

"Fat lot of good that does me."

Jack adjusted the receiver in the crook of his neck. "Look, maybe we should drop it."

"You really know how to grab my interest, Jack. Why drop it now?"

"No reason."

"This Sekrine character is no longer important?"

"I don't know."

He hung up and stared at the wall. Was he doing the wrong thing? The Professor seemed to know so much. Why couldn't he ask the old man directly?

More than that, Jack felt he already owed Louise twice an apology and was intruding in a domain none of his business.

#138

An interminable ringing woke him, its source the ancient black Western Electric Model 202 telephone on his bedside table. Jack'd never heard a peep from the bugger, but apparently an almighty clanging at five minutes past two in the morning was its specialized party trick. He juggled with the overlarge handset, as he rose to a halfway decent upright position in the dark.

"Hello?"

There was sobbing on the other end — a girl? — and then he heard a soft voice pleading to somebody, a scream, and two shouted words: "No! No!"

"Louise...?" He couldn't tell. Neither tone nor line was clear.

"Monarch Theatre — Pearl Street — oh, God, please hurry!"

After that the connection went dead. Jack sat on the edge of the bed, wearing green-and-white checked pyjamas, mulling over what he'd awoken to while he quickly rubbed sleep from his eyes.

He didn't go collect the others. The Equalizer flew solo, taking a lonesome yellow cab downtown, paying, and climbing out of his suit in a back alley. Didn't want to get the thing dirty, so he wrapped it in two vinyl bags and tucked the package carefully under a gap in the fence.

Mask on, Jack guessed he was ready. Going it alone sounded stupid, but if Louise were involved he had no choice — something to do with the reckless things one gets up to in the name of love or infatuation or whatever it was they had between them.

Next door to the Hotel Excelsior, the Monarch Theatre was a huge, glitzy hall that'd seen better days, but still looked a million bucks. There were art-deco details highlighted in silver against black tiles and a lighted diamond sitting atop a single tower.

On the marquee out the front was a poster of a vampish girl in fishnets promoting some musical called *Footlight Frenzy*, but at three a.m. the place was closed to business.

Down a narrow side street that ran alongside the theatre was parked a fancy silver, hard-top 1937 Saoutchik Hispano-Suiza H6C 'Xenia' Streamliner, looking more like an airplane than a car since it was commissioned by André Dubonnet — a World War I fighter pilot and heir to the Dubonnet aperitif and cognac business — with styling done by aerodynamics expert Jean Andreau.

Near that, some fool had kindly left a side door unlocked.

It was dark inside, but minor illumination here and there allowed Jack to see. He wandered into the central aisle of an auditorium likely to seat a thousand. After scanning the shadows, he then strolled slowly toward the stage. Like the phone call, none of this rang right at all. He'd just reached the orchestra pit when there was a loud clapping sound and two spotlights switched on somewhere far above — one highlighting him, the other the stage.

There were three people on a podium, soaking up the illumination. One of them he recognized — Prima Ballerina.

Beside her was a tall, Teutonic-looking male bodybuilder in a tight jumpsuit, with flaxen curls shaped in a Prince Valiant cut, a coiled whip at the right hip, and a large Nazi swastika on his chest.

Rounding out this posse was a wiry guy wearing an olive-green, mid-twentieth-century communist army uniform, drab as dust. He had his cap down over his eyes and a tight brown belt around the waist — could've been Cuban or North Korean, for all Jack was able to tell.

Behind them were a painted set and a few props that looked like they described a rural medieval hamlet in Bavaria.

The Nazi clearly aspired to be ringleader. He stepped forward with a self-satisfied mien and poked a big handgun, something like a German Mauser, in Jack's direction — using the flag on his costume as a bull's-eye.

"Make no sudden move. Stand as still as the wind."

The man said this with a cartoon-cut-out inflection that predictably made his Vs sound like Ws and Fs — 'move' became 'moof' and 'wind' segued into 'vind'. It was also inconsistent, like he forgot to persist with the charade.

"The wind is still?" asked the Communist, with far better pronunciation, over the shoulder of his Kraut accomplice.

The Mauser dipped a few inches. "Hush, General Ching." Then the pistol bounced back up. "I am Baron von Gatz. No doubt you have heard tell of me. The estimable Southern Cross, I presume?"

"Bingo. You'll get extra gold stars from teacher for that quip."

"Another smartarse," sighed von Gatz's henchman.

Jack noticed the Communist was hefting an assault rifle he'd never before had the pleasure of meeting. While taking a leaf out of the AK-47 design manual — there was a long, curving magazine beneath — this particular hardware was far from pretty.

"A simple bullet in the head will end the shenanigans," added the man toting the eyesore.

"*Donnerwetter!* I said be quiet!" hissed von Gatz in a voice anyone could hear a mile off. His jaw muscles momentarily bulged, and then the Nazi took up a confident pose and even louder bluster. "*Nein*, General Ching. My way is far more complicated, time-consuming, und thereby...rewarding."

"For whom?"

"For myself, of course."

"Ingrate," the other man sneered.

"Buffoon."

Jack fought off a yawn. His watch said three-thirty — what did they expect? "Whenever you boys are ready."

"Liberty-loving *schwein*," said Baron von Gatz, apparently having returned his attention to the Equalizer since Jack couldn't picture General Ching being a liberty-loving anything, "your ultimate fate is assured!"

"Mm-hmm. Don't bet on it, Fritz."

"Bah! Your false bravado cannot impress us now. We are here to take revenge for Black Owl — you know you put him in a wheel-chair? Und there ist the unfinished matter of Iffy Bizness and Sinistro...cold-blooded murder."

"In case you haven't heard, we've also been losing people like flies."

"Pfaw! You Equalizers crossed the line. Let this be our answer to the scoffers und der doubters — to those who think the League of Unmitigated Rotters has lost its resolve!"

The Nazi threw back his head and laughed heavenward, and then he took time out to unravel a banner of that poorly rendered, three-legged black turkey logo of theirs.

"Wherever the deadly spectre of heroism looms, the spirit of villainous men—" Prima Ballerina coughed discreetly behind him "—oh, und of *fräuleins* too, together proud and united, will drive it from our streets."

Von Gatz started waving the flag, like he was stuck on the tail-end of a Third Reich propaganda reel.

"You sure like to waffle," Jack decided.

"That pathetic barb counts for nothing, bumbling fool! This moment belongs to Baron von Gatz! Now all that remains is to determine the manner in which you will die."

"Where's Bulkhead? He and I are old mates."

"That dolt refused to come — said he wanted no invitation to a lynching party."

"The man has manners." Looking over at Prima Ballerina, Jack nodded. "Can't say the same for you."

"I'm just along for the ride," the girl murmured, without any particular conviction.

"Shut up!" shouted von Gatz.

"For crap's sake, get it over with — use the gun," his Communist teammate urged.

"Never! A bullet is far too quick und easy for the likes of him."

"Then I will use mine."

"That thing? It's hideous. The *verdammt* Norinco Type 86S was a commercial failure precisely because it's so ugly." Von Gatz glanced at Jack. "Made in China," the man said, by way of explanation. He even winked.

"I am sick to death of your cultural stereotyping!" General Ching stepped up to his colleague and held him by the scruff of his costume's swastika. "Don't you know the pistol you're flaunting is Chinese? That's no Mauser — it's a Shanxi .45."

"Rubbish."

"Shanxis are noticeably bigger than their Mauser 7.63mm brethren, with the ten-round magazine extending beneath the trigger guard. See? If you don't believe me, pig — it will be inscribed with 'Type 17' in Chinese on the left-hand side of the gun. Take a look."

Baron von Gatz did just that and he blanched. "*Scheisse.*" Then he karate-chopped General Ching's assault rifle. It clattered on the floor and snapped in two.

"Look what you did to my gun — you broke it!"

"Well, I think it's safe to say that's now kaput. Mass-produced trash breaks so easily, don't you think?"

"Then I'll take that mass-produced pistol!"

The two men comically tussled on stage as the Nazi tried to keep his mock-Mauser out of the Communist's fingers.

"Oh, for goodness' sake," Prima Ballerina sighed, pushing forward. "*Gomene,* Southern Cross — I'm sorry you have to put up with such idiocy. Let me take care of this."

Jack knew he had to act, and do so post-haste — having previously copped a dose of the woman's spellbinding body language, he was not sure he wouldn't again cave in.

So, as he leapt across the space, the Equalizer fired off a controlled plasma blast at Prima Ballerina's feet — preferring not to break her legs, but sufficient to knock the girl off the raised platform.

Jack'd counted on the Nazi and his ideologically opposite sparring partner being too preoccupied to take pot-shots at short notice, and was proved right — by the time he ducked beneath an apron, the two men were still struggling and their ring-in Mauser was pointed at the roof, fully loaded.

That was when the shooting really started.

The rat-a-tat-tat came from a rich patron's box with velvet curtains, to the front and above the level of the stage, about two hundred metres away.

Jack saw the first muzzle-flash in the corner of his eye and ducked — since he was completely exposed in his position — but nothing ended up hitting him.

The Nazi and the Communist, on the other hand, were not so fortunate.

For at least thirty seconds, they danced a romantic jig together up on the podium, held aloft by the impact of several hundred rounds. Once the firing ceased, they leaned against one another and slowly slid down to the boards. There was a red wash over everything in proximity, with Prima Ballerina nowhere to be seen.

Jack was barely able to breathe.

He peered over his shoulder at the distant theatre box, wondering when it would be his turn. He blinked several times, quickly, holding back tears he knew were ready to run riot. Why didn't the person shoot? Why drag it out in such a way? At least for von Gatz and Ching it'd been quick.

This was how he spent the next fifteen minutes — waiting to die. Only after that quarter of an hour did he cotton on that death was not here and the killer had gone.

Police entered the theatre, about a dozen of them — pistols drawn, a couple of Tommy guns ready, torches out. They found Jack huddled beneath the stage. His legs were cramping and he shook.

"You all right?"

This was a plainclothes asking, one of two who'd positioned themselves next to where Jack slouched in a fold-down theatre chair far from the mayhem. What made this particular plainclothes stand out was the black leather patch covering his left eye.

The Equalizer tried not to stare as the man handed over a paper cup of lukewarm coffee poured from a Thermos he had in his coat pocket. Aside from the patch, this was a mostly dark-haired cop with salt-and-pepper to either side, pushing fifty, ruggedly handsome and bearing a slightly lopsided nose, broken at some stage in the distant past. He had on a long, mustard-yellow trench coat and olive-green pants, and surprisingly the combination worked.

His partner, a beefier individual with a pot-belly, sandy-coloured hair and a moustache, same age as Eyepatch, hovered a few feet away in a clothing combo that failed.

"You all right, mate?" the first officer repeated.

"Yeah. Yeah, I think so. Just shaken up."

The Equalizer dragged off his mask. Sure, it was against regs — but after all he'd that evening experienced, Jack didn't care about any of it. He huddled there with the cup between both hands.

"Scared shitless, actually. Thought I was a dead man."

"Part and parcel of the territory," the cop said, "but you never, ever appreciate it. Funny, that."

He threw out a hand and Jack reached over to shake it.

"Lieutenant Robert Kahn. Call me Bob."

"Jack."

"Say, aren't you people supposed to keep your names a secret?"

"Something along those lines."

Kahn chuckled. "You want a splash of whiskey with that there coffee?"

"No, I'm fine."

Behind him Kahn's partner whistled. "He's fine, he says."

"Shut up, Irv. Jack, you'll have to excuse Detective Forbush's manners." Kahn then pointed over to the distant stage. "So. What happened here?"

"Looks like it was a set-up," Jack mused, bewildered still. "Meant to be a trap for me, but instead the tables got turned."

"By you?"

"No." He looked into the cop's single eye. "Someone else. With a whole lot of spare ammo."

"Any witnesses?"

"Another Cape — goes by the name of Prima Ballerina."

Kahn scribbled in a small, dog-eared notebook. "Prima Ballerina.

Where is she? I, uh, presume we're talking up a sheila?"

"With most o' these Bops it don't seem to matter," Detective Forbush said. "Fuckin' freaks."

"Irv — give us a moment."

"Sure thing, boss." The other man wandered away with hands in pockets. Kahn watched him go, and then turned back to the Equalizer.

"Guy has a serious problem with Capes," Jack said.

"Unprofessional, yeah, but a good cop. So, tell me — what happened to this Prima Ballerina? Dame, right?"

"Yep. And I don't know. After the shooting started, she skedaddled."

"Smart lady." The cop raised an eyebrow and stopped writing. "Too smart?"

"Good question."

"Even better if you could answer."

Kahn thought for a while, eyeballing the middle distance with his good peeper, and then he looked like he remembered something.

"By the way — we're long overdue returning Sir Omphalos' effects to the Equalizers. Can I pass them on to you now?"

"What, you carry them round?"

"Not much to carry, sadly." He produced a small, sealed plastic bag and handed it over. "Just this."

Inside was a piece of notepaper folded several times to be about two centimetres by two centimetres — the perfect size to fit in the hidden pocket of a costume like Jack's. As he unfolded, the cop continued talking.

"The Words and Pictures Museum of Fine Sequential Art requisitioned his costume — didn't think you people would object. They see it as a state treasure."

The note itself was simple.

THERE ARE 6

"Six," Jack mused.

"Yep. Half a dozen," Kahn chimed in.

"Of what? — People? Eggs? Geese a-laying?"

#139

After half an hour's more waffling, note-taking and cross-referencing, Jack went directly to Louise's apartment — couldn't care less if it was five in the morning. He had to be sure she was okay.

The Professor answered the door and didn't look like his visitor had woken him.

"Jack. Either you're an early-riser, or you have important business with our girl," he breezed, as he showed the man in without further ado.

Jack apologized repeatedly, until the older man cut him off.

"Nonsense, there's no need to say that. I was up anyway, pottering with my Vita-Rays — and, I say, you missed all the excitement!"

"I did?" Frankly, Jack was feeling like he'd had sufficient excitement to last him into his sunset years.

"Oh, very much so."

The elderly man swept up a pipe and began packing it as they stood in the middle of the room. He peered at Jack with a rascally grin.

"Yesterday, Louise clocked her employer — laid the man out on the showroom floor, so to speak — and she then handed in her resignation to leave that financial doss house! She finishes up at the end of this week and I, for one, could not be happier. Last night, Mister Winkle dropped by to pass on his respects and hearty congratulations. He told me that our girl broke Henry Holland's jaw. Not much chin there to fracture, to be sure, but bravo, what?"

It was possible Jack appeared stressed, flustered, or both, and the Prof silenced his patter. He led the younger man to a settee and urged him to sit.

"Stay here, my boy. I will go to get Louise."

The Professor hadn't yet lit his pipe but puffed away on it as he left the room.

Minutes later, his daughter-in-law appeared in the loungeroom.

Alone. The girl's hair was in disarray and she was wrapped only in an oversized men's tuxedo shirt that must've belonged to her husband, but she looked prettier than ever. There was concern and apprehension all over her face. She came before the man and took his hands.

"What is it, Jack? What's happened? Are you all right?"

Jack stood and hugged the girl to him. "Thank crap, you're okay."

"Course I am, aside from morningitis," she whispered in his ear. "What's going on?"

"I — I had a nightmare," he said. "Sorry for barging in like this, I just needed to be sure you were safe."

"I think I'll always be safe — now."

Her arms tightened, and there was no mistaking the relief ricocheting about inside Jack's head. He returned the strength and found himself smiling.

"From what I hear," he mused into her shoulder, "you can handle yourself pretty damned well, regardless."

Louise leaned back a fraction and pretended not to look pleased. "The Prof mentioned yesterday."

"He did."

"I've been dying to slap Henry Holland for days."

"Did you really deck him?"

"Exaggerations. It was nothing more than a light tap."

"That so? I pray I never give you cause to 'tap' me."

"Impossible."

#140

Louise lightly snored beside him. The girl was lying on her front without the white shirt, arms thrown over the pillow, face turned his way. She looked angelic.

Jack parked himself on one elbow to gaze. God, he loved her, even as it dawned upon him that this wouldn't — couldn't — last. One day soon, they'd fix the Reset and everything'd go back to square one.

"Louise," he said. "Louise, are you awake?"

Silence, aside from the sound of sleep.

Then he kicked himself.

What was he going to say? 'There's something I need to tell you about. It's called the Reset.' Sure. Would he end up confessing every-thing about Heropa — including her own intransience? So that she would sit there, desolate, and say, 'That's it? I'll forget everything? Go on working at the bank, putting up with Henry Holland, smoking cigarettes thereafter, on a twenty-four-hour cycle forever? My whole world is a sham, a game?'

And what would Jack do in return? Protest, 'You don't under-stand. This world has so much more than mine. Mine is a place on its last legs, one single city left, and we can't see it surviving long. People have no rights, oppression is everywhere, and we have no heroes. Nothing, aside from ever-present rain and a daily grind of death, dying, loss — and of trying to find scraps of food in rubbish skips.'

No. He couldn't tell her.

Couldn't destroy what she'd achieved in so short a time, all in the name of sharing the burden. Couldn't degrade her opinion of him with a few short sentences.

#141

When Jack opened his eyes in the morning, some time round sun-up, Louise was awake. She was naked — discreetly covered by a sheet — and they'd swapped positions overnight. She had her head propped up in one hand, watching him with a mysterious half-smile.

"More bad dreams?"

Jack nodded. "Always."

"Can you remember what?"

"Prefer to forget." He pushed fingers through the girl's golden hair and gently held the back of her head. "Good morning. How'd you sleep?"

"Like a rock, darling," she said, before pecking his lips, "though I too get nightmares, from time to time."

"How is that possible?"

"Doesn't everyone?"

"I guess." Jack straight away regretted his comment. It'd slipped free prior to thinking it through — insensitive stuff. "What do you dream about?"

"Mine usually involve a building falling on me, or being buried alive."

Jack rubbed his face. "Not surprising — in Heropa."

"And I dream of him sometimes."

"Who?"

"My husband. Lee." Louise sat up, her back to Jack, started to pull on a white bra. "I'm sorry," he heard her say.

Jack placed a hand on her shoulder. "Don't be. I have no problem with you dreaming of him. I don't have a problem with you dreaming, period." He reached over with his other arm and pulled her close. "You have to go to work?"

"Don't *you*?"

The man briefly put his hug on hold. "Sure."

Louise manoeuvred away.

"Funny. You know what I do and where I live, you sleep in my bed. You know I smoke, what kind of flowers I like, my favourite champagne. You know I drink too much coffee, I have pet seahorses, I hate my boss and have an eccentric father-in-law. But I've no scoop on you — have you noticed you've told me so very little?"

Jack struggled with the right thing to say. "Hey. You know I like Roy Lichtenstein."

"You also told me your parents are dead. Maybe. I'm not sure that story is true. It seemed like a convenient way to shut me up."

She stood, went to a dresser, and pulled out a slip and underpants. Then she flicked through clothes hanging in the wardrobe.

"I've noticed. The sweet nothings, I mean. I thought these little details would come naturally — but they haven't. Lichtenstein isn't enough."

She was right. Jack understood that. The girl had every right to be frustrated and annoyed. He grabbed his undershirt from the bed-end.

"I'm sorry. I didn't realize. I've been so wrapped up in you that I didn't think it through. What do you want to know?"

"Everything."

"Where do I start?"

"Your problem exactly."

Louise had zipped up an ivory crepe and chiffon dress, adjusted her stockings, put on a pair of death-defying pumps. All the while, her eyes stayed off the man sitting on her bed, and when she was finished she went to the doorway.

"I'm in love with you, Jack — but I have no clue who you really are. Anyway, I'm late. You can show yourself out."

The door slammed.

#142

When Jack stepped out of the elevator at Timely Tower around eleven o'clock, bad news had apparently inscribed itself into the *carte du jour*.

"Congratulations — you're famous."

Pretty Amazonia shoved a copy of the *Port Phillip Patriot* into his hands and, upon unfolding the paper, the Equalizer discovered his sketched mug on the front page, *sans* mask.

A good likeness.

There was a huge headline he barely noticed, asking:

WHO IS SOUTHERN CROSS??

Beneath was an obligatory sub-header in speech-marks, like always.

"Equalizers not available for comment."

Jack rubbed his jaw as he twisted his mouth sideways (to the right), kicking round this newspaper revelation — while trying to kick the repetitive melody of 'A Walk in the Black Forest' and still overwhelmed by Louise's behaviour that very morning.

"Oh, boy," he finally put out on the line. "Bad?"

"Bad?"

In return PA was fuming, blood having fled her generous lips — which she compressed into a horizontal line in between spurts of dialogue.

"You'll be lucky if you're not thrown out of Heropa," she lashed. "You broke one of our cardinal rules. Bollocks. You idiot. I warned you, did I not?"

"You did."

PA seemed to run out of steam. She flopped onto one of the couches. "Dammit, SC, I told you to stay in costume while on duty out there."

"You don't wear a mask."

"I don't need to."

Jack peered along her length. "How do you hide seven feet?"

"As I mentioned once before, you'd be surprised. I look completely different in my Sunday best. No one would have a hope of recognizing me. But you — with those golden locks and the perfectly chiselled chin — people will finger you straight off the bat."

Her partner carefully sat on a stool next to the coffee table. He focused on the death masks up on the walls and felt like they were laughing at him.

He was guessing the big reveal had happened at the Museum of Antiquities, when he'd removed his mask after the explosion that ripped Sinistro in half. Alternatively, it was the doing of that cop Kahn. Or Gypsie-Ann? She worked for the *Patriot*. Jack'd definitely been liberal in his many reveals — aside from showing anything substantial to Louise, who mattered most.

"Look, I'm sorry." Jack shook his head. "I wasn't thinking. I took off the mask after a man was blown up right there in front of me. Yes, it was a stupid thing to do. I'm new at this."

"Sinistro wasn't a man, he was a shade."

"Same end result." He glanced at her. "So what happens now?"

"The powers-that-be—"

"The mayor?"

"Course not. That man's a nobody. The real powers — the leaders of the Capes and the Rotters — would usually get together with Donald Wright and one of the four other Chief Justices to hash out the misdemeanour. They'd decide whether you stay or go. In the past, this kind of thing always resulted in expulsion, and it's not going to help your case that you clipped Black Owl's wings and the Great White Hope is dead."

"They'll expel me?"

"I don't know. Probably."

"So what do I do in the meantime?"

"There's nothing to do. You're suspended."

Pretty Amazonia grabbed back the newspaper from him and tossed it across the living space. Her anger then subsided and she slapped back down into the couch.

"Crap. The Brick and I talked about this. We tried to work out some way to salvage the situation, but rules are rules. All we can do is wait. Dammit."

"Where is the Brick?"

The woman nodded her head in the direction of the next floor. "In his room, brooding. He's overly fond of you. God knows why."

#143

Jack was all prepared to rap on the entrance to the Brick's private quarters — one part of Equalizers HQ where he'd never before set a single toe — when he became aware of music drifting from within.

The same score he'd heard at the Satori Dance Studio the other night.

Unsure why he again intruded on the man's privacy, Jack pushed the door slightly ajar. The music came out of archaic Hallicrafters Model R-12 console speakers in each corner of the suite.

The Brick was hunched over on a big, reinforced couch, dabbing his eyes with a pale blue handkerchief that had a pink cherry-blossom design.

The seated man didn't notice his partner's intrusion, Jack felt like a fool, and he silently closed the door.

Andrez Bergen

#144

When Jack popped into the bank an hour later, Louise closed off her till.

He thought she did that in order to dash out into the foyer and meet him, but after he'd been waiting twenty-five minutes, he realized she wasn't coming.

So the man joined the queue to Mister Winkle's window. Once he got there, the old coot smiled in wan fashion.

"Miss Starkwell refuses to see you, sonny."

"I kind of realized that. But — if possible — I'd like to know why. Or talk with her."

Mister Winkle looked past Jack to the next customer. "I'm sorry. I'm afraid that won't be possible. We're very busy today."

"Look." Leaning on the counter, Jack lowered his voice. "I don't want to start a commotion. I just want to talk to Miss Starkwell — straight after that, I'll be out of your hair and commotions will be a thing of the distant past. But if you refuse to let me see her, I promise you'll have the mother of commotions on your hands."

The old man leaned away. "Are you saying you won't cause a ruckus?"

"You meet my terms? — Cross my heart."

"Hope to die?"

"Sure," Jack frowned, feeling like he was back on the playground, "if that makes you feel any better."

"Try the smoking room. Down the corridor over there, third door on the left."

Jack walked along a narrow hallway obviously intended only for staff, straight past Henry Holland — who had his jaw wired and looked miserable. The Equalizer knocked on the third door.

When no one answered, he pushed it open.

As promised, Louise was in there, alone, next to a barred window. She had one arm, her left, crossed over her chest as she dragged in on a cigarette she'd recently lit. Several drowned

233

brothers were stashed in a small bowl of water on a table in the centre of the room.

Jack could see the girl had been crying, the telltale signs some screwed up tissues lying abandoned next to the improvised ashtray.

"Congratulations — you're famous," Louise said.

This was the second time he'd heard the very same words, on both occasions bearing a certain degree of venom.

"No wonder you told me nothing about yourself. I'm so stupid. So naive. I can't believe you're a Cape."

Walking straight over to her, Jack held her arms and looked into those vivid greens. "What difference does it make?"

"We can't — I don't — " Louise broke away from him.

She stared out the window at a yellow Plymouth parked on the other side of an alley, in front of a warehouse with signage that read Carson Chemical Laboratories.

"I want you to leave."

"What difference does it make?" Jack repeated, voice now flat.

"Just go."

"Louise."

"Go."

"Listen to me—"

"I said, just go!"

By the time she would've finished the current cigarette, Jack was out on a busy street, pushing through an ocean of people he didn't know.

BLACKJACK

#145

"Psst — mister!"

He'd been walking the streets of Heropa in relatively aimless fashion, dodging other pedestrians and avoiding the occasional glance of recognition — despite the fact he wasn't in costume.

Things were unravelling so damned fast.

His career as a Cape was, according to Pretty Amazonia, pretty much on the rocks; his relationship with Louise finished before they'd had the chance to truly begin.

At some stage in this ramble, Jack bumped into Gypsie-Ann Stellar on an intersection near the offices of the *Port Phillip Patriot*.

She walked beside him, head down, nose almost to the ground, and her eyes occasionally glancing at her colleague as they walked.

"Wasn't me who published the picture," she said, like it mattered and Jack cared. "I tried to block them using the image, but I only have so much pull. I know the rules, and I realize this could seriously imperil your career."

"So I've been hearing," Jack muttered, hoping she couldn't keep up with his pace.

He may have had longer legs, but the woman was better on high-heels than he figured.

"Look, I know Chief Justice Fargo is in consultations with my boss and Black Owl re: your case. Unfortunately, you didn't make a good impression on either Wright or the Owl, but don't fret — everyone knows they're dipsticks. Joe Fargo is a fair man, maybe the fairest in this city."

Gypsie-Ann punched his shoulder.

"Hang in there, okay? I've been snooping about a fair bit regarding your Sekrine lead...figured you'd need a professional hand. Nothing to report — as yet — but 'tis early days."

"Forget about it."

"I'm never one to forget a budding story. Anyway, must go. Good luck."

With that, she crossed the lights against the traffic and had a bunch of old cars honking and swerving.

In a side-alley next to a bookshop with elegantly flowing writing on its signage, a man caught Jack's attention when he stumbled past.

"Psst — mister!"

Jack looked over and saw a tall figure in a buttoned-up brown trench coat that hung down over grey wool trousers with red pinstripes. What grabbed him most was the red Stetson the man had down low over his eyes, so he couldn't see the face clearly.

"C'mon, mister!" the stranger urged. "Step over here. Just for a sec. I won't bite. You're that Cape — Southern Cross, right?"

Jack came marginally closer. Hell, at least he'd have someone to whine to.

"Supposedly. Like the hat. Seen it before."

"It's a pre-war Bross and Clackwell. Only one of its kind in town."

"That so?"

Jack didn't see the blackjack until the thing had passed across his eyes — on the way, a split second later, to dance a frolicsome jig on his left temple.

#146

The Equalizer came to inside a cramped, dark place he quickly realized he'd prefer not to be. His legs were folded up, wrists tied together, suit crumpled, and his head ached.

From within what he sussed out to be a metal locker, through the grille beside his face, Jack could espy partial glimpses of a big room proper, filtered with red light.

First thing he made out was Bulkhead.

The Rotter was settled in the same interview chair Jack'd occupied days before at the headquarters of the League. Those decorative chains from the ceiling had been put to good use — binding Bulkhead's metallic torso, arms and legs dozens of times over.

There was another individual walking around him.

This man wore an innocuous tan trench coat that made him look like just about every other male Blando in the city, but the hat on his head — a pillar-box red, wide-brim Stetson — stood out a mile.

He had the hat pulled down low, so that shadows played around his cheeks and eyes.

Even when this individual occasionally faced the locker during the course of his circular route, Jack could not see any features clearly.

The man in the red hat stopped for a moment, his back to Jack, and clicked a lighter. A plume of smoke headed towards the high ceiling.

"Man, oh, man," his voice remarked, as he took up looping the loop again, "I'd swear these were real."

Bulkhead sounded disgusted: "You're a tobacco-fiend."

"Yep."

"On ya."

"Hard to find the real McCoy back in Melbourne."

"Then you're a Cape?"

"Nup."

238

Ineffectual as it was, the Rotter writhed a lot and there was the scraping of metal on metal. "Yeah, well — enjoy the experience, arsewipe."

"Oh, I will."

"Get me outta these chains, and you'll enjoy a whole new ballgame."

"Think I'll skip out on that particular pleasure, mate."

"What d'you want? The other Rotters will be back shortly. They'll fry your balls."

"Yeah, I reckon they would, so time to end this. Besides, I reckon our prize spectator," the man in the red hat nodded in Jack's direction, "has likely woken up by now."

"What happened to the Peter Pan policy?" Bulkhead demanded, swivelling one eye and then the other to ogle his captor. "You abiding by it?"

The man in the red hat chuckled.

He leaned in close to Bulkhead, all cosy-like, and said something Jack couldn't make out.

At the same time, he saw the man push a small, cylindrical object into the midriff area of the bound tin-man, and then he strolled away whistling a tune Jack thought he recognized — what was it?

The door slammed shut.

Gone.

Jack breathed easier, getting set to kick open the locker, when he heard Bulkhead shout out, "I do believe in fairies! I do, I—"

The roar and flames of an explosion consumed everything, flipping Jack's cabinet several times — and causing him to black out for the third time in two weeks.

When the Equalizer came to, something hard was cradling the back of his head. It took him a moment to realize this was a handful of small bricks. His eyes burned, a stench of smoke seared his nostrils as he dragged in for breath, everything spun.

Strangely enough, prior to oblivion settling back in to roost, the Equalizer had a flash and thought he remembered the name of the whistled tune: Ary Barroso's 1939 number, 'Aquarela do Brasil'.

"Kid! Kid!" the Brick's voice pleaded, somewhere very distant. "Goddammit, are you awright—?"

6° OF TREPIDATION

#147

Louise Starkwell had been happy.

For the first spell in any time she could recall, contentment had channelled her way. Then again, Louise supposed she'd been happy in the past, but any experience of that kind remained strangely removed.

This often left the girl wondering if some illness — dementia, Alzheimer's, attention deficit disorder or a variation of it — were playing havoc with her brain. She'd heard that symptoms of ADD included forgetting things on a daily basis, misplacing keys, locking oneself out, and leaving the lights on — none of which she did.

But chronic forgetfulness in general? Most certainly this, and there was the subconscious procrastination about leaving her job.

Yet things she'd evidently studied, like art and accounting, also the basic act of whipping up a pasta dish off the top of her head, remained fresh and accessible. Louise wished she could remember having boned up on these in the first place.

There was a time, close to the moment she met Jack, when things that happened the day before were shrouded in mystery. The feeling had declined as their relationship bloomed, and it was only the more distant past that was now beyond her.

A time involving a husband who appeared in dreams — even if she was not so sure this man was Lee. There were no pictures to check, no memories to tick off, nothing to compare or contrast.

Not that this mattered.

None of it did.

The recent bout with happiness? Short-lived — as usual, it had all too quickly decamped. While she felt a fool, worse still she had this uncontrollable melodramatic belief that her heart had been mashed beyond repair. Louise thought about slapping herself. She had stupidly trusted Jack, believed in him, loved the man. A vacuous rollercoaster that was over inside two weeks — some kind of new record.

Damn it, Jack, she mulled, *why couldn't you be honest?*

Was she to blame for that? After all, she'd brought up Lee's death at the hands of other Bops. No wonder he didn't want to mention his career choice. And it wasn't his fault he was naturally reticent and shy — that's what she liked about him in the first place.

But what were those more recent awkward moments, his thoughts obviously elsewhere, and the lie about his parents?

At least, she believed it was a lie. Jack had been safe-harbouring too many secrets, not allowing her to glimpse his real self, and then one major truth exploded onto the front page of a newspaper. She had every right to react the way she did. He couldn't be trusted. He'd lied. Hadn't he?

The Prof always said it took two to tango.

Who was it that moaned her dead spouse's name in the middle of a particularly poignant moment? Louise closed her eyes. No wonder the guy acted strange.

And she'd played the jealousy card by paying too much attention to Karl Burgos at the restaurant, had seen Jack squirm. Now she felt disgusted with herself. He'd behaved almost...human.

When a relationship goes right, she decided, everything sparkles. Life is so grand you could carve it up and generously give portions to the needy. When a relationship goes wrong, every niggling doubt shoves its way to the surface. You close up shop, embrace bitterness, and denounce the world.

Louise looked up, shook away the vacillating debris, and held up a hand to order a glass of Bollinger from the waiter. She then produced cigarettes from her bag.

Flicked one out of the pack, grabbed it with her teeth and struck a match. Breathed in hints of sulphur and burning wood along with the tobacco smoke.

Exhaled in the direction of the ceiling, with it's gorgeous French-style chandelier, thinking as she did so — and saw the middle-aged gentleman standing there between dinner tables, dressed in a long raccoon coat, a black bowler hat between his hands. While his shiny scalp was unadorned with hair, the man had a fine moustache, was passably handsome — and he was staring straight back at her.

"Hello, Mitzi."

Louise glanced over her shoulder at the other patrons, even while knowing the man had addressed her. "I'm sorry? Are you speaking to me?"

"It's been a long time, baby. Perhaps you've forgotten."

The mention of long-term memory gaps gave the girl pause, but the name 'Mitzi' still threw things. "I think you have me confused with someone else," she decided, presenting the kind of smile she usually gave to customers in the bank. "My name is Louise."

"Of course it is. My mistake." The man responded with his own artificial beam. "And yet the likeness is uncanny. So — are you, or aren't you?"

"Am I, or aren't I, what?"

"A phony."

Louise dragged on her cigarette. Something about this individual was unsettling — likely it had to do with being labelled a phony — but curiosity won out. "What do you mean?"

"Well, now. Would you mind if I sat?" He indicated the vacant seat on the other side of the table.

She'd only recently broken a scoundrel's jaw. Why not? "Sure."

The gentleman took off his coat to place it on the next chair over, depositing his hat on top. Beneath, he wore a tailored black jacket, grey vest, and dark-grey satin ascot tie, in the centre of which was a flashy diamond. He settled down opposite the girl, reached into a jacket pocket, and took out a fat cigar that was wrapped in cellophane and the words Coronas del Ritz.

"Would you overly mind if I smoked, Miss Louise?"

"Just Louise. And go ahead — I am. Or was." The girl stamped out her cigarette in a glaring white plastic ashtray that had on it mystical-looking mountains and the words 'Shangri-La' in an Asiatic-style typeface.

"Cigar?"

"No, thank you."

"I could order you another glass of champagne, or better yet the entire bottle. What are you drinking there, kid — Moët?"

Louise placed her hand over the flute. She despised Moët. "I'm fine. Thank you. I don't mean to sound unappreciative, but weren't you going to tell me something?"

"Oh, yes — of course, of course, of course..." The 'of courses' trailed away as the newcomer lit and road-tested his cigar. He sat back, slid his right leg over his left thigh, and smiled again. "So lovely to see you."

The smile came across less than affable and quite a distance sinister. This man knew something, was playing a game. Louise held his eyes, maintaining a placid expression, something she'd mastered while working with Henry Holland.

Lighting up another cigarette gave a few seconds to consider options.

It would be easy to walk out of the restaurant without further word — either cough up the cash on the way to the front door, or leave this strange visitor to foot the bill. He looked rich enough.

But there was a possibility he genuinely knew something about her past, something she'd forgotten or lost grip on.

Louise also sat back. "I'm still waiting."

"Yes, so you are. Excuse the manners."

The man placed his cigar on the ashtray, took out an ivory cigarette-holder, and proceeded to squeeze into it the end of the cigar, which was too big. Finally, the slightly bent thing sat in precarious fashion in the holder. That accomplished, he leaned closer on one elbow, eyes glittering.

"You could easily be her," he murmured softly, appraising the girl anew. "Change the hair colour and style, tweak the makeup, get rid of the silly glasses. Slap some exaggerated confidence into your expression."

"This Mitzi you mentioned." Louise ashed her cigarette.

"That's right, baby."

"Who was she?"

"Oh, a complete bitch."

Having killed the ciggie and emptying her glass, Louise then slid the packets of Paul Jones and matches back inside her purse and stood up.

"Well, well, look at the time," she announced.

The stranger smiled more. "Must you go, Louise?"

"I do. To be honest — I've had enough of strange arseholes in my life and, while I don't mean to be rude, would you go find some other patsy to mess around?"

The girl didn't look back as she strode away. Nor as she went to the cashier's desk, certainly not while waiting for change, and she looked straight ahead in the process of walking out of the restaurant. She waltzed down the street at a leisurely pace, pretended to admire shoes in a shop window, and then turned the corner.

Only at that point did Louise fall back against a brick wall, out of breath, feeling faint, and light up another cigarette. She took off the glasses, to rub her eyes with her left hand — mascara be damned.

#148

Captain Robert Kahn sat slumped at his desk in the cluttered premises of police headquarters, a place buried in the basement of City Hall, and he was also unhappy.

He stretched the muscles in his shoulders, heard a couple of bones crack, and then leaned back in his creaky leather swivel chair to stare at the files and boxes assembled haphazardly across a nearby tabletop. Ten different cases, apparently related, all of them still open, unsettled, ongoing. He sipped from a mug of thick black coffee, which had turned lukewarm while he pondered.

"How many now, boss?" Detective Forbush asked, from his miniature desk diagonally opposite Kahn's larger one. The officer was supposed to be composing a report, but had obviously noticed the other cop's distraction.

"Ten."

"Double figures it is, then. Ten Bops. Half a pack of ciggies' worth — the list grows bigger."

"On a daily basis."

"No wonder we're bloody busy."

"Let's hope the guilty parties take a weekend off."

Kahn checked his calendar. Eight in the past week alone. No suspects, no decent lead. The Capes were falling like flies while he dogged down dead-ends.

Detective Forbush had been chewing on a toothpick that he carefully laid on a dish. "Me an' the boys, we've been talking about the Bops. 'Bout how to deal with the ones that're left, the stragglers — unofficial-like, I mean."

"I won't have vigilantes on the force, Irv. You hear me?"

"Sure, boss."

"Tell me you're not involved in these deaths."

"Our hands're clean, I swear. But what about the Bops? They're the vigilantes from Hades."

"They don't wear a police uniform or a badge."

"So if I put on a pretty costume and mask, it's okay?"

"Of course not." Kahn sighed. "Right now, we need them. It won't always be like this."

The other cop picked up his bent, saliva-logged toothpick and began masticating again. Kahn wondered how much longer the thing could last.

"I guess all we've gotta do is wait for them to polish off each other. Equalizers, dumb-arse Rotters — I don't care. But if it's the Equalizers that win, we're in luck. In case you lost count, there's only three of them now. Dunno about you, boss, but I've been waitin' a long time to take down the bastards."

Kahn frowned. "Don't be in such a rush. We need the Equalizers, Irv. Who else can stand against the Rotters? We don't have the firepower."

"Which is why we wait, like I says. But you're wrong. We do have the firepower." Forbush lifted a well-fingered piece of paper. "In the evidence-room armoury, all the leftovers from Bop fights — nutty things like an atom igniter, a Vacutex, remote-control gravi-polarizers, an MCD99 pistol, demolo and negato guns, a cosmic rod an' cosmic cube, and something grandstandingly calling itself the ultimate nullifier — whatever the heck that is."

"You're forgetting the vibra-gun and several pairs of x-ray specs."

"Oh, yeah. Different list."

"And you have instruction manuals for them?"

Forbush looked down as he folded the paper into quarters. "No."

"You realize you could vaporize half the city with any one of those gadgets?"

"I guess. 'Nother coffee?"

"Sure. That's safer."

Detective Forbush got up, headed to the tiny kitchenette, and started manhandling a large blue, orange, white and red tin of Maxwell House roaster fresh.

While he was thus occupied, Kahn allowed his eyes to wash over the assembled desks and the other officers — good people, all of them, but worked to the bone.

Typing up something nearby was Inspector Rudd, for example, a fine man with a family of six hungry kids he never saw. The ever-restless, unacceptably long-haired Officer Norrin Radd had shelved plans of quitting the force to pursue his dream of a professional surfing career — for what? Some miguided loyalty to his mates here?

And Detective Dan Carey, who sat on the other side of the room, loading and unloading his police pistol with an agitated look, an expression he'd nurtured since his wife Marla had eloped with a man calling himself Albino Joe.

Too many cases, generating myriad personal problems, without sufficient boots on the ground. Yet still the mayor talked of cutbacks.

On the wall next to a sagging mantelpiece crowded with plastic Tiki gods and a pair of kissing dolls, on the other side of a legit picture of public enemy #1 Hogarr Ditko, there was a hand-drawn poster with a black silhouette of a Cape crossed out, and 'CAPE-FREE ZONE' written above in a thick red texta. Near that, an Equalizers logo had been converted into a dartboard — haggard from overuse, currently with a yellow plastic dart dead centre, skewering the lightning bolt, it sat next to a poster for a local bout that announced 'Fight!! Karnak vs. Krushki!', with betting odds beneath.

He should have taken down all three things days ago. But better to have this shit out in the open than festering somewhere private-like.

Kahn had his reason for sticking up for the Capes — the Big O saved his life.

Copped a bullet meant for him, fired from his blind side by some low-life gutter monkey robbing a grocery store; the Cape took it in his stride, obviously hurt, but disappeared into the sky after first knocking the crim senseless. Kahn had seen the hero's blood on the street, never got a chance to thank him.

The funny thing was that he remembered this, when not so long ago no one else would.

There was a time everyone — bar himself — forgot everything on a daily basis. He'd rise and shine at four a.m. before work, look out the window at dawn, and see a brand new Heropa City that sparkled — all and any damage from the previous day's shenanigans restored. And he noticed, whereas none of his friends or co-workers batted an eyelid. For a long time, he believed Capes did this overnight as a kind of service, like the elves and the shoemaker story.

Kahn told no one. Didn't wish to rock the boat or disquiet other people. Briefing his officers on the same cases every morning — with nobody recalling a goddamned detail — could be a drag, but it was the way things were. He knew no differently.

Recently, however, there was no need for the morning briefings. Kahn felt a hole in his routine, it made him uncomfortable.

Recently, everyone else did remember, and that was when this Cape backlash got in full swing and well out of hand.

The meeting the day before at Mayor Brown's office, upstairs on the thirty-ninth floor, was supposed to be a briefing about the case.

In front of the mayor, Chief of Police O'Hara, District Attorney Paul Garrett, State Prison Warden Williams, and financial bigwig Donald Wright — along with Garrett's secretary Edith, who took minutes — Kahn gave an abridged rundown on the progress of Cape killings, their hypotheses (unfounded guesswork) and police-artist sketches of the bodies that could still be sketched. In the case of Kid Kindle it was a charred skeleton — ironic, since the teenager's talent was manhandling fire.

After the detective finished his speech, the chitchat swivelled on an oily dime to one of recrimination.

The mayor had put on a song and dance about what a nuisance the Capes were, how they threatened public safety. The fact that elections neared probably prodded the man into action.

"Things were better when Sir Omphalos was in charge — at least he kept them in check," Garrett said. "Now it's chaos out there, only a matter of time till those people do something very, very stupid.

And civilians pay the price."

"You need some kind of control mechanism," Wright piped up, looking at no one in particular as he rubbed his bald head. "A leash, if you will."

"How? I don't have the resources," Chief O'Hara complained.

"When you're ready to outsource, and trust me on the matter, I believe I have the appropriate contacts."

"And what will this cost us?" asked the mayor, ever the penny-pincher — aside from his infamous personal budget.

"Well, these things don't come cheaply," Wright said, feeding a lady finger banana to a small monkey he'd brought along in a cage. "Let me get back to you on that issue, Mayor Brown."

Once the meeting was adjourned, Kahn had walked with Chief O'Hara back to the elevators.

"Needless to say, what was said in that room remains there," the chief advised, all cautious tone. "I understand you have a soft-spot for the Equalizers, and I know they've done us their fair share of favours. But the Capes' time is over, Robert. You need to remember that — remember whose side you're on."

"Yes sir."

"May I have your hand on it?"

They shook, just as one of the elevator's doors opened and dinged.

"There'll be a bigger playing field for the police force once we clean out the old order. More space for people like you and me to move up."

"Yes, sir," Kahn had repeated by rote — his worries increasing every damned second.

#149

Gypsie-Ann Stellar was somewhat happier.

She'd spent several hours of the afternoon up in the newspaper archive, and finally tracked down Southern Cross's John Doe.

There was a dossier, misfiled under 'E' with the name SEKRINE, L. on it, behind another misfiled report for ROGERS, Sarah and Joseph.

The Sekrine portfolio was unusually complete. It told of a fatality in a fight between Funk Gadget and Prima Ballerina, one of several deaths, thanks to a stray sonic musical blast — Funk Gadget's signature mojo.

But the signature on the report, while indecipherable, was also one the reporter didn't recognise. She knew the handwriting of all the cadets she assigned to do the menial, thankless task. This writing did not match theirs. The question was, who filled in the report, and why had it been completed with such care?

There *were* omissions — no coroner's report, no police-artist sketch of the corpse — so how had a fresh newspaper recruit compiled this much information at a time when the twenty-four-hour Reset window still existed?

Gypsie-Ann flipped through the details.

Height, weight, address, age, hair colour, driver's licence number, criminal record (none): all the information was present and accounted for.

Next of kin: a spouse, Louise Sekrine *née* Starkwell, and a father named Abe J. Sekrine.

Funnily enough, they'd forgotten to write in the actual victim's first name or middle moniker — there was only that lonesome 'L-full stop'.

Misfiled under 'E'. Next to a report recording the deaths of Sarah and Joseph Rogers.

The reporter thought about that, and then she started reassembling the characters of SEKRINE, making one of the 'E's the first letter:

EKRINES/EREINSK/ESKINER/
ERSKINE/ERKSIEN/EINSKER

One of these stood out — *Erskine*.

Gypsie-Ann underlined it. Could be an anagrammatic coincidence, but she didn't believe in those. The dad's name was the clincher.

Abe. *Abraham*.

An hour later, some time around four, she hopped out of a cab on the corner of Burnside and Monroe, in Hymie Heights.

The address was on the second storey of a nearby brownstone, above an antique store.

Gypsie-Ann looked at the windows. Late afternoon, a Thursday, and the blinds were drawn — nothing strange about that if the people who lived there were out to work.

The security door, sitting above a small flight of brick stairs, wouldn't budge. An easy matter to pick the lock, but the reporter preferred not to resort to such tactics in broad daylight, on a main thoroughfare like this one.

She decided instead to head into the antique shop.

A bell rang overhead, and as she weaved through various kinds of junk, a pocket-sized old man stuck his noggin — boasting a shock of white hair — above the edge of a cedar desk in the corner.

"Good morning, madam. Are you looking for anything in particular?"

"Just browsing," Gypsie-Ann said as she ran her finger over dusty books on the shelf.

"Then enjoy yourself, and let me know if you need anything."

The owner had started to turn away when the woman spoke again.

"You wouldn't happen to know Abe or Louise Sekrine, who live on the second floor of this building?"

He stopped straight away and glanced over his shoulder.

"Why do you ask?"

"The name is Sigerson. An old family friend." The man's eyes further told her he didn't believe a word, so Gypsie-Ann decided to ditch the ruse. "Actually, that's not true."

"I was not inclined to believe so."

"I'm a reporter—"

"A reporter?"

"Working with the *Port Phillip Patriot*."

She held out her right hand but the man didn't move. Not the first time the gesture had been refused. Out of practice, she dropped her arm and placed the hand on her hip.

"My name is Gypsie-Ann Stellar, and I'm working on a story that may or may not involve Louise Sekrine's husband."

"Are you now?" The old man's voice sounded flat as a proverbial tack.

"Possibly. I'm looking into the details. So, would you know either party upstairs?"

"I would. I am Professor Sekrine. Perhaps you should come with me, Miss Stellar. We can talk privately in the back room."

The reporter followed her elderly tour-guide through a minor maze of boxes to an office, where they settled into the same two chairs Jack and the Professor had shared only days before.

While he surprisingly retrieved a pouch of tobacco from the toe end of a Persian slipper, Gypsie-Ann leaned forward with notebook and pen.

"Do you mind if I ask you some questions, Mister Sekrine?"

"By all means."

"How long have you and your family lived in this building?"

"A very, very long time. My son was born here."

Gypsie-Ann looked sharply over. "Really?"

"As was I, my dear."

"I see." The reporter wrote nothing — this was nonsense. "Could you please tell me your son's name?"

"I don't remember."

The old man studied the tips of his fingers. A hostile witness, then. The reporter smiled to herself. Hanging on the wall behind the man was a large oil painting of a young lady with a lamb.

"Nice picture," she said, with a nod in that direction.

"An original, by Jean-Baptiste Greuze. *La jeune fille à l'agneau.* Beautiful, is it not? I plan to give it to someone special for her birthday."

"Your daughter-in-law."

"Yes."

"Does she still live here with you? Or did she move on, after the accident?"

"Louise continues to reside here. But it was no accident."

"Are you saying your son was deliberately killed? Murdered?"

"I'm not sure. I forget things. I'm an old man."

"Oh, you seem to me sufficiently on the ball." Gypsie-Ann sat back and crossed her legs. "Correct me if I'm wrong, but your real name is Erskine."

The Professor lost interest in the fingers and one of his arms poked behind while he sat up straight, looking at the reporter.

"A final problem, for which I must apologize," he said.

"I don't understand. For what?"

"For this." A weapon had appeared in the old man's hand, a snub-nosed .450 Webley Metropolitan Police revolver — compact in most people's grip, but exceptionally large in his tiny fist. "Believe me, I am so sorry."

Before the woman could think to move, this gun-toting pensioner shot her in the stomach, from a distance of only six feet.

The impact knocked both her and the heavy divan backwards, where she lay amidst a mess of books, knick-knacks and her own blood.

Trying desperately to rise, Gypsie-Ann railed at the pain ripping through her as much as the stupidity of blundering into this. She somehow got to her feet, the room spinning, gut gushing, flashes of

O and his flickering smile now entering her head.

"Lee," she gasped, as she fell back to the floor.

#150

Psyborg-9 had well and truly had enough of Heropa, what with the recent spate of murders. He'd decided to pack his bags and leave, but neither the open sesame nor a flurry of ill-conceived swear-words had opened the door for departure.

This, before him, was the final straw.

The Cape scanned the crowd, his inbuilt abacus counting out one hundred and twelve individuals: eighty-two adult men, nineteen women, and eleven adolescents.

Who brought children to this kind of rally?

The mob in the plaza looked on edge, with zero police officers in sight, and there were placards made to varying degrees of professionalism. One had 'Give a Bop the Chop!', another 'Down With Fascist Capes'; the most inventive, so far as Psyborg-9 was concerned, read 'Once You Bop, the Fun Does Stop'.

At the back of the crowd he spied two young boys setting fire to an imitation Equalizers banner.

While he might've been unceremoniously evicted from that group, along with two-dozen others, enough was enough.

"Citizens," Psyborg-9 announced on his automated loudhailer, as he stepped up to a plinth in front of one of Heropa's supposed founding fathers, a statue of Joseph Kubert, "disperse this place in orderly fashion or there will be...trouble."

"More trouble than you know, mister," hissed a nearby individual in a red hat. This man also jumped onto the podium to shove at the Cape.

"Stand down," warned Psyborg-9.

"Make me."

The man unexpectedly tossed into the Cape's face the contents of a paper cup of coffee, short-circuiting his electronic vision. Straight after, the coffee-thrower turned back to the mob.

"Oi! Everyone! — I know this guy! This is the Bop that massacred all those innocent people the other day, the ones near Harvey's

Gems!"

The throng hushed while Psyborg-9 struggled to clear his eyes —
and then they surged forward, all hell breaking loose and spinning
asunder.

#151

The Brick glared at the images spilling across his portable Meteor black-and-white television, over on its tripod stand; listened to the commentary with repressed anger.

"...Scenes of bedlam at the Simonson Centre today [cue: hand-held, panning visual of abandoned placards in an empty public space], where a freelance Cape was attacked by a wild mob of civilians, over one hundred in number. By the time the police intervened to break up the crowd [this time stable footage of uniformed cops picking about], the part-android Psyborg-9 had been irreparably damaged and passed away shortly before ambulances arrived [a long-shot of blood-drenched pavement and an ambulance]. Mayor William Brown [Big Bill, looking flustered and irritated] made this brief statement: 'Citizens, remain calm. That's all I have to say at this juncture — get that camera out of my face!' [And a dissolve to the male announcer in the studio, simple cardboard cut-out backdrop behind him] There were no arrests made by police, and we'll have further updates for you as they come to hand."

The Equalizer reached over to pull the button on the telly, watching the image shrink to a white dot in the middle of the screen. He sighed, long and loud. Then he walked out of the room, the weight of the known world on his shoulders.

If only she were here.

Prima Ballerina had disappeared, not so much as a farewell my lovely. His reaction slayed the Brick more than her absence — made him feel like his heart was in his mouth, that he could spit the thing out in the sink. He could taste the loss, and infused that with the brewing rage inside.

Meanwhile, the kid'd suffered, and good people like Psyborg and Kindle were being slain out there on the streets.

Disgusted with himself, the Brick kicked a hole in a wall and went back to his room.

#152

The Professor?

He sat in his armchair, the warm gun on his lap, while he studied the body decorating the floor on the other side of the small, cluttered office.

He wasn't certain, but it looked like she was still breathing. One foot shifted. It would be courteous to put the poor woman out of her misery, but he found he could not move.

He'd broken his trust, done something very foolish. The sound of the shot was bound to attract attention this time of day, and in fact he could hear the whine of approaching sirens.

Still, there was one thing to draw out of all the brouhaha — he'd been reacquainted with his first name.

GUN HAPPY

#153

The colours lined up in polite order for presentation first: vague washes of purple, orange and yellow that blurred into one another, with shadows diplomatically hanging back, moving somewhere behind. A stronger, more shocking smell came next, the unmistakable scent of ammonia and a second fragrance, pleasantly floral in nature.

The first kosher thing he saw was fuzz, insubstantial and wandering.

Light drifting above, glare from some window to his right. He could hear blipping nearby, and the distant sound of strange traffic.

Once his vision cleared, he understood he was lying on a bed in a hospital room. The walls and the ceiling were white, as were the curtains.

When Jack fully awoke and managed to turn his head, he found Gypsie-Ann Stellar sitting in the next bed, also all in white, less makeup than usual, and she was peering back.

"A bit of an empty house we share here, so I'm glad you're awake. Hello, stranger," she said.

"I...didn't know...we were rooming together," the Equalizer fought to squeeze out. His throat felt like sandpaper and there was a dull pain throughout his body. Having tried to get up, he realized he couldn't.

"We've been bedfellows since you passed on your ticklish lead and I hit pay dirt," Gypsie-Ann was saying. "Better to lay still, Jack. We have matching bandages, but I'm in better shape." The reporter raised the hospital gown she was wearing so he could see the wrap looping her torso. "The Brick told me you had a chunk of Bulkhead embedded in your abdomen — you really don't want to know which part."

"Bulkhead. He's dead...?"

"In little pieces."

"The explosion."

"Something like that. I don't know the full details."

"Crap." Jack felt like he was on fire. "I need water."

"No need for subtlety."

Gypsie-Ann climbed out of her cot, grabbed a tumbler off a small table, poured from the plastic jug there, and walked it over to her pyjama partner.

"Thanks," he said, after completely finishing the glass. Swallowing had become marginally easier, but it still hurt like hell.

"What happened to you?"

"Someone shot me in the stomach."

"Jeez. Did that hurt?"

"What do you reckon? I thought I was going to die." Obviously tired of standing, the reporter settled down on the end of the other patient's bed.

"Me too," Jack muttered, and then he stopped to think. "How long've I been out of it? I mean, since the explosion."

"Pretty Amazonia says three days."

"Then when did you get shot?"

"Yesterday arvo."

The Equalizer stared at her as she sat there. "And you said you got shot in the stomach?"

"I did."

"In that case, you look remarkably peachy."

Gypsie-Ann laughed. "I do, don't I? When it came to choosing baggage before downloading into Heropa, I was smart."

"You're invulnerable."

"No, no. Since we can't have the option of invulnerability — believe me, I harried them — I thought I'd go with the next best option."

"Which was...?"

"Wolverine's healing factor."

"Ah-hah."

"I have no idea why no one else here has chosen it — if you look at Wolverine in comicbooks, he's been on death's door dozens of times, yet always recovers. I know it's not the most realistic mojo to have, but this whole place is make-believe."

"Isn't that cheating? It makes you virtually invulnerable."

"Not really — since I go through all the pain before my body decides to heal itself. You have no idea how excruciating it is to get shot. Still, I'm alive."

"Wish I'd thought of that, but the '60s're more my speciality."

"Meh, I'm more of a bronze-age-comic fan. It's what I grew up with, thanks to my dad — who had a great collection of the stuff."

"Some good yarns tucked away in there," Jack admitted, "though the Avengers, from the late '70s, had this rabid policy of superhero overpopulation."

"That so? I hadn't noticed, since I was more into the X-Men. How many are we talking?"

"Eighteen members of the team, along with respective spouses and nemeses."

"Yep," the woman agreed, "that is a spot of overpopulation. Kind of kills the idea of 'the more the merrier', right?"

"Probably because you don't care a single iota about anyone since the individual protagonists're watered down."

"It's tricky, when you have so many characters."

Gypsie-Ann mulled over the geeky concept, surprisingly without objection. Jack had expected to be slapped down but all he got was a vague glance.

"To be honest," the reporter continued, "the Wolverine thing always made me scratch my head."

"Why's that?"

"Well, if you think about it seriously, in order to fix the point-blank bullet wound in my tummy the surrounding cells would have to multiply themselves at an insane rate, causing a form of hypermitosis. Instead, there's a trigger mechanism somewhere here inside me that tells the cells to play ball, and thereby make up for any loss of structure, dividing at extreme speed when needed — giving rise to the creation of new blood vessels and neurons, *et voilà*.

Look," she unwrapped and revealed her stomach, "not even any scarring. I never road-tested this before. Thank Christ, it works. I was beginning to wonder, since — and this really annoys me — the knack only kicks in with major injuries. Trivial things like blisters from new shoes take the old-fashioned route. In the good old days, they'd heal inside twenty-four hours because of the Reset, but now no such luck. Remember this?"

The reporter held up a finger wrapped with a white plastic patch that had little anime girl characters dancing across it. They looked like Pretty Amazonia.

"*PreCure?*" Jack guessed.

"Not the Band-Aid, the finger — the Band-Aid is PA's, and beside the point."

"Ahh, that paper cut."

"Yep. Same one I showed you the other day. The thing got infected, meaning it's taken longer to fix than a gunshot wound to the stomach. The buggers who gave me the unbalanced self-healing power told me this was its Achilles' heel, but I think they did it as a twisted joke."

"I thought your power was to be a super-snoop. The Brick told me."

"Everyone believes that, but the Brick also isn't the sharpest knife in the drawer. Doesn't take any special skill to be a journalist, or a hack detective. Shame is, I didn't end up with Wolverine's retractable claws — they'd make great letter openers."

"So which doctor do I have to thank for saving my life?"

"My sister."

Jack raised his eyebrows. At least that didn't hurt so much.

"Pretty Amazonia. Yes, we're sisters — go figure. She was a surgeon once, before being struck off for what the government said was unethical behaviour."

"If you don't mind me asking, what kind of unethical behaviour?"

"Saving the life of someone the authorities had blacklisted.

Anyway, back to the here and now, PA stitched you and me up both."

Gypsie-Ann shrugged. "Me, she didn't need to sew. As I mentioned, I would've healed all by myself — but I think she got her jollies sticking in the needle."

Precisely then, Pretty Amazonia strode into the room, still in costume, but with a medical smock tied over the top.

"Ahh, my two favourite patients are awake."

"Your *only* patients — since we were unconscious when they delivered us to you."

"You never looked prettier." PA squinted her eyes in the reporter's direction and delivered up an insincere general-practitioner's smile. "By the way, I pinched some of your blood."

"What are you, a vampire?"

"Not for me, idiot — it was for SC — to help speed his recovery."

"Like I don't need to speed my own."

"What're you complaining about? You'll live."

"I hate doctors."

The taller sister glowed triumphant.

"Oh, there's something else, before I forget," she said, as she came back to earth, delved into the single pocket on her smock, and held up a silver object between two fingers. "Here's the bullet. Thought you might want to keep it."

"I'm not one for sentimental jewellery."

PA ignored the comment to stroll over to Jack's bed. "How're you feeling, hon? I can imagine there's still some pain."

She slapped his forehead with the back of her hand, possibly checking for signs of a fever, and then shoved a thermometer under his armpit. The woman had the bedside manner of a bear.

"Yeah, I'm aching all over — but thank you. Really," Jack mumbled during the rough check-up. "Where are we? A hospital?"

"Are you kidding? The Blandos won't allow us anywhere near a regular hospital — too afraid of reprisal attacks by other Capes, they say, but I suspect they think we're dirty or something. We're in a side-wing of Equalizers HQ, a clinic the Big O put together. Never thought we'd need it."

"I need to use the loo," Gypsie-Ann piped up.

"Go ahead. You're not getting a bed-pan from me — out in the corridor, second door on the right."

After the reporter left the room, PA dragged over a chair to sit beside Jack.

"You know you had us worried for a while there? The shrapnel wound, smoke inhalation, two busted ribs, a punctured lung. Quite a collection."

"Thank you."

"You keep saying that. For what? Worrying?"

"For saving my sorry arse."

"We're a team."

"We are." Still, the man sighed. "By the way, you were right. About Louise, I mean."

"I'm often wrong. You sure, hon?"

"She hates me."

"Only if you let her." The woman put her large, elegant hand over his and she granted him a minor smile. "Get some sleep. You need it."

"Okay. But tell me something."

"What now?"

"Anything."

"You want a bedtime story?"

"That'll be the day." Jack pried himself loose and smiled back from the pillow. "So. Tell me about your *Pretty Cure* shindig — Brick's warned me I'll be bored stiff, but I'm up for the grand master challenge. Might help me sleep, anyway."

The woman shook her head, laughing. "He's right. And you *do* want a bedtime story."

"C'mon, why not? It's about time I learned something more about you — in the name of trust and all that jazz."

"You sure about that?"

"The evening is young."

"That sounds disturbingly suave. Don't you have better things to do, like roll over?"

"Right now, there's nothing better than getting to know a teammate who sweetly patched me up not so long ago."

"All right, all right — don't make me ill."

PA leaned back, hands clasped behind her head. She blew her cheeks out, and then sighed.

"When I was a little kid, my dad was transferred to Tokyo on business. He was a specialist in beetles — don't you dare laugh — and the Japanese islands had a lot of these. My mum, my sister and I went with him. We ended up spending several years in Japan. This was way before the Catastrophe."

"How many years are we talking?"

"Don't be cheeky. You want me to stop?"

"No. Understood."

"Good. The most popular girls' anime series on TV when we arrived was a show called *Pretty Cure*, or *PreCure*."

"Based on a manga comic?"

"No, they skipped that route." She pursed her substantial lips. "At the time — I later learned — things were dire for televised animation in Japan. Most of the innovative studios were stuck in hibernation or kept their claws sheathed. Looking back now, it's clear the industry was going through a rough patch like that which crippled the newspaper, magazine and music industries — but I'll leave appraisal to better qualified people."

"Ancient history," Jack said. Before he was born.

"Still. There was a bright note here, one series on the telly that kept me amused and more than a little infatuated."

"*Pretty Cure.*" Jack frowned, suddenly less confident. "*PreCure?* — Which one should I be using?"

"Either is okay. I tend towards *PreCure* in spite of my name. Anyway, the series had different story arcs and my favourite, the one I first watched, was *HeartCatch PreCure!*"

"How old were you again?"

"Four."

"Ah-hah."

"Don't mock, SC — it doesn't suit you."

He laughed, and then grimaced. "Ouch. Point taken. Physically as well."

"Karma."

"I know, I know. But it's your fault. I'm still awake."

"Then prepare to be bored senseless as I run through the season synopsis of *HeartCatch*."

Pretty Amazonia untied her smock, took a deep breath, and plunged straight in.

"The yarn started with our shy, upright schoolgirl heroine Tsubomi, who is suddenly magically endowed with special powers and becomes Cure Blossom, swathed in a pink costume. Trusty neighbour and fashion-minded sidekick Erika, as the all-blue Cure Marine, joins her. Five months into the series, the third heroine emerged with the gold-hued, androgynous Itsuki, Cure Sunshine, who dressed in boy's clothes but shone in her girly Pretty Cure persona. Later on, a reticent, quietly cantankerous and quite possibly bitter senior high-school student, Yuri, was revealed to be the purple-shrouded Cure Moonlight — the predecessor of our other three champions. Turns out she lost her powers in a big battle with Dark Pretty Cure. That's a long story for another day — or not."

The man's light snoring was her only response.

"Mister B was right," she muttered, "it does bore people senseless." That was when she noticed the hand on her right shoulder, and she looked up.

"I never thought you had it in you," Gypsie-Ann said. "You do care."

Hesitantly, Pretty Amazonia placed her fingers around her sister's. "He's a good kid."

"You're not too shabby yourself."

"Quiet, you."

#154

"Junior — wake up."

Jack came to with a pile of shoddily paved cobbling and a pair of blue eyes six inches from his face.

"The stuff that dreams are made of," he muttered.

"Awright, wiseguy. Rise an' shine."

With some assistance from his partner, Jack sat up on the cot. The sun outside the window was low on the horizon, mostly obscured behind other skyscrapers.

He noticed Gypsie-Ann standing in the doorway to the room, fully clothed and completely recovered. She raised her small felt hat as a greeting.

"Where's our erstwhile doctor?" Jack asked.

"Off checkin' into some leads," said the Brick. "Broad saved yer life, y'know."

"I know. But I seem to remember you coming to Rotters HQ to get me."

"Yeah, well." Jack believed the Brick would have blushed, if that were possible. "Gave me ample opportunity t'knock some heads together an' souvenir their flag. Shame 'bout Bulkhead — we had some classic tussles in our time, levellin' entire city blocks." He looked around the room. "Now I wonder how many Blando casualties ended up in a hospital or morgue. But we have news, big bloody news, that I been itchin' t'share with ya both."

The Equalizer paced the room, footfall reverberating.

"They've had the bastard locked up overnight at City Hall. You hear me? *That* bastard. The one we've all been lookin' fer. Kid was blamed well right — it is a Blando responsible."

"The man in the red hat?"

"Dunno 'bout his preference fer headwear, but the cops caught 'im red-handed with the smokin' revolver, sittin' next to Gypsie-Ann here's twitchin' body — before you recovered, I mean."

The reporter shrugged. "If twitching was all I did, that's okay.

You mean that tiny old man is the Cape-killer?" Disbelief decanted in her tone.

The comment was, however, a surprise to Jack — who remembered a face not particularly ancient beneath the brim of that red Stetson. "What tiny old man?"

"Your lead," Gypsie-Ann reminded him. "The Sekrine thing."

The Equalizer's eyes widened as he shot over a look. "The Professor?"

"You knew about him? You could've warned me, Jack. Turns out the name wasn't Sekrine at all — it was Erskine. The Professor's first name is Abe. *Abraham Erskine.* Ring any bells?"

"Creator of the Super-Soldier Serum...and thereby Captain America." The Prof's liberal use of 'Vita-Rays' pounded inside Jack's head. God. Louise.

"Hang on, hang on," fussed the Brick. "Do I get a say? I thought Josef Reinstein was the bloke behind that nutty Super-Soldier whatsis."

"Reinstein's an alias," Gypsie-Ann shot his way.

"Alias, schmalias. If I could just get me paws on 'im fer a sweet second..."

"But this doesn't make sense." Shaking his head, Jack looked at both people. "We're talking about a fictitious character from a comicbook."

"In case yer forgot, cuddles — the whole damn domain's a work o' four-colour fiction."

"Not to mention, this is a fictitious character so alarmed by our discovery that he put a slug in my gut."

"*He* shot you?"

"From as close as you are to me now, using an old British gun, a Webley."

"Don't make 'em like they used to. An' guess what? This crumb-bum Cape-killer's askin' fer you, junior."

"Me?"

The brickwork on the Equalizer's face formed a remarkably fluid sneer. "Won't speak to no one, he reckons, 'cept fer Southern Cross."

His partner balked. "Bloody hell."

"Tho' he calls you Jack, like you an' him're old mates."

"Are you?" Gypsie-Ann demanded to know.

"No — not really. I mean, I guess we're kind of friends."

The woman bristled. "You often buddy-up with homicidal types?"

Jack stared straight ahead, confused. "I had no idea."

"Cops're spittin' chips," the Brick went on. "They already didn't trust us — now the buggers're demandin' to know the connection, but more important they want a confession from the ol' man. So. You up to headin' down there tonight?"

"Tonight? Thought I was under suspension — about to be shipped back to Melbourne?"

Gypsie-Ann's ire turned to laughter, like the earlier spat didn't matter. "Right now, none of us can go back, even if we wanted to."

"An', even better, we got a call from head-judge Fargo an' his lawyer buddy Paul Garrett — Erskine's goin' before a grand jury tomorrow mornin', bright an' early, and they need him talkin' before that." The Brick summoned up a token grin. "So, La Suspension's waived — pendin' yer li'l chat."

"Convenient," muttered the Equalizer, stretching to his right and wincing with the pain coming from his abdomen.

"Innit?"

"Still hurt?" the woman in the doorway inquired.

Jack nodded. "Like someone roundhoused my insides with a four-by-two. But I think I'm cool. No choice." He was fretting about Louise and, to an admittedly lesser degree, her father-in-law. Even so, he did like the guy. This was screwy. "I have to get down there, right?"

"I'll give you a lift," the reporter said.

"Thanks, that'd be great. You coming, Brick?"

"Nah, not sure I could control meself. By the by, y'better change clothes, junior — much as you look dashin' in them there hospital duds."

"Suit?"

"Costume."

"Fuck that."

"*Nada*. Judge Fargo's explicit orders, an' even I don't go up against that fella. He has a wrath that puts Khan's t'shame."

"Straight?"

"Fair dinkum."

"All right, all right — now I'm on edge, but no mask. Everyone knows what I look like. Where the hell is the outfit, anyway?"

The Brick lobbed a plastic bag onto his lap.

"Thing was a torn-up mess after the accident, but PA got Phineas to fix a newbie fer ya. Looks better'n ever. He even added in the missing star."

#155

They barrelled up at City Hall some time around seven-thirty and were thereafter escorted to the basement by two uniforms bearing bronze badges that read Sydney Nicholls and James Bancks. Otherwise, the duo aped mute or declined to speak.

Jack noticed the poster with its 'Cape-Free Zone' motif as they walked through cluttered space on the way to the holding cells. Captain Robert Kahn was awaiting them there, a warm expression planted on his face amidst the overall chill.

Nicholls and Bancks made themselves scarce, leaving the visitors with Kahn and Forbush.

"Stellar." The police captain nodded at the woman.

"Kahn," she said, returning the gesture, with a smile attached.

"Jack."

"Bob." The two men shook hands.

"Irv," Jack added, but was greeted with silence.

Kahn moved straight on. "Thanks for coming."

"Ta for the invite."

"I'm his plus-one," appended the reporter.

"Remarkably lively, for a corpse. Thought you would've been two feet under by now — you looked on death's door yesterday, when the medics carted you out of that antique store."

"I recover quick. Don't sound so sad."

"Freak," Detective Forbush finally growled under the moustache, from his guard-position by a nearby metal door.

"Shut up, Irv."

"Right you are, boss."

"Anyway," Kahn reflected, "one less case for us, and one less murder on the old man's rap-sheet."

Jack stopped before a large glass window — standard issue police interrogation room stuff, no doubt with a mirrored surface on the flipside — that looked onto a bland, Spartan room brightly lit with fluorescent globes. The only furniture there was a table, two chairs, and a pint-sized old man.

"Do you have some kind of bugging/intercom device for the room?" the Equalizer asked.

"We have this."

Kahn opened a cupboard to reveal a batch of wires, a single speaker, and a German Magnetophon reel-to-reel that was already recording, spooling a 7-inch reel of $\frac{1}{4}$-inch-wide Fe_2O_3 tape.

"Switch it off."

"What?"

"I said switch it off — or I'm out of here."

Kahn studied the other man's face for several seconds. "I could lose my job or my other eye if something untoward goes down in there. You're not planning to do anything untoward, are you?"

"Trust me."

"Not the easiest thing to do when it comes to your garden-variety Capes."

Jack nodded. "I know — so let me take responsibility." He reached over to rip out all the wiring. The speaker fell off the wall and the Magnetophon stopped rolling.

"Untoward," said Gypsie-Ann from over his shoulder.

Kahn inspected the damage and tut-tutted. "Judge Fargo won't be happy."

"Yeah, I can imagine. Think he'll already have complaints about my choice of wardrobe — sorry."

"Tell him that. He demanded something for the Grand Jury tomorrow."

"I'll get the Professor to talk to you. Let's see what he wants with me first." Jack went to the door but found Detective Forbush's arm blocking his path.

"You hurt him, I hurt you," again growled the officer. Jack wondered whether, were he to shave off the moustache, he'd still be able to do that.

"Shut up, Irv," Kahn ordered.

"No," the Equalizer responded as he looked at both men. "Irv's right. I'm glad to see the Prof is being looked after. Thanks."

With that, Jack opened up, strolled into the other room, and shut the door.

Gypsie-Ann flew straight to the looking glass, pressing her nose close.

"What're you doing, Stellar?"

"Shhh."

#156

In the centre of this room, Professor Sekrine was planted at the well-worn, stained pine table, his hands palm-down on top of it, wrists held close together by a pair of metal handcuffs.

He was wrapped in a baggy, beige-coloured cardigan that had leather patches on the elbows, and a white shirt beneath with the top button done up.

There was a half-full paper cup next to him, a Jolly Roger-brand teabag label hanging out. He looked chipper for someone accused of multiple-murder, and who'd spent the past twenty-four hours in the pen.

Even so, the man's hair was more awry than ever before.

"Jack!" he called out, while he ran eyes from his visitor's head to toe. "I say, this is wonderful. Nice to see that you dispensed with Captain America's little wings and bright-red apparel — although I notice you kept the stars, and they have multiplied."

The Equalizer settled into the chair on the other side of the square table. A perceptive look passed between the two men and they smiled.

"You knew I was a Cape."

"I had my suspicions."

"Why?"

"The unusually broad shoulders, the strong jaw line. You aren't built like regular people, Jack, and I couldn't picture you dabbling with steroids or being a fitness nut."

"Ah."

"Oh, and there was a slip you made, referring to Capes as heroes. Most people here wouldn't think so."

Jack laughed. "Are you okay? The cops are looking after you?"

"Although the tea they serve is rather — er — wishy-washy, the police have been most civil."

"Possibly because some of them sympathize with what you've done. Killing Capes."

"Is that what you believe?"

"You shot Gypsie-Ann."

"Who?"

"The reporter."

"Oh, yes. A necessity."

"What about the others?"

"I have only Miss Stellar's blood on my hands."

"She recovered."

"She did?" The Professor looked genuinely relieved. "Good show!"

"Thought you said her death was a necessity?"

"Given how things ended up, with my presence in this place, it doesn't really matter. Tell me, how is Louise taking all of this?"

"I don't know."

"Pardon?"

"The last time I talked to her, she made it clear she doesn't want to see me. I think we're finished."

"Oh. She did not tell me." The elderly man allowed his eyes to wander, before fixing them back on his visitor. "The Cape business."

"Mmm."

"Jack, you must — you *must* — ensure she is all right. Promise me."

"I'll do what I can."

"That sounds unpleasantly like a brush-off."

"It's not a brush-off. A lot depends on her willingness to see me."

"And on how persuasive you are."

Nodding, Jack had other matters to discuss. "Professor, I need to ask you — why'd you shoot Gypsie-Ann? She's a friend, a good guy."

"Are we being recorded?"

The Equalizer shook his head. "Switched off."

"Are you sure about that?"

"I kind of ripped out the circuits."

"Bravo." The Professor leaned forward on his leather-cushioned elbows. "Well, then, allow me to make my point: there is no such

278

thing as a good guy. I can trust nobody, not with this."

"With what?"

"There's the rub. If I tell you, I defeat my own philosophy — I trust in you. And yet, given the circumstances," he sat back and raised his cuffed wrists, "I believe I shall have to do just that. Jack, I made a mess of things. I was not supposed to draw any attention, but when the lady reporter came snooping about the shop and sprouted the Erskine name, I panicked. Unforgivable. I was simply trying to protect our girl."

"Louise? — Why?"

"Because," the old man said in a soft voice, barely audible, while he leaned as far across the table as he could and Jack moved closer to meet him halfway, "she's the Aerialist."

#157

By the time she arrived home, Louise's world had turned upside down, as well as inside out and frayed some.

She'd met up with a recently divorced friend, former model Millie Collins and her artist sister Ruth, and crashed the night at the girls' place, consuming cocktails while commiserating together about lost love and the stupidity of men. When she went to work in the morning — her last day at the bank — it was at the mercy of a hangover and an uneasy stomach.

Straight after she finished up and packed a box of her things, Louise stepped onto the street and saw a newspaper headline on a placard at a nearby street kiosk:

SUSPECT CAPE-KILLER IN CUSTODY!!

While the girl normally shied away from the broadsheets, on this occasion she wasn't able to resist. After she looked at the picture on the front page and blanched, she bought a copy, rapidly skimmed through the accompanying article — and then reread it more carefully, horror seizing her.

Worse was to come.

Over on page two was a smaller story, a recap about a bombing three days before at the League of Unmitigated Rotters, one in which one Rotter had died, several others were wounded, and an Equalizer — Southern Cross — seriously so.

Louise didn't know when, exactly, she realized she had her knuckles in her mouth and was snivelling. She'd wiped her cheeks with a handkerchief and took off at a run.

Now, the paper was closed, folded and tucked under an arm as she fetched the house keys from her bag, unlocked the security door, slowly stepped upstairs, and went to the apartment.

She couldn't — wouldn't — believe what the article said, with all the 'alleged', 'claimed' and 'possible' disclaimers holding together the text. That the Prof had been systematically murdering Bops over the past two months. That he was a cold-blooded killer, a vigilante, a complete stranger.

And Jack — she had to know if the man was all right; prayed he was.

Louise would've gone directly to City Hall, except for some bizarre impulse that told her to swing by home to make sure it wasn't all some rude coincidence, to see if the Prof wasn't there, fiddling with his contraptions and his Vita-Rays, and whether or not Jack had called.

Instead, she found this darkened apartment, and the shop downstairs had yellow police tape across the entrance, along with an official poster warning people to stay away from these premises.

Outside in the quiet evening, standing smoking a cigarette beneath a streetlamp near the front door to the brownstone, was a man in a brown coat and red hat.

"Hey, miss," he said as Louise stepped past. "There's only two things in this world that a 'real man' needs: a cup of coffee and a good smoke. Got the ciggie, but not the Joe. Can you lend me a dime?"

The girl stared at him, blinking, wasn't sure she understood the question. "I'm sorry," she said. "I have somewhere I need to be."

"Sure you do. Well, aside from the Joe, my head honcho wants to have a chinwag."

"Is that so?" The mention of chins made Louise suddenly aware she was in the frame of mind to bust another jaw.

"My boss says to tell you that the lives of the two blokes in your life — the old codger's and that poor excuse for a Bop, Southern Cross — hang in the balance." The man pushed the hat to the back of his head, revealing an unremarkable face. "Says to tell you he can help save both of them."

"Really?" the girl uttered, resolve broken in an instant.

"I have a car over there, the yellow Plymouth. You coming?"

"This man...your boss...he can really help?"

"Sure as houses, miss. C'mon."

#158

"Hang on — stop. This is insane. How can a Blando be a Cape?"

"Allow me to explain," the Professor said while Jack sought to grapple with the lowdown he'd been thrown in the old man's previous sentence. "You're closer to the truth than you realize. The Reset is equitable with a disease, and as with any disease there are those who are immune. In this case, not the body — cutting oneself shaving would always mend overnight compliments of the Reset — but the electrochemical signalling of the mind. In here."

The old man tapped the right side of his forehead.

"I am one of those people. For some time, I self-indulgently believed I might be the single person in Heropa who could remember and think with complete continuity beyond a twenty-four-hour timeframe — save for the Capes, of course. I was a scientist in the employ of Metro College. While my peers would begin work each and every morning, puzzling over devices and formulas they'd started assembling the day before — scratching their heads, with absolutely no memory of these things — I was blessedly able not only to encode and store, but to retrieve this information and work on my projects for weeks on end."

The old man suddenly sneezed, and wiped his nose.

"Excuse me."

"Go on," Jack urged.

"Well, it goes without saying that such behaviour was eventually noticed. The chancellor of the college, Mister Wright, got whiff of my progress—"

"Donald Wright?"

"Yes, that's the man. Mister Wright summoned Major Patriot to the campus one afternoon. A Friday, I remember, and he deigned to meet me at the Kozy Kampus Koffee Shop."

Sitting up straight, Jack nodded. "Major Patriot? I've heard about him. Wasn't he was the leader of some older Heropa super group? Can't remember their name."

"The Crime Crusader Crew."

"Yeah, that's it. So all this was — when?"

"Four years ago, less than a year after Heropa went online. Back then my memory was so much more competent — I could also remember that big baptismal event. Oh, my. All the pretty lights, out of darkness."

The Professor looked wistful.

"Anyhow, I believe I mentioned — didn't I? — that Major Patriot stepped in for a chat. I did mention it, yes, and the man was extremely alarmed to learn of my immunity. The Reset was a form of control, you see, of maintaining the status quo and preventing Blandos from getting ideas above their station. We were created in the image of our designers. All the same flaws and failings, but also similar dreams and aspirations. The Major, as the original designer of Heropa, did not wish his creations to develop any further along these lines than the basic programming window allowed for with the Reset."

Jack recalled his discussion with Gypsie-Ann. The Equalizer was itching for this old man to get back on track, to address his daughter-in-law and what the hell had happened there — the Aerialist? — Louise? But he still had other questions that needed answering.

"I thought Sir Omphalos was the co-creator of Heropa."

"No, no, he was a junior partner in development. Important, to be sure, but the real creative genius rested with the Major."

"So what was the outcome of this fireside conversation you two shared?"

"Major Patriot realized, through my existence, that the Reset was not infallible. He therefore gifted me a task, a commission as it were, to discover an alternative means to complement the Reset, one that could be used to control other people we found to be resistant or immune. That was how I cobbled together a machine that gave out certain emissions. 'Vita-Rays', the Major called them — his sadistic joke, since these emissions do nothing to revitalize and empower the body or the soul. Rather, a direct opposite. They act as a sedative, a memory-loss agent, and I was coerced first of all to employ myself as a guinea pig, and then others like me."

"Coerced...how?"

"The Major was a very persuasive man. I was under no delusion that he would not kill me if I refused to collaborate in his schemes."

"But he was a Cape."

"Precisely. Not all people see them as heroes, and most of them hardly act that way."

"So you collaborated."

"For several months, about a year, yes."

"And then?"

"I could not continue. This was channelling God, without accounting for the consequences — and then having me play Satan's little helper when the consequences jumped up and bit them on the *derrière*. I was appalled with myself, as much as with this evil man. Evil, Jack. Pure and simple. The Reset was a cheat, a programming blink that kept things from naturally developing the way they should. Vita-Rays added to this cheat. Not only against us, but also undercutting Capes — without a fear of demise, how can any person truly appreciate the value of another's life? Finally, I'd had enough. I approached a third party, a different Cape. Sir Omphalos I believe you knew."

"Only by reputation."

"Well, that is a shame. This was an individual far more humane, understanding and appreciative of the situation. I told him about the Vita-Rays project, and the man was scandalized. He helped me to escape from the university, provided a new identity, and set me up in the shop. Lee was a good Cape, a bright spark in this madness."

Mention of the name floored Jack's wayward thoughts. He focused again on the old man's mush, eyes wide. "Lee — ? Louise's husband?"

"Oh no, dear boy, that was a ruse, something I cooked up to appease the girl when her memories started to bubble back to the surface one time."

The Equalizer sat back. "What does that mean?"

"It means I'm getting ahead of myself, so let us do just that, since time is precious. Allow me to fast-forward. There was a day, around two months ago, when Sir Omphalos came to visit me. I had not seen the man for three years, and on this occasion he was not alone — over his shoulder Lee hefted another Cape, one dressed in a flight suit and a helmet that reminded me of the Rocketeer. Did you ever read *The Rocketeer*?"

"No."

"You should. Marvellous stuff. Well, anyhow, this helmet reminded me of the comic. Once I removed the thing, I discovered a pretty redhead and she was unconscious. Lee told me that the turbulence of a long fall from high altitude had knocked her senseless — said he barely had time to reach the girl before she struck terra firma. That was when he showed me something truly shocking — the gentleman pushed back her hair and there, on the spine, between the shoulder-blades, was a black letter 'p'."

"A Blando."

"Yes."

"But I still don't understand — how?"

"The lady was a unique case. No special powers, obviously, but a spark, a drive to make her mark in this world. Lee had recognized that passion, inducting her into the Crime Crusaders Crew as Bullet Gal. She was a brunette then, and people believed she was from Melbourne, just like all the other Capes."

Struggling to get his head around this revelation, Jack zeroed in on what he already knew. "The Big O busted up the Crime Crusaders to establish the Equalizers, at which stage Bullet Gal changed her costume, name, and obviously her hair colour — became the Aerialist. Why?"

The Professor nodded while he rapped his fingers on the wooden surface of the table. "This is indeed where things get murky. When he came to my house, as I say two months back, Lee told me the woman had switched identities to elude somebody, but that the secret got out and this person, this pursuer, had discovered the truth."

"The attempt on her life — sabotaging the jetpack."

"I believe so, yes."

"Did the Big O give you a name?"

"No."

Jack thought hard, attempting to put everything together, but there were too many loose ends. "Prof, do you think this somebody, this pursuer, was Major Patriot?"

"The man I remember was certainly capable. He was furious about the dissolution of the Crime Crusaders Crew three years ago, and very publicly stormed off — it was in all the papers, though the next day everyone forgot. The Reset did have its uses."

The Professor chuckled.

"After that? I'm not sure. No one has since seen or heard from the Major. I doubt he stayed in Heropa, but Lee certainly feared somebody. It was trepidation I saw in his eyes, an unusual mental state in such a man."

Leaning on the table, face in his hands yet still watching the prisoner, Jack sighed. "So. What did the three of you cook up? ... About the Aerialist and her stalker problem, I mean."

"Lee asked me to take her in, to hide her," the Professor responded. "I complied, of course, since there were things I'd done that did not make me proud. This was an opportunity for penance, if not redemption. Lee knew about my work with Vita-Rays and together we hatched a cunning plan. Though she was immune to the Reset, prolonged exposure to Vita-Rays had the desired effect — the Aerialist forgot all about her old life of heroics and derring-do. She became a far simpler individual, placed out in public where no one would dream she'd hide. Became the bank clerk you met. A tub of bleach and a pair of glasses from the shop made the world of difference — and little did Major Patriot realize we'd use his precious Vita-Rays in such subversive fashion, to hide and protect someone he'd despise."

"Louise." Jack pulled away, horrified. Louise.

"Mitzi was the real name. We changed that, obviously, too."

"And what about her?" The Equalizer glared over the table at the older man. "You said she was unconscious when she was brought to you — did she have any say in this improvised witness-protection scheme? Did you stop to ask her?"

Lowering his gaze, the Professor shook his head. "No. Lee knew she'd refuse."

"So you decided for her."

"Yes, but as I say—"

"Making you both no better than Major Patriot."

"Well, yes...and no. Lee said this felon on Mitzi's tail had contacts. She couldn't exactly leave Heropa, her life was in danger, and we had to act fast. As fast as possible, before something happened, do you understand?" The old man was dithering now, his fingers entwined and eyes losing focus. "It was this or probable death, I think."

"You think?"

Jack kicked back the chair and got to his feet.

"From what I see and hear, she was more than capable of looking after herself — even after you stole her memories, she broke a man's jaw. I can't believe you did this. I can't believe I looked up to you. You had no right to put her through that, say what you will. We're done here."

"Wait, wait, wait. What about our girl?"

"*Our* girl? Don't ever use that expression round me again. I swear, I'll knock you out — I don't care how old you are."

"You're right. Of course, you're right. Yet she remains in grave danger."

"I'll handle it."

"Thank you."

"Not for your sake, for hers."

The old man nodded, his head bowed and eyes on the table.

"Jack, a piece of advice," he said in a small voice. "You should not judge people so quickly, without first taking a long, hard look in the mirror."

Jack exhaled, short and sharp.

"Don't worry yourself, mate. I've done my fair share of that." In spite of better ideas, his anger diminished as he first glanced at the mirrored window on one wall, and then down at the miniscule man at the table. "Listen, give the cops what they need to know. Tell them you didn't kill the Capes — hell, maybe even tell them the Big O stuck you in hiding. But leave Louise out of the yarn. The police might go easy on you, if they believe your story and Gypsie-Ann doesn't press charges. But I'll tell you one thing — this will be all over the news, and people won't forget anymore. If he's still in Heropa, Major Patriot would know about you by now and he doesn't sound like the forgiving kind of guy. I'm not sure I like your chances, but we'll try to keep an eye out."

"That's fair enough. I understand. Please find Louise. Please protect her."

Crossing to the steel door, Jack nodded.

"I will."

#159

Jack zipped straight past Kahn, the other cops, plus Gypsie-Ann —
"All yours," he breezed — and then thought twice and doubled
back. "By the way, the guy you're looking for isn't the Professor. The
real trickster wears a brown coat and a red hat, a Stetson."

"The old man told you this?" Kahn asked.

"No, I knew already."

"You did? Could've saved us some trouble by disclosing this a
quarter hour ago." The police captain was eyeballing his busted-up
recording equipment.

"Sorry — I wasn't sure then."

"But you are now."

"Yep."

"Great. And Sekrine isn't our man?"

"Nah, he's a couple of generations too long in the tooth."

"So," piped up Detective Forbush, rounding out the commentary
with a sneer, "what fancy shade of red are we s'posed to keep our
eyes peeled for?"

"Fire engine. You won't miss it."

"Hard to," Kahn agreed. "What do you have on him?"

"Saw him kill Bulkhead, and possibly he planted the bomb that
did in Sinistro. The others I'm not so sure about."

"Working alone?"

"I don't know."

"Bop or civilian?" That was Forbush, lobbing in his two cents
again.

"I'd put even money on this being a Blando."

"Blando... Pfft."

"Civilian, then. But I haven't asked the fella."

Kahn poured himself coffee from a nearby vacuum brewer.
"Nothing else to go by? No silly walks or — better yet — facial
scarring? No eyepatches like mine?"

"Hard to tell. The hat's always running interference, and the only time I saw him without it was in a darkened street. Average height, average build. Average everything, aside from the Stetson. Didn't see a patch."

"Okay, I'll put out an APB on the red hat. Round up all the usual milliners."

Jack grinned, but kept the applause in check. "Funny. One thing, though — maybe keep it on the sly. Tell only officers you trust."

Pushing forward from his place by the door to stand toe-to-toe with the Equalizer, Detective Forbush tried his best at intimidating. "What's the matter, bub? You don't trust Heropa Police?"

"Sure I do," Jack muttered, unimpressed. "More worried the bastard will ditch the hat, if word gets out regarding a public witch-hunt for his peculiar headwear. Then he'll be just another—"

"Blando?"

"Face in the crowd."

Throwing up chubby hands, Forbush grimaced. "Boss, this's ridiculous. You really going to have us buskin' round town for a red-coloured boater?"

"Bet your bottom dollar I am."

"Next thing, these Bops'll have you lunging through loops."

"Enough, Irv. You have a job to do." Kahn's subordinate backed away, catching hint of the impatience. "All righty, we'll keep it under the hat."

Gypsie-Ann let out a groan. "Can we ditch the Panama puns?"

The police captain grinned. "Yeah, yeah, I know. Sorry — slipped out. Moving right along, we'll get on it."

"Thanks," Jack said. "And one more thing — be careful. From what I've seen so far, he packs everything from explosives to a blackjack."

Kahn chuckled softly. "Understood. If push comes to shove fireworks-wise, we'll hand-pass him to you lot — once we succeed in tracking him down, I mean."

"Fair enough. D'you have a phone I can use?"

"Corridor. Try not to break it."

The Equalizer left them outside the Professor's interrogation room and located an old, boxy Western Electric 234G 3-Slot payphone on one wall in the passage.

After pushing in a coin and dialling the operator, he was put through to Louise's apartment address.

Jack had a half-baked idea about what to say, but the girl had left no delusions of patching up their short-term romance. He'd decided to play it business-like instead, warn her of possible danger, and offer to lend a hand.

Conflicting with this in his head was the revelation that, in all likelihood, Louise didn't need his help — especially if she recovered her memories. He wasn't sure the Vita-Rays had a permanent effect, and hadn't thought to ask.

Once again, however, the Equalizer dithered while the phone continued to ring. Should he tell her everything? 'Hi, just found out you were once a Cape yourself, even though you're a Blando'? She'd hang up in his ear — hell, he would do the same if the tables were reversed. But the danger to the girl could be far more than merely possible. Whatever the telephone discussion, he needed to see her urgently.

After the twentieth ring, the operator squeezed back onto the line.

"I'd say the lady isn't home, wouldn't you?" she offered in a cheeky drawl, and then severed the connection. Jack placed the phone back on the hook, mulling as he retrieved his coin.

"So the Aerialist is still with us?"

Jack turned to find Gypsie-Ann leaning back against the beige plaster wall, legs crossed in a relaxed pose, but a dark look in her eyes.

"You heard?"

"Didn't need to — an old talent, one I picked up once upon a time when I worked as a rehab officer at a school for disabled kids."

"Lip-reading."

"You'll make reporter yet."

"You told Kahn?"

"Surely you jest? I don't want to kill the story before it has time to unfold. What is this woman to you, Jack?"

"It's complicated. Can you drive us over to Hymie Heights?"

"Back there? I'm not overly fond of the place — in case it slipped your mind, that's where Erskine shot me."

"Are you in or out?"

"Sure I'm in. Nothing wrong with a whine every now and then. Besides, you'll be able to bring me up to speed regarding everything on the way over. About time, too."

#160

There was a large metal box under the glove compartment, pressed against Jack's leg, and this suddenly started to ding-a-ling.

"Can you get it?" asked Gypsie-Ann, hands on the steering wheel, a stiff breeze ruffling her hair.

"Get what?"

"The annoying ringing thing next to your knee."

When Jack bent over to peer closer at the box, he saw the words 'Motorola Bell System Pulsar IMTS Mobile Car Telephone' and discovered a chunky handset. Upon lifting this, the clamour and vibration ceased.

"Hello? ... Hello?" emitted a tinny voice.

"You're supposed to speak into it," the woman beside him muttered, as she turned a corner close by Swanson's Garage and Sam's Market. "The wonders of modern science."

Jack smiled at his own stupidity and stuck the handset against his ear. "Gypsie-Ann's car speaking."

"Kid?"

"Brick."

"Did you nail 'im?"

"False lead."

"Rats! That's crummy." Jack heard some kind of crunching on the line. "Was a report on the radio," the other Equalizer remarked, between what sounded like mouthfuls of food. "Mmm! Not bad. Anyhow, seems there's a full-on riot happenin' on Marty Goodman Drive, over near the harbour."

"A riot?"

"That's what I says. Capes — heroes fightin' Rotters, and by all reports trashin' the place." Louder chewing ensued. "Prob'ly bad blood over the unsolved murderin'. We're talkin' massive casualties to Blandos in the surroundin' area."

"Crap." Jack had twisted in his seat, felt a stabbing pain in the stomach, and flinched.

"You all right?" Gypsie-Ann asked, having glanced over from watching the road.

"I'm okay."

"Wuzzat?" That was the Brick.

"Nothing. We'll meet you down there, yeah?"

"Yep. PA is headed over. Prob'ly already made it, the way she clocks in her sprints." A loud click, and both the munching and the line went dead.

"Meet whom, where?" the reporter quizzed.

"The Brick and your sis — d'you know Marty Goodman Drive? Apparently, there's a crazy Cape riot underway."

"Do tell? Thought we were going to check up on the Aerialist."

Jack pondered that. "I know. But she wasn't home when I called from City Hall — can I try her now on this phone?"

"Sure, I'll charge it to my boss. Work-related, and all."

Going through a thankfully different operator, Jack let the phone ring ten times, before hanging up.

"I'd say she's out for an evening of champagne and cigarettes." Jack half-snarled this remark, a sour taste in his mouth, brewed with memories of Karl Burghos at the restaurant across the road from Louise's place and 'Handsome' Harry next door. There were plenty of fish to trawl, just outside her window.

"You really have it bad, don't you?" the reporter said, bearing half a smile as she drove.

"Doesn't matter how I feel. To Louise, I'm nothing more than a Cape."

"Have you told her anyway?"

"I tried."

"Obviously."

Looking out at the shop fronts they passed, Jack sighed. "I think she'll have to wait until this blows over. The Brick said there're a lot of innocent people being hurt."

"Your call, but there's nothing like a good bout of street anarchy to help sell papers."

Gypsie-Ann suddenly put her orange convertible in tyre-squealing reverse, and then did a U-turn — right in front of a truck that had to slam on its brakes.

#161

Having parked overly close to the corner of Newton Place and Maxwell Avenue, Gypsie-Ann Stellar shoved open the driver's side door and was all prepared to climb out, but then stopped and instead craned her neck. "Is it going to rain?"

"Why're you asking me?" Jack complained. "I have no idea." He hopped gingerly from the car, pausing at the kerb next to a waist-high portable pole. It was shaped like a lollipop, with signage on the bulbous round bit at the top reading NO PARKING FROM HERE TO THERE, and someone had scratched into its paintwork that 'Heidi Sladkin loves Frederick von Frankenstein'.

"Think I'll bring my brolly just in case," decided the reporter, just as Jack noticed the lollipop sign had started to wobble unassisted.

"Um...can I ask a question?"

"Not sure that's fair — you weren't so friendly with mine. But go on."

"Heropa doesn't cop earthquakes, does it?"

"No stress there."

"Really? Ground's shaking."

The reporter stepped up with a man's black umbrella over her shoulder and slowly looked about at other vibrating signage. "Oh. Yes."

"Not my imagination?"

"Not unless you're sharing it round."

"There's your reason." From out of nowhere, Pretty Amazonia had flashed to Jack's side and pointed to the sky. "All hell's about to bust loose and kick in some poor sucker's false teeth."

"Ye gods."

Roaring over the skyscrapers were a collection of magnificent flying machines.

Jack spotted three huge dirigibles, an overlarge biplane with ten propellers, a Botanachi DRHC Tilt Rotor, several anti-grav two-seaters, and a baker's dozen of individual Capes with jetpacks, rocket suits, strap-on helicopter hats, or jerry-rigged hang gliders. There were two distinct waves coming from north and south, and they were headed for one another — directly overhead. More would undoubtedly be approaching on foot.

"Heroes there," PA nodded in a northerly direction, "Rotters in the south-east. Looks like Rocket Scientist has been busy."

"He made all those contraptions?" Jack asked, stunned.

"I guess so."

"This doesn't augur well." Gypsie-Ann had been busy counting. "At least forty people — not including however many are inside those blimps."

"Getting together for a fun-filled reunion?" Jack optimistically suggested.

"Nah. More a second round o' fracas an' bloodshed." The Brick locked up his car a few metres away and joined the others spectating on the sidewalk. "First time round, they gutted half the neigh-bourhood, two blocks down, an' there were only a dozen of 'em. Now we got more'n twice that number. Nuts. Awright — clear as mud what we gotta do."

"Hide?" the reporter suggested.

"Wise sentiments. That, an' we ought'a deposit our cars some place safe."

Watching the forces about to converge, Jack shook his head. "No running, no hiding, and no parking elsewhere — we have to stop them."

"How, kid? Got yer own private army corps tucked up in yer pants?"

"And we haven't exactly got wings," cut in Pretty Amazonia. "Don't say you want us to join in this debacle — there're only three of us."

Gypsie-Ann glanced up at her sister. "Four."

"Gee, whiz, I feel so much safer. What difference can a quartet make, one of whom is armed with an umbrella?"

"Five minutes with me and this brolly might surprise you," the reporter muttered. "I've been brushing up on *yubiwaza*, the secret, amazingly easy art of self-defence that turns just one finger or your hands into a potent weapon of defence without any bodily—"

"Contact. And it only costs $1.98. For God's sake, if you're going to poke your head in anywhere, make it a gas oven rather than the classifieds of old comics."

Jack breathed out, barely listening, stumped, considering the lack of options. This was a busy part of town. There were office buildings and stores all round, cars bumper-to-bumper, and a flood of pedestrians stopped on the sidewalks, rubbernecking impending doom.

"No choice," the Equalizer began to say — but before anything substantial passed through his lips, a loud, rousing orchestral score drowned out everything. *What the hell?*

"Well, this's surreal," PA shouted above the ruckus, pointing to a speaker at the top of a nearby lamppost. "They're playing a bloody waltz on the city's emergency siren system."

"I know the music," bawled back the Brick. "It ain't a waltz, it's a polka — 'Hungarian Dance No. 6', by Johannes Brahms." He looked sheepish when he found the other three staring. "What? I seen a recital or three in me time."

"Fair enough," Gypsie-Ann said.

More proactively, Jack ventured, "Some kind of message?"

PA shook her head. "Some kind of pisstake, if you ask me."

Which was when all hell busted loose, above and beyond the raucous music. The Brick was hammered by some kind of explosives charge, he toppled back onto Pretty Amazonia, and she lay flattened on her back, red in the face, pinned beneath portable cement-work.

"Get off me, you big lug!"

"Soz, dollface," he muttered, trying to rise with Gypsie-Ann's assistance. "Do me a favour an' nail that bastard, junior."

Down the street Jack spotted the culprit, some kind of armoured robot on four legs, two mechanical hands sporting three fingers on extensible arms.

"Is that bastard a person?" he quizzed the others.

PA, who'd dragged herself free of her concrete paperweight, was busy straightening her bows but spared a moment to look in the same direction — and then rolled her eyes. "Oh, for crap's sake. It's Otaku Fuchikoma."

"Who?"

"Don't worry. Inside all that fancy military hardware and futuristic armour is one exceptionally dim-witted Rotter. We haven't got time for his annoying antics. Can you take care of this, hon?"

"Sure, I guess."

The Equalizer pointed his arm in the direction of the machine and blew it back the way it'd come — just as lightning bolts zigzagged between buildings, gale force winds erupted, plasma arced across the sky, and Capes of all shape, size and colour started brawling in the air.

Straight after a shop across the road exploded, a telephone pole slapped down at the Brick's feet the moment he regained them, forcing him to backtrack a few steps, while a crowd of people began pushing blindly past — screaming and shrieking as fire rained.

Sheltering both in the Brick's shadow and beneath her opened umbrella, Gypsie-Ann looked reasonably dismayed. "Um... I hate to come across chicken-hearted, but have any of you given further thought to high-tailing out of here?" she shouted to no one in particular.

Her sister laughed without mirth. "P'raps you could use your parasol, Mary Poppins."

"Crap that, and dispense with the jokes," Jack yelled back, clearly annoyed by the loud music, "we have to help these people."

Still dusting herself, Pretty Amazonia frowned. "This riffraff?"

"Now," Jack urged. "Come on, guys. Move it — let's get them headed down that street over there." He pointed to a narrow avenue that was partially sheltered by the tall buildings to either side. "Probably the safest place in all this madness."

"Right you are, boss-sir," responded the Brick, as he gave a brief look to PA. "You heard the man, lady — if ya got a few minutes to spare, it's time fer us to save humanity again." Strolling out in time to the waltz, holding aloft his big arms, the chunky Equalizer took up yelling at men and women while debris fell about. "Beat it, ya bums! Thataway!"

Jack was set to go lend a hand when he sensed PA hovering behind him. Glancing round, he noticed how her expression simmered.

"Since when did you start giving orders, *Jack*?"

"Any better notions?"

"Number one, we're way out of our league — and, secondly, you're hardly the type to be in charge."

"Not saying I am — so you take the lead."

"Why bother?"

Impatient to help the poor sods under attack, and equally steamed up, Jack turned a speedy circle to face the woman. "Because it's our job, our responsibility — to save innocent people."

"Not mine. I don't remember signing up for such rubbish."

There was a sonic boom, like someone nearby had broken the sound barrier, and the entire façade of a skyscraper crashed down with a roar onto a nearby street, concrete dust filling the air. Once it cleared, Jack saw people hanging from naked girders several storeys up; others stood, shocked, in offices now open to the elements.

"Shite, we haven't got time for this." He glared up at the woman. "For God's sake, make yourself useful, right now, or go home."

"Touché," Gypsie-Ann chimed in from over Jack's shoulder.

In answer, since she was wordless, the other woman quicksilvered it off the street. Jack caught a blur of lavender, and then there was neither sight nor sign in either direction.

The reporter leaned in close, speaking above the sound of squealing violins and peppered shouting. "Don't judge her just yet. In the meantime, let's try and do what we can."

Someone in a Technicolor cape fell out of the sky to slam headfirst into the asphalt in the middle of the road near the Brick, just as a hardware store went kablooey and showered glass and garden tools on people luckless enough to be nearby.

"Lightning bolt at eleven o'clock!" the Brick shouted from the other side of the street.

Jack and Gypsy-Ann looked about. "Bollocks!" Southern Cross yelped, "which bloody way is eleven o' cl—?"

A fork of electricity that danced across the boulevard cut him short, missing the Equalizer and his umbrella-wielding companion by only a metre, while several bystanders were sautéed.

Now pushed against him, the reporter had lost most of her calm. "Least we now know what time it is. This is getting really bloody hairy," she whined.

"At least you stayed."

"I always was the stupid sister."

Flames sizzled across rooftops as Capes laid into one another in mid-air. One man caught on fire and another dived beneath a plasma blast, straight into a wall. There were screams, insane cheers and jeers, all of this above and beyond the switch in music to 'Hungarian Dance No. 5'.

While they tried to round up stragglers, Jack and Gypsie-Ann were almost bowled over by a police officer on an Indian Chief motorcycle — Jack saw the hysteria etched into the cop's face as he raced past — but the reporter successfully fended him off with her brolly.

Of course these people were panicking. They needed a restorative.

With this fancy in mind, the Equalizer again pointed his arm straight, directed at the sky. Having performed a quick look-see to ensure no one was flying overhead, he then fired off his biggest explosive bolt yet. This might've almost removed his fingers, but it lit up the street, giving the terrified pause.

"Head that way!" Jack yelled, shaking his right arm in pain at the same time that he pointed with the left. "Stay calm! We're here to help, okay? Help us help you!"

"Fer the luvva Pete — move it, bozos!" boomed the Brick.

Once the three established some vague sense of order, even while the battle raged on in the wild blue yonder, Jack heard a crack and a scream above the rollicking chorus of stringed instruments in FA minor.

At first he didn't know which way to look, but seconds later saw that a boy had stumbled, or been pushed over, in the mad scrum — fifty-odd metres away. This kid sat there on his bum, tears in the eyes, nursing a bleeding knee. Above him, formerly secured to the third storey of an emporium, a huge neon-lit billboard sagged. Sparks flying, it broke away from the wall, dipping down at an accelerated pace toward the kid.

The Brick was closer, but he hadn't noticed — and there was no way his bulk would cover the distance in time. Jack and Gypsie-Ann were too far and could do nothing to stop this horror-in-motion.

"Oh, no," the reporter mumbled.

In a strange kind of slow-mo, the boy looked up, paled, covered his head with his hands — and then vanished inside a purple flash a split-second before the huge sign smashed into the ground and a veil of debris billowed.

Jack blinked several times.

"Knew you'd need me," Pretty Amazonia announced right beside him, to his left.

When Jack spun, he found she cradled the bewildered kid. "Jesus...you cut it close," her partner muttered, a grin etching itself into his face.

"Needed to get the tantrum out of my system."

"An old habit," Gypsie-Ann said. "I knew she'd be back."

"You could've told me," Jack responded.

"Think I inferred."

Meanwhile, the boy seated in PA's arms was staring up at his saviour. "You — you're Pretty Amazonia, ain't you?" he finally said, eyes huge.

"Yeah, yeah," the woman muttered, remembering to put him down.

"Wow — it's really you! Wait'll I tell the others! I'm Willie Marston, ma'am. Me an' my pals, Harry and Liz, we're putting together our own comicbook, honest to gosh, an' we've almost finished issue 1 — with you in spots as the main star."

"Get over it, kiddo. Not impressed."

"For you, ma'am, I'll roll over an' stay dead." The boy laughed out loud.

Sure, PA sounded more indifferent than ever, pushing supremely bored, but when Jack looked again he would've sworn she'd teared-up.

Then again, maybe it was the smoke.

The war between the Capes took a total of eight minutes to end. The pretty music trailed on thirty seconds longer, before it too subsided and there was an eerie silence.

Soon, sirens wailed and people screamed or moaned or cried, while further buildings collapsed. Entire city blocks had been ravaged, cars burned out on the streets, and there were dozens of bodies amidst the rubble.

In this context, the number of people the Equalizers had saved hardly mattered.

A crowd gathered at both ends of the street, helping survivors and clearing detritus, but when Jack approached to help they responded by pitching rocks at him. This forced the Brick to run interference, stones rebounding off his hide, as he shuffled his partner away from the scene and back to the others.

"Jack, you're such a bleeding-heart sentimentalist," PA complained, back to her best. "You remind me of the Big O. These people don't want your respect — they want you off their damned property."

#162

On the near horizon, fires still raged.

After a quick call from an undamaged payphone to see if Louise was home (she wasn't), Jack let Gypsie-Ann get on the blower to the *Patriot* with her eyewitness scoop, and he joined the other two Equalizers at an adjacent bar, since they'd shot down the Brick's recommendation of the chicken shawarma place next door.

A black sign above its front window spelled out the Neon Bullpen in baby blue luminous tube lights, and the owners had topped it off with a picture of an HB pencil. On their in-house sound system they were spinning Tom Jones's 'What's New, Pussycat?', an upbeat full stop to a long-winded evening.

"Think I need t'order one thousand, five hundred an' seventy-four gin an' tonics t'get over this inord'nate stink," bellyached the Brick, squeezed as he was into a tiny chair.

"Large ones?" Pretty Amazonia helpfully suggested.

"Let's go with jugs. Only way I'll feel jolly again, Christmas be damned."

Jack hopped onto a bench seat closer to the window and ventured a glance into the twilight. The skeleton of a zeppelin smouldered atop a ruined skyscraper three blocks down, and there were four red fire engines tackling the blaze. Hundreds more were down by the waterfront.

"All quiet on the Western Front," said Jack, "aside from all the people fighting fires."

"That's 'cos most o' the Capes're dead-meat."

"And a whole bunch of other people." Jack wasn't wearing his mask. There didn't seem any point.

"Gotta admit — I never seen anythin' like it."

"Soak it up. Doubt we will again," said PA.

Jack nodded. "Agreed. God, I hope not. The costumed moppets broke way too many toys."

"And service here sucks."

The Brick searched about for a waiter, head swivelling this way and that at a rapid pace, which remarkably made Jack laugh.

"I wouldn't serve us, either."

As 'What's New, Pussycat' segued into 'It's Not Unusual', the woman on the other side of the table focused in on him.

"You did good, Jack."

"You too."

"Eventually."

"Fat lot of help any of it was, though."

"Don't beat yourself up. You were right to coerce us into making the stand." PA looked down to the red and white chequered table-cloth, carefully sliding a fork next to a butter knife. "I think Mister B and I learned something from you — yeah, I'll admit it, you showed us our prejudices, and now we're trying to play catch-up."

"Glad we're together on this."

"Even so, learn something from us. About the girl — Louise. You have to let her go."

This subject again. The last thing he needed to hear right now. "Why the blazes would I do that?"

"Why? Because one day soon, the hopeless techs back in Melbourne will fix the Reset — and because when she forgets, it'll break your heart."

Next to him, the Brick fussed over a serviette but said zero. Agreement hung in the air.

"PA," Jack muttered, "just drop it."

"All right."

The unmasked Equalizer looked around this bar, thinking hard about nothing in particular and trying to shake the gloominess. "I doubt any of it matters, anyway — I'm pretty sure we're washed up."

"Still," PA insisted.

"I get you."

"But you don't like our lectures." She sighed.

"Shoo, Jack — go on, then, scoot over!"

Before the three knew what was afoot, Gypsie-Ann had muscled into a seat beside Southern Cross, and she turned to examine his face.

"Why the moping? You're alive, aren't you?"

"Debatable."

"Well, you look reasonably functional, more so than my poor umbrella."

"So your investment in *yubiwaza* didn't include accessories?"

The reporter tilted her head to one side. "Appreciate the moment. You could easily be one of those corpses out there — speaking of which, we missed the fun and hastily organized games of the funeral for all those dead Capes."

"They did that already?" Pretty Amazonia frowned. "The fight ended only, what, two hours ago?"

"I'm guessing the locals think good riddance to bad rubbish. I got this from a reliable source — they tossed the bodies into a mass grave in an abandoned lot that's stuck away on a no-nonsense back street at the edge of town. Witnessed by a miniscule crowd who gave no shit. Or so I hear."

"Classy," decided the Brick, as he began to tear a paper napkin into neat strips. "Least they would'a skipped them annoying musical interludes."

"Not all they skipped. No tears, no flowers, no car horns, and definitely no love lost. Another eight Capes are in intensive care — yep, at a hospital. The rules were bent. Have their own wing to themselves, but I do wonder about any 'priority' they'll be granted."

PA shifted closer. "Anyone we know?"

"Nana Mouskouri's Spectacles, Dick Drone, Atomic Autocrac, Callous Claude. A couple of others I hadn't heard a peep from before."

"Word on Prima Ballerina?" delicately prodded the Brick.

"She wasn't on the list."

"Saint Y?"

"Nope."

Jack sighed. "Civilian casualties?"

"Last count, six hundred odd — two thirds of that number dead."

Gypsie-Ann spotted a waitress, hailed her over, and ordered a bottle of Les Gouttes de Dieu merlot with four glasses.

"Hard to say how many for sure. The police're still counting and playing jigsaw with the remaining pieces. Bob Kahn's in a rage and Chief of Police O'Hara is on the telly, demanding new legislation to control Cape activities — basically pitching to lock us all up. By the way, I do love this relaxing of the stupid rules. Haven't drunk this much in years."

She grabbed the bottle from the waitress, before the woman could pour, in order to do a faster job herself. "Here we go. To the end of a stupid era."

They clinked glasses filled to the rim, but before she drank PA stared into the red wine. "You reckon there'll be others?"

"Stupid eras?"

"You know what I mean."

"Other fly-by-nighters from Melbourne?" Jack asked after a big sip.

"Yeah."

"Always more suckers back there," said the Brick.

After finishing off her drink in a few quick gulps, Gypsie-Ann shook her head. "Oh, I doubt it. The system's down, Blandos waking up. Heropa is not exactly attractive now. I'm loving it, but fact is we're the stragglers, along with a handful of other bozos out on the streets."

Pretty Amazonia downed half her own glass, and then pulled a face. "You make me feel like that survivor of the three hundred Spartans."

"Aristodemus? He actually skipped out on the final battle — eye infection. That's how he lived."

"Figures. Maybe that'll be my excuse. When the system is Reset and we can get out of here," Jack looked at the reporter over his glass, "are you staying?"

"Bet your life I am. Someone has to tell the stories, and thereby keep the perverse spirit of heroism alive."

"This wasn't heroism. It was madness."

"Precisely — aside from the actions of three people I know right here, Jack. Cheers. Which brings me to my real reason for popping in to hound you all."

"What, I thought hounding us was your hobby," her sister responded.

"True, but I also spoke to Kahn."

Jack flinched. "Has he seen Louise?"

"I mentioned her — but, no, he hasn't. The man is understandably spitting chips and his officers have their hands full, but he still found time to mention something he found out before the riot. They have a lead on this man we're after."

Now Jack shot his head back up. "What? Where?"

"Entering a building downtown, in South Erebus — I have the address here." Gypsie-Ann placed a piece of paper on the table, expression thoughtful. "I double-checked. There are no Capes we know of — alive, dead or M.I.A. — residing in the area, though I can't account for secret IDs. This may, and I stress may, be the guy's base of operations."

Sweeping up the paper, Jack read an address he didn't know, and then showed it to his two teammates. "Kahn is sure?"

"The Stetson. Red rag to a bull."

"PA?"

"On it, sahib."

A second later, the other woman's chair was empty, gently rocking back and forth a few times until Gypsie-Ann reached over to stabilize it.

"Haste, less speed," she muttered.

"Dollface can handle 'erself," said the Brick.

"Oh, I know that — I'm more concerned about our suspect."

"Yeah, come to think o' it, I don't want her t'get first dibs. Garçon!" The man snapped his fingers in the air, very nearly deafening the two others at the table. "Where's our blamed bill?"

#163

While Stellar bee-lined back to the *Patriot* building — "Vital stuff to catch up on," she claimed — Jack hopped into the Brick's Delahaye, and they drove at speed.

"Yer with us, kid?" asked the roughly sculpted chauffeur.

Tightening his seatbelt, Jack produced a slight shrug. "Yeah, just thinking. I should've tried calling Louise again."

"I'm not stoppin' yer."

"But you don't have a telephone in this crate — do you?"

"Only what'cha see. PA says I'm a skinflint, but why on this earth would I need a natty phone?"

Jack glanced at his driver. "How soon till we get to South Erebus?"

"Few minutes. We're on Iger Street now. Hang tight."

"The bastard is mine."

"Join our extended queue, junior. I'll leave yer the crumbs."

Ten minutes later, they pulled up at a kerb — the Brick turned the corner far too quickly, took out a road sign, and lodged a back wheel up on the gutter. Outside stood an unremarkable redbrick block of flats with the words Randall Arms in fading print above the entrance.

"344 Yancy?" the Brick wondered, as he looked about.

"Maybe you need spectacles — says so right there, on the sign you knocked over."

"Let it ride, huh?"

"Nice choice in comebacks, B."

The streets were empty, to be expected this time of night, riot or no riot. The Brick locked up his car and the two Equalizers walked over to the flats, where they met Pretty Amazonia by a broken post-box. Sporting the beginnings of a nasty black eye, the woman toyed with sheepish.

"This bastard had some fight in him," she muttered, "even while I was moving at 299,792,458 metres-per-second."

"I give up. Can't begin to get me head round how fast that is," the Brick confessed.

"It's fast. But he still hit my face, and the idiotic mojo works against me in that situation." The woman smiled anyway. "Don't worry, speed does have its advantage. The loser is trussed up like a Christmas turkey in apartment 3-D — all yours, boys."

Jack glanced at her. "Where're you going?"

"Home to bed. I'd prefer not to witness what happens next." She was off like a shot.

"Smart lady — gal got that right," the Brick chuckled.

"Now you sound sinister."

"C'mon. We're late fer a very important date."

The two Equalizers headed upstairs, stopped at the third floor, and paraded to a door marked 3-D. It was open. Jack diplomatically stood aside while the Brick barged through.

An empty living room welcomed them. In the adjoining bedroom, amidst a chaos of overturned furniture and several abandoned handguns, carefully positioned next to a single bed, they found their quarry: a man in a red Stetson on a kitchen chair, arms tied with rope, and a pair of men's blue underpants stuffed in his mouth.

"Classy," Jack decided.

The Brick had the gag off in a second.

"Yer the prick that offed Bulkhead!" he boomed.

"That sad-sack metal tosser?" The man in the red hat rotated his jaw, testing it out. "Jerk believed in Never Never Land."

"How many other Capes?"

"Huh?"

The Equalizer grabbed him around the throat. "How many others've you killed?"

"Brick?" said Jack. "Maybe take it easy."

"Lemme paste 'im one — lemme use 'im as me very own ninety-nine cent giant, life-size karate practice dummy."

Their prisoner pulled free from his fist. "Ow! Leggo! I'll talk.

310

Fuck."

Suspicious, the Brick stood back.

"Let me think now," the man deliberated, hardly appreciative. "Gotta be at least one dozen I know about. Tin man. Guy in a bath, another in a billboard. The man we roasted, and the one we refrigerated. That was funny — oh, you haven't found him yet? Called himself Bonfire, so we thought it ironic."

Jack was staring at him. "We?"

"Me. *Me*. I'm crazy. Always mixing up my pronouns."

Fed up, the Brick leaned in again and shoved forward the man's head, making his hat fall off onto the floor.

"Shite, you were right again," Jack's partner said, indicating the three-by-two 'p' just below the shirt collar at the back. "Bloke's a bloody Blando. Think me whole belief system's gone bust."

"Hold on," Jack responded.

He stuck a finger in his mouth, and then reached over. The man formerly in the red hat looked horrified — "Keep your saliva to yourself," he yelped — as Jack rubbed at the 'p'. It smudged, like all good tattooed letters don't.

"Counterfeit."

"Fuck you!" Their prisoner spat back, a globule hitting Jack's boot, and then he peered at the ceiling. "*Googly!*" When nothing changed, his face skidded from a sneer to a close cousin of crestfallen.

"Lemme guess," Jack said. "Password doesn't work."

"Yer tellin' me 'Googly' is the creep's open sesame? Corny as."

Jack forced a smile. "Since things've been screwy here in Heropa over the past few days, I guess it goes both ways — for them, as much as us."

The Brick glanced his way. "But who's *them*, kiddo?"

In return, the other Equalizer raised one eyebrow. "Let's find out. No emergency exits for this bugger, Mister B."

"Lovely."

Straight away, the Brick cuffed the man across the face. Jack could hear a cheek bone snap.

"Who the flyin' fig are ya?"

Their prisoner merely glared back, some of the defiance returning. "Say...don't you losers know what your little world has become?"

"Pray enlighten us," muttered the Brick, and then he slapped again.

"*Hurts*," the prisoner said in a small voice.

"Don't worry, tough guy. It ain't gonna hurt fer long."

Jack wasn't comfortable with this, no matter how much he pretended otherwise. "Just tell us 'real men' what we want to know."

"Okay, okay."

Silence.

"We're listening."

Nothing.

"Still listening."

No word at all. Jack looked at the Brick. "The man's whistling Dixie, wasting our time. Rearrange his face."

"Okay! Okay! Stop!"

"So — why're you here?"

"Why? Why, you ask?"

"Brick."

The man latterly in the red hat shook his head. "It's a testing ground. The bigwigs at security services must've stumbled across the place 'cause, next thing you know, we get a memo at Management Control Division, yacking about a new direction in road-testing for its agents, something a little offbeat and fun to boot — offing superheroes with offensive taste in dress-sense."

"Ouch," the Brick muttered, attitude channelling bored. His eyes, however, told Jack otherwise.

"You lot are pathetic. What, you thought you could trade off Melbourne for this dumb, walking/talking board game? You're nothing more than goons, canon-fodder to improve our killing skills."

"Sonuvabitch..." The Brick glared, quickly raising his giant mitt to strike again. Jack stopped him.

"He must have an insider," he said.

"He must?" The Brick looked confused.

"Someone here. Someone to help — remember how disorienting it can be, when people first arrive in Heropa?"

"True," Jack's teammate agreed.

"Plus, he needs a private stomping ground to lay low, stock weapons, whatever. Somebody is helping him. We want names, places."

"Why the fuck do you reckon I'll tell you anything?" piped up their man tied to the chair.

The Brick glowered at him. "Don't see anyone talkin' yer way. D'you?"

"Besides," Jack threw in, "we have a little bartering tool called the Brick's fist." He glanced at his teammate, who now beamed. "Well, maybe not the fist *per se* — we don't want to kill him," Jack changed his mind. "A bit of open-hand surgery instead."

"Oh, goodie-me. Fun."

The Brick used just two fingers, one wave left, one wave right. Thereafter, blood gushed from a broken nose and a couple of shattered teeth spilled to the carpet.

Jack winced. This looked real enough. "Okay. Let's start with who you are."

The loser folded quickly.

"Yeah, name's Colt. Denny Colt," he mumbled, pronunciation now a little off. "MCD Services, registration number 01042011 back in Melbourne. I'm staying at the Hobart Arms, on Franklin Avenue near North Kenmore Avenue."

"That's the spirit. Who's your point person here?"

"Fuck you." The Brick flexed his fingers, and Colt winced. "I don't care one way or the other." The Brick formed a fist. "Please don't hit me again!"

"Aw, gee. After all this is over I'll send you a crying-towel size no-prize — that way mebbe you'll forgive us while you wipe yer baby blues. Fair 'nuff? The name, bozo."

"Donald Wright."

"Wright? The newspaper head-honcho?" Jack's teammate glanced at him. "Bloke behind the *Port Phillip Patriot.*"

"I know. Blando or a Cape?"

"I thought Blando — tho' I'm beginnin' to realize it's easy t'get one's wires crossed. How d'we even know this bastard's on the level? Mebbe it's a red hernia."

"Herring," Jack said. "And maybe you're right. Why don't you have some more fun with his face, Brick?"

"No, no!" Colt cried, writhing inside his ropes. "Wright is the bloke we report to! Honest! Swear to God!"

"Yer not convincin' us, dickwad."

That was precisely when they heard a faint noise from the next room, the sound of metal on concrete. At the same moment, their prisoner's expression switched to crafty.

"What... What time is it?" he quizzed, gazing at the flattened red hat on the floor. The Brick had obviously stepped on it.

"Oh, you'll like this," the Equalizer announced, cracking rocky fingers. "Ding-dong — time t'do the Mussolini head kick. Why? Expectin' an audience?"

"Just him." Colt nodded past them. "You turds might wanna meet our self-styled Cape," he yammered through broken teeth, a red mouth, and much unnecessary laughter, "something we call the Kapitän 'cos of all the Kraut munitions. Perfect timing, Dolan."

While nowhere near as fast as Pretty Amazonia, Jack did get the split-second chance to look over his shoulder.

He thereby glimpsed a tall figure in the shadows by the open door, took in the black Kerberos Panzer Cop-style body armour — its varying angles, abundant grooves, detailing and perfect symmetry — that completely covered this person's body, dolled up with four Model 24 Stielhandgranate 'Potato Masher' stick grenades, a Luger pistol in a holster, an antenna, backpack, metallic gasmask with breathing tube, a German World War II army helmet, and glowing red eyes.

While he or she carried no kitchen sink, there was a huge piece of hardware in the newcomer's hands, some kind of demented machine gun well over a metre in length, with an endless belt of cartridges attached.

The man formerly in the red hat had taken to sniggering. "Dolan and I swap turns carting this stuff round. I get to sit it out today. Lovely. Say hello to the good Kapitän's 1,200 rounds-per-minute 7.9mm Maschinengewehr 42."

Jack realized he'd been acquainted with the gun before — this was the brute that'd butchered Baron von Gatz and General Ching.

"Oh, crap," he squeezed out.

Just as the Kapitän clicked a switch and opened fire, the Brick stepped between Jack and the gun. Pieces of cinderblock joined bullets ricocheting across the room.

"Whenever... yer ... ready," he heard the Equalizer yell above the ruckus.

Jack'd been stunned, too surprised to think, but his teammate's comment — and the selfless act of placing himself in the way of the barrage — reminded him that he wasn't unarmed.

Quickly steeling himself, Jack appraised distance and trajectory, and then jumped clear of the cover offered by the Brick, to fire one bolt. Something tore through his thigh, but the other person's shooting ceased.

Having blown the Kapitän — or Dolan, or whoever he damned well was — clear through the wall, Jack doubted this terror would be stepping back any time soon.

The Brick was on his knees, Colt cut to ribbons. So much for the cavalry.

After quickly wrapping his leg with a handy towel, Jack placed a hand on the Brick's broken shoulder. "Bloody well saved me, B. You all right?"

"Yeah, sure, sure," the Equalizer said, head down. "Yerself...?"

"Leg's fucked. Looks like the bullet went right on through. Hope so. Hurts like buggery, but I'll live — I'm way more worried about you."

"Our...whacko prisoner?"

"El Bastardo won't be telling us anything else."

"Bollocks." The Brick collapsed heavily onto his backside. Jack could now see the extent of damage that'd been done to the Equalizer's torso — entire bricks were missing or shattered. "Silenced...you think?"

"Maybe. Killed by his own mate."

"Then it's up to you, kid."

"What d'you mean? — I can't do this alone."

"You're gonna have'ta." The man grabbed Jack's fingers in his big mitt. "You owe PA an' me nothin'," he said, and then coughed. "I'd like yer t'do it fer us... But if not us, do it fer yerself. An' Louise."

Jack finally nodded, a slight smile on his face. "For love, eh?"

"Zip it. Fer you, her...fer everybody."

"All right, all right. Where does Wright live?"

"Gimme a moment...the world's spinnin'. Prick has a pretentious mansion, named Hatfield House, somewhere on South San Rafael Drive. Rich prats round there... Not up on where, precisely, since I'm not one of 'em. Wanker cruises about in a '48 Talbot Lago T-26 GS Saoutchik coupe — one o' those crates that won Le Mans, in 1950 I think it were, blue...two-tone..." Even in his bullet-riddled state, the Brick realized he was losing his audience so he pulled up stumps. "Ahh, crap it. Get Stellar t'help ya find 'im."

"But she works for this particular prick."

"No matter — y'can trust her. Pay no heed to PA's jealous tirades." Jack could see his partner was vagueing out, becoming distant. "We had fun times, right-o...?"

He wasn't sure if the Equalizer meant during the short period he was here — something he very much doubted — or the other man's over all stay in Heropa.

"You need me to get you to hospital? I can take you there now. I'll call PA."

"Can still walk, kid...an' methinks I need a stone mason instead o' some silly quack. Don't you worry yerself, I'm not ready to start praticin' Banquo's ghost just yet — but I need'ja to get the hell outta here...do our job. Now. Pronto, like..."

#164

After contacting Pretty Amazonia to urgently come collect the Brick, and then popping into a chemist's to grab bandages and a quart of Cream of Dixie Straight Rye, Jack piled into a taxi, numberplate 7077. On the back seat headed uptown, while the cabbie nervously checked a rearview mirror, the Equalizer got changed from his partially shredded costume, mopped the blood, wrapped the wound, poured whiskey over it, drank the rest — and spat most of the rotgut out the open window. He'd steeled himself anyway by the time the Cadillac pulled up to the *Port Phillip Patriot* building.

Upstairs, Gypsie-Ann didn't need too much arm-wringing.

Once Jack'd bounced through her office door and weathered a degree of abuse about smelling like a brewery, he plopped her down to brief her on the interview-cum-interrogation-cum-massacre of the man in the red hat. She sat up straight, eyes sparkling.

"I knew it," she said, possibly more to herself. "I knew Wright had feculence hitching a ride beneath his coattails."

Like Jack, who'd donned a suit in the cab, the reporter had changed outfits. She was wearing a grey and black tweed wool herringbone double-breasted jacket — Basil Rathbone playing up Sherlock Holmes, with a feminine flourish.

"The Brick's okay?" she asked, at the same time as she fetched a bag from under a pile of folders.

"I don't know. Hoping so."

"Shit. Well. My lovely boss is here." The woman looked heavenward. "In his offices." A moment later, Gypsie-Ann checked inside her satchel and Jack noted the presence there of a small, silver Walther 9mm pistol.

"Think you'll need that?" he asked.

"Even Sherlock carried a firearm — and I don't intend on getting caught unawares a second time. Now," Gypsie-Ann muttered under her breath, "where on earth did I put my deerstalker?" Her roving eyes caught Jack's. "Only joking, by the way."

"I kind of figured that."

They proceeded along the corridor to take up the single elevator. While ascending, Gypsie-Ann put a hand to the wall of the contraption and stroked the surface.

"Did you notice the walls are inlaid with twelve varieties of local hardwood? Extravagant stuff. This building cost $2.3 million to build — $1.1 million over the original budget. That's so bloody Wright."

The publisher's secretary Joanie, in the reception area, intercepted the two and she made a brief telephone call. As they waited, Gypsie-Ann pillaged a nearby umbrella-stand — "Shhh," she whispered, "I need a new one!" — and requisitioned a chocolate-brown parasol that matched her hair.

Almost straight after, a tall man with short black hair and a boxer's complexion came out to meet and greet.

"Hello, I'm Art Cazeneuve, Mister Wright's personal assistant." The man shook Jack's hand, but ignored his companion. "He'll be ready to see you shortly. Would you mind waiting?"

"El Presidente always makes me wait," Gypsie-Ann grouched. "Nothing new there."

Cazeneuve stared her way. "Should give you time, Miss Stellar, to put that umbrella back where you found it." Then he marched off.

They sat on the padded divans and Jack instinctively crossed his legs — causing him to double-up in pain.

"You still hurting from the explosion?" the reporter asked, concerned.

"A different memento. I'll be okay. You still want that umbrella?"

"Nah, I've decided it's tainted."

Five minutes later they were shown into the offices proper.

Donald Wright, dressed in a tan naval military jacket and pants, walked across the plush rug with a debonair grin. His monkey, Miami Beach, was AWOL. "What a surprise," the man announced.

"Nice outfit, chief," Gypsie-Ann said. "Very Gary Cooper."

"Why, thank you, baby." Wright stopped before Jack. "I have to

say, I do also like the suit. Snazzy — three-piece navy wool Benham
& Co double-breaster, if I'm not mistaken. Far better than the splashy
superhero costume. The white cotton shirt and navy silk tie are a
lovely touch. You would be Southern All Stars."

"Southern Cross."

"Ahh yes, of course — apologies, and all that. I recognize you
from your picture in our paper."

Jack cursed himself. So much for incognito.

"Why don't you cats take a seat? Or separate ones, if you're shy."

His two visitors remained standing while the publisher circumnavigated the desk, walked behind it, and pushed back into his
throne.

"You did a wonderful job protecting those people during the
Cape hostilities. So, what can I do for you, SC-baby? Have you given
any consideration to my proposal?"

"You could start by telling me why the hell you're killing all the
Capes of Heropa."

"Oh ho, and here I was thinking they were doing that to
themselves!" the man chuckled.

"Along with giving comfort to gung-ho security types from the
real world."

Wright looked at Jack, head cocked. "Am I?"

"I have it on good authority that, yes, you bloody well are."

"This 'good authority' wouldn't happen to be a recently-deceased
individual with a predilection for the wearing of garish red
headwear?"

Ah.

"Personally, I'd ensure I had decent source material before I went
about accusing persons of foul play — one thing we learn in the
newspaper biz, isn't that right, Gypsie-Ann?"

"Mm-hm," the woman beside Jack responded, in a noncommittal
tone.

"By the way, baby, how's the leg?"

Wright looked directly at the Equalizer's injured thigh. The publisher couldn't have spotted the injury, given the change of clothes and Jack's fairly commendable effort not to limp or favour the other leg.

"Fine," he said.

"Swell. Allow me to show you something of my own. You'll dig this."

The publisher reached over and pushed a button that Jack fretted might open up the floor beneath he and Gypsie-Ann, but instead one of the floor-to-ceiling bookcases slid aside.

Behind an exposed steel door tagged Lock 41, inside a sterile-looking cubbyhole with a flickering fluorescent light, was a plexiglass tube in which sat a costume atop a chisel-jawed mannequin. There was a red skullcap and half-mask with a big white star, a blue uniform boasting more stars shaped like a v-for-victory across the torso, yellow gloves, red boots, and a red belt on a pair of underpants that rode too high. The kind of get-up the Professor would've complained about.

Jack recognized the costume from a picture Pretty Amazonia had once shown him — these were Major Patriot's threads. While he also felt he'd seen them somewhere else, so far as Wright was concerned? This guy looked way too old.

The publisher apparently picked up on the confusion.

"You know the adage, the one about absolute power corrupting absolutely? Well, that's a rort. I wasn't corrupted, I was bored senseless! Do either of you have any idea how ageing boredom can be?"

"I don't get it," Jack heard Gypsie-Ann cut in.

"Too much for your fabulous powers of deduction?" Wright chuckled. "Why, oh why, doesn't that surprise me?"

"You could be generous enough to grant better clues."

"Tart as ever, too. When will you learn to know your place?"

"Oh, dearie, p'raps I left the knowledge in my other suit?"

Jack glanced at her. "Time for quips later. He's one of the original Capes — a member of the Crime Crusaders."

"Crime Crusaders *Crew*," Wright corrected. "Why you people always feel the need to shorten things drives me to distraction. Doing so robs them of full flavour."

"The CCC was well before my time." The reporter shrugged, but she had a smirk. "I heard they washed up. Not worth doing the homework."

"Oh, huzzah. A dash of heroic repartee to raise my spirits."

"So you're a Cape," Gypsie-Ann posited. "Big deal."

"Not quite." Wright kicked back to place his feet on the desk. "I'm not the same as you people. I didn't go through all the smoke, mirrors and pulleys they use to keep the safe house safe — you know the place, back in Melbourne. I've heard it's quite a shithole. Five years ago, when Heropa was placed online, I came in through a backdoor, since I was the original designer of this platform."

Now walking gingerly, hardly disguising the limp, Jack went to a mantelpiece and examined the bust of a black bird he'd seen before. "Mister Wright, you wouldn't know a Professor Erskine?"

"The creator of Captain America?" This crack came back sticky with sarcasm.

"No. The one here in Heropa."

"Interesting. Actually, I do."

Jack glanced over at the man. "Go on."

"Rather a bright spark, for a phony."

"A phony?"

"That's what we called common folk before 'Blando' became *de rigueur* — hence the letter 'p' you'll find on the back of their necks." Wright mirrored Jack's visit to the mantelpiece, to straighten up the avian statuette. "I had Erskine do me some technical work a few years back — the humdrum things I was too busy to worry about." Wright frowned. "He started getting idiotic notions, ideas beyond his call. I'm a very sensitive fella and had to let him go."

"As one does," Gypsie-Ann said.

She was looking at the costume in the secret compartment, the smirk still on her face, but her comment appeared to incite her boss.

"Will you stop with that incessant prattling?" he demanded.

"So, why'd you quit being a Cape?" Jack said, playing for time. "Why the whole Donald Wright sham?"

"Playing for time is not going to help you." Wright's eyes held onto Jack's. "Don't you realize you stand no chance?"

"So indulge the poor kid," Gypsy-Ann sighed.

"Yes, why not?" Skipping back to his desk, Wright pushed aside some paperwork and sat down on top. "In the early days, one had free range. This was a brave new world, baby. When I established this secret identity, it didn't make sense to be a menial reporter like Clark Kent or Gypsie-Ann here — no offence, darling."

"None taken."

"Anyhow, I elevated myself to publisher. We ran the place then, everything, riding roughshod over the hoi polloi. And then Sir-*bloody*-Omphalos came along with these ridiculous notions of changing Heropa, of making it a 'better place', as he ranted to anyone that'd listen. Better for whom, I ask you? He broke up our Crime Crusaders Crew, cavorted with phonies, and set up the Equalizers. Installed that arrogant oaf the Great White Hope as second-in-charge, while I didn't receive any invitation at all."

"Hence the sour grapes."

"Far from it. As I say, I was bored. The change suited me. I settled into my new alter ego, starting to manipulate things from here."

"And now you're killing Capes."

"As the dear old GWH would have said, boring me to tears: 'Par for the course, good fellow, par for the course', et cetera, et cetera."

"Then you admit it?" Gypsie-Ann cut in, her fingers playing with the steel catch on her bag.

"But — hang on," Jack said as he held up a warning hand to his colleague. "Surely you still have to play ball by the same rules as us. If the safeties are off, what's to stop me blowing you through yonder window?"

"A twenty-one storey drop."

"Unless you hit something on the way down."

"Decidedly messy," Wright mused.

"Right you are."

The publisher stood up, opened one of the multitudes of drawers lining his massive bureau, and took out a squareish Colt M1911 automatic — the standard-issue sidearm for American military types from 1911 to 1985. He racked the slide, switched off the safety.

"Alternatively, I could do the chore myself." Having lined up the rectangular silver barrel by his right temple, Wright prepared to pull the trigger. "BANG!" he shouted.

Jack and Gypsie-Ann jumped; the man roared with laughter.

"What?" he finally managed, drying tears with a floral hanky. "Did you seriously think I'm some kind of suicidal nutcase?"

"The thought had crossed my mind," Jack muttered.

"To shame!" Wright then spun the revolver with an adept nod to Western gunslingers, and this time the barrel stopped between his jaw line and throat, pointed upwards — which was when he really pulled the trigger.

"Crap!" Gypsie-Ann yelped.

Jack didn't get to squeeze out any sound. Probably he was stunned, since his face had been redecorated with the older man's blood and brains.

"Also messy, as you can see."

Another Donald Wright slunk into the room, wearing the exact same faux military outfit, his grey matter intact, and sat on the edge of the desk to survey the suicide diorama.

"Gore everywhere. Not pretty at all. Oh, I'm sorry, baby — did I mess up your suit?"

This second Wright was watching Jack's distress with an amused expression, so Gypsie-Ann pulled herself together. "Not mine," she said. The reporter pursed lips, studying both Wrights in return, dead and alive. "Twins," she deduced.

Wright tut-tutted, wagging a finger her way.

"Oh, far more than double-trouble. Duplication is my signature gift. One of me dies, another takes right up and continues the

324

charade. Rather like the HYDRA terrorist organization in Marvel Comics: 'If a head is cut off, two more will take its place' — one way in which I've been able to wear so many professional hats. I'll admit it's spread my intellect rather thin, however — you see, the power is supposed be a temporary trick, not permanent. There are numerous copies, and I have my rather schizophrenic moments — but that adds to the challenge, and levels the playing field a fraction for you cretinous people."

"Humility is obviously something you don't have to worry about," Jack said, back on top of his wits and clearing his eyes with a sleeve.

"You should try sitting in on the humbug's three-hour divisional meetings — end of every bloody month," Gypsie-Ann responded.

"Complaints, complaints. This is all I hear."

"When you complicate things, of course you're going to have complaints running interference."

"It's actually all very simple." The elderly man took out a cigar, unwrapped the thing, and coerced it into his cigarette holder. "If you really knew your comicbook history — I mean *really*, not just the 1960s Marvel fodder you seem so enamoured with, Southern Cross — you'd have figured this out already. You'd know about a hero named Captain Freedom."

That name snagged Jack's attention, just as he finished wiping down his face. He glanced over to the wall covered with 1930s and '40s junk. At one of the old, framed collectibles — *Speed Comics* issue 17, the one with the unnamed Captain America rip-off individual on the cover.

Wright noticed the Equalizer's look. "Right on, baby. In primary-colour glory, on that cover there. I modelled Major Patriot on Captain Freedom. Of course, to my mind a Captain wasn't authority enough — 'Major' has a much nicer ring to it."

"Yeah, well. I guess once Captain America hit the big time, copycat patriotic heroes became abundant," Jack said.

Wright looked at him, all straight face. "Pot-Kettle-Black."

"Whatever. But your costume's slightly different from the one in the picture."

"The good Captain had a few wardrobe switches over the years, depending on the artist. This was my favourite."

Gypsie-Anne glanced at her boss. "You didn't have the imagination to conjure up your own?"

"I was a hero, not a haberdasher." Wright chuckled. "Allow me to provide a brief history."

"Do you have to?"

"Yes," said the publisher, Mark II, as he swept up the Colt pistol from the Mk. I on the floor. "Captain Freedom was first published in 1941, through to 1947, by a little-known company called Brookwood Publications, and then Harvey Comics."

"Quality. The home of Richie Rich and Casper the Friendly Ghost," deadpanned Gypsie-Ann.

Jack produced a tentative smile. So — she did know her comics. "And let us never forget Baby Huey and Wendy the Good Little Witch."

"Absolute classics," the reporter agreed.

Wright now squirmed a fraction. "Whatever. You know, it's likely your artistic hero Jack Kirby designed that cover there, alongside Joe Simon. The duo was reputed to make use of the alias 'Jon Henri'. Can you see it in the lower left-hand corner? So, laugh all you will."

The picture was crude, ugly stuff — Jack marvelled at how much better Kirby's work had gotten by the height of the swinging '60s. Still, the old comicbook was likely a collector's item, worth a king's fortune in the real world.

"I hear nobody laughing," he said.

"Then shut up and allow me to finish my rant. Newspaper publisher Don Wright, physically perfect and blessed with incredible willpower, dons a mask to fight the Axis enemies. When AC Comics briefly revived the character in the 1980s, Captain Freedom also became a set of clones."

The man lit his cigar and puffed.

"I'm positive you both would've noticed him, if you weren't goddamned narrow-minded in your choice of hero-worship. As for the 'Patriot' part of the name, I wanted to give some hint as to who I might be — since I run a paper called the *Patriot*. But no one picked up on the clue. How mundane."

"So you're a nihilistic clown," Gypsie-Ann decided.

"Sticks and stones."

"With a dire range in come-backs. No wonder you prefer geriatric golden-age comics, chopped together when things were much — simpler."

"You want simple? You have no idea how many of me there are, or where we all might be at any given time. Getting down to the nitty-gritty, you can't hope to stop us."

Jack had finally finished wiping gunk off his face. "We can still fight."

Wright smiled. "That, I'm banking on."

"We prevented the Reset. That's not going to happen anymore."

"So you have all the more to lose. What were you thinking — that I'd care about the Reset? I've decided I don't give a donkey's arse. Blandos shouldn't feel pain, sweat, cry, scream, and fornicate — yet they do. Why? These are not true human beings. Phonies were all born to be slaves. They're not worth your idiotic concern. Yet here we are and, Jack, I'm certain you're well-qualified to debate the point."

The Equalizer's fist was curling before he knew it, but Gypsie-Ann laid a restraining hand on his arm.

"Don't. He's not worth it."

Donald Wright leaned on the desktop and examined them both with contempt.

"Worth? I'll give you worth. They say audacity is a true hero's weapon, contempt for Blandos another. You people want to get into bed with the local population, so it stands to reason you have to protect them. Every Blando that dies will be a scar on your conscience. Rather pathetic, really. But worth every moment."

"Speak in plain English," the reporter muttered.

"Certainly. I decided to open up the field, to make things more —
interesting. This also boosts my wallet in the real-deal world, so I'm
hardly complaining."

Jack studied him. "You went to the government back in
Melbourne."

Leaning back, cigar clenched between his teeth, Wright beamed.
"Precisely what I did, baby. I told them all about Heropa and gave
them access via my backdoor, even have a trans-barrier phone to stay
in touch. They're now using this as a training ground to harden up
recruits. Oh, they have their own idInteract programs, but Heropa
offers something a fraction more...exotic."

"The man with the red hat. Denny Colt..."

"All these 'Colts' — it's bound to become way-out confusing,
don't you think? Anyhow, he and his partners will be the first of
many. I have other guests lined up on the agenda, all of whom you'll
have to entertain — or Blandos will die. I rather dig the arrangement.
Now, would you two like a drink, or prefer to play indignant and
leave? I'm a busy man."

"We're going to defend Heropa," Jack said, "and I'm going to kick
your arse."

Wright looked at him from beneath his bushy eyebrows, pointing
the gun in the Equalizer's direction.

"Good luck with that fool's assignment, lover-boy. Now beat it, or
I'll place a bullet in your belfry. Hail HYDRA!"

Just as the man clucked away at his lame gag, he accidentally
inhaled cigar smoke, and then stooped over to cough.

Despite the existence of these duplicates — who could lurk
anywhere nearby, likely also armed — Jack was about to make a
move, when Wright sat up straight, rubbing his chest, the gun again
pointed in the direction of his two visitors.

"By the way," Wright said, "give my best to Mitzi. Oh, wait, I
believe that's already being taken care of. Can you give her this?"

Tarpé Mills flew across the space and landed in Jack's right hand.
Her eyes had been gouged out.

#165

No one was home when Jack banged on the door — or else Louise had taken to avoiding him. But he had seen the lights were all off from out on the street when arriving in Gypsie-Ann's car. Since the security entrance had been open, they'd been able to head straight upstairs.

Beside him on the doormat, the reporter produced a hairpin.

"I think, in this situation, we're allowed to pry," she announced.

"Wouldn't do that if I were you."

Both were startled by this comment, coming as it did from the very next doorway along. Louise's neighbour 'Handsome' Harry Phillips stood there in his purple satin dressing robe, puffing on a cheroot.

"Mister Phillips."

"Louise's friend," the man nodded back.

"Do you know where she is?"

"Kid isn't home. Saw her come and go earlier this evening — I'd say she was headed for City Hall."

"Cheers." Jack decided on the spot to broach something troubling him. "Not that we don't appreciate it, but why're you being helpful?"

"One gets to recognize the signs. I have eyes. Can see Louise likes you and know when I'm licked. Aside from that, she looked upset — crapper chat, who wouldn't be in the circumstances? Her world is gone to hell, with the old man being locked up." Phillips studied the stains on Jack's shirt collar. "By the way, what happened? Looks like you've been in a warzone."

"Kind of."

"Well, if I were you, I'd invest in a change of wardrobe. Nothing like carnage to turn off a lady."

Jack nodded, before hobbling down stairs with Gypsie-Ann. His leg was cramping and it felt like the improvised bandage was soaked through, but he didn't have time to get the thing redecorated.

"What a honey," the reporter muttered, her cheeks an unfamiliar pink.

"One more thing," Harry called over the banister above. "I have to say — Louise accepted a lift from a pretty dodgy-looking chap."

Jack froze. "What? When?"

"When she left here. Out the front."

"Taxi driver?"

"Didn't seem that way. Drove a yellow Plymouth, though, so maybe it was unmarked. I think it was a '38, registration BBP589, and one other thing — he wore a particularly tasteless red hat. Good night." Harry's door slammed.

At the same time, Jack had entirely stopped breathing for several seconds, and then he fell down onto a step. Turning straight back, Gypsie-Ann crouched before him.

"The guy in the *rouge feutre* you were telling me about?"

Panting now, trying desperately not to panic, Jack thought about all the angles this might not be — but kept returning to the one it probably was. "Maybe, if you're talking up the man in the red hat." He swallowed hard. "Likely. Too much of a—"

"Coincidence?"

"Yeah."

So wrapped up in heroics that Jack hadn't done what he'd promised the Professor — look after Louise. Too scared anyway to talk to her after the fight. Jack knew he would live with both failings, and the personal inadequacy, the rest of his years.

"God. Then they have her."

"Who're they?"

"I don't know."

"Wright and his cronies?"

"I don't know! Bloody hell... What if something's happened? What're they going to do with her, Gypsie-Ann?" He felt paralyzed, rended.

The reporter leaned in close with her beak.

"We don't know anything yet. Nothing. You hear me? But we can't sit here bunting hunches all night — are you coming, Jack? Move it, mister — you and that busted-up leg."

#166

Gypsie-Ann decreed that the two of them needed to regroup with the other Equalizers to nut out a 'team response', even if it was against her better judgement.

"Don't forget we're in this together, Jack," she said as she drove, eyes narrowed. "Strength in numbers, and all that jazz people tend to waffle on about."

"What if the Brick isn't okay?"

"Let's deal with everything as it comes. And you really need to get PA to look at your wound."

"I'm fine," Jack muttered.

"I don't care."

When they arrived at Timely Tower, the clock said it was after midnight and the building was minimally lit. Having pushed through the big glass door, the two of them were intercepted by a security guard Jack had never seen before, a man younger than the usual breed, animated and bearing a smile.

"Excuse me, sir," this guard said, as he came close. "Southern Cross, right? I recognize you from your picture in the paper. I'm Ford Davis."

Jack nodded, thoughts plumbing elsewhere, but Davis handed him an envelope that smelled of citrus.

"There's a young lady in the penthouse — she came earlier this evening. Said she's a friend of yours and asked me to give you this. Didn't do the wrong thing allowing her up there, did I?"

The guard appeared nowhere near as contrite as he pretended, and he winked at Jack while the Equalizer tore open the letter.

The note inside was short — and sweet. 'I'm so sorry, Jack', it said in Louise's elegant hand, albeit a little shaky. 'Upstairs. Let's make up.' Jack read the words a second time, his heart beating fast, and then smiled too. He breathed out, relieved.

"She's here. She's safe."

"You-know-who?" Gypsie-Ann inquired, a suspicious eye on the uniform before them with his eager-to-please expression.

"Louise. Yes." Already looking over at the elevator doors, Jack nodded. "She's waiting."

"You want me to come? Or have I become a third leg?"

"I think we can talk about everything tomorrow," Jack said in a vague voice while he gazed up at the ceiling, still milking that silly grin. "With PA and the Brick, I mean."

"Oh, sure — why be rash today, when you can put off everything to the morrow?" Still, the reporter remained leery. "Are the other Equalizers back yet?" she asked the guard. This fellow seemed put out with her query and the charm wavered.

"Not that I know, ma'am."

Gypsie-Ann decided to try the Neon Bullpen or the Brick's car phone — she had no way of getting directly in touch with her sister.

"All right, Jack, I'm out of your hair. But for crap's sake be careful, you hear me? Don't forget what we learned tonight."

"All up in the old coin locker." Tapping his forehead as he limped to one of the metal concertina doors beneath the Equalizers banner, Jack laughed. "She's here. She's safe. And thanks, Gypsie-Ann — for everything."

Davis, the security guard, faded into the shadows near his desk while the reporter strode away from the foyer, shoved through the entrance, and headed for her convertible.

#167

The first thing Jack spotted when he entered Equalizers HQ were the flowers — hundreds of yellow roses sprinkled across the white floor, petals everywhere, making a path from the door, across the living space, and ascending the staircase.

Jack again smiled, deeply touched. He wanted to run along the trail, to take up the girl in his arms and shower her with kisses aplenty, and then to just hold her — for hours if need be. She'd forgiven him. She'd returned to him. She was safe. Even the death masks on the wall looked jolly.

He stopped, picked up a rose, sniffed it, and the smile became a beam.

Skirting alongside the other flowers so as not to damage a single one, Jack galloped upstairs — pain be damned— and tossed his hat across the room below. On the landing were additional roses, lined up leading straight to his bedroom door, which was partly ajar. Orange candlelight flickered within. Jack sneaked over, his heart pounding more than before. She'd forgiven him. She'd returned to him. She was safe, just when he'd begun to believe the worst.

He knocked softly. "Louise?"

There was a soft sound of music, something out of place in the circumstances, yet familiar all the same. Ary Borroso's old song 'Aquarela do Brasil'. Jack pushed the door forward. Lying on top of the bed, apparently asleep, was Louise.

Strangely, her fish tank — the one with the seahorses — also sat in the room, on the table beside her. Jack could see half the water was missing. There were seahorses flipping about on the surface of the table proper, next to a pair of cat's eye glasses. Louise's head, hair and shoulders were wet, her face deathly pale.

As he embraced these details, Jack's smile evaporated.

A ROSE BY ANY OTHER STAIN

#168

The woman felt like she'd throw up. "That's it, then. Game over."

"Stellar, this isn't no game," snapped Robert Kahn, the police officer seated to her left. He'd taken off his beige trench coat, had it draped on the back of the chair, and he slouched over, fiddling with a cigarette he refused to light.

"Depends on your perspective," she said.

"Depends on a lot of things — but a game? No."

On the reporter's right, Pretty Amazonia quietly stared at the ceiling, ignoring the others. Finally dropping her chin, she surveyed the trampled foliage all about and suppressed a rising anger. "This is too much," she hazarded. "This is despicable."

The three sat together in the meeting area downstairs at Equalizers HQ, although they'd renounced the big round table in favour of more intimate placement on the settees. Even so, it felt like a mausoleum. Huddled amidst crushed yellow flowers, they spoke in low tones, scarcely able to fathom what had taken place here only an hour before.

Gypsie-Ann shivered. Maybe a lining on the stomach was required? How long had it been since she'd eaten something? "All this makes Melbourne feel like a tea party."

"Where?" asked Kahn, placing the cigarette back inside its Camel box.

"Forget it. PA, what are we going to do?"

"We?"

"We." Stellar worried about her sister. She'd never seen her this rattled.

Roughly pushing fingers through her hair, Pretty Amazonia peered back and sighed in loud fashion. "I'll tell you what we need to do — we need to find Jack. In his state, God knows what he'll do."

"Agreed. How's the Brick?"

"Touch and go — the damage was massive, and Polyfilla's never going to be adequate. Mister B's out of it now — I pumped him full of drugs I had to administer orally, since there was no way to get a needle through his thick hide, diluted them with whiskey so the bugger would drink up. Hate to tell you, but it looks like more of your blood is required."

"Again?"

"We need the Brick back on his feet."

"I'm beginning to suspect I picked the wrong power — I feel like a blood-bank."

"Stop whining. As you like to badger people, at least you're alive." PA diverted her attention to the floor and started counting rose petals, before she told herself to stop. "Shit, I tried so hard. Really I did. CPR, adrenaline, AED — God, I so wanted to help her."

"I know you did." Stellar glanced at Kahn, who nodded as he opened a small, leather-bound notebook. "We know."

"Screw your sympathy."

"We were aiming at empathy. Misfire?"

"I'll say. Either way, I don't want that shit." The Equalizer jumped up, acting edgy. "We need to clean this place. These flowers. Jesus."

"Priorities, sweetheart. First we have to go get Jack. Any idea where he might've gone?"

"None at all. The Brick may be better at answering — they tended to hang out together. Turns out Jack pinched Mister B's prize motorcycle, but I think I'll skip telling him that part."

"Jack can ride one?" the reporter muttered.

"The Brick gave him lessons."

"Great."

"But, before nicking the wheels, Jack was here when you arrived?" This was the cop speaking.

"Yeah. He'd just found her."

Kahn glanced over his notebook. "What happened next?"

"Girl was laid out on his bed, flowers scattered all round, and some kind of evil attempt at romantic Latin jingles on the stereo. A howling success, that was." PA closed her eyes. She didn't want to venture back there.

"Go on."

No choice. She knew the cop would hound her. "Jack was in the bedroom, as I say, but he also wasn't."

"What's that supposed to mean?"

"I guess this was shock. No. No, the horror, more like it. He just sat there in the middle of the floor, staring at nothing, like he'd already given up the ghost. His face was... Bloody hell. The girl's brain had been deprived of oxygen by the time I got her breathing again. I have no idea about Blando physiology — we needed to get her to a proper hospital, so I dialled an ambulance. And then you."

"What about Jack?" persisted the officer.

"Jack was gone, right before I called. I looked up, after the AED got the girl's pulse back, and he wasn't there. So far as he knows, she's dead. Might as well be anyway, but we have to find him, have to help him. I can't imagine what he's going through. No one deserves this."

Gypsie-Ann slowly scratched behind one ear, lips compressed, before she broached another unsavoury topic. "You realized he'd been shot?"

"What? — No! Where?"

"In the leg, earlier this evening, when the Brick copped it."

"Anyone patch him up?"

"I think he did that himself."

"Home medicine for a bullet wound? God, more to fret about."

The police officer leaned forward, clearing his throat.

"We haven't forgotten you," Gypsy-Ann snapped.

"Well, we need to go back a degree, get the full details, so I can try to help."

"How do you think a Blando flatfoot can help?" asked Pretty Amazonia, her face lacking enthusiasm of any sort — making Kahn wonder whether this was a deliberate insult or a genuine query.

"Ladies, I'm not completely useless. I know *taekwondo* and *jūjutsu*, was an amateur heavyweight champion in my twenties, I have a gun, and an entire police force at my disposal. You people need all the assistance you can get."

The reporter nodded after the speech. "Yeah, fair enough."

"Okay, talk to me. PA, do you know what exactly was done to the victim?"

"I told you. Someone tried to drown her. Almost succeeded, too, since she was minus a heartbeat before I arrived. Same end result — they got what they wanted. The girl isn't going to recover from that kind of necrosis of the cerebral neurons. There were abrasions around her wrists, so I'm guessing she'd been tied up at one point. Also bruising on the collarbone and neck, skin beneath her nails. Kid put up a fight." PA looked at her sister. "By the way, I *did* notice. She's the Aerialist. I have no idea why I didn't see that before, whatever the hair-colour. But how can this be? She's a Blando — I double-checked."

"I know."

"Why didn't anyone bother telling me?"

"Long story. Only found out tonight, but we don't have time to go into it. Later, okay?"

"All right. But you better fill me in. Who put the bite on her?"

"Good question. I'm thinking the security guard downstairs," Stellar mused. "There was something off about him — and he'd scarpered when I came back."

Kahn jotted more notes. "Give me a description. I'll get my boys on it."

"What's the point? We all now know who's ultimately responsible: Donald Wright."

"Our very own fucking Lex Luthor." Pretty Amazonia wandered away to pick up a stray fedora from the floor; recognized it as Jack's and almost cried on the spot. She was trying desperately hard to avoid doing that. "The perennial arsehole."

Kahn frowned. "And a former Cape."

"Don't remind me."

"Wright will be a challenge," appraised Gypsie-Ann, "since we still don't know how many of him there are."

"Perhaps we do." The police officer edged forward on his seat, eyes slit. "Did Jack share with you the Big O's final effects?"

That snagged the reporter's attention. "No — well, not with me. PA?"

"Not us either."

"Maybe he forgot. It was a small matter, and I mean that literally, just a tiny, folded-up piece of paper with an obscure message written there. We found it in a secret pocket in the Big O's costume."

"Well?" asked Gypsie-Ann, impatience making her voice shrill.

"It said 'There are 6'. Nothing more."

"Six? Six what?"

"That's what Jack asked. The note didn't say."

"Then why are you telling us this?"

"It could be a clue as to how many duplicates Wright has."

"Lordy — clutching at straws, aren't we?" The reporter shook her head. "Does this mean we're completely desperate?"

"Six is a possibility."

"Or not."

She contemplated the notion, rolling it round the hay inside her skull. This would be just like O, finding out something vital, and then neglecting to take adequate notes — unlike Kahn, who wrote down everything.

"Well," she said, "five, six, or more — Wright will still be a problem, along with all the accoutrements he's shipping into this city. Fat chance me doing an exposé, given he runs the paper and we have no evidence. Kahn, we need Prof Erskine here. Jack told me he's worked with Wright. He may know something we don't."

"I thought you'd be pressing charges."

"Did I say that?"

"No, but he shot you down in cold blood."

"Stop trying to read my mind."

"Whatever." Kahn used his pen as a bookmark and closed the tome. "Not an easy thing to arrange in any case — Judge Fargo wants him to stand trial for the assault."

"Leave Fargo to me."

"And Chief O'Hara? I'd have to go above his head, but you should know that he and Wright are in each other's pockets."

"I'm sure you'll sort something out. You're usually inventive at that sort of thing — for a law-enforcement official, I mean."

The police officer smiled. "Flattery, with a caveat, goes far."

"I knew it would."

Having propped herself on the edge of the large round table with the Equalizers logo in the centre, Pretty Amazonia flaunted a pair of scissors and started snipping away at her hair, leaving great wads of purple on the floor, in between crushed orange flowers. Stellar and Kahn stopped quarrelling to stare at the sight.

"PA?" Stellar said, more worried. "Are you okay?"

"Sure I am." The woman grabbed a fistful of tresses and hacked them off just inches from her scalp. "But there's a time for gung-ho, as much as there is for glamour. I'm going to kick Wright's bum, and I don't think he'll worry while I bounce round looking pretty. What he did to Jack and his girl is...just vile. I'm going to paint his life vile. Hence the time for gung-ho."

#169

Jack rode straight over to the *Port Phillip Patriot*, crashed through the glass entrance, grabbed an elevator up, and blew out the twenty-first and twenty-second floors. Didn't realise he had that much power. Innocent people might've got hurt, but the place should have been empty this time of night — not that he gave a shit either way.

Next up was Hatfield House, at 380 South San Rafael Drive. This time Jack taxied it, remembering nothing from the drive, how long it took, or how much he paid.

Left the neoclassical mansion shattered and ablaze. Didn't know if one or more of Donald Wright's clones were caught in either maelstrom.

The Brick found him near dawn, wandering the streets downtown, raving at the heavens like a madman. The Equalizer weathered a wild plasma blast, and then pulled his partner to him, hugging for all he was worthwhile Jack plucked out hair and howled.

Eventually, the Brick drove to Heropa City General Hospital where — after much protest, followed by Brick-like intimidation — they x-rayed Jack, patched the ballistic trauma (stitching the entry and exit wounds in his thigh), shot him up with antibiotics and a merciful amount of painkillers, and placed the man in a private room far from other patients, unconscious, on an intravenous drip of isotonic fluids.

Precariously seated in the waiting room, dressed only in his undies, the Brick caught up on fretful sleep for an hour or so, and then rifled through old dailies and frayed magazines sitting in a wire rack.

One in particular caught his fancy when he recognized a pair of costumed legs on a folded newspaper. The Equalizer opened up the broadsheet, written in some foreign lingo like Hungarian, and took in another drawing of Southern Cross in action — without his mask, precisely as Jack preferred.

The Brick smiled.

Local artists seemed to like the whole headline-ripping theme —
and in this case he couldn't make any sense of the headlines. This
would cause the kid to laugh, surely.

Or not.

Carefully refolding the paper, the Brick breathed out noisily. A
sourpuss old lady, across the aisle, acted annoyed by the sound but
what did he care? Silly battle-axe.

The Equalizer's body ached all over. Still alive, which was
surprising. PA said he had Stellar to acknowledge for the small
mercy, thanks to that miracle blood of hers. Blood that'd do nothing
to thaw this heart or fix up the kid's broken one.

Call in.

He needed to call in, let Pretty Amazonia know that Jack had
been found. She could tell Kahn and Stellar.

The Brick felt like he was pinioned to the flimsy chair, which
squeaked as he shifted — probably it was about to collapse anyway,
so no choice. After rising to his feet, the Equalizer stomped along a
wide, cream-coloured corridor with many staring people and found
a payphone, an old AMT with Russian lettering on it.

The problem with the underpants was no space for a dime.

#170

When he opened his eyes, Jack found Pretty Amazonia hovering over him.

"Don't you get altitude sickness?" he mumbled.

The woman smiled in a roundabout way — an expression as forced as it was relieved, while she cupped his face in both her hands, and then leaned in close.

"You're okay?"

Jack blinked, removed the fingers, and turned his head away to stare at venetian blinds that were open by the window, allowing in strips of sunlight. "Sure. Yes. No."

He could hear the rustle of her costume behind him.

"I understand." She blew out air. "You really did some damage, by the way. Took them hours to put out the fire at Hatfield House."

"Is he dead?"

"We don't know. They're still sifting through the ruins there and at the *Patriot*. Gypsie-Ann's on it."

"You heard about Wright?"

"Yes. We'll get him, Jack. I swear it."

The man slowly peered over his shoulder. "I like the hair. Short suits you."

"Thanks." PA looked through the open doorway into the hospital proper, obviously uncomfortable, skittish. "She's here."

"I know." Jack's tone revealed nothing.

"Then you know she's—?"

"I know. The Brick told me."

#171

Jack found his suit hanging in a small closet. One trouser leg may have been caked in dried blood, but given it was navy blue, you'd barely notice. Other specks — from Wright's dead lookalike — peppered the jacket and shirt. He didn't care. After changing, the Equalizer grabbed a pair of crutches and made his way, thanks to various nurses' directions, to Intensive Care.

The Professor was in a chair beside a bed upon which Louise lay.

She was plugged into an ICU monitor, an arterial line and IV catheter, and had a fat tube coming out of the side of her mouth that connected with a ventilator.

"Our girl is brain-dead, Jack. She's left us."

The little old man's wrinkled face was whiter than ever as he leaned in to kiss the hand of a girl who looked — despite the medical paraphernalia — like she was simply sleeping.

"Turn off these machines and she slips away from us forever."

Jack put his head into his hands, turned a circle, and ripped the curtains from the window.

"No!" he shouted at the wall, and then, with far less intensity: "No." The anger and the rage vanished. All that remained was an overpowering exhaustion. Annoyed looks were tossed his way by nearby medical staff, before they went about their business. Jack felt he'd keel onto the linoleum floor in the middle of the ward.

"Bring yourself over here, son."

The Professor patted a chair beside him, lined up next to the cot and closer to Louise's face. Jack didn't argue. He collapsed into it to stare at the girl for a long time, thinking but saying nothing.

"You were right," the Prof said in a quiet voice. "Miss Stellar refused to press charges, bless her. The police considered going with unlawful possession of a firearm, but I have a licence for the Webley since it's an antique and part of the shop's inventory. Instead, they may press charges related to false identity. We'll see. Captain Kahn gave me the time-worn missive not to leave town — our brave police

348

don't appear to realize yet that Blandos cannot leave Heropa, even if one chooses to do so."

"Neither can we."

Aside from his clutch of exclamations at inanimate objects, this was the first time Jack had spoken in almost twenty-four hours. The process felt odd, the pitch wavered while he rubbed his jaw, and he felt numb.

Jack wasn't able to tear his gaze from Louise's face. She was so close, and yet he couldn't touch her; he wasn't aware when, precisely, the Professor had coerced his hand into holding the girl's fingers.

"Heropa has a magnifying effect on the personality traits of those who reside here," said the Professor as he packed a pipe. "Good becomes great, bad becomes worse, and so on and so forth. Louise was a shining light."

"Is." Jack squeezed her hand, smiled a fraction. "She's still here, still alive."

"Of course." The Professor patted the other man's shoulder before leaving.

#172

He returned to the Warbucks & Erewhon Union Trust Bank on Fawcett Avenue.

Initially he stood outside, staring at the grand building, almost turned on his heel. Stopping him was something distantly related to a backbone.

He had on something old, a three-piece suit by Walter Plunkett he'd worn the first time he met Louise, the one he'd borrowed from the Big O (hadn't that been destroyed?) and wondered if, maybe, he should've tried something in blue.

Having pushed through the plate-glass door, he hoofed it up to the customer-service area. No Louise at her desk, meaning he was forced to join a long, zigzagging queue that crossed the tiled floor and had no end — but before he knew what was afoot, Jack was looming over a till occupied by the elderly Mister Winkle, never one for speed.

Jack forced himself to smile, yet Mister Winkle looked more alarmed than pleased — perhaps because Jack's fabricated grin had come across gruesome. No mirror to check, so he eased off on the charm.

"I'm here to see Miss Starkwell," he announced.

"Really, now?" Mister Winkle said in languid fashion. "Do you have an appointment?"

"I do."

"Then I will have her paged. What is your name, sir?"

"Jacob Curtiss."

"Just a moment, sonny — please wait over there." Mister Winkle lifted an ancient claw to point to the other side of the open space, which was when Jack noticed all the other customers had vanished. Was it closing time?

While he waited, Jack did some browsing. First there was the wall Bulkhead had crashed through — it was still an airy mess that looked out onto the street — and next up sat an oddball lump of metal on a perch over near the main entrance.

"*Twilight Over Hoboken.*"

Jack briefly closed his eyes.

She was behind him, just like the second time they crossed paths. He could feel a cautious smile shimmy across his face and prayed it didn't mimic the one that had scared Mister Winkle.

"Sorry?" Jack said finally, as he turned about to face Louise — who, straight off the bat, was back to being the business-like Miss Starkwell.

Behind tortoiseshell cat's eye spectacles were a pair of wonderful emerald-green eyes that didn't know him from, well, Jack.

The girl was wearing a green and white leaf-patterned sleeveless dress and black silk shoes, with silk baby blue pom-pom ribbons on the toes. Her hair hung straight, with the ends curling upward. While she also had a smile, it was a polished and friendly number, not in any way related to recognition. She was being courteous to a complete stranger.

"That sculpture you're looking at. It's *Twilight Over Hoboken*," Miss Starkwell went on, "by famous Italian-American artist Pierre Picolino. Do you know him?"

"I've heard the name." Jack found it difficult to breathe, but he knew the rest by rote and allowed the words to spill out. "I don't see it."

"You don't see what, sir?"

Throat dry, he could barely swallow. "The twilight."

"It's an abstract sculpture. You're supposed to use your imagination."

"Still."

"There's always something there, sir, if you look closely enough."

Jack scrutinized the girl's face. No, there wasn't. Not anymore. Never would be again.

"Please...call me Jacob." A flailing plea was in his heart, if not in the wonderfully steady tone he used.

In return the girl looked through him. Only seconds had passed and Jack was already losing her attention. "Mister Curtiss, isn't it?"

"That's right."

"Is there something in particular you needed to see me about? We're quite busy."

The truth? He wanted to see beyond her spectacles, right down into places he'd recently traversed and where he'd discovered such — what? Bliss? Bliss. Yes. He pined to hold her and kiss her and tell her everything would be fine; tell himself the exact same thing. Lie to them both.

"Mister Curtiss?" Miss Starkwell tilted her head. She looked cagey.

"Yes. I wanted to say thank you."

Jack heard a veiled exhalation of relief.

"I'm so happy to hear we could be of assistance." Miss Starkwell had no clue what he was talking about. As always, she covered beautifully, even held out her hand. They shook right there next to *Twilight Over Hoboken*.

"Goodbye then," Miss Starkwell said. "Please call, if ever you need our help." The girl was turning away when Jack stopped her with a lie.

"I want to take out a loan," he fudged.

Miss Starkwell hesitated. "Mister Winkle is our loans expert."

"But I trust *you* to manage my accounts. I don't know Mister Winkle."

"I'm sorry, sir. Loans are not my jurisdiction."

"We're talking a considerable sum."

"Even so." Miss Starkwell gave the man an apologetic look.

"Then I'll take my business elsewhere."

Jack had no idea from whence all this rubbish was sprouting, but it had the desired effect — the girl appeared to be mildly alarmed, although it was hard to tell how this complete stranger really felt.

"There's no need to do that," she said, as if it mattered. "I'll talk to Mister Winkle right away, explain the situation — I'm sure I can sit in on the meeting, if that would make you more comfortable?"

"It would. Thank you."

Without thinking, Jack stretched out his left hand and placed it on Miss Starkwell's right shoulder. She stiffened, but said nothing. He noticed her lips lost their colour.

"Is there somewhere we could go? To wait for Mister Winkle, I mean?"

"Certainly, sir."

She scrutinized Jack's hand, a clear message he should remove it. Once he did so, Miss Starkwell turned around, and the Equalizer studied a glorious pair of shoulder blades he'd once held and caressed naked.

"Please follow me." Her voice icy now, akin to the one he'd heard her throw at her boss Henry Holland.

Jack followed around the staff receptacles, through a swinging butler's door. He could smell perfume lingering behind her, peppermint mixed with strawberries and a vague scent of disinfectant.

The slightly dipping corridor diminished into the distance, with dozens of doors to either side, composed of different shapes, sizes and colours. As they walked, Jack had to step over a two-headed brown snake coiled on the carpet. He frowned, glancing back. Meanwhile, Miss Starkwell had finally stopped, took out a set of keys to unlock a door — a white one, number 4, with 'BOPS GO HOME!' stencilled across the surface and this slogan surrounded by yellow roses shaped into a wagon wheel.

They entered a shadowy cubbyhole with wood-panelling on the walls, a small, tidy pine desk, a two-tone green mohair channel-backed chair with a throw pillow on top. Jack picked up the pillow to test it — feather stuffing — and then he very quietly closed the door.

Miss Starkwell had stopped moving.

She was in the centre of this small room, staring fixedly at the desk. "Did you know," she murmured, in a soft voice Jack barely made out, "that the pine tree symbolizes creativity, life, longevity and immortality?"

"No. I didn't."

Jack went up close behind the girl, pressed against the shoulders. He brought his left arm around her waist and with the right hand pushed the pillow to her face, so that her mouth and nose were covered. She didn't struggle, though he felt her body tense up. After a couple of minutes, her limbs relaxed and Jack noted she'd ceased to breathe.

He placed the pillow back on the sofa-chair while gently easing Louise onto it.

Her lips were slightly apart, the eyes closed.

Jack sat on the arm of the chair, looking down at her face, her hair, her neck, her arms, her hands. Almost choked on the wails he repressed, and buried these deep down inside. No need for that nonsense here. Not now. Later.

That was when he woke up.

Louise was asleep in the hospital bed beside him. A long slumber from which she'd never awake. Kept alive by the ventilator, with its awful sound of artificial breathing. In-out. In-out. In-out.

Still, it was evening, and even here in the Intensive Care unit of Heropa City General Hospital — up on the fifth floor — he could hear the additional noise of cicadas. Was it supposed to be late summer in Heropa? There were no trees nearby and they were deep inside a modern structure of concrete and glass. The sound settled him, somehow buttered up his pain.

Jack rose from the chair, wiped a film of sweat from his brow, stared in the half-light at Louise's peaceful face. No. There had to be another way. This place wasn't real — why did they have to stoop to real-world answers? Surely there was another way.

Jack grabbed his jacket, along with a single crutch, and left the room.

Decided to go for a hobble to find those cicadas.

He took a lift to the ground floor, went out through automatic doors, crossed a sizeable carpark, and emerged into a main street that was reasonably quiet for nine-thirty.

There was a small park a block from the hospital, only twenty square metres. About the same size as his flat in Melbourne. Three trees, elms, dominated the place above a sandbox and a slide. Jack sat down on the wooden edge of the sandbox, listening to the cicadas' chorus from the branches above.

He wasn't sure when he realized one of the creatures, lime-green in colour, had placed itself on his shoulder. He gazed at it for a long time — the oddball beauty of its bulbous shape, the tiny black eyes, the see-through wings.

He'd never seen a cicada before. There weren't any left in Melbourne. So much for Gypsie-Ann's theory that creepy-crawlies didn't inhabit Heropa.

The insect climbed along his upper arm, and then took to the treetops. Watching it fly, Jack got to his feet with the crutch, dusted off his backside, and began to walk some more. The sound of sirens drowned out the cicadas.

A few blocks further along was a ring of six police cars — 1940s-style black numbers that the Brick would be better able to describe — with 'HEROPA CITY POLICE' painted on the doors and overlarge lights on their roofs flashing.

Officers were standing behind, revolvers drawn. The object of their attention appeared to be a bar with a raucous neon image of a woman in a suspender belt, stockings, and very little else.

"Come out! With your hands in the air!" demanded a police sergeant via a loudhailer, and then he signalled to two of his number. After some hesitation, they proceeded across the sidewalk into the building.

Well, why not?

Jack needed to clear his head — perhaps do a Brick and damage others. He didn't have his Southern Cross rags, wasn't sure where they'd got to with the bullet holes in the leg. Being a Cape seemed to take a lot of unnecessary effort and Jack pined for the Flash's costume ring.

Then he changed his mind. Who needed a costume?

With his crutch under his arm, Jack ambled over to the ruckus, heading straight for the authority figure with the beaten-up loudhailer.

"What's the problem, officer?"

"Sergeant," the man bridled, pointing out the stripes on his sleeve at the same time that he gave Jack the once-over. "Donnegan, of the 31st. Nothin' we can't handle. Beat it, cripple."

The flatfoot had just full-stopped this fitting riposte when his two subordinates exited the building via a plate-glass window, sailed over the heads of their mates, and ended up on the road behind the squad cars.

The sarge looked at the unconscious, muttering men, rolled his eyes, and folded. "Meet Officers Freddie Wertham and Carey Kefauver. Usually they have more to say."

"I'll bet."

"It's Crosshairs again, drunk and disorderly — by all reports he's injured six patrons in there. Now add two fine police officers to the list. These Capes are outta control."

"Good Cape or bad?"

"Does it matter, bud?"

"Nope — you're right. Let's see what I can do to help."

"You're kidding me. What, you and that crutch? Swell."

Jack actually grinned, something he would have thought impossible only a day before. "Forgot my costume. I'm Southern Cross."

"The hell you are." Then the sergeant thawed, a glint of recognition on his face. "I'll be — it is you, isn't it? Seen your mug before. You did good yesterday, helping all those bystanders in the Cape War."

"Just doing our job — like you."

The police sergeant smiled widely. "You're all right."

"Guess I have my minor moments. Can you and the boys hold your fire? Unless this Crosshairs bastardo trounces me, of course."

"You okay?" The cop glanced at the crutch.

"Luckily my power comes out of my arm, not my leg."

"Then we're right behind you.

"Counting on it."

"Southern Cross, right?"

"Got it."

"I'll remember this. Thanks."

Jack left the police sergeant's company and hopped closer to the bar with its gaping, broken window. Difficult to see inside, and he had no idea what to expect. This left the Equalizer wondering when he'd learn to brush up on a Cape's powers before trying to take him or her down.

"Hey, Crosshairs!" he called. "Drinks on the house out here. Short-time offer only."

There was much commotion inside the building, and then a shadowy figure pushed through the door out into the police spotlights, where he became crystal-clear.

This individual was at least ten feet tall — despite bowlegs — with a barrel chest and brawny arms dangling down to the knees. His entire body was covered with downy fur that reminded Jack of a chinchilla, but round the neck was a coarser lion's mane. 'Crosshairs'. Ahh.

The simian-feline-rodentia staggered a couple of steps, banged back against the doorframe, and laughed in slurred fashion.

"Well, well, if it ain't Mister Southern Cross, the Red Skull know-it-all," he chortled. "You brought along your snazzy pink purse to shout me some rounds?"

That comment caught Jack off guard. No way — this was the Rat, from back in Melbourne? He stared at the ape-like character for a few seconds, and then spoke again.

"Give it up, okay? You've done enough damage."

"Damage...? Whoa! Why so serious, man? This is all — every-thing, y'know — a joke, you know that, don't you?" The giant staggered out a few steps. "Lighten up! So where're these freakin' free drinks you promis—"

An extra eye, a bright red one, suddenly appeared between his other two.

Crosshairs froze, frowned, and then reeled backwards onto the cement with a dull thud. Half his grey matter was spattered over the glowing girl and her stockings.

Jack stared, aghast.

"Fuck—!"

MARVELLOUS MELBOURNE

#173

"—it easy there."

He found himself sitting up, tottering anyway, dizzy, violently shaking, and a fevered perspiration covering most of his naked form.

Naked — *What kind of hateful gag was this?*

Not only trapped inside a room the size of the closet, but no suit, no costume, just wiring and electrodes aplenty — scattered all over a tiny, skinny white body with freckles and very little in the way of muscles. This was like being Steve Rogers in reverse. Of course he started to panic.

"Take deep breaths," the same voice commanded in his right ear. "Come on. Calm down. You're hyperventilating. Breathe...breathe. Steady, now. There's a lad."

"I... What—? Bloody hell, what is this shit?" shouted out Jacob, in a higher pitch than he was used to, while he yanked at the wires and his fingers became entangled in their net.

"Take it easy! Stop that! You'll break them."

Strong hands grabbed his wrists. Then again, maybe they weren't so strong — more likely he was now weak. Jacob found himself looking at Gonzo with the long green hair, wearing another of his Ralph Steadman tees and a bent pair of thick-frame glasses.

The man had started to tenderly remove each and every electrode from his charge's body.

"Thataboy. We need this gear," he was saying, focused on the task, "combined with amino acid therapy, a proteolytic inhibitor and the standard iconometric-frammistat, so your muscles don't atrophy. For every person here we use an eight-channel FES device that culti-vates hundreds of these little surface electrodes and cables, two interconnected four-channel stimulators, and a reconfigured Mitt-Mate for stimulator programming and processing compliance data. They don't come cheap or grow on trees. Automated and extensive training of eight muscle groups of the upper and lower extremities is performed six hours a day, with one second on and two off tetanic contractions, at twenty to thirty percent of maximum tetanic muscle force. We need to take loving care of these things."

Jacob blinked several times, his thoughts confused and his eyes partly out of focus. No amount of waffling was ever going to get this information to make sense, but the boy got the feeling it wasn't intended to — Gonzo was more trying to bring him back to the here and now, perhaps by boring him stupid with outlandish jargon.

"What...reeks?" the boy asked.

"You do. *Pfew!*" Gonzo grinned, as first he fanned himself, and then wiped Jacob's brow with a filthy rag. "I'm used to it, but otherwise you gave me a scare. Had enough of those lately. Now I'm all done with the electrodes, I'll just unhook the colostomy bag — let's keep the drip in for a bit."

There was a rusted steel pole beside the cot, dangling a half-empty IV pouch.

"Reckon you can stand, Jacob?"

"I think so." His voice sounded shrill, distant. "Don't know. I feel dizzy."

"That's normal, agonize not. You should see how people react after months of downtime — you were in Heropa only two weeks. C'mon. Try it."

With Gonzo's assistance, Jacob pushed up and, while he found his body lighter than expected, the legs felt like jelly. Once on his feet, he tottered, but Gonzo gave additional support.

"Problem with standing, or are you playing drunk?"

"Not drunk. Someone shot me."

"Ow! What the hell is going on down there?" Gonzo appraised things anew. "It takes time to get used to the fact this all happened in your noggin, that in actual fact you have no injury at all. Give it twenty-four hours, more or less. Incidentally — how'd you get out of Heropa?"

Thinking took effort. "I swore," recalled the boy.

"No kidding? Cool. Glad to hear the cuss-words work again,

though it means an auto two-day penalization — not that you'll care."

"Where am I?"

"Safe. Back in Melbourne, of course."

"Safe?"

"As houses."

While Gonzo proceeded to chuckle away at some unshared joke, Jacob shook his head, attempting to clear the cobwebs.

"Fuck," he whispered. Nothing happened.

"Come with me," Gonzo said, giving Jacob his arm. "You need to start walking this off, get the circulation flowing. You can carry the IV."

The two of them moved out of that miniature, ill-lit room into a familiar hallway, filthy-looking, with broken floorboards and mildewed, peeling wallpaper that had Victorian illustrations of angel's trumpets or moonflowers. The atmosphere felt heavy, humid, and the sound of torrential rain was somewhere close by.

"You joined Heropa at a bad time," Gonzo disclosed. "We've been having no end of hassle with the mainframe — thing went rogue on us. We use old gear, hand-me-downs and complete junk, so I'm hardly surprised — William Gibson would roll in his grave. Hitting reset doesn't seem to work anymore. I'm sure we'll get the glitches ironed out, but meanwhile there've been some...complications."

"People dying."

"Hell, no! Nothing that serious. Not exactly — but, well, complications."

"Like the Rat?"

Gonzo stopped assisting and looked down, eyebrows knotted, as he wiped hair from his face. "Are you talking about Tom?"

"Kid my age, resembling a rat? We met when I came here, and he was with you when I showed my picture of Southern Cross."

"Tom. What do you know?"

"Pretty sure he doubles-up under the name of Crosshairs in

Heropa, right?"

"I'm not supposed to say."

"Well. Looks like some sniper killed Crosshairs — using their own crosshairs."

Staring up at the distant ceiling, Gonzo chewed his lower lip at the same time he rubbed his chin. The man needed a facial. "Shit, so that's it. Sometimes you get a day like this when nothing goes right."

"Let me guess — this isn't the first 'complication'."

"No. Dammit!"

Gonzo helped Jacob to the next room along, another tiny, partitioned-off cubicle. A familiar figure with terrible skin laid prostate on a camp bed, a blanket pulled up to his neck. The Rat/Tom/Crosshairs. This teenager appeared to be alive, eyes half open, but there was nothing behind them — dead without being clinically proclaimed thus.

"How long?" Jacob asked.

"About ten minutes before you woke up. I know the symptoms. Seen them far too often lately."

"Ten minutes? There was only a second or so between his...demise...and me accidentally hitting eject."

Gonzo shrugged. "For some reason, it takes longer to revive naturally than via unnatural means. Can't account for the glitch."

"Will he recover?"

"I doubt it. No one else has. We now have twenty people like this — what the fuck is happening down there?"

Still looking at the Rat, Jacob murmured, "Someone was killing off the great Capes of Heropa."

"Jesus H. Christ... Murder? — In Heropa? Is that possible?"

"What were you thinking? That twenty people copped fatal accidents at the same time?"

"No!" The man acted sheepish. "Then we need to shut down the system."

"Don't do that." Jacob held onto the other man's shoulder, still frail, and looked him in the eye. "Listen to me — not yet. I don't think it's appropriate. There's a lot at stake."

"Why the hell not? People are dropping like flies out here!"

"I think we nailed the culprit. But I need to be sure."

"You? You're out."

"No, I'm going back in."

"Are you crazy?"

"Working on it. But we need time to sort out what's going on. Can I return to Heropa early?

"Server won't let you — you need to pay the piper for the swearing misdemeanour, even if every other online system's gone snafu."

"Can't you override it?"

"I'm not a magician. The only way would be a complete shut-down."

"Crap." Jacob blew out benumbed cheeks, trying to get some sort of feeling happening there. "Okay, I'll have to wait. Is the Reset working again?"

"Offline, like the passwords. Then again, I thought swearing was out, too." Gonzo eased Jacob down to a wooden box on which to sit.

"I need to see the Big O."

"Me too. He's still in Heropa — right?"

Jacob looked up, checking the man's face for some sense of sarcasm, but saw only confusion. "You do know he was the second victim, not long after the Aerialist?"

"Huh. Her too?"

Flirting with full disclosure — that she was further still a Blando — Jacob realized he didn't have the strength to go into it, not now. "Yeah," he muttered. "But why isn't the Big O here, if he was killed off in Heropa? Where's his real self?"

Gonzo cocked his baffled head to one side. "In Melbourne?"

"Obviously — but where?"

"Same place as the Aerialist?"

"Now you're confusing me."

"Welcome to the club." From out of the back pocket of his jeans, the man produced a hipflask, took a long swig of something, and then dragged over a milkcrate to sit. "The original developers of Heropa have their own access points into the place — only the plebs that came later, like us, use this dump." Gonzo waved around him. "We have no idea where those people really are. I always figured the Aerialist was one of them, since she was there pretty much from the beginning and I never met her here."

The two gazed at the still-life Rat on the camper bed.

"A swell kid. Could be downright annoying, but he cared about people. Worked with me for months looking after the place — this was his first trip to Heropa, same as you. I told him not to go. Now look at him. Self-indulgent madness. Knew there was a reason I stayed out of there."

Jacob looked at his companion anew in that moment. The ragged pants, the Docs, his choice of seating, the coat he wore the day the boy first arrived. "You were Milkcrate Man, weren't you?"

"Ancient history, mate. But how'd you figure that out?"

"Didn't exactly alter yourself much for Heropa, or so I hear. The affinity for milkcrates and alcohol helped."

Holding aloft his hipflask, Gonzo bowed while seated. "Happy with who, and what, I am."

"So you knew Major Patriot."

"Major Pain, you mean."

"Original."

"Don't be sarcastic, kid — it doesn't suit."

"Sorry."

"Water off a duck's back. Anyway, Major Patriot and the Great White Hope were in a competition to be the biggest pseudo-intellectual ball-breaker, though MP was more smarmy about it."

"You didn't like him."

"Like him? He's the major reason I left — pun again intended."

"What was his power?"

"Outside his own head? The despot could duplicate himself — six or seven times. I don't remember. Six or seven times too many of this bastard, that I do recall. Him and Sir Omphalos had some serious issues — there was definitely a power play going down when I arrived, about a year after they launched Heropa. A bizarre triangle between the Big O, the Major and Bullet Gal."

"Triangle?"

"They were both obviously smitten with her."

"Why'd you leave?"

"You have to ask? I spent two years in Heropa, trying to make the place better — a losing cause when you think of all the egos prancing about in tights."

#174

Gonzo closeted himself away with a litre of synth-brandy, two bags of grass and a salt-shaker half full of ground Clodualdo. Said he was depressed and wanted to be left alone — "Screw Heropa!" — but, prior to locking the door, assured Jacob that someone named Midori would monitor the dozen remaining downloaders.

Having briefly wondered which of these sleeping beauties were the Brick, PA and Gypsy-Ann, or even Saint Y, Jacob decided against snooping about the small rooms amongst people still plugged in. Seemed too personal and far too weird, even if he could win the next round of *Whaddaya Reckon This Person is Really Like Out There?*

The other thing he skipped out on visiting, like a plague virus, was the back room. His host had warned that's where the catatonic ones were placed, most recently the Rat.

So, after Gonzo slammed his door, the boy borrowed some of the Rat's clothes — a disturbing habit he'd acquired, nicking accessories from dead and/or incapacitated types — and headed out into the rain, in the direction of the Tower of the Elephant in Thornbury. Jacob had a busted-up orange umbrella that offered minimal protection, and after five minutes he was drenched. Half an hour of walking later, the itching began.

But Jacob had purpose, something to focus on other than the black hole in his chest. This purpose involved an old school-chum who owned a computer and, given the time of afternoon, he knew where the boy would most likely be.

While it was true that idInteract venues peppered Melbourne, the more famous one in Jacob's neighbourhood was the Tower of the Elephant, inside Beet Street Arcade, where most kids — aged eight to eighty — hung out. There was a permanent queue spilling from the arcade onto the footpath, and then circumnavigated the block. The owners had installed flashing neon signage and screens everywhere surrounding the building, along with a set of diabolical fifteen-inch, 1800-watt speakers booming out classic rock like the number that roared and echoed along the street as Jacob neared — AC/DC's 'Jailbreak' — above the sound of the downpour.

Running across the road in front of an archaic, speeding double-decker bus wasn't an impulse of great genius as his leg still played up, and the boy almost fell beneath the vehicle's wheels. At any rate, he was further swamped with a wave of muddy water. Dripping, Jacob began to inspect the hundreds of usual suspects in the idI line-up.

John wasn't there, but on a corner nearby, beneath an awning, he spotted three pre-teen kids he did recognize: Roy, Sal and Barry.

Twelve-year-old Roy wore a t-shirt with 'Alter-Ego' splashed on it, and he had a blond, jagged-cut fringe hanging over misshapen glasses. Barry, the youngest at about ten, was the son of English émigrés, clung to his Britishness — even though he was born in Melbourne — and had an obligatory scowl framed by long black hair that'd possibly never been introduced to a brush. While Barry bossed his elders round, Roy was the brains of the outfit. Easier-going Sal, who had slicked-back dark hair and ears that stuck out quite a distance, was John's younger brother. Bingo.

A girl with a blue 'do, a banged-up bowler hat and a single set of false eyelashes hanging from her left peeper was busy cajoling the boys, flaunting a disc in her hand.

"—A real kick-starter, y'know? Heavy, heavy, heavy, heavy stuff," she raved on.

While this girl puttered stop-start fashion through a wayward sales pitch, Jacob asked, in one of their ears, "How's Johnnie?"

"All right," Sal said "Ain't seen you in a bit."

"Been busy treading water."

"Reckon he's pissed off with you, J. Says you become a hermit-freak."

"I'm out of my box now."

"Still."

"Sure I'll live to tell the tale."

"D'you eat?

Jacob smiled at that. "Better than ever."

"You look like a scarecrow."

"Blame the metabolism."

Some guy walked right up close behind the blue-haired hawker, wearing a frayed-looking Stetson and coat that made Jacob enact a double-take. He couldn't see the face properly since it was hidden in a dark shadow produced by glaring overhead spotlights.

"What d'you want, Georgie, huh?" the girl asked when she finally noticed him.

"Let's talk, sweetheart. Scatter boys." The man grabbed her arm and tugged her away into the rain.

A few seconds' startled quietude was subsequently broken.

"Girl was some serious spaz," Roy shouted above the deafening din of an Angus Young guitar solo, coming out of one of those all-powerful speakers above them. This particular box was wrapped in plastic to shield it from the rain, and the material rattled. "Brain-fry stuff. You see her eyes? Glazed as."

Barry: "What'cha reckon? IdIot, plain and simple."

Sal: "Who was the old fogie in the hat?"

Roy: "Dunno. Her dad? Wasn't that old—"

Barry: "Bollocks! More like her idI-pimp."

Sal: "They have them?"

Roy: "You're kidding, Sal — what the hell does Baz know?"

Barry: "Well, now, that's just cracking foxy, innit?"

Roy: "Cracking peanuts, more like it."

Barry: "Oh, ha-de-hah. IdI-gimp."

Roy: "IdI-tosser."

Barry: "I'll toss you in a minute."

Roy: "You, and what slackarse army?"

Jacob waited with patience for this pointless stream-of-consciousness to blow over, and then blundered back into the fray.

"Sal, I need to see Johnnie."

"So, see him."

"Is he home?"

"Dunno."

"Yes, or no?"

"Guess he might be. Maybe," the boy murmured, his attention distracted and held by a nearby screen displaying some kind of idI extreme sport snowboarding romp. "I hate waiting. Boring!"

Jacob left the trio to their suffering and headed for John and Sal's place two streets away, in another Housing Commission complex. When he arrived, his friend wasn't home but the mother was. She opened the door, looked a picture of washed-out concern as she invited him in. Their flat was more bare-bones than Jacob remembered. Without saying much beyond a hello, the boy asked if they still had a computer and if he could use it — needed to do a spot of research, he told her.

This mum asked high-pitched, stressed-out questions while he worked online. 'When're you returning to school? Who's looking after you? Are you eating enough? Do the authorities know you live by yourself?' ...That kind of barrage.

Jacob fielded the flak, gave vague answers he hoped would make the busybody happy, and after a couple of hours and a quick bite to eat of bland, thrice-heated leftovers, he set back out into the elements for home.

The water had stopped itching and begun to sting by the time he reached the building, took several flights of stairs past dozing denizens in rags, and trudged along the corridor to his flat.

Two men lingered there right beside the door. They looked out of place on the litter-covered cement with their neat raincoats and hats, one plump and the other skinny.

"Jacob Curtiss?" the fat man asked.

"That's me."

"Swell to hear," piped up his partner, the wiry one. "We're not bothering you, are we? Tell us we aren't."

"No."

"No, we aren't bothering you, or no — we are?"

Jacob shivered. What would the Brick say in a situation like this?

"Whichever you prefer, twinkles."

"Hey, a tough guy."

"Not at all."

"I'll say. Looks like you'd blow away in a stiff breeze. Well, now. Juvie Services sent us along. Not our usual jaunt — we have way bigger fish to fry — but what the heck, job's a job, right?"

It looked like the skinny fellow was reaching for something beneath his coat, making Jacob renounce the shiver and tense up instead.

The fat man chose then to intervene, placing his considerable bulk between the boy and the thin man.

"Crosley, shut the fuck up and relax. There's a good laddie." He swivelled attention back to Jacob. "Listen, son, word's got out you quit school and're destitute. These are not good times for either road. I know what happened to your parents, so let's avoid it happening to you. Re-enrol. Go to Juvenile Services and plead the case — you're entitled to benefits, food-stamps, that kind'a thing."

"Fuck that!" declared the other fellow. "Why give any thought? Let's cut the crap and take featherweight in."

"I have seniority here, mate." The fat man glared at his partner. "Chill."

"All right, all right. Whatever. Grumpy-bum."

The fat man rolled aggravated eyes, and then returned to the boy. "Anyhow, I know the system sucks and they'll give you shit-all help. But do what I say, make them happy. If ever you need advice, call me." He shoved a card into Jacob's hand. "For fuck's sake, stay out of trouble. C'mon, Crosley. I have to go buy some kitty litter."

"Didn't know you had a cat."

"Do now."

"Guess so." The rakish man took one last glance at Jacob. "Grab something to eat, kid — you look like a goddamned skeleton."

That said, the two walked away towards the elevator without a backward glance.

Jacob examined the satin-finish plasticard: 'Harry Jones' it read,

'Seeker Branch', followed by a telephone number.

Jacob pushed this card into the Rat's pocket, removed a key from under the doormat, and unlocked the door.

#175

The next two days took an eternity to pass.

During those forty hours it never once stopped raining outside. Initially, Jacob squandered time doing exercises to get his new, frail body functioning properly — but then got tired of doing that and went through old comicbooks, scoured *The History of Art* — anything to keep the defective grey matter occupied.

He also spent an hour at the window, watching the rain pelt down across a grey, hazy metropolis floodlit in places by gussied-up neon marquee sign advertising. Traced his finger along the greasy glass, following each fresh rivulet of dirty water on the other side.

His stomach's rumbling reminded Jacob there was nothing here to eat and the out-of-action fridge housed paperbacks, but he ignored the hunger. Eventually the other thing, the thing he'd been ignoring all along, came home to roost and he couldn't brush up anymore. The textbook read stuffy, the comics lame, the view depressing.

So Jacob eventually fled his flat, spent a few hours at the old, abandoned railway siding near Batman Station — a name that now struck him as funny, if he were in the mood to laugh, given recent experiences in Heropa — off Renown Street, close to Sydney Road in North Coburg.

There was a Southern Cross Station in Melbourne too, inside the Dome, but he'd never seen it and never would. Jacob could just make out the Dome in the distance, through a pall of rain, lit up like an enormous, grubby snowglobe.

Mostly, he thought about Louise.

About her face, so clear still when he allowed himself to remember. Her casually husky laugh and the way in which she toyed with her glasses as she thought something through. Lighting up, cigarette held between straight white teeth, while she poured another glass of champagne. The queen of caffeine. A bouquet of peppermint and citrus.

He kept at bay the still-life images — Louise in the hospital bed, these mannerisms and eccentricities diminished to nothing.

Finally, Jacob looked around.

In Melbourne, midnight and noon were little different. It rained through the day and pissed down all night. The illumination at three a.m. was pretty much the same as three o'clock in the afternoon, there were no seasons aside from this single, humid one, and there would never again be any cicadas. This was the sum total Jacob had known since his earliest rememoration.

The rain wore down buildings as much as it did the people. Gutters overflowed; there were sometimes corpses in stagnant ponds. Children starving to death after their parents were rounded up and disappeared.

The boy wandered back streets on the way home, through the downpour and bumper-to-bumper traffic, and people with umbrellas — suicidal, as they flew past on bicycles. Some shops shuttered, others bearing smashed windows and vandalized signage. Deals and beatings and sex going down in laneways, police glaring at everyone but ignoring everything.

When, finally, the next afternoon the two-day deadline neared, Jacob set off at a run.

Frequently checking over his shoulder, doubling back and crossing busy streets to ensure he wasn't followed, Jacob wound up on the verandah of the Victorian terrace house and rapped at the door with the lightning bolt knocker.

He was dripping wet (again) but that didn't matter. The short, queasy silence was followed by a furtive voice coming through damp wood. Not the Rat's, of course — this was female.

"Hello?"

"Comicbooks."

Someone coughed. "Who killed Professor Abraham Erskine?"

This question took Jacob by surprise. He stared at the door, at the peeling pain and specks of mould, thinking about the Prof and his shock of white hair. He'd promised to look out for the old man — had he failed that too?

"Well?" the voice asked, on edge. "Don't you know your Captain America lore?"

"You're talking up in the comic?"

"What else would I be talking about?"

"Thank crap." The boy leaned against the doorframe, pulling himself back together. "Okay, I know this — a Nazi spy, Heinz Kruger."

The door was unbolted and a pale girl's face peered out, hard to see in the shadows. "What d'you want?"

"Heropa."

"Heropa's finished."

"Not so far as I'm concerned. Let me in."

"Why're you here?"

"I told you."

The door swung open and Jacob marched through. There was a gangly, teenage Asian girl standing sentry, pretty enough from what he could see under a mop-top fringe that covered most of her face, but the most striking aspect was that she looked bent in the middle, like someone had folded her waist sideways and forgotten to straighten it out. This girl refused to engage in eye contact and had an anorexic edge — then again, he was equally malnourished, so nothing new there.

As Jacob entered, the girl slipped awkwardly to one side. "Haven't you heard?" she said, in a flat voice that pushed inaudible. "The system's down."

"I heard. What's your problem?"

"Huh?"

"Your posture looks off."

"Gee — subtle. Thanks." The girl momentarily looked up and her bangs parted. Jacob saw one iris grey, one brown. "Didn't your folks ever teach you discretion?"

"I don't see the point anymore."

"No beating round the bush for you, then?"

"The last time I did so, it caused a lot of pain to someone I care about."

"Oh."

Jacob sighed. "Do you have a towel? I'm leaking on your floor."

"Sure. Come with me."

While he followed the limping caretaker, it dawned on him that this was the person the Rat had truly been mimicking the first time Jacob came to the house. Meanwhile, the girl was humming something Jacob recognized. He'd heard it that night he spied on the Brick and his paramour in the dance studio.

"What's the tune?"

She stopped briefly to glance back. "Johann Strauss II — the *pas de deux* shared between Bella and Johann after he's freed from prison in Act 2 of *Die Fledermaus*, 'The Bat'. You wouldn't know the ballet. Why?"

"It's beautiful." And so it was.

The girl detoured into a grungy bathroom and pulled down a towel that she tossed to her guest. It was threadbare and stank to high heaven, but did the job.

"Anyway. Heropa," he reminded her.

"Thought you said you knew the problems? Safeties offline, passwords dysfunctional. Even though they're patchy, expletives appear to be the only escape route — that's the way I got out."

"Me too."

"Birds of a feather. So, what are you really doing here?" he heard her quiz, still monotone, but louder-voiced while he dried his hair.

"I've got unfinished business." Jacob threw back the towel. "Where's Gonzo?"

"Who?"

"Guy with the green mane."

The girl sniggered, at the same time covering her mouth with a hand. "Oh, you mean Brion."

"That's his real name? Huh. Can I see him?"

"Not here. Probably, he's passed out somewhere."

"Who're you?"

"Midori."

"Nice to meet you. I'm Jacob. Otherwise known as Jack, a.k.a. Southern Cross."

The girl teetered back a few steps, gaze on the terrain at her feet. "Southern Cross? Oh. Southern Cross."

"Try not to wear it out."

Her eyes — admittedly attractive — swung up then. "And why would I do that?"

"Well, correct me if I'm wrong, but you're Prima Ballerina."

"Was."

"Running away from what's going on down there?"

She breathed out in loud fashion. "I have a condition known as adolescent idiopathic scoliosis — it's not the easiest thing for me to do a spot of jogging anytime. Besides, I never thought Heropa would get so crazy."

"Midori...Prima...crazy is *here*. This place. You know that as much as me. At least, in Heropa, we make a smidgeon of difference."

"It's scary. No."

"You can dance."

The girl closed her eyes. "True. That was something."

"And what about the Brick?"

"What about him?"

"He's still there."

"So what?"

Voice assuming a defiant tone, the girl had an expression steering in the direction of a sneer — the Prima Ballerina he remembered and precisely what Jacob, right now, held dear.

"My point. So what?"

She turned about, head suddenly held more erect even if her spine was not. "Are you implying something?"

"You two are pretty much common knowledge — well, were, before Bulkhead died."

"Meaning?"

"An item."

"What — me and that lump of rock?"

"We knew."

"Really?"

"Really."

After returning the towel to the bathroom, Midori shuffled back into the dim passageway. "What're you talking up? A silly rescue attempt?"

"Not just that, but we sort out what the fuck is going on. Call it justice or revenge or whatever you bloody well like — we go back and kick some serious arse."

Midori laughed, her bi-coloured eyes dissecting Jack, taking out his innards and examining each individual organ. "I had no idea you'd look like this."

"Scrawny and inconsequential?"

"No, right now you appear to me like you do in Heropa."

"Probably I sound tougher, because I get to swear more here."

"Likely, that helps."

The door at the other end of the hall suddenly burst open and Gonzo was trudging in their direction, a half-empty wine bottle in one hand.

"It works!" he shouted to them, then at the walls and the high ceiling. "You buggers hear me? It works!"

"What works?" Midori asked, startled.

"What do you reckon? The Reset's back online! I am, it goes without saying, a bloody miracle worker — can't believe I fixed the thing. It'll kick in at midnight, Heropa time. You bloody beauty!"

#176

Jacob squatted on the rancid, carpeted floor in front of a man in one corner in a 'wheelchair' — a yellow Series 7 number that'd seen far better days, castors gaffer-taped to the stainless-steel legs, and a belt encircling his waist to keep him seated.

There were other people strapped into similar, improvised contraptions around this spacious room and the air was not only stale, but also damp, ill-lit. The place had a heady fragrance of human effluence.

Jacob never once looked at the others. He felt that would be too much. The Rat was in here, Bulkhead, Sinistro, Iffy Bizness, Baron von Gatz and General Ching. Hell, even Marat/Rabble Rouser.

The boy continued to squat and stare into the face of someone he knew well, without having ever met, that Gonzo had reluctantly fingered.

While he needed a shave two weeks ago and his skin was too pale, this was a good-looking man, fortyish, thin face, strong chin. Light brown hair, with silver pushing through on the sides. There were wrinkles around the eyes, suggesting a sense of humour that'd scarpered.

The Brick was wrong. This wasn't the loser his partner had conjured up in their game in the park. Given an absence of expression in the sitter's eyes, Jacob doubted the Great White Hope would now care if he were tucked into an undersize baby chair. This man's observational powers were like the Rat's — a fat zero. It was like peering into a pair of glass eyes.

Jacob took the GWH's warm left hand in his.

"What did you know?" the boy asked. "Was it possible you found out the truth? Is that why they blinded you?" He flexed the other man's limp fingers. "I just wanted to say something. I'm sorry for the way I treated you. I hope you one day understand that."

The GWH's expression registered nary a morsel.

Getting to his feet, Jacob kicked away pins-and-needles in the leg that'd been shot in Heropa — it still played up — and unbolted the door to this room. He opened it to an overgrown, flooded back yard bathed in a combination of darkness and artificial light. The rain was loud on an overhead corrugated roof, and the outside air, though hardly pristine, began to diffuse the stench in this place.

Where out there was the Big O, and was there anybody to look after his comatose body?

"The people of Heropa didn't forget," Jacob announced to the rain. "They gave you a right royal send-off. Enough to make a person proud."

What was his name? Truly Lee, or was that an alias he used in Heropa? Did this matter anyway?

"Like you, I'm going to betray that faith. I know you meant to do the right thing with Louise — with Mitzi. Doesn't mean I agree with it at all, but likewise I'm going to try to do something that rectifies matters. People's memories will be sacrificed in the process. I know I'm being selfish. I think you did, too. Right? There're times when idealism needs to take a back seat."

Jacob stepped out into the rain, pushing through brittle, waist-high weeds, peered up at the sky, and got wet all over again.

"So, turns out I'm no better than you."

Andrez Bergen

THE KNOCK-OFF

#177

Jack and Midori touched down precisely where Jack had wound up on his first visit to Heropa — the busy sidewalk next to the travel agency, amidst late-afternoon pedestrian traffic. A gaily-coloured banner across the agency window read 'Holiday in San Gusto!!'.

The sky above was a deep blue, the sun relatively low on the horizon, and temperature-wise a perfect twenty-three degrees Celsius, or seventy-three-point-four in the old Fahrenheit system.

Adding to the déjà vu, that same dizziness was there, riding shotgun with a mild sense of panic. Once again, Jack tore off his mask. Obviously in the woman's case there was an additional touch of nausea, since she bent over and threw up into an alcove between the footpath and a brick wall.

When she recovered, Midori wiped her chin and had an embarrassed smile.

"Always the same reaction to the download," she said in an alluring, melodious tone, rotating her shoulders and stretching her back in the black swan leotard, "but, my, it's nice to stand up straight."

"Well, you can turn off the charm." Jack looked down at his chest, couldn't quite see over the now-protruding *pectoralis major* — being brawny had its drawbacks. "How many stars do I have?"

"Five. One more than the last time I saw you."

"Then the system remembers replacement costumes."

"Whatever makes you happy, Jack. All you now need is a shield."

"Nah, too much effort to lug around — besides, I have the Brick."

Adjusting her mask, Prima Ballerina continued to smile. "You know, we ought to be fighting right about now."

"Nice to take a break from that silliness."

"Agreed."

"You feeling okay?"

"Getting there."

Timely Tower's doorman Stan waltzed up to them, and he

examined the two Capes with a keen eye and rascally grin.

"Here's something to marvel at," he announced, genuinely pleased. "An Equalizer and a Rotter arriving together — as comrades-in-arms. It's very good to see you both."

"Thanks, Stan. Likewise."

"Mmm," said Midori, suspicious. "How do you know who I am?"

"I'm Stan the Doorman. I see all." Having clicked his heels, the man's snow-white moustache twisted into a tighter grin. "I have to say I happen to be quite the fan — I always did have a soft-spot for the ballet, and your offensive use of the *balançoire* is sublime."

"People aren't supposed to like me. I'm a villain."

"With a heart of gold. Always the best kind."

"Huh."

"I don't suppose you would be kind enough to autograph this for me?" The elderly man reached into his starched red miliatary jacket and produced a glossy, rolled-up parchment that had a caricature on it in pencil, looking like Belle Époque poster art.

Jack laughed. "Stan, please don't tell me you carry that around with you just for occasions like this?"

In response Midori punched his arm. "Hush, you." She swept up the picture, pressed it against a convenient brick wall, signed away, and then passed it back. "Here you go, you old darling."

"Excellent. The lads on nightshift shall be green with envy." The doorman again inspected his two young charges. "Coming home?"

Jack nodded. "For now."

As before, no one save Stan could see the new arrivals, so they were forced to weave amidst oblivious types as the three of them crossed the park, past the fountains and a flock of white doves, and then a newspaper stand with a headline that grabbed Jack's attention: 'Big Bill Blows It'.

"What's the deal there?"

Stan chuckled. "Our illustrious mayor was arrested yesterday for mob connections and graft. I dare say he won't be running for

another term."

"Politicians always get off scot-free," Midori countered. "Haven't you people learned that lesson?"

"A degree of optimism never, ever goes astray."

After waiting for a tram to rattle through the intersection, the trio crossed over and entered Timely Tower. In the foyer, the Equalizers banner was absent from its perch above the elevators — replacing it was a 75 x 45 cm brown coir doormat with the Equalizers logo on its 15 mm brush pile.

Stan followed Jack's gaze.

"Stolen," the doorman said, shaking his head.

"The doormat is a nice touch."

"We had to improvise. I don't know what this world is coming to."

Midori harrumphed. "You were the one singing about being optimistic just now."

"Even so. The flag was taken the other night, when Mac over there," Stan nodded in the direction of a security guard with a noticeable black eye, "was knocked senseless by thugs-unknown, trussed up in the broom closet...and that terrible business went down. I'm so sorry, Jack."

"Forget about it."

Midori leaned in close. "What terrible business?"

"Later," Jack replied, a frown pleating his forehead.

"You know, we could have the banner replaced," said Stan.

"It's only a piece of material. Besides, I think the thing has had its day."

"A very good philosophy."

"Our old friend optimism," retorted the woman with them.

From there, Jack and Prima took a lift to the penthouse, accompanied by 'A Walk in the Black Forest'. It had the girl humming again.

"This tune drives me bananas," Jack muttered.

"Oops. Sorry."

"And enough with the optimism quips."

"Never entered my mind."

When he pulled the concertina door across, they found the headquarters of the Equalizers curiously quiet and barely illuminated. It was dusk outside the windows, which added to the gloom, but Jack was more than grateful to note that the flowers from his last visit had been removed.

They stepped out into the hallway, memories flooding through Jack's mind — things he'd much rather forget — just as he saw the drawings of all the Equalizers, past and present, mostly dead and gone. He attempted to smother these diversions as he checked for sign of anybody, and the two of them entered the main room.

"Never thought I'd set *pointe* shoe in Equalizers high command," Midori said lightly. "The place is like a crypt."

Jack tore his eyes from the gloomy, totemic masks on the surrounding walls. "What makes you say that?"

"Let me think now — because it's so lifeless? Like a concert hall minus the audience."

"I guess you're right. Hello?" he called out. "Brick? PA—?"

"Where the *hell* have you been?"

The two newcomers recoiled. Slap-bang before them, in a space a split-second before devoid of life, was a seven-foot giant of a woman with hands on her hips and an angry, expectant expression planted on the kisser.

"Hello, PA." Jack returned her a languid smile.

"Hello, my foot. Answer the question."

"My, that's a lovely haircut," Midori ventured, sounding edgy all the same.

Pretty Amazonia flicked a glance the other woman's way, and then whipped it back to Jack. "Also, what're you doing with her? Well?"

"Easy, now. Prima's okay."

"Nonsense. She's a Rotter. A dangerous one."

Jack looked from one to the other, brandishing the same half-mast smile. "I think those old distinctions are dead and buried."

"Really?" His teammate, he noticed, was impatiently tapping one boot.

"Yeah — really." Moving diplomatically between the two women, Jack faced his teammate. "Sorry I disappeared on you."

"We didn't know what to think. Thought you might be dead, or worse. You could have called."

"Not from where I've been. I was back in Melbourne."

"What—?" PA dropped her hands from her hips. "How?"

"Swore at an inopportune moment."

"And it worked?"

"Two-day penalty, and all."

The woman's mouth twitched — and then PA guffawed, acting as if the weight of this world had been lifted. "Oh, that's right," she managed to squeeze out, between peals of laughter. "I did once warn you, didn't I?"

"You did." Without thinking, Jack covered the distance between them to give her a hug, left ear pressed against her sternum. "Man, I missed you."

"Sure, sure," PA protested, even while her arms tightened and he heard her heart beat faster, "don't go getting all mushy. Thought you didn't trust me."

"I learned."

"Swell. And you're okay?"

"I am, surprisingly." Jack released her, as he peered up. "The Brick?"

Gravity returned to the woman's expression, as she lost the smile. "He's had a relapse. Gypsie-Ann's blood wasn't enough — only a temporary effect. I can't explain it."

"What?" Prima Ballerina pushed forward and closer to them both. "What are you saying? B's going to be all right, isn't he?" Silence. "Where is he?"

"Here. In the clinic." Pretty Amazonia dissected the Rotter with her eyes. "Took Jack a while to learn how to trust me — how're we ever going to trust you?"

Herself angry now, Midori stared up at the other woman, and her voice possessed none of its singsong charm. "What the hell do you think, lady? You think you can stop me finding him?"

PA's cheeks dusted pink. "Are you threatening me?"

Once again, Jack pushed between them. "Enough with the schoolyard behaviour, kids — we have more important stuff to think about. PA, Midori has a point and we all need to know. Is the Brick going to be okay?"

Pretty Amazonia swivelled to face the big, dark windows that rounded one side of the Equalizers' meeting area. The sun outside had already set and Jack could see that a fire still licked part of the city over near the harbour.

"If he survives the night," she said in a soft voice, "I'll be surprised."

Where had the optimism fled?

#178

Lying on his back, on a reinforced steel bed that still deigned to sag in the middle, the Brick had his eyes closed.

He'd apparently fallen asleep listening to classical music, since an orchestral tune (in mono on black shellac) spun at 78 rpm towards the finish of the single track. The record rotated atop a stained, wooden 1930s Zenith tube player beside him, a cumbersome thing much like the patient — a big, rectangular box with a bronze dial at the front and a deco-style grille covering the single speaker.

A rash of intrusive behaviour by Midori — who rushed over, snapping up his massive four-fingered right hand in both of hers, and then putting on the weeps — revived the ailing Equalizer. Petrous eyelids flickered, there was a soft groan, and seconds later he gazed up at the girl.

"Hello, sunshine," he squeezed out, all feeble voice.

"Shhh, B. I'm sorry I left. Didn't mean to. I'm so, so sorry."

"Forget it. Yer here now."

"I am."

"That's what counts."

While she reached over to give him a hug, the Brick's blue irises, faded in colour, moved across the room and found Jack and Pretty Amazonia in the doorway.

"Kid. Yer back. Knew you'd be back... Grand t'see you."

Jack inclined his head, forcing a smile. "You too, Mister B."

"Word is yer loaned me Henderson — looked after that li'l beauty, right...?"

Jack distantly recalled a bent-up and smashed motorbike in the ground floor front lobby of the *Port Phillip Patriot*. "Sure thing," he said, nodding too quickly.

"And we're a team again." The Brick wrapped his rocky arms around Prima Ballerina, squeezed his eyes shut. "We're a team. Together."

Midori showered kisses all over the craggy brow while he tittered, at which point Jack and PA chose to do a runner. After closing the door, they walked silently together, carousing with thoughts each preferred not to put out on the line.

The woman ruptured this silence first. "I can't stand to see him like that."

"He looked okay."

"It's all front, for our sake. So, ends up I'm glad you brought the girl."

"Didn't seem like it."

"We're old enemies. Gallons of water under the bridge — but right now the Brick needs her."

"PA, he doesn't have to die."

"You know a miracle cure I don't?"

"Maybe."

The woman slowed her pace as they descended the stairs, head cocked to one side. "And you. Are you really all right?"

"Sure."

"Sure?" PA rolled her eyes, trying her best to look annoyed but obviously relieved. "You like playing it minimal, don't you?"

"I guess. Any news? — About Donald Wright, I mean."

"Plenty."

"Go on."

"The police found five cadavers in his burned-out offices."

"Five...?" This morsel made Jack uneasy. Had innocent people lost their lives? "Who?"

"We don't exactly know, not yet. They're with the coroner — but the on-scene quack reported some striking similarities between the skeletal structures of all five victims. Kahn says he'll let us know as soon as they finish with autopsies and have a verdict re: cause of death."

"Killed by Cape," her partner mumbled, lost in thought. "And they'll let us know their identities?"

"And their identities, if possible."

"So this could be Wright," Jack hoped aloud, "or his lookalikes."

"Maybe."

He narrowed his eyes — was PA now having a shot at playing it bare bones? "Do we know yet how many versions of Wright there are?"

"Our beat cop Kahn has a pet theory: Six."

"Six? Why six?"

"All to do with a note the Big O was packing when he died, apparently."

A thawing smile worked its way onto Jack's face. Gonzo had mentioned that number. "Half a dozen? It's possible." Then he remembered something he'd noticed the first time he met Donald Wright at the *Port Phillip Patriot* — over by one window had been that tall, antique wooden hat-stand with six identical black bowlers. "You know, I think he might be right."

"Minus the suicide you and Gypsie-Ann witnessed would leave five."

"The five corpses at the *Patriot*?"

"We live in hope."

"That's for sure. Where's Gypsie-Ann?"

"Out doing her thing: Snooping. I swear this has given her a new lease on life." The Equalizer stopped and looked down at her colleague. "What happened in Melbourne?"

"I met Milkcrate Man, saw the GWH."

"The GWH? You spoke to him?"

"No. I tried, but it was a one-way street. He's gone, like you and the Brick figured."

"Dead?"

"Next best thing."

"Ah."

"But Gonzo — Milkcrate Man — is looking after things out there. He has the Reset back online."

With her jaw hanging open, PA aped the spitting image of shocked. "You're kidding me?"

"About the Reset? Or the fact that we have to rely on Milkcrate Man."

"I don't know — a portion of both?"

"Live a little." Jack winked. "I think we can strike Milkcrate Man off the suspects list. He's going to help, and we Reset tonight. One final time."

"Why only the once?"

"We can't save a single soul in Melbourne, but these people here deserve the chance to develop on their own."

"When they do...they tend to hate us," the woman sighed.

"Then we have to earn their respect."

"Do you know a recipe for that?"

"Think we'll need to write one ourselves."

"Ye gods. So. What on earth have you cooked up?"

Jack rubbed his jaw. "We hit Reset this last time, just to put things straight in Heropa — save the lives of any people in hospital, Cape or Blando; resurrect this city. I'm praying it's also in time for the Brick."

PA started walking again, leading her partner to the kitchen. "And Louise."

"And Louise," said Jack.

"She won't remember you."

The Equalizer shrugged, but he had an honest smile when Pretty Amazonia glanced back. "She doesn't have to."

#179

Jack didn't have the gumption to set foot in his quarters, not after what'd happened there, so PA set him up in a spare room at the other end of a long corridor, and then delivered an armful of clothes — which, for anyone else, would have been two.

Just before eight o'clock, switching to a suit that was slate-grey and a burgundy-coloured tie with geometric designs on it, Jack went downstairs. While he stood between the doorways to Las Palmas Luggage Shop and A.G. Geiger Rare Books & De Luxe Editions, Stan stood on the kerb to hail him a taxi — a 1940s Chevrolet, all yellow aside from red fenders and a chequer-pattern strip along both sides. It had Green Top Cab Company signage.

The cabbie at the wheel was sucking hard on a series of cigarettes that she flicked out the window when they became a stub.

"Guessin' you'd be a Bop," the woman said while she looked straight ahead. Her driver's card on the dashboard read Joy Barlow.

"Why?" Jack asked, tired.

"The pick-up address."

"Sorry."

"No need to apologize, mister, job's a job. I'm your girl, and a customer's a customer — so long as he coughs up at the end of the ride." The girl glanced back over the bench seat, with the brass numbers 132 sewn into her jaunty hat.

The streets were busier than usual; mostly people in suits and skirts headed home from work, along with others more gaily dressed arriving for a night on the town. The bars and restaurants were fairly rammed. The overhead neon signage flickered on and off, creating a stop-start, glorious haze of pink, baby blue, purple and lime-green.

The Equalizer went straight to the hospital and fished out of his wallet an extra five bucks for the broad-minded driver.

"Thanks, mister!" the woman enthused.

"Likewise. Have a good one."

At some stage while Jack was in Melbourne, Louise had been shuffled out of ICU and into a shared room on the second floor of the building. At that time of evening the interior lighting was subdued and the other ladies asleep. The only sounds came from a snorer, the beeps of a heart-rate monitor — and a respirator that huffed and puffed.

Having pulled a curtain across to get a foothold of privacy, Jack flopped on a chair next to the patient. Someone had placed a vase of starflowers atop the small chest of drawers paired with the bed. The man stared at them for a few seconds, before taking up the girl's right hand and gazing at her face behind the respirator tube.

"Christ, I missed you," Jack murmured. "I was away. Some place you would never want to go. Hope they've been looking after you here."

He leaned over the armrest to peck the girl's cheek — cool to the touch — and, once settled back in his seat, Jack found himself smiling.

"We're going to try something tonight. Don't know if the plan'll work. It should work, but I think it's better not to promise anything. If it does, you'll be out of here, on your feet, alive, kicking and back to yourself. The way you should be — would be — if I hadn't screwed up. Thing is, you won't remember me. Maybe that's a blessing. You can start afresh, find the partner you deserve, someone who doesn't lie and keep secrets. A better person, you know?"

Jack drew away, annoyed. He was rambling.

"I don't know why I'm telling you this. My plan was to keep it simple, to remain enigmatic and all that, but instead here I am throwing out my stupid heart onto the sleeve of a jacket I didn't pay for myself. Don't listen to me. What I'm trying to say is this: whatever happens, Louise — live life, love life, and be happy. You deserve that. You hear me? Yes?"

Right then, the curtain pulled aside and the Professor peered in, his hair and eyebrows more cockeyed than previously.

"Oh, I do apologize. I'll give you some privacy."

"Prof, it's okay. Stay. I know Louise would want you to be here."

The old man didn't move, but he didn't leave either. "I would prefer not to intrude."

"You're not, honestly. I've said what I needed to. Drag over that chair."

He did as requested and sat down on the other side of the cot. "You were missed over the past two days. I don't care what the medicos say, Louise was aware of your absence."

"Nice of you." Jack offered a slight inclination of his head. "Who're these flowers from?"

"My doing. Louise grew them in the small garden behind the shop."

"Hers?"

"Yes. You don't like the touch?"

"Let's just say I had a recent bad experience with flowers."

"Then you would prefer for me to remove the things?"

"No, it's fine. They're hers, after all."

The Professor mused for a few seconds, apparently debating whether to ask his next question — and did so regardless.

"Would you mind if I asked where you've been?"

"Melbourne."

"Ahh, the motherland."

"Once, maybe. Now — no."

"Are you planning on leaving us?"

"I don't know. There're things I need to finish up here, before I pass judgement. Donald Wright, for one."

"We haven't heard a peep from that man since you destroyed his places of abode."

"Still."

"And there's Louise, of course."

"Yes."

"The doctors have asked us to make a decision — according to them, she is not going to recover. They can keep her alive indefinitely, via these mechanized contrivances, but recommend we switch off. Allow nature to take its course."

"I have a better idea."

The Professor looked over. "What, precisely?"

"I'm going to channel a little bit of you, Wright and the Big O. I'm going to play God, just for one night. There won't be any reruns."

Andrez Bergen

#180

Waiting up for the Reset was like trying to stay awake to catch a glimpse of Santa Claus — no matter how strong one's willpower, you passed out right beforehand and woke in the morning with the presents already chucked together under the tree.

Not that Jack's parents had ever once invested in a shrubbery to encourage Yuletide season shenanigans, but he got the gist.

In this case the city sparkled. Every scrap of evidence that there'd been a destructive Cape war harbourside had been erased, the shops and buildings down there raised from obliteration. The Equalizers banner was back downstairs in the lobby and the table the Brick had damaged — in a meeting a couple of weeks before that included the late Great White Hope — fixed itself.

The hospitals and clinics emptied out, even if the mortuaries remained fully booked, and Tarpé Mills got her eyes back.

All of which possibly accounted for why the Brick whistled a jaunty Christmas tune (it was 'Jingle Bells', and gave good chase to Matt Munro's vocals in the song playing on the café sound system, Quincy Jones's 'On Days Like These') when he bundled into the Neon Bullpen at eight-thirty the following morning. The elegant woman in the tutu, attached to his arm, was likely another reason.

Southern Cross and Pretty Amazonia were already seated with Gypsie-Ann Stellar. The Equalizers had on their costumes — Jack without his mask — while the reporter wore a smart, tweed pants-suit number. All three were tucking into coffee and flapjacks.

"What'cha celebratin'?" the Brick inquired, having cut the whistle as he approached their table.

"Renewal," PA said, adding maple syrup to her breakfast. "A bona fide second chance, or at least a good kick up the bum."

"Nice t'see you waited fer us."

The woman glanced over a dangling pancake on her fork. "Quit grouching, Casanova, and sit down. You eaten yet?"

As she leaned in close to her partner, Midori laughed. "B woke a bunch of restaurant staff at six this morning, all in the name of demanding they cook him up something called the King Henry VIII Steak."

Jack chuckled between mouthfuls. "Oh, wow, I remember that — was too scared to try it, though."

"You kiddin', bright eyes? I was ravenous!" Straight after kissing the girl's forehead, the Brick joined in the bonhomie. "Still am — order me a wad o' jacks, will ya?" The girl pulled up a chair, while the man positioned himself on a more secure bench-seat.

Pretty Amazonia leaned back to inspect him as he did so. "You're looking dapper, hon."

"Feelin' mighty fine too. Blessin's o' the Reset, eh?"

"One-time special, according to Jack."

"Once were enough fer me."

"I'll say. He's well and truly back on form," Prima Ballerina agreed, eyes all over her chunky beau.

"Prima was sayin' the swearin's out — again."

"Yep," confirmed Jack.

"Fer f's sake. How 'bout boozin'?"

"I think that's still okay."

"Bonza fer small mercies."

"By the way, in case you're curious, we're waiting for Bob Kahn to join us," spoke up Gypsie-Ann, while she applied to her dish a liberal blend of tomato sauce, black peppercorns, French Dijon mustard, salt and maple syrup.

Studying the resultant concoction, Jack felt vaguely ill. "Are you going to eat that — or just play with your food?"

"Don't knock it till you try it, buster. Yum."

With a bass-driven chuckle, the Brick unwrapped a fat cigar and lit up. "So, what's Dick Tracy want?"

"He has the autopsy report."

"Whose?"

The reporter rolled her eyes. "Whose do you think?"

"The dead geezers at the *Patriot*."

"Spot on. My blood runs in your veins yet."

"Sure the fella'll remember to bring the thing — or come at all? I seems to remember a Reset happenin' last night."

This time Gypsie-Ann produced a mysterious smile. "Kahn won't forget. He's a special case."

His attention having wandered to the clasped hands shared between Prima Ballerina and her boyfriend, Jack felt — what? Jealousy? Natch that. Sadness. Happy for his teammate, to be sure, but a general sense of the lonely prevailed.

"Whatever the verdict," he decided, "we have each other, a pretty hefty little consortium. But I understand if you bail out and go back to Melbourne, now you can."

"And why would we do that?" Pretty Amazonia had grabbed the Brick's cigar to take a drag, glare challenging — which gave Gypsie-Ann ample opportunity to lean forward and insert her two cents.

"Nothing wrong with running away, dearie, your tail between your legs."

"Fat chance, Lois."

"Well, then." Jack placed his right hand, palm-side down, on the linoleum surface of the table, between drops of syrup. "We're a team in this?"

"Shit-a-brick. D'we have'ta indulge in the Three Musketeers shtick?"

"I agree," complained PA. "It's so bloody passé."

"Four. Four Musketeers." Midori stuck her free hand atop Jack's.

"Let's make it a round five," Gypsie-Ann said. "I don't pack a firearm, but I have an umbrella, miracle blood, and you people need some brains."

"Oh, great." PA rolled her eyes. "Now I have competition. I liked being the only girl."

"Stop whining and give me your hands."

"No, I'm not doing it. I'm in, but you can stick the musketeers thing up your arse."

The Brick blew several smoke-rings toward the ceiling.

"Speaking of which, can we change the name o' the group, an' ditch that dumb logo?"

"Priorities, Mister B."

"C'mon, dollface — we can at least put it to the vote."

"Let it go, you big oaf. We can do this, right, Jack?"

PA playing deferential surprised her less experienced partner. "Don't quote me, but I think we can." Jack looked at Gypsie-Ann, followed by Midori, and then the Brick and Pretty Amazonia. "With the smallest amount of help from you lot."

"Gee, thanks."

The Brick twisted over the table. "Okay if I get drunk now?"

#181

An hour later, Captain Robert Kahn still hadn't shown.

Getting stuck into his twelfth beer, the Brick was increasingly rowdy, Prima Ballerina remained unable to tear gaze from her paramour nor scrub the silly grin from her face, and Pretty Amazonia and Gypsie-Ann were quarrelling up a storm that'd put the standard cat-and-dog shindig to shame.

Jack kept glancing at a Swiss chalet-style cuckoo clock affixed to the wall, something the Brick noticed in spite of any bleary vision.

"Got somewhere yer gotta be, kid?"

The man initially shook his head — "No," he said — but straight after leaned back against the cushioned wall, mouth pressed into a beleaguered straight line. "Maybe. Am I that obvious?"

"As obvious as yours truly skinny-dippin' without me trunks."

Having overheard the hesitation, Pretty Amazonia took a welcome break from sisterly altercation. "Let me guess — Louise."

Jack nodded. "The bank will be open by now. I'm not sure she works there anymore, and I'm not going to interfere. Just want to make sure she's all right."

"Haven't you put yourself through the wringer enough yet?" muttered Gypsie-Ann.

"Oh, shush," PA responded. "You could always pay our rent early. That would make the bank happy — fresh start, and all that. The recipe for success you mentioned."

"G'on," the big ceramic man beside Jack urged. "We'll hold down ye olde fort while yer off stalkin' — well, actually, you gals can. Prima an' me are goin' t'take our mornin' constitutional. Soak up a bit o' life."

PA looked put out. "You don't think we need some living?"

"Stop fussing," cut in her sister. "Run along, children. We'll fill you in."

"Will we now?"

#182

Once more, Southern Cross was lodged in a queue.

He gazed at the architecture holding up the domed ceiling dozens of metres above, watched the fans spin, ventured a peek ahead. First a young woman haggled about her account balance, and then an old lady took a month of Sundays to retrieve a bankbook from her bag. The man in front of him, in a greengrocer's get-up, was much faster and peeled away in silence.

Which placed Jack at the front of the line, left hand touching the counter, staring at a girl behind the grille as she looked back. Same outcome as last time. The Equalizer lost everything in mind — all he perceived were a pair of big green eyes, still the most precious articles in any world.

"May I help you, sir?"

It took a second or two to remember she'd asked this before.

What was his answer, that first time? "Um. I want to make a deposit."

The emerald eyes did a quick wash over, no recognition there. After he pushed closer the Gladstone he'd fetched from Equalizers HQ, it was opened to check, and Jack took time out to examine the woman's downturned face.

"Could I have your passbook?"

"Here you go." On cue, he slid the document across, this time ensuring no physical contact. Anyway, his face burned, so he looked down to her hands — superb, as he knew only too well — while she sorted through the bills. Jack blinked rapidly. He didn't know where to focus. The clothes again?

She was dressed in that fitted navy blue box-cut jacket, the one with grape-rose coloured buttons boasting rhinestone accents.

The mother-of-pearl badge was there too, with her name.

"Oh, Mister Winkle," she was saying to the elderly coot at the next stall. "I have a deposit here for $5,000. Would you mind confirming the amount?"

"Certainly, Miss Starkwell."

The Gladstone again exchanged hands.

"We won't be long, sir," Miss Starkwell assured her customer with a charming smile.

Henry Holland, all annular nose and decorative moustache, sauntered up to the woman's side. The facial wiring was sadly amiss. He placed one hand on the girl's shoulder, the resurrected smirk verging on patronizing, and those fingers on the navy blue material held Jack's attention as before.

"Everything dandy here, Louise?"

"Yes, sir."

The girl refused to look up at him, clearly bothered. Henry's stare passed over Jack and the other customers, like they did not exist. Jack wasn't wrong the first time — this rogue was more intent on pawing his subordinate, and the fingers on the shoulder had started their cloying massage.

"Henry," Jack remarked in a loud voice.

Distracted from his reverie, Mister Holland looked straight over at the Equalizer. "Yes, sir?"

"Don't push your girl too far — she may bust your chin. Just a friendly warning."

The manager stepped back, face ashen and that fragile jaw of his gaping. Meanwhile, Miss Starkwell put a hand over her mouth to smother a laugh. With an awkward twirl, far from suave, Holland retreated to his dimly lit cubbyhole.

That done, Jack relaxed. "You okay?" he asked the teller.

"I am, now. Thank you."

"Anytime."

Mister Winkle had apparently finished his counting. "All done, Miss Starkwell," the ancient cadaver croaked, as he laboured under the Gladstone's weight and placed it upon her desk. "And, I must add, sir, well said."

—Which was precisely when the wall, the same one as last time, caved in amidst the cacophonous racket of an explosion.

Horrified customers, intermingled with equally alarmed bank staff, dispersed screaming and shouting while bricks, mortar, and a billowing veil of dust settled. This time, rather than a three-metre beast standing by the gaping hole, there was instead an underwhelming, middle-aged 5′ 8″ individual, dolled-up in a gaudy, ill-fitting, blue, red and yellow costume.

More memorable was the pistol planted in his right mitt, the silver Colt M1911 automatic Jack had seen in action at the offices of Donald Wright.

"Hello, baby."

"You." As Jack backed away — even so ensuring he remained between the newcomer and the tellers behind him — he champed at his lower lip, attempting to nut out a course of action post haste.

"Me. Why surprised? Thought I'd drop by for Devonshire tea." Wright veritably purred while placing the gun in the left hand, and then straightened his mask over the moustache. "So, Southern Cross. We meet again."

In spite of better judgement, Jack couldn't resist a wry grin. "Sheesh. I have to say — you really need a new scriptwriter. Who pens such archaic lines?"

"That's right, laugh it up. A fitting epitaph: 'The cat indulged in cheap comeback tomfoolery, right before Major Patriot placed a slug in his skull.' Which I'm going to do, by the way."

"And yet, you felt the need to wax pompous before hand."

"Not at all."

"Well, there's a surprise."

"Indeed. The only long-winded diatribe you'll get from me is a brace of bullets."

The first shot hit the same region as the bullet Jack had taken before bailing out to Melbourne, tearing through trouser material and then the *gracilis* muscle in the inner thigh of his left leg. The second round passed through his shoulder pad, hitting no flesh, but the next one clipped the bone in his upper right arm and took out the *brachialis anticus*, rendering the limb useless from the elbow down.

Andrez Bergen

Not that the Equalizer was aware of any of these details at that very moment. If he screamed, yelped or stoically stayed mum, Jack had no idea.

Having been thrown backward a good two to three feet by the impact of both shots, he tottered, and then slumped onto his backside on the marble before the bank-teller windows.

Everything was spinning in slow motion inside his head, but there was no mistaking the unyielding pain from arm and leg. Warm blood streamed down inside the shirt and pants, collecting together on the floor in a dark pool, and his vision began to randomly whiteout the edges.

Donald Wright stalked the area around the fallen man, taking care not to stain immaculate red boots.

"Any other facile quip you feel the need to toss my way?" The only response was Jack's panicked, erratic panting. "Go on, then. Lay it on me. No? Funny, that."

"Give me...time," the other man managed to say as he battled for breath.

"Good boy — you're a son of a gun."

While he greased bystanders cowering nearby, possibly fishing for applause for his witty use of an idiom, the publisher showed off and spun the revolver, Wild West-style.

"Any of you cringing, craven cowards moves — bang, bang! You get it? Call me gun crazy — I've flipped my wig! *Comprende?*" Wright roved the tiles, keeping one eye on his victim, even as he continued to wind-up the others. "You're all pathetic. What a waste of electrons."

Jack wasn't sure if this was theatrical pontificating on Wright's behalf — making him a poor-man's ham actor — or whether he'd misplaced his marbles. Either way, the old guy was tossing that gun about and, pain or no pain, the Equalizer had to intervene. Didn't care if these surrounding people were made out of shrimps and snails and puppy dog tails.

"Stop," he simply said.

The older man paused to look down at the Equalizer, who was also struggling (none-too-successfully) to get to his feet. "Did you utter something meaningful, Jack?"

"I said...stop."

"Ahh, the people's champion awakes. Why don't you make me? What a gas — we could indulge in a classic, rousing slugfest of superhero derring-do. You think you're up for playing big man on campus?"

"Tricky."

"Why?"

"Are you forgetting you used me for target practice?... I can't exactly stand."

"There is that, yes."

"You're also hardly a hero."

"Mootable."

"And these are innocent people."

"Innocent? You mean insignificant."

"They've done nothing wrong."

"How honourable you sound, yet how mistaken." Wright let out a great sigh. "Nothing wrong? You do know this bank owes me a great deal of money, lent at a discounted rate of twenty-one-point-two percent? Late on debt repayments — I ought to shoot the lot of them. Bang, bang, bang."

"Oh, come on... And you lecture me on insignificance?"

"Easy with the tongue, tiger."

"You know what I mean. Let them go."

"Eh?"

"Let them...go," Jack repeated. He stopped trying to rise and simply sat there on the ground, peering up, face pushing pale to the limit. "Your beef — it isn't with this crowd. It's with me. I'm the one that polished off your pug-ugly twins."

"Right on, baby. I'll say the beef's with you."

Wright pushed the barrel of his gun into Jack's forehead, almost knocking him off balance.

"Does this hurt? I have four bullets to go — three for play and one to finish the job. Thought you would've packed your toys and gone home," the man was saying, "after what my men did to poor little Mitzi. Remember her?"

"I remember."

"Course you do. You should. Aren't you racked with guilt? Ahh, golden silence."

"I'm thinking," Jack mumbled.

"How wet! Oh, and I do believe your phony got her feet wet also. What's the matter? Can't raise your arm to fire off one of your magical lightning bolts? What a dying shame!"

In response, the Equalizer started laughing. It began as a low, cough-like whisper, but in seconds, Jack had his head back and he was chortling aloud.

"I wasn't *that* funny," Wright said, uncomfortable, as he lowered the gun a few centimetres.

"No, no, not you."

"Not me? What, then?"

Rubbing his eyes with his left hand, laughter subsiding, Jack suspected he was about to pass out — but he needed to hold on, fight this sensation. Louise was somewhere behind, in danger, and Wright hadn't noticed her.

"It's this whole situation," he said. "You, me, Heropa. Everything."

"What in blazes are you talking about?"

"Well, for starters, I thought we'd wrapped your chapter. But here you are, a fossilised loser still getting round in tights. Hope I know better at your age — it's not a good look, mate. Embarrassing."

"You forget who has the gun."

"Who cares? The entire world has Reset, yet you remain an old fart on his last legs..." Jack chuckled, a lousier effort this time. "And only a sixth of one, if you want to get real finicky."

Standing over him, Wright lashed out with the pistol, this time bringing down its handgrip on the top of Jack's head. As the

Equalizer hit the floor, hard, someone screamed nearby, and followed up with hysterical sobbing.

"Shut up!" shouted the man formerly known as Major Patriot. "Shut your cake holes, or I'll kill you all! In fact — I'll probably do that, anyway. Rub you out, the wrong way, whatever takes my fancy."

Hot on the heels of this tantrum, he looked down again and booted Jack in the ribs.

"You still with us?"

#183

It was a further half hour until Bob Kahn dashed into the Neon Bullpen, a manila folder of paperwork under his arm. He found Pretty Amazonia and Gypsie-Ann Stellar in the middle of a row about who was going to foot the excessive bill.

"Ladies," he said as he joined them.

"Fashionably late or unfashionably tardy?" PA muttered before turning back to her sister. "I don't exactly have room for a purse in this skimpy bloody costume."

"Hardly my fault," the reporter snapped back. "Why don't you offer to wash their dishes? You could get them done in, what, two seconds flat?"

"I'm not one for dish-pan hands. Just fork out the cash, for Heaven's sake!"

"Temper, temper." Gypsie-Ann winked at Kahn, who smiled just a fraction. Neither gesture escaped the Equalizer's notice.

"What's up between you two?"

"Nothing."

PA wasn't sure which annoyed her more — her sister feigning innocence, or the one-eyed police officer staring down at the papers he was spreading across the surface of the next table — a cleaner place to do so.

"Where's your coat hanger?" she asked.

"My what?"

"Forbush."

"I left him back at the cop-shop. He doesn't remember a goddamned thing about recent events."

"Yet, you do."

"You got it."

"Ahh, Heropa. Full of surprises."

"Anyhow," the man braved, "we have the autopsy reports."

"What took so long?"

"For one thing, a discrepancy."

Leaning forward, PA searched amid the medical jargon, ugly penmanship, photos and findings outlined there. "A bullet," she quickly discovered. "Fished out of the *parietal lobe*."

"Say again?" piped up her sibling.

"The rear-end of the brain."

Nodding, Khan pushed the paperwork toward the reporter. "All here. Doc McCoy discovered the slug stuck in the head of one of those John Does from the *Patriot* fire. Oh, yeah, they're not JDs anymore, by the way. We matched dental records with Donald Wright — for all five."

Gypsie-Ann frowned at the disclosure. "What, they've been eating the same food over the past five years and followed exactly the same regime of dental hygiene? Isn't that kind of strange?"

"The stranger thing here, in the circumstances, was the bullet."

"I suppose so." She rifled through photographs of corpses on five different slabs. "You can barely recognize these people. Ouch. Skin burned away. Old Henry did a swell job identifying them at all."

"This was before the Reset. Doc McCoy also couldn't remember anything this morning. Thanks for the heads-up, Stellar — nice to be forewarned for a change."

"You're welcome."

"What about the bullet?" PA asked.

"I took it this morning to Ballistics, which is one of the reasons I'm late — the other being that McCoy mislaid his report, since he couldn't recall doing the autopsies. We had to scour the morgue from top to bottom, not the best place to do a spot of scouring. Ended up finding the folder in a toilet cubicle."

"*Ew.*"

"Don't worry — only reading material, I think."

"We hope. And the bullet?"

"It's a .45 ACP, which I suspected. Used in Colt pistols."

At this news, the reporter stared. "Like an automatic?"

"Could be. Or a large calibre sport shooter."

Gypsie-Ann sat back, thinking. "Wright had a Colt automatic. It's

what he used to kill one of his doubles in front of me and Jack."
Straight after, she jumped up, sending her chair flying backwards
and clattering across the floor. A nearby waiter looked peeved, but
she didn't notice. "Oh, crap — suicide guy was one of the five!
Which means, if there are six—"

"One of those losers is still on the loose." PA stared at her sister.
"Jack. The Brick. We have to warn them."

Nodding, Gypsie-Ann had started to say, "There are times when
you do have your moments," but Pretty Amazonia was gone before
'times' had spilled past her lips. "And I do wish you'd let me finish
my compliments," the reporter added into empty air.

#184

"You still with us?"

"...Yep..."

"Grandy-doodee."

A kick to his ribcage was nothing compared with the pain emanating from the top of Jack's skull. At least his leg and arm were dull throbs — useless limbs, sure, flopping about like they belonged to someone else — but the migraine was immediate and overwhelming.

The Equalizer knew he had to retain the old man's attention, keep him from looking too closely over the bench behind him and thereby espying Louise beyond the grille. Hopefully she'd ducked down low, out of sight, but he had no way of knowing if this were so.

Talk, you idiot, he told himself. *Any old thing will do.*

"You wouldn't have any...pain killers on you?"

Donald Wright pretended to pat himself down. "Sadly, the medicine cabinet is dry. Tell you what, though, I have another funky idea. Why don't you resort to an old-fashioned four-letter word of ill-repute? My sources tell me that this escape clause is back on the cards."

"Go to hell."

"Oh, there's no doubt there — eventually. You, however, can stop the pain, here and now. You can live, Jack-o-mine."

"With a catch?"

"Of course, of course, of course. There is the silly two-day handicap, giving me plenty of time to exterminate your twee chums: Stellar, Pretty Amazonia, that brute the Brick, old Erskine. I'll throw in the police officer, Captain Kahn, for good measure — I know you've been buddying up. Even if you resort to another Reset, I have until midnight to mop up these folk. The day is young. You may have killed all my clones but left me, the original and the best."

"Jeez...you have ludicrous tabs..."

"On myself? You already told me. Yawn. Well, go on."

"Go on, what?"

"Laugh some more. A slug in the labonza will knock any remaining wind out of the sails — let's see how well you snicker after losing that member of the family."

His gun was already moving down in this direction. Confused and disoriented as he was, Jack grasped he had to stall the fiend. If only he could think clearly — everything was yellow-starred, wonky, a flux of extreme agony from various points in his body.

"I don't get it," the Equalizer managed to say, but it came out too soft. The weapon was still on the prowl. "I don't get it," he reiterated in a louder voice. Bingo. The pistol paused.

"Don't get what?"

"You..."

"Me? You want an explanation? A confession? Some kind of villain's soliloquy?"

"No. Not that."

"Oh." Wright sounded disappointed. "What, then?"

Jack crawled to the wall beneath the counter and pulled himself back up to a sitting position. "There were six of you." He offered this as a statement, rather than a question. They had to be certain.

"There weren't six."

Bzzzt—! So much for the note, Milkcrate Man's memory, and that collection of bowler hats.

"You think you intuit everything, daddy-o. We were seven."
Huh?

"Did you know that seven was a lucky number in Japan? No? Don't sweat it — people in general are ill-educated these days. Such a shame. In my past life, in Melbourne, I had an interest in things Japanese. A fascinating, hip culture, albeit a dead one. Ahhh, seven. What an intriguing number. There are the seven deadly sins, the seven dwarfs, seven samurai — and the magnificent seven. We believed we were the latter, all decked out in our identical Major Patriot duds."

Over where he lay, Jack barely listened. He was on the verge of unconsciousness, grappling with the thing at the same time that he manhandled nausea and dizziness, trying to dodge all three and evaluate what to do next.

"But seven is *not* lucky!"

Wright suddenly punched a wall, and directly after removed his red gauntlet and flexed the fingers of the hand, staring at them, apparently in some pain himself.

"Our kinship was undermined," he blathered on while examining each digit, "by one of our own, in league with another, a corrupting influence from this place. A phony. One of our magnificent seven started to get other thoughts, began questioning. Not a freak out *per se*, but thinking independent of the other six." Satisfied nothing was broken, Wright put the glove back on. "He fell in love."

Blame the searing pain, but Jack had a flash of lucidity in that moment, realized something he'd never suspected and would hardly have dreamed up at any other point in the narrative.

"Shite. The Big O..."

"Hah! 'Big O', my foot — we tried to put the kibosh on his developing liaison with Bullet Gal, but the man was too far gone. Betrayal by one of your own, your psyche rebelling against itself — can you imagine such a thing, Jack? Our own flesh, blood and spirit. He betrayed us! Us!" Now continually striking himself in the head with the automatic, Wright turned full circle several times, spinning like a wound-up whirling dervish. "The candyass!" he yelped between blows. "The prick!"

His mask tore and fell aside; nasty welts appeared across the man's leathery forehead, nose and cheekbones, until finally he stopped smacking. A look of surprising clarity then entered his eyes.

"He passed judgement and denounced the other six. Took on a new costume, a new name, refused to rejoin us. Thought himself a better person. All because of *her* — that brat Mitzi. A phony, for Christ's sake. Who did he think he could be? The prodigal-bloody-son? We were never the same after that. We lost a significant part of our soul."

"But Sir Omphalos was — looked — younger than you."

If he was offended, Donald Wright forgot to show it. "Yes, yes, all right. Perhaps he discovered a better moisturizer."

A trail of red seeped down Jack's face, so he wiped it away with the suit-sleeve of his left arm. This was nothing — beneath him spread a lot of blood on the floor. He refused to examine further. Knew he'd already lost too much of the stuff.

"Still, there were six," Wright mused. "Six being sufficient to run the roost. We took up an alias our brother didn't know, this new identity as the publisher of the *Patriot* — along with all those other hats — and slowly and surely drew our plans against him."

"And murdered the guy."

"That's right, baby. After all, we had a panting public to amuse."

"Taking self-loathing to new extremes."

"Not at all."

"Then you had one of your other duplicates kill himself. Why?"

"A demonstration of our power — an example, and a warning."

"To who? ...You or us? The Big O was already dead by then."

"Let us say all interested parties."

"Bit excessive, don't you reckon?"

"Well, SC-baby, you people didn't know how many of me there were. Casually offing one of my selves like that would intimate a lot more clones — I have to say, I'm surprised you came close to guessing the correct number. How did you?"

"Little things."

"Such as?"

"Hats."

"Well, well. A smart guy."

At that point Jack closed his eyes, almost let go. Then he remembered Louise, and snapped back to rag-doll attention.

"Which left five of you," he spoke up. The Equalizer was struggling to focus on the man hovering above. "After I gutted your offices at the *Patriot*, the police — well, what was it the police said? That they found five bodies...?"

"Ahh, I see your confusion."

It was Wright's turn to guffaw, his self-abuse a thing of the recent past.

"Funny thing. We were in the midst of a ceremony — usually careful to stay far enough apart in order that one or two of us would survive any attempt at assassination. This was the first time in years we'd congregated together, and the reason? That same, self-sacrificial doppelgänger we were just talking about. You attacked us during a private wake for the man — which accounts for five identical cats being found, even after I escaped the terrible maelstrom. If you look closely, you'll find that one of them has a spent .45 in his head."

"You sure like to waffle on."

"A winner's prerogative."

Police sirens were getting closer, and maybe the mayor would lift a lazy, tobacco-stained finger to employ his Equalizers laser-signal doohickey, and alert Jack's comrades — this, after all, was a Reset world in which people still mostly respected the team, there was a miscreant in a costume who'd blown through the wall of one of main bank branches, and a bunch of people were now held hostage. Only a matter of time — something Jack suspected he didn't have.

"God," he grumbled.

"Yes?"

The Equalizer very slowly glanced up. "Fair enough. Okay. I guess you really are, since you designed all this, right?"

"Of course."

"Or did you...?"

"What is the meaning of that crack?"

"Well," Jack managed to go on, "how do we know it was you?"

"Bet your bottom dollar it was I."

"But how d'you know you're the original...? Like, where exactly were you when I attacked the *Port Phillip Patriot* the other night, when your — your 'brothers' carked it? I blew the place to smithereens."

"Why, I'd stepped out to get refreshments."

"As the original would stoop to doing."

Doubts flooded the man's half-masked mush. "I see your point. How embarrassing."

"And... What's to say that the Big O wasn't the archetype all along—?"

"Pah!"

"—fed up with his corrupted clones' poor behaviour?"

Wright frowned and then grinned in maniacal fashion, at the very same moment Jack lost the capacity to smile at all.

"Perish the thought. I think — at least I presume I'm the original. Sometimes, it got confusing as to who was who, but none of that now matters. Does it?"

"You tell me."

"I believe I am." Wright peeled away the tattered red remains of his mask and tossed them into a nearby trashcan. "By the way, was it you that pulled this Reset stunt?"

"Yeah."

"Then perhaps you could fill me in — why is it I haven't been restored, along with everything else?"

"You mean...you and your better halves getting back together, thereby making you young and pretty?"

"Exactly."

"We're following your rules, moron... Dead electrical impulses don't Reset."

Clicking his tongue, Wright then glared at Jack while he very carefully placed the gun level with the injured man's left eye.

The sirens had stopped wailing.

Beyond the barrel, Jack could see flashing lights through the hole in the wall. Some fool was on a loudhailer, but none of the words made any sense.

"I'll keep the extra bullets for your friends, baby," Major Patriot said at his silkiest, far more coherent. "Time to die."

"I don't think so, arsehole."

That was when the sculpture *Twilight Over Hoboken* reared overhead, from behind Donald Wright, and crowned the man. He dropped the gun, staggered a few steps, shrieking, hands clutching his head, and then turned to ogle at his assailant.

The screams ceased. "Impossible," he instead mumbled aloud. "You're dead."

Taking advantage of those precious seconds, Jack used his left hand to prop-up and level the right one, pointing it in the direction of the other Cape's set of stars.

"Don't you know yet that anything is possible in Heropa?" he said, just before letting off a blast that lifted Donald Wright, taking him and his offensive, unshapely costume clear through the wall.

Straight after, Jack collapsed.

Other fingers were raising him, gently this time, onto aching buttocks. The Equalizer found himself gazing into Louise's deep, emerald-coloured eyes.

"God, Jack. Are you all right?" she asked, distress etched into a beautiful face no longer bespectacled.

"Hey. What happened...to your glasses?"

"I ditched them." The girl checked over his injured, blood-spattered form; started tearing strips off the slip beneath her skirt, to use as tourniquets for stemming the flow — all seasoned professionalism.

As he was manoeuvred about in this manner, Jack had no idea where he rediscovered the strength to toss back both a grin and a quip.

"Aren't you people...s'posed to give better customer service?"

"I don't play by the stupid rules," Louise said, a smile sharing space with concern while she tied another knot, "and, you know what? Now I remember everything."

"You do?"

"I do." Louise pecked Jack's cheek. "Can we start afresh?"

Andrez Bergen

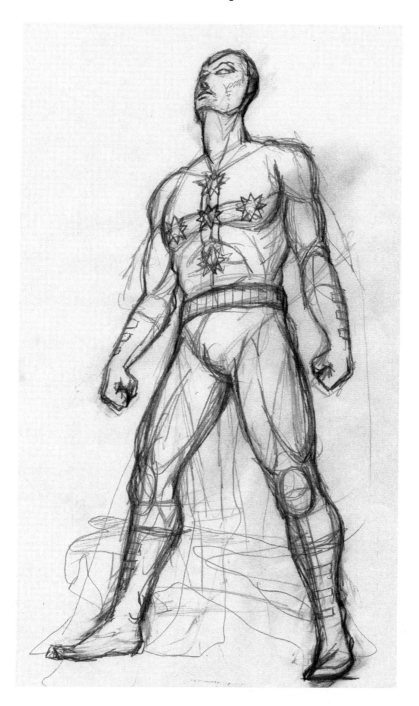

423

ROGUES GALLERY + ENCYCLOPAEDIA COMMIX

Andrez Bergen

Glossary

Everything you wanted to know about comics, the movies, Aussie slang, obscure nomenclature and some of the oddball colloquialisms you'll find in Heropa.

Adamantium: indestructible metal alloy in the Marvel universe — Wolverine's bones are made from the stuff

Amazing (Adult) Fantasy: anthology comic series published by Marvel in 1961/62, culminating in final issue 15 — which introduced Spider-Man

Arse: British/Aussie English for 'ass'

Balançoire: A movement usually with grands battements or attitudes, in which a dancer swings the leg front and back through first position

Beano, The: British children's comic published from 1938 to the present time

Belle Époque: French golden age, 1871-1914, famous for musical theatre art

Black Panther, the: African superhero created by Stan Lee and Jack Kirby in the 1960s

Blue Max, the: 1966 British WWI flick about a German fighter pilot, directed by John Guillermin & starring George Peppard

Bonnet: British English used for a car's hood

Bronze Age of Comics: from 1970 to 1985

Bushidō: 'the way of the warrior' is a code of honour that the samurai followed

Buster Crabbe: American athlete and actor. Starred in *Flash Gordon* and *Buck Rogers* cliffhanger serials and one Tarzan movie, *Tarzan the Fearless* (1933)

Captain America: iconic superhero created by Joe Simon and Jack Kirby for Timely Comics in 1941, made into a theatre serial in 1944, and resurrected by Kirby with Stan Lee for Marvel Comics in 1964. Gets about in a costume with an American flag motif,

427

with powers endued by the Super-Soldier Serum & Vita-Rays

Cark it: Australian slang, meaning "to die"

Chicago typewriter: .45 caliber Thompson submachine gun (a.k.a. a Tommy gun)

Chrysophylax: the name of a wily dragon that invades the Middle Kingdom in J.R.R. Tolkien's *Farmer Giles of Ham* (1949)

Clodualdo: Illegal depressant

Coir: natural fibre extracted from the husk of coconuts

Comics Code Authority, the: de facto censor of U.S. comics from 1948, banning violence, gore and sexual innuendo, amongst other things

Cool McCool: U.S. TV cartoon series (1966-69) created by Bob Kane — of Batman notoriety — and used as a throwaway variant of just plain 'cool'

Coot: a foolish old man

Cor!!: British humourous comic launched in 1970

Cure Blossom (aka Tsubomi Hanasaki): Lead magical supergirl in Toei's 2010-11 Pretty Cure anime series, *HeartCatch PreCure!*

Dada: iconoclastic art movement from the early 20th century

Dashiell Hammett: created iconic noir character Sam Spade and alcoholic detective duo Nick & Nora Charles

Dell Comics: published comics in the U.S. from 1929-73, including *The Funnies* and *Kona, Monarch of Monster Isle*

DC Comics: est. in 1934 and therefore one of the largest, longest-lived American comic companies—the publishers of Superman and Batman

Démagogue: a political leader who seeks support by appealing to popular desires and prejudices rather than by using rational argument; a rabble-rouser

Der: Australian slang — mocking exclamation indicating faked and exaggerated stupidity or bewilderment

Derro: Australian slang, derived from the word 'derelict': hobo, bum, no-hoper

Dick Tracy: police detective comic strip created by Chester Gould in 1931

Docs: famous British Doc Martens lace-up leather boots

Domino mask: small mask covering only the eyes and the space between them, as worn by the Lone Ranger, the Spirit, Hit-Girl and Robin

Dosh: currency, money, cash, moola

'Drowning Girl': Roy Lichtenstein used an image from a romance story in DC Comics' *Secret Hearts* #83 (November 1962) by artist Tony Abruzzo as the basis for this iconic Pop Art image

Erskine, Dr. Abraham: German biochemist & physicist who developed the Vita-Rays and Super-Soldier Serum that created Captain America in 1941

Exegesis: the act of analyzing passages from a document — often the Bible — to understand what it meant to its author and others in the author's culture

F.A.B.: a call-sign used in the British action marionette show *Thunderbirds*; there's some debate as to whether this means 'Full Acknowledgment of Broadcast', 'Fabulous', 'Final Audio Broadcast', or 'Fully Advised, Briefed'

Fear and Loathing in Las Vegas: first published in 1971, a novel by Hunter S. Thompson with illustrations by Ralph Steadman

Fedora: felt hat associated with Prohibition era gangsters, Sam Spade and Indiana Jones

Flash Gordon: 13-installment 1936 sci-fi/action theatre serial starring Buster Crabbe, based on the comic strip created in 1934 by Alex Raymond

Frida Kahlo: famous Mexican surrealist painter

George Peppard: Hollywood actor, best known for for *Breakfast at Tiffany's* & *The A-Team*

GHB: grievous bodily harm, a.k.a. "wounding with intent", according to English crimal law; also a name used for gamma-Hydroxybutyric acid, an anaesthetic used for recreational drug purposes — and in date-rape

Ginger Meggs: Australian newspaper comic strip created in the early 1920s by Jimmy Bancks.

Golden Age of Comics: from the late 1930s until the late 1940s or early '50s

Gomene: an apology in the Japanese language; "sorry"

Great Gazoo, the: a pompous green, floating alien who was exiled to earth in the 1960s TV cartoon *The Flintstones*

Grit: "America's Greatest Family Newspaper" — at least according to the ads they stuck in 1960s comicbooks

Harvey Comics: American comic publisher, 1941-1994, with titles like *Casper the Friendly Ghost, Richie Rich,* and *Captain Freedom*

Hoon: Australian expression used to refer to anyone engaging in loutish behaviour; in particular used to refer to people who drive in a manner considered anti-social or reckless

Hylax: a large corporation specializing in plastics

IdInteract: virtual reality-based portable gaming console

In good nick: British English expression meaning 'in good condition'

Jack Kirby: legendary comic book artist and innovator active since the 1940s, most proactive in the '60s at Marvel Comics. Co-created superheroes Captain America, the Fantastic Four, the Avengers, Thor, X-Men, Silver Surfer, and the Black Panther — along with stunning villains like Doctor Doom, Galactus, and the Red Skull

Joe: coffee

Joe Simon: created or co-created a slew of important characters in the 1930s–1940s, including Captain America and Manhunter. Frequently worked with Jack Kirby, and was the first editor of Timely Comics

Joseph (Joe) Kubert: founder of the Kubert School in the U.S.; created *Tor* in 1953, and worked (as artist) with writer Robert

Kanigher to create DC title *Sgt. Rock*

Kármán line, the: lies at an altitude of 100 kilometres (62 miles) above sea level, used to define the boundary between the earth's atmosphere and outer space

Kerberos Panzer Cops: 1988-2000 manga series about special armoured police, written by Mamoru Oshii, illustrated by Kamui Fujiwara, and with mechanical designs by Yutaka Izubuchi. Oshii also used them in his movies *StrayDog* and *Jin-Roh*

Khan: Khan Noonien Singh, shortened to Khan, is the villain in the 1982 movie *Star Trek II: The Wrath of Khan*

Labonza: the belly, stomach

Lex Luthor: long-time arch-fiend in the *Superman* universe

Lois Lane: intrepid reporter for *The Daily Planet* and Superman's long-time love interest

Loo: toilet

Maltese Falcon, The: Dashiell Hammett's famous 1930 detective novel featuring Sam Spade

Mandrake the Magician: syndicated American newspaper comic strip created by Lee Falk (The Phantom) in 1934

Marat, Jean-Paul: physician, political theorist, scientist, radical journalist and politician during the French Revolution; more famous for being stabbed dead in his bath in the painting by Jacques-Louis David

Marat/Sade: 1967 movie directed by Peter Brook, adapted from the play by Peter Weiss

Marvel Comics: American comicbook company originally named Timely in 1939, Atlas Comics in the 1950s, and its better-known

incarnation from 1961

Matthew 24:27: the Gospel According to Matthew is the first book of the *New Testament*

Mauser C-96: German pistol introduced in 1896 and first used in the Boer War, later adopted by the German Army

Milk Bar: Australian term for suburban local shop

Mitt-Mate 1187: Hand-held computer and communications device

Mr. Sparkle: in Season 8 of *The Simpsons* (the episode 'In Marge We Trust'), Homer stumbles across a Japanese dishwasher detergent called Mr. Sparkle with his face on the box

Nancy Drew: perennially popular fictional girl detective created in 1930 whose books have sold 80 million copies

Noggin: head

Norinco Type 86S: AKM-type assault rifle produced in China in the 1980s

Ornithology: the study of birds

Peplum effect: a short overskirt usually attached to a fitted jacket. Popular as a design in women's suiting in the 1940s

Phantom, the: long-running American adventure comic created by Lee Falk (Mandrake the Magician) in 1936

PreCure: also known as Pretty Cure

Pretty Cure (aka PreCure): Japanese animated magical superhero girls' series, screening from 2004

Qípáo: body-hugging one-piece Chinese dress for women

Rain: 1932 film starring Joan Crawford, adapted from a story by W. Somerset Maugham

Ralph Steadman: iconic British cartoonist who worked extensively with author Hunter S. Thompson

Red Skull, the: Nazi supervillain and Captain America's arch-enemy since 1941

Ridgy didge: Australian slang, meaning the real article, not false or pretentious

Rock Hudson: Hollywood leading man in the 1960s-70s

Roy Lichtenstein: prominent American artist in the 1960s; with

Andy Warhol, helped to define the Pop Art movement

Sailor Moon: 1990s Japanese manga series and anime that set the standard in the magical-girl genre, in which mild-mannered teenage girls transform into heroines to fight evil

Sheila: colloquial term for a girl or woman in Australia

Silver Age of Comics: from 1956 to about 1970

Spider-Man: Marvel superhero created by Stan Lee and artist Steve Ditko in 1962

Stan Lee: American comicbook writer, editor, actor, producer, publisher, television personality, and the former president and chairman of Marvel Comics; in the 1960s he co-created the Fantastic Four, Spider-Man, Thor, the Uncanny X-Men, and the Avengers

Steve McQueen: Hollywood actor and racing driver. Starred in *The Magnificent Seven* and *Bullitt*.

Steve Rogers: Captain America's civilian, out-of-costume real identity — at one time a frail young man transformed via the Super-Soldier Serum & Vita-Rays in World War II

Stetson: iconic hat worn by Humphrey Bogart in *The Big Sleep*

Super-Soldier Serum: The drug from which Captain America, Isaiah Bradley, Patriot, Protocide & Josiah X get their enhanced abilities, developed by Dr. Abraham Erskine

Swandooly: Australian slang for money

Thomas Nast: nineteenth-century German-born American caricaturist, sometimes called the father of American cartoons

Timely Comics: predecessor to Marvel Comics; in the 1940s they published Captain America, the Human Torch, and the Sub-Mariner

Tiny Tots: British comic published 1927-59

Tolkien, J.R.R.: English writer, poet and professor responsible for the fantasy outings *The Hobbit* and *The Lord of the Rings*

Tony Nancy: famed American drag-racer and custom vehicle upholsterer

Toodle-oo: British/Australian English expression meaning 'farewell'

Tyre: British English 'tire'

Ukiyo-e: Japanese woodblock prints produced between the seventeenth and twentieth centuries

Un bel di vedremo ('One beautiful day, we will see'): an aria from Puccini's opera *Madama Butterfly*

Uvidimsya: from Russian language, meaning "we'll see each other again"

Vegemite: dark brown salty paste made from yeast extract, used as a spread

Vibranium: fictional rare metal from the Marvel universe, used to construct Captain America's shield. Wakandan Vibranium has the ability to absorb all vibrations

Vickers machine gun: water-cooled .303 British machine gun produced by Vickers Limited, from the First World War to the 1960s

Vita-Rays: part of the Super-Soldier Serum that speeds up the potion's effects

Von Dutch: custom vehicle painter and pin-striper

Walter Plunkett: prolific costume designer and among Hollywood's great style designers

Walk in the Black Forest, A: Oft-parodied instrumental easy-listening tune by Horst Jankowski, released in 1965

Wonder Woman: Amazonian DC heroine created by William Moulton Marston, with artist Harry George Peter, in 1941

Zorro: dashing, black-clad Robin Hood-like masked outlaw and master swordsman living in the Spanish colonial era, created in 1919 by pulp writer Johnston McCulley

Andrez Bergen

ACKNOWLEDGEMENTS

First up, the shout-outs to relatives and mates — specifically my wife Yoko and my daughter Cocoa for their constant support, encouragement and indulgence, since without them none of this would be bound, on screen, or still gracing little scraps of paper.

Thanks to mum Fée, dad Des, and nan June (who once procured copies of *Ripley's Believe It or Not* from the local book exchange in Burleigh Heads), Peter (original owner of that Richmond stash), cuz Zoe, Briony, Tim, Seb, Alby, Dames, Devin, Pete, Kris, Danielle, Nikki, Mikey, Jason, Wolfgang, Trish, Bas, Baz, Camille, Marce, the IF? Records posse, Yoshiko & the ETM crew here in Tokyo, and Brian Huber (the *real* Milkcrate Man).

Much appreciation must also punt in the direction of the editors, fellow authors, artists, critics and people who bother to read my stuff — and let me know how they felt about it. In particular, Marcus, Elizabeth, Fiona, Renee, Stefan, Mihai, Katy, Josh, Heath, Chris, Dakota, Jack, Dan, Guy, Joe, Kevin, Jacob, Zoe, Lee, Jessica, Lori, Liv, Travis, Josh, Mckay, Lloyd, Gordon, Craig, Caleb, Tony, Benoit, Guy, Chad, Chris TM, Gerard, Jonny, Ryan, Liam, Bernard, and the original browsers of this particular manuscript (you know who you are, since your monikers appear in God-hopefully bold type print elsewhere in this tome!) — each of whom gave invaluable feedback.

I'll doff a quick hat to the Jack Kirby Museum, Comic Bastards, The Momus Report, the Booked Podcast, Forces Of Geek, Crime City Central, ComicsOnline.com, Sons Of Spade, Angry Robot, LitReactor, Books and Booze, Nerd Culture Podcast, Zouch, Farrago, Bleeding Cool, Shotgun Honey, Longbox Graveyard and Slit Your Wrists.

But I wouldn't be hammering together this hack acknowledgements section of a published book without the belief of people like Another Sky Press — who gave me my first bona fide break with *Tobacco-Stained Mountain Goat* in 2011 — and Phil Jourdan and everyone else at Perfect Edge Books...who gave me my next. Phil in particular has proven himself as much a best buddy as he is an ally, like-minded sod and publisher, while my editors Dominic C. James and Trevor Greenfield do a great job tidying up my wayward prose. Wunderbar support has also come from John Hunt and Maria Maloney.

I owe a sizeable debt to the international cast of artists involved here, stellar talent unto themselves: Rodolfo for the fantastic cover concept, and other cool art by Paul, Giovanni, Maan, Javier, Juan, Harvey, Fred, Hannah, Loka, Andrew, Dave, Kohana, Saint Y, Carlos, Marcin, Joe, Tsubomi, Drezz, Van, Milton, Yata, Wally, Israel, Lorrie, Sho and Cocoa.

In order to gain clarity regarding the future dystopia of Melbourne, the nature of the politics, idInteract, Wolram Deaps, the Richmond comics stash, 'Deviancy' and some of the characters that flit through these pages, it might be worthwhile checking out my previous novels *Tobacco-Stained Mountain Goat* (you can grab a free digital version from anotherskypress.org) and *One Hundred Years of Vicissitude*, also out through Perfect Edge.

And there's still more for me to offer up their dues.

This novel would never have brewed, infused and decanted without two essential ingredients that first grabbed me as a child and have continued to stalk my senses as a somewhat older kid: American comicbooks from the silver and bronze ages (basically the late 1950s to mid '80s) and the noir/detective yarns of Raymond Chandler and Dashiell Hammett written a couple of decades before that.

Chandler's short stories 'Goldfish', 'Finger Man' and 'Killer in the Rain' figured lightly; also in the mix are several different Sherlock Holmes stories by Arthur Conan Doyle, *Erewhon: or, Over the Range* by Samuel Butler, Hammett's *Red Harvest* playing minor fiddle, H.G. Wells' *War of the Worlds*, E. H. Gombrich's *The Story of Art*, and Dr. Seuss' *I Wish that I Had Duck Feet*.

Getting back to the comics, I was always (mostly) a Marvel fan, forever enamoured with the written words of Stan Lee in collusion with Jack Kirby (script/pencils) and Joe Sinnott (inks) when they together worked a kind of magic on the mid '60s direction of *Fantastic Four* from #44 (which coincided with the unveiling of the Inhumans). I also love *The Avengers* yarns in 1968 concocted by writer Roy Thomas and artist John Buscema — along with the astounding artistic inroads of both Kirby and Jim Steranko later that decade on *Captain America* and *Nick Fury, Agent of S.H.I.E.L.D.*

But it wasn't just the Americans who made an impression. I remember spending hours in the school library entranced with the adventures of Tintin, and my dad bought me subscriptions to British comics *Cor!!*, *Action* (with the brilliant strips 'Hook Jaw' and 'Death Game 1999') and finally *2000 AD*, when it kicked off in 1977.

There's so much I could waffle on about here, if I haven't done so already, without meaning to bore you senseless. Each and every facet deserves the acknowledgement; it's just going to have to be compressed.

So, here is a list of the more worthy TV stuff: Disney's *Zorro* (1957-59), *Star Trek* (the original series), *Comic Strip Presents*, *Department S*, *PreCure* — especially the 'HeartCatch' season (2010-11) — *The Goodies*, *Kamen Rider*, *Blackadder*, *Buffy the Vampire Slayer*, *Space: 1999*, *Buck Rogers in the 25th Century*, both gigs of *Battlestar Galactica*, *The Mentalist*, *F Troop*, *Monty Python's Flying Circus*, *Doctor Who*, *Lost in Space*, *Mickey Spillane's Mike Hammer*, *UFO*, *Spyforce*, *The Twilight Zone*, *Batman*, *The Lone Ranger*, *Adventures of Superman*, and *Red Dwarf*.

I also grew up with Americanized versions of Japanese anime classics like *Janguru Taitei* (Kimba the White Lion), *Tetsujin 28-go* (Gigantor) and, later on, the original Japanese videos of *Project A-Ko*, *Akira*, *Ghost in the Shell*, *Patlabor* and *Macross* — while discovering the joys of manga done by Yukito Kishiro, Katsuhiro Otomo and Masamune Shirow. After finishing uni, over brekky before working a horrendous corporate job, I was mesmerized by the telly romps of *Sailor Moon*.

But whom am I kidding?

Anyone who knows me would skip into a long harangue that I'm a movie buff more than much else, as inclined to gush about John Huston's take on Hammett (*The Maltese Falcon*) and Howard Hawks' interpretation of Chandler (*The Big Sleep*) as I am Blake Edwards' dust-down of *Breakfast at Tiffany's* and Basil Rathbone de-vilifying himself to squeeze beneath Sherlock Holmes' deerstalker.

Further cinema/DVDs making tsunami in this tome? *Singin' in the Rain, Peter Pan, Johnny Guitar, Paprika, Inception, Dark Knight, Take the Money and Run, Matrix, Mr. Winkle Goes to War, The Lavender Hill Mob, Stray Dog: Kerberos Panzer Cops, Dark City, Hard Boiled, Chitty Chitty Bang Bang, The Third Man, Rain, Niagara, The Blue Max, Magnetic Rose, Taxi Driver, Millennium Actress, Jin-Roh, RoboCop, Batman, X-Men, Thor, Forbidden Planet, Batman Begins, You're in the Navy Now, The Avengers, Captain America, Casshern, Raiders of the Lost Ark, Avalon, From Russia With Love, Dark Passage, Mystery Men, Star Wars* (only episodes IV-VI), *Innocence, Watchmen, Seven Samurai, Iron Man,* Sam Raimi's *Spider-Man, Superman and the Mole Men, Blade Runner, Star Trek* (the 2009 reboot), *Perfect Blue, Brazil, Kick-Ass, Nausicaä,* the *kaiju* classics (Godzilla, Mothra, et al), *Gone with the Wind,* and *La Chauve-Souris* with Alessandra Ferri & Massimo Murru.

And yet, yep, this novel wears cheap comic-paper art on its soiled shirtsleeve.

Comicbooks and strips — along with those publications' creators — that I've directly riffed on, nipped, tucked, and/or misleadingly winked at include multiple issues of Kirby & Lee's run on *Fantastic Four*, as well as the duo's work with *Captain America, Strange Tales, Avengers, Sgt. Fury and His Howling Commandos, X-Men,* and *Tales to Astonish.*

Also I should mention DC Comics' *Mr. District Attorney,* the Skrull Kill Krew, Marvel's *Rawhide Kid* and *Two-Gun Kid,* Harold Gray's *Little Orphan Annie,* DC's *Secret Hearts* #83 (the issue Roy Lichtenstein plundered for 'Drowning Girl'), Warren Publishing's *Eerie* comics, Wonder Woman, *Barbarella* creator Jean-Claude Forest,

Pete Loveday, Judge Dredd, and even *Uncle Scrooge* comic #17.

Hergé's work remains a favourite years after I should've grown out of it, and I'm not inclined to forget *American Splendor* creator Harvey Pekar, Bob Kane, the illustrious Joe Simon, Jerry Siegel & Joe Shuster, *The Fabulous Furry Freak Brothers*, June Mills (a.k.a. comic artist Tarpé Mills) with *Miss Fury*, Jerry Robinson, Bryan Talbot, *Battle Angel Alita*, the Franklin Flagg (real name unknown) creation Captain Freedom, *One Piece*, Timely Comics, Mark Millar, *Action Comics* #1, *Les Gouttes de Dieu* (a Japanese manga series about wine) created by Yuko and Shin Kibayashi, N.C. Wyeth, Yoshihiko Umakoshi, Moira Bertram, the 1940 Porky Pig cartoon *Africa Squeaks*, Carl Burgos (creator of the original Human Torch), Fawcett Comics' Bulletgirl and Baron von Gatz, Holyoke Publishing's Chop Suey, Standard Comics' Faceless Phantom, Marty Goodman, artist Morris and writer Rene Goscinny's fictional outlaws The Daltons (who regularly appeared in the Franco-Belgian cowboy comic *Lucky Luke*), War Picture Library, occasional copies of *The Flash* and *Supergirl* in the '70s — and the great Will Eisner's *The Spirit*.

While I still cherish Roy Thomas and Barry Windsor-Smith's work in the first twelve issues of *Conan the Barbarian* from 1970, especially when Sal Buscema was doing the inks, influence from comics later than the 1960s and early '70s (in the era people these days call the bronze age) helped fuel my teenage inclinations. Following on from Conan, I dug the early issues of Frank Thorne's run with *Red Sonja* that started in 1977 — the same year a young Canadian named John Byrne lent his art to writer Jim Shooter and dragged me right back into *The Avengers* with #164.

By 1980 Byrne, with Chris Claremont doing spot-on scripts, made the *Uncanny X-Men* his own over #108-143, and their collaboration on the Dark Phoenix saga was a staggering thing to go through at the time. And then there was *Daredevil*. Artist/writer Frank Miller's work with inker Klaus Janson on that title from 1979 was breathtaking, culminating (for me) in the superb #181 three years later. I also loved Miller's subsequent work in 1986 on DC's *Batman: The Dark Knight*

Returns, with Janson again doing inks and canny colours courtesy of Lynn Varley.

Growing up in Australia we had Lee Falk's *Phantom* comics published fortnightly via Frew Publications, while in the Melbourne *Herald* newspaper John Dixon's strip *Air Hawk and the Flying Doctors* was printed almost daily. Speaking of newsprint, I'd be remiss to ignore *Calvin and Hobbes* and the early (funnier) strips of *Wizard of Id* and *B.C.* Johnny Hart's *B.C.* was a huge influence on my first and only comic strip 'funny' *Up the Front*, created in school — and since safely buried out of sight.

Cameo-ing in this novel are denizens of another strip: Escape Goat, Air Gal, Capitol Hill and the Felon Fighters are the creations of cool American artist Denver Brubaker. I asked him for permission to give a shout-out here. The same with contemporary Aussie comicbook heroes Vesper (Matt Nicholls/Ross Stewart), The Soldier (Paul Mason), McBlack (Jason Franks) and That Bulletproof Kid (Matt Kyme/Arthur Strickland), who squeeze in for a deserved wink.

Further thanks to Maxwell Newton's Newton Comics (set up in Melbourne in the mid-1970s to re-release silver-age Marvel), pioneering Aussie strip creators Syd Nicholls (*Fatty Finn*) and Jimmy Bancks (*Ginger Meggs*), and the B&W *Giant Batman Albums* of the 1970s that reran classic '50s Batman & Robin yarns, published by Planet Comics/KGM in Australia. Melbourne is pivotal here, not just in the novel. Like Jacob, I discovered a treasure trove of silver-age Marvel Comics in a shed in a back yard (my grandparents') in Duke Street, Richmond — packed in snail-trailed cardboard boxes beneath crates of my nan's burnished kitchen utensils and a seriously disturbing ventriloquist's dummy.

Dummies aside, most of all here I intend to pay respect to the creators — the writers, pencilers, inkers, and occasionally colourists — who made the most impact because of the astounding work they did in the 1960s.

Yep, the kids Jacob meets in this novel, back in Melbourne at the idl arcade Tower of the Elephant — Roy, Barry and Sal — are vaguely modelled after Roy Thomas, Barry Windsor-Smith and Sal Buscema (John Buscema's younger brother), who did such creative, mind-bending stuff at Marvel in the late 1960s and early '70s.

While I was mostly influenced by the Marvel Bullpen in New York (dominated by North Americans), some outstanding DC and Gold Key types, a few oddball Europeans, Brits and Australians, and a couple of Japanese slip in here as well.

This book is therefore dedicated to Lee, Thomas, Steranko, Windsor-Smith, Sinnott, Colletta, Tuska, Klein, the Brothers Buscema, Don Heck, Steve Ditko, Gene Colan, John Romita, Syd Shores, George Roussos (a.k.a. George Bell), Stan Goldberg, Artie Simek, John & Marie Severin, Jack Keller, Carl Burgos, Sam & Joe Rosen, Paul Reinman, Dick Ayers, Wally Wood, Bill Everett, Chic Stone, Mike Esposito, Gary Friedrich, Neal Adams, Dan Adkins, Carmine Infantino, Gardner Fox, Joe Kubert, John Tartaglione, Jack Davis, Larry Lieber, Steve Parkhouse, Frank Giacoia (a.k.a. Frank Ray), Herb Trimpe, Sol Brodsky, Johnny Craig, Len Wein, Archie Goodwin, Dennis O'Neil, Julius Schwartz, Tom Palmer, Robert Bernstein, Bob Brown, Joe Orlando, Arnold Drake, Joe Certa, John Celardo, Dan DeCarlo, Dick Giordano, Ross Andru, Mike Sekowsky, Sy & Dan Barry, John Dixon, Irv Watanabe, Maurice Bramley, Stan Pitt, Bill Lignante, Ramona Fradon, Sid Greene, Tony Abruzzo, Roy Lichtenstein, Hergé, Will Eisner, Mœbius, Osamu Tezuka, Lee Falk, Jean-Claude Forest, Mitsuteru Yokoyama, Joe Colquhoun, Don Lawrence, Hugo Pratt, Ron Vivian, and all the other unmentioned, toiling masters behind 1960s comicbook bliss.

But most of all? For Jack 'King' Kirby — thank you.

Essential comicbook back reading: Some highlights

X-Men #1 (Sept. 1963)

I got wrapped up in the early antics of the X-Men — namely Beast (the stand-out for me), Angel (number two), Cyclops, Marvel Girl & Iceman — and the way in which they were feared and misunderstood by regular people in the burgeoning tale first unfolded by Stan Lee and Jack Kirby. Once the title was revived in 1975 it took me some time to adapt — although I did pick up #94 for just 10c at a school fête in Melbourne and sadly sold it a few years later for $150 to help pay the rent. In this baptismal issue, we had the blue-and-yellow-clad teen mutants up against the mightily evil Magneto, their ongoing nemesis — and a fellow who looked pretty neat in a scarlet Corinthian helmet.

Avengers #4 (March 1964)

I picked this up in black-and-white thanks to Newton Comics' re-release in Australia in the mid '70s, and here we had golden-age hero Captain America revived from suspended animation after a nap that took the better part of 20 years. While great to see the fledgling Avengers at play, as handled by Stan Lee and Jack Kirby, it's more fun witnessing Cap's first moments as a man-out-of-time.

Fantastic Four #25 (April 1964)

The Thing versus the Hulk — subtitled 'The Battle of the Century!'. 'Nuff said. But we also have some of blue-eyed Benjamin's best ever one-liners, mesmerizing fisticuffs that destroy a few city blocks (along with a speedboat, a bus, and a bridge), the rampaging Hulk, a shoe-in from the Avengers, and Jack Kirby *really* starting to find his visual voice. I never get tired of this one. You'll need to get #26 to see the finale, but #25 is better.

Fantastic Four #27 (June 1964)

Story and art by Stan Lee and Jack Kirby, inks by George Roussos (as George Bell), and lettering by Sam Rosen. Basically Reed Richards, the group's leader, flies off the handle in an uncharacteristically jealous rage when his girlfriend Sue Storm is kidnapped by the Sub-Mariner — a man she digs perhaps as much as she does Reed. This was the first *Fantastic Four* comic I read, part of my older half-brother's collection at Duke Street, Richmond, though his was lacking the front cover. I discovered it when I was about 6, fell in head-over-heels with the quartet (and Kirby), and never looked back. While the Human Torch appealed to me, it was Benjamin J. Grimm, a.k.a. the unfortunate-looking, orange-skinned Thing that won me over. He's remained one of my preferred characters ever since. Lee and Kirby had him pushing perfection from about #21 onwards.

Avengers #21 & #22 (Oct. & Nov. 1965)

Another discovery in the Richmond treasure-trove in a box in a spider-ridden shed, this time we had Stan Lee (writer), Don Heck (pencils) and Wally Wood (inks) relating the messy break-up of a bickering super team I hadn't encountered previously. The sense of pathos was fascinating here, and the part where the Avengers disband rocked the pre-adolescent me — even while I wondered why Captain America had fish-scales on his costume. I only later realized the scales in fact represented chain mail.

Fantastic Four #51 (June 1966)

For me one of the best ever issues of *Fantastic Four*, subtitled 'This Man... This Monster!' A Jack Kirby cover, with Jack Kirby's art inside inked by Joe Sinnott wrapped perfectly around Stan Lee (and likely some of Kirby's) words. And what a story of angst and redemption. Some of you may have guessed that the Thing was a heavy influence on my character the Brick in *Heropa*. Here — as well as in #25 — you find out why.

Avengers #52 (May 1968)

Of course a mad-looking guy with a scythe on a cover done by John Buscema, with the tags 'The Grim Reaper' and 'The Man Who Killed the Avengers' would drag forth any impressionable kids. But inside the mag, the story by Roy Thomas and further art of Buscema (inked by Vince Colletta) was a stunning romp in which new arrival the Black Panther is accused of — yes — doing away with three of our heroes. Thomas and Buscema tweaked a stunning run on the title, with other standouts being #53, #55, and #56-61.

Nick Fury, Agent of S.H.I.E.L.D # 7 (Dec. 1968)

Jim Steranko's best frontispiece for Marvel in a field of stiff competition (from himself — #4 in this series also comes close) sees this brilliant artist pit war hero and secret agent extraordinaire Nick Fury against... Salvador Dalí's *Soft Watch at the Moment of Explosion.* And this was the cover alone. Worth framing.

Captain America #109 (Jan. 1969)

I'd go so far as to declare this is my favourite comicbook propaganda cover — an iconographic piece by Jack Kirby (with Syd Shores) displaying our hero tearing through a 1940s newspaper and ready for action. In fact I love this so much that I have it on a t-shirt I picked up here in Tokyo, and I commissioned most of the artists doing Southern Cross in this novel to model their images around the superb piece. The story within, by Stan Lee and possibly Kirby as well, has Steve Rogers relating to Nick Fury his rousing origin tale and the tragic death of Bucky Barnes. It's like Shakespeare rendered in four-colour art.

Silver Surfer #4 (Feb. 1969)

For years I had the cover of this issue on my bedroom wall: John Buscema's rendering of the Silver Surfer and Thor about to embark in mutually destructive hostilities. The issue itself was great, too, with Stan Lee providing another good yarn and John's pencils embellished by his brother Sal.

Captain America #111 (March 1969)

1969 was a very good year and Cap, as redefined by Jim Steranko, was a brief, sublime moment. He took the character beyond the rough-and-tumbling tragedy of Kirby's vision, and applied hallucinogenic menace, especially with the evil organization HYDRA — and the shattering 'death' of our hero at the conclusion. Innovative and essential.

Conan the Barbarian #4 (April 1971)

Barry Windsor-Smith-wise, I considered slipping in his artistic efforts for #12 of *Nick Fury, Agent of S.H.I.E.L.D*, written by Steve Parkhouse and an old fave — but already had Steranko's issue here. So I went for the best ever Conan story. 'The Tower of the Elephant!' was adapted by Roy Thomas from Robert E. Howard's original story and gloriously brought to life thanks to Barry Smith, with inks by Sal Buscema and lettering by Sam Rosen — making this the best of the series. Less focused on barbarism *per se*, robbing a tower was never so tricky.

The Flash #215 (May, 1972)

I had to squeeze in some DC here, just so they're not too neglected — and I loved this issue as a wee tacker. It was one of the first comics I bought myself, with a story by Len Wein, pencils by Irv Novick, and Dick Giordano on inks. I remember the opening was an unusual one involving a possible hangover and unintended wife-swapping, we had two Flashes, and the 'Death of an Immortal'. The cover alone (by Neal Adams) is fantastic stuff, and one of the reasons I grabbed the mag.

Amazing Spider-Man #121 (June, 1973)

I have so much respect for Steve Ditko and the artwork he did, especially covers in the '50s for things like *Science Fiction Space*

Adventures and *Outer Space*. One of the best comicbook short stories — 'The Worst Man On Earth', in *Tales to Astonish* #40 — was published 50 years ago last February by Ditko in collusion with Stan Lee at Marvel. And yet... I never really warmed to his art on *Spider-Man*. His idea of Aunt May scared the willies out of me. Much more my style, also probably because I came to the character first via his character designs, was John Romita, Sr.'s version after he took over in 1966. Even more surprisingly, my favourite issue of the series, although it had a Romita cover, was drawn by Gil Kane with Romita and Tony Mortellaro on inks and Gerry Conway writing. A 'Turning Point' indeed, as the Green Goblin returns and one of the central characters dies — for real. As shocking as it was moving, and Spidey's happy-go-lucky attitude would never quite be the same.

2001: A Space Odyssey #1 (Dec. 1976)
My dad did my head in early — he took me to see a screening of Stanley Kubrick's *2001: A Space Odyssey* when I was four years old. So when my childhood hero Jack Kirby tackled that baffling movie head-on with his own bamboozling series (which he wrote & drew), of course I was going to become hooked. By 1976 Kirby's style had become an exaggerated version, almost a self-intended parody of exploding imagination, of what was arguably his peak artistic period in the late '60s. Everything here buzzes with mad foreshortening and shorn-off square fingertips. I actually haven't had the chance to read this again (nor my other Kirby fave as a kid, *Kamandi*), but the first issue beautifully bludgeoned my senses — and I nicked 'Decker' as the name of my hero in a short story I wrote that eventually became *Tobacco-Stained Mountain Goat*.

2000 AD #2 (March 1977)
This one's simple — only two words. Judge Dredd.

The Avengers #164 (Oct. 1977)
I'm not sure why, but I fell out of Marvel Comics for a year or two

(probably this had to do more with a lack of spare pocket money) — but this issue dragged me right back in. With a cover by George Perez and inside art by John Byrne, (inked by Pablo Marcos) and a script by Jim Shooter in which the Lethal Legion attack our heroes, this was beginning of a love affair with Byrne that would continue right through his run on *Uncanny X-Men* but ease off when he took over *Fantastic Four*.

X-Men #137 (Sept. 1980)

Writer Chris Claremont and artist John Byrne (with help from Terry Austin) handled the run up to this double-issue with absolute aplomb, teasing out the plot over the course of a couple of dozen issues — but most especially from #122 (June, 1979). Wolverine stands out all by himself but the real clincher takes place from #132 through to this finale. And what a finale it is. After being defeated and then laying waste to the Hellfire Club, Jean Grey finds the absolute power of the Phoenix/Dark Phoenix all-consuming — which then leads to the gut-wrenching, self-sacrificial death of a hero.

Daredevil #181 (April 1982)

Another double-issue blockbuster helmed by Frank Miller (script/pencils) with Klaus Janson (pencils/ink/colours) that redefined for me the idea of a 'comicbook'. The way in which the tale starts and ends, narrated as it is by antagonist Bullseye, and the fate of Matt Murdoch's flame Electra, shattered illusions and rejigged the way I looked at narrative in my own fiction and art.

Batman: The Dark Knight Returns #1-4 (1986)

In a completely crap, messed-up future Gotham City, Batman has disappeared, Commissioner Gordon is about to retire, and Bruce Wayne leads a bitter, self-destructive depth-charge into his sunset years. While gangs run riot, the Joker escapes from Arkham Asylum, Two-Face gets a new face, and a nuclear winter kicks in, the Batman returns — older and not necessarily wiser — to kick-start a crusade against all these ills...and to have a tussle with government lackey Superman. Writer/artist Frank Miller again collaborated with inker Klaus Janson and colourist Lynn Varley to unveil one of the most staggering mini-series sagas I've ever consumed. Brilliant — simple as that.

Gunnm (Battle Angel Alita) Vol. 1 (1990)

Somewhere along the line in the 1990s I drifted into reading more Japanese manga than American comicbooks, though I always kept an eye on Marvel. When her dismembered but still-functioning body is discovered in a junkyard, Yukito Kishiro's character Gally (renamed Alita in the English translation) has no memory of who or what she is. This single volume covers not just our heroine's journey toward self-discovery and new body parts, but also the nature of humanity and the squalid effects of violence in a dystopic community gone mad.

Kōkaku Kidōtai (Ghost in the Shell) (1991)

If I have one complaint about Marvel and other American comics from the 1960s it was the frailty of the female characters (Sue Storm continuously describing situations as "hopeless", Alicia Masters fainting, Jean Grey pictured in a related swoon, etc, etc), so it was enlivening to discover their relatively stronger counterparts in the 1970s and '80s. But in manga they went further still — such as here, which I picked up in English translation in about 1996. While Major Mototo Kusanagi might have a few too many curves, and creator Masamune Shirow is renowned for his *hentai* (basically, perverted), techno-fetishist pin-ups of buxom gals, the fact is that the Major is more kick-arse than the trio of Hit-Girl in *Kick-Ass*, Tank Girl, and Makoto's direct descendant Trinity in *The Matrix* — combined.

Memories: The Collection (1995)

I was lucky enough to live in Australia when the local Random

House publishers released this 250-page compendium of short manga tales by someone I respect a great deal: Katsuhiro Otomo (*Akira*). The stories veer wildly from surprising twists verging on *Twilight Zone* to silly slapstick, but it's the title-tale 'Memories' that always grabs me. A space salvage vessel with a cranky crew finds a drifting Marie Céleste with plush carpets, chandeliers, empty books and homicidal robot watchdogs — not to mention a mummified cadaver reaching out from beyond the grave. A bloody brilliant mix of philosophy, comedy, action and meaningful drama.

300 (May-Sept. 1998)

What can I say? I grew up on swords 'n' sandals epics like *Ben-Hur*, *The Golden Voyage of Sinbad*, *Ali Baba and the Forty Thieves*, and... *The 300 Spartans* (1962), directed by cinematographer Rudolph Maté (*Gilda*). Something Frank Miller also apparently relished. Here Miller takes his *Sin City* work — another classic — to a new extreme thanks to the colour palette of Lynn Varley. There's no wonder it won three Eisner awards. A rousing, macho homage to pig-headed bravery in the face of enormously unbalanced odds, the story may at times hang outlandish, but the art — ahhh, the art.

Kick-Ass #1 (Feb. 2008)

I actually approached this out of respect to John Romita Sr., since his son — another Marvel veteran called John Romita — did the art, inked by the rather legendary Tom Palmer, with a story from Scottish writer Mark Millar (*Civil War*). And it was, indeed, kick-arse. The sheer audacity and the violent exuberance here reminded me of a geek-teen, comicbook *A Clockwork Orange*.

A LAST WORD FROM (SOME) OF OUR ARTISTS' MOUTHS*

*the others were too shy to join in the chorus.

Harvey Finch

"Harvey Finch grew up in the vast desolate forests of the Pictish Wilderness, fending off ghost snakes, savages, and saber-toothed tigers. He likes to draw comics of his exploits in his spare time." (harveyfinch.com)

Rodolfo Reyes

"Born in Mexico City, I graduated from the Universidad del Valle de México with a degree in graphic design. My work has been published in two books of illustrations and as limited edition prints in the U.S. and the U.K. I've done the covers of several magazines and books as well as quite a few logos. In recent years being a finalist in several national and international contests earned me the opportunity to display my artwork at MUMEDI — the Mexican Museum of Design." (rodolforever.tumblr.com)

Paul Mason

"Paul Mason is the creator/writer/artist of *The Soldier Legacy*, an Australian action-adventure/superhero comicbook series published by Black House Comics. Illustrated work published here and there, a doctoral candidate in the comics field at the Queensland College of Arts, a World Championship ITF Taekwon-do fighter, and lifts heavy things like a jerk. Therefore, a Jack Kirby nerd *and* a jock, he sometimes gives himself wedgies." (thesoldierlegacy.com)

JGMiranda

"I've been drawing ever since I can remember — self-taught and stubborn. I love character design and concept art (it's always great fun to imagine a monster or a prop from zero). After drawing for several Spanish fanzines, I started my professional career with the roleplaying game publisher Herogames, working for *The Monster Hunter International Employee's Handbook*, inspired in the Monster Hunter International novels by author Larry Correia, and then incursed into the comic-book industry with Zenescope's *Robyn Hood vs Red Riding Hood*. I am currently getting work from Zenescope in their Grimm Fairy Tales series. Oh, and I do caffeine. A lot of caffeine." (jgmiranda.daportfolio.com)

Giovanni Ballati

"I have always drawn and fantasized stories, my notebook integers. One day, someone told me I had to copy. So I did it for a long time, I copied everyone for years. And here I am...not doing it anymore. Instead, I draw to stem the flood of words."
(giovanniballati.blogspot.it)

Maan House

"Digital artist, began at a young age to work as a book illustrator and comicbook artist, specializing in horror. Currently he's finishing a sixth book of illustrations of urban legends, a bestseller in his home country, Uruguay."
(maanhouse.deviantart.com)

Carlos Gómez

"Born in Madrid, Spain in 1985. Worked on comics since I was 18 years old, at first with small publishers — and then, from 2008 to 2011, I drew *Spectacular Spider-Man* for Marvel UK. My most recent work has been for PathFinder, mostly covers."
(carlosgomezartist.deviantart.com)

Fred Rambaud

"I got my lucky break when I landed a concept art job in Norway, at a game studio called Funcom. I then moved to Singapore, to Imaginary Friends Studios, then Volta Studios and Activision, both

in Canada. I am now a freelance concept artist and illustrator."
(artoffredram.com)

Andrew Chiu
"I'm a freelance illustrator, working primarily in the field of comics
and children's books. After a break of about 10 years, I returned to
drawing just over two years ago and am loving every second of it.
Current projects include a children's book for Franklin
Watts/Hachette, a children's book series for Wayland Books/
Hachette, a graphic novel for Raintree, and comic strips for
Benchmark Education." (andrewchiu.co.uk)

Hannah Buena
"Hannah is a freelance artist and comic creator based in Naga City in
the Philippines. She picked up a pencil since she learned you can't
eat crayons, and has been drawing ever since. A self-taught artist,
Hannah does pretty girls in dresses and of characters she likes. On
her off days, she's a fan of good books and classic videogames."
(sketchamababble.blogspot.com)

Saint Yak
"Not so much to say... Well, I'm 30 years old, everything I can do in
art is a result of self-teaching. Most of all I like to draw superheroes.
I live in Russia, but I wish to move to the USA, because in Russia I
have no chance for the future as a comicbook artist."
(saintyak.deviantart.com)

Dave Acosta
"Dave Acosta is an illustrator and sequential artist living in
suburban Detroit — and yes, he would like some more coffee, thank
you." (davedrawsgood.com)

Juan Saavedra
"I started in this line of work with the co-creation of Invasor Art

Studios, from which I have excellent memories — it was a fun, successful time. Over the past 3 years I've been a part of ATAKA-MALABS Game Studios, owned by DeNA, where I work as the lead artist." (atakamalabs.com)

Drezz Rodriguez
"Many moons ago in a small community in the Great White North, Drezz Rodriguez literally made his mark. When all of the kids in his preschool shouted that they wanted to be astronauts or cowboys, Drezz would just shrug his shoulders and draw on stuff. 20 years later he is an award-winning creative director for a design firm, author of a long-running online graphic novel (El Cuervo), owner of a bursting design and illustration portfolio and article columnist at Webcomic Alliance." (drezzworks.com)

ABOUT THE AUTHOR

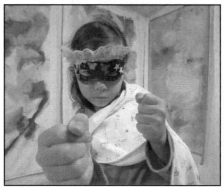

PHOTO BY CASEY CRIME

Andrez Bergen is a Melbourne-born expat Australian writer, journalist, DJ, and occasional comic creator who's been entrenched in Tokyo, Japan, for the past decade. He makes music as Little Nobody and ran groundbreaking Melbourne record label IF? for 15 years.

Bergen has also written for newspapers such as *The Age* and the *Yomiuri Shinbun*, as well as magazines like *Mixmag, Anime Insider, Australian Style, Remix, Impact, Beat, 3D World* and *Geek Magazine*.

He published noir/sci-fi novel *Tobacco-Stained Mountain Goat* in 2011 through Another Sky Press, as well as the surreal fantasy *One Hundred Years of Vicissitude* and a recent anthology *The Condimental Op* via Perfect Edge Books in 2012/13.

Over the past two years Bergen collaborated with artists Drezz Rodriguez, Andrew Chiu, Marcos Vergara, Michael Grills, Harvey Finch and Nathan St. John on a series of sequential noir vignettes.

Bergen has published his straight short stories via Crime Factory, Shotgun Honey, Snubnose Press, Solarcide, Weird Noir, Big Pulp, Full Dark City Press, Pulp Ink and All Due Respect, and worked on translating and adapting the scripts for feature anime films by Mamoru Oshii, Kazuchika Kise and Naoyoshi Shiotani with Production I.G.

He married artist Yoko Umehara in 2005 and they have one child, Cocoa.

http://andrezbergen.wordpress.com

PERFECT
EDGE
BOOKS

"There are many who dare not kill themselves for fear of what the neighbours will say," Cyril Connolly wrote, and we believe he was right.

Perfect Edge seeks books that take on the crippling fear of other people, the question of what's correct and normal, of how life works, of what art is.

Our authors disagree with each other; their styles vary as widely as their concerns. What matters is the will to create books that won't be easy to assimilate. We take risks, not for the sake of risk-taking, but for the things that might come out of it.